You Were Summer

Enjoy my
story
Love

Rachel C.
Goodhand
x

You Were Summer

Published by The Conrad Press Ltd. in the United
Kingdom 2023

Tel: +44(0)1227 472 874
www.theconradpress.com
info@theconradpress.com

ISBN 978-1-915494-87-0

Typesetting and cover design by:
Michelle Emerson, michelleemerson.co.uk

The Conrad Press logo was designed by Maria Priestley

Printed and bound in Great Britain by Clays Ltd, Elcograf
S.p.A.

You Were Summer

Rachel C. Goodhand

For Ma and Pops

Chapter One

Have you ever included any of your own romantic encounters in your twelve best-selling novels?

The lonely cursor flashing in the reply box is like the tapping finger of a city trader queuing in a sandwich shop with a pre-packed baguette. With four minutes left of their guilt-laden ten-minute lunch, they're stuck behind someone whose life isn't controlled by performance targets; to add insult to irritation, they're paying with a mountain of loose change. It's what they've held back from collection tins. Charity begins at home, they believe – with a bespoke steak brioche roll.

I, however, don't care how many minutes they have left.

I pick up my empty cup and stroll down to the staff kitchen. It has one of those fancy bean-to-cup coffee machines, which means my procrastination doesn't even have time to add up its Scrabble score. All too soon, with a latte in one hand and a stack of my favourite brand of ginger biscuits in the other, I am forced to return to my literary agent's private office and his clutter-free workspace.

Honestly, there's bugger all on his desk to distract me from what I'm supposed to be doing.

Have you ever included any of your own romantic encounters in your twelve best-selling novels?

Oh, hello, Sarcasm. Better late than never. Autopilot could do with a hand.

No, I've never saved an evil millionaire from a drug overdose and mistakenly married his twin brother. I've never enjoyed mind-blowing sex with an Irishman in Italy, either. And I have never met the perfect man in a record shop.

In fact, let me correct that: I have never met the perfect man.

I rarely include first-hand adventures in any of my rom-coms. Come on, readers. Where do you find my books? That's right. The *fiction* aisle.

Trust me, my sexual relationships rarely have 'romance' in the job description; they're usually pushed to include the word 'relationship'. Then, if you rounded them up and wheedled out the boring parts, the story might fill a half-page spread in a Sunday colour supplement.

If they used a large font.

And they included photos.

And an advertisement—

'Jo, you can't send that,' says a voice behind me.

'I know.'

I highlight the text and delete it.

Have you ever included any of your own romantic encounters in your twelve best-selling novels?

I blend three cups of imagination with a pinch of

personal experience and a splash of humour. I then add a little spice before spreading the mixture over many pages.

With no objection this time from the well-paid voice of reason, I send my response.

What can we expect from Olivia J. Lawrence's next book?

This question is easy to answer.

Probably the same old, same old—

'Jo.'

Highlight and delete.

***

After two more lattes and three of my five a day (the leftovers from Cal's routinely overambitious bowl of fresh fruit salad), the live Q&A session is done. I stand up and tie my sweater around my waist and my scarf around my neck.

My agent reclaims his chair. 'We have the itinerary for the tour to go over.'

'Email me.'

'You won't look at it,' he says to the hefty pile of paper in front of him, massacring the top page with his favourite colour pen.

'Maybe I will.'

Or maybe I won't. In fact, forget the 'maybe'. I know I won't; Cal knows I won't. Ask a Magic Eight Ball if you like, and its sources will say no. But I am both the woman and the talent in this writing partnership, so I get the last word. And the first word.

Plus the majority that sits in between, if we're counting.

Calder Johnson and I have been a unit for eight years now. He came on board when my writing took on a fantasy genre sideline, which meant I had to work with two negotiators. Not long after, though, my original agent of five years announced she was choosing family over romantic fiction. This sullen, serene American then took responsibility for both fields of my writing. It was a decision, I believe, made *for* him – and one he seemed less than thrilled about. Despite this, he quietly got down to business, showing ruthless expertise that earned him my limited trust.

Cal soon noticed how my career was being handled, which was something I didn't have the knowledge or strength to do. With no fireworks or hidden agenda, he took over the running of my professional life. Since then, I've entrusted him with many things, from getting more money for my work than I think I deserve to signing off on the shoes I wear at a book signing. The man is, without a doubt, as vital to my business as my overactive imagination.

In exchange for his invaluable service, it is my job to hand in my manuscripts on time, show appreciation to my readers, and ensure his yearly bonus. If his silence is a measure, I do these tasks 'adequately'; therefore, peace and harmony prevail.

I haven't dedicated a book to him, but his name always appears in the acknowledgements. That's because we work closely together, but we are not close.

I don't know Cal's political views or where he stands on immigration, or if he has a favourite emoji. Or who he thinks should have gone out this week on *The Great Pottery Throw Down*. It's also why we've never swapped birthday cards, critiqued the John Lewis Christmas advert over hot chocolates, or asked what the other one is doing at the weekend.

I guess it's no surprise then that his relationship status is a mystery to me. I don't know whether Cal likes women or men. Or both. Or neither. Or perhaps he prefers not to be labelled. However, judging by the absence of button-festooned clay blobs that resemble nothing living or dead on his boring desk, I don't think he has kids.

'Katrina will be over Thursday afternoon,' Cal informs me.

Katrina makes sure I pack outfits that still have their price tags on – and nothing that's been washed to within an inch of its hemmed life.

'Our flight Friday morning is at ten a.m.,' he continues. 'The taxi will pick you up at six-fifteen. I will call you at five.'

'I'll be up.'

'I will call you at five.'

Cal hasn't stopped thumbing an essay on his phone while he's been talking, the deadly red ballpoint still between his fingers.

'When can I expect the final draft?' he asks.

'Wednesday.'

'Wednesday. Thank you.'

Conversing, electronically replying, editing *and*

listening all at once. Now's your chance. Swipe right.

I pick up my bag. 'Are there brownie points for getting it done three weeks early?'

'A chocolate brownie…' Cal checks something on his iPad '… when we're in Washington.'

'Which will be…?'

He taps his pen. '*If* we were to go over the itinerary, Jo—'

'See you Friday.'

***

I emerge from the tall office building with a few hours of daylight left. It's a sunny Saturday in mid-February, with temperatures up again on what they were last year. Daffodils brighten up all the roadsides and parks, waving their jazz-hands petals. They don't seem to mind tagging on to winter. In fact, they've grabbed the season by the waist this year, not by the fringe of its scarf.

It takes approximately fifty minutes to get to my apartment on foot. Cal could tell you how long it takes on the underground, but London's pavements allow me my semi-skimmed milk. Also, getting from A to B this way doesn't cost me a monthly membership. Having never stepped foot in a gym, I plan to keep it that way. Those places require commitment as well as the ability to sweat *and* look good simultaneously. Only one of those I can do on my exercise bike – and in bucketfuls.

With three Starbucks on my route, it's lucky number two who gets my order. No, not a refreshing

6

juice for a change. I had Cal's fruity remnants, remember? I also have some blitzed goodness in a lovely shade of snot green sitting in my fridge to 'look forward to'.

My next stop is the bookshop, and it's not just to reunite my takeaway cup with its comrades. Once a month, I need to be among other book addicts who like getting high on the scent of new releases. Those who also believe that wasting two hours surrounded by print and imagination is better than blowing a free afternoon on sex.

I know some of you will disagree with that statement. I probably would've done too until two years ago, when I hit forty-two. That was when I stopped concerning myself with what *Cosmopolitan* claimed I was entitled to in the bedroom.

And yes, it's been a while. Don't look so horrified. I assure you, going a day without complaining is ten times harder.

While I'm swapping my prescription sunglasses for spectacles, I pass the poster for Olivia J. Lawrence's latest book. On the second floor, I keep going until I get to a particular author's body of work. I'd like to snuggle up with another of his books, following the sabbatical required after the 983-page epic that—

'Have you read his first book?' someone asks.

A man is standing within touching distance, his nose buried in a hefty paperback. I check to see if we're the only ones in this aisle before sneaking a look at him. There's no chance of guessing his age, not when a furry hot dog bun is the majority shareholder in the space above his top lip. But who am I to judge? Maybe he's a big fan of Mark Twain or Friedrich Nietzsche.

Or Yosemite Sam.

'Yes,' I answer. 'I have read it.'

'Hypocritical and scapegoating,' facial-hair faux pas informs the pages.

'Now they are two guests you don't want to get stuck on a table with at a wedding,' I joke, moving my bent elbow in a nudge-nudge movement.

I don't actually nudge him, but he isn't willing to take any chances. He shuffles to his left, almost doing a pratfall over the tumbleweeds that my attempt at humour blew in.

'I thought it was good, but it was tough going,' I don't mind confessing – and aloud for once, instead of just with a star rating on Amazon. 'Especially that mountain climber's soapboxing. His forty-page speech? Hell's teeth! And I thought eating dry crackers was—'

'The author was nothing but a narcissistic ladies' man.'

Cutting people off was rude even before it became the calling card for breakfast television presenters. And I know we live in a fast-paced world, but I feel it will still be viewed as bloody disrespectful by the time I get an invitation for my first mammogram. But seeing as I still have some fabulous coffee left, my enhanced mood will let it go.

Just this once, mind you.

'And that's an insult?' I query. 'Sigmund Freud may have disagreed with you on the—'

'He believed that conservatism was his free ticket to—'

'I'm *terribly* sorry.' Count again on one finger how many times I agreed to let it go. 'But the middles of my sentences keep getting in the way of your interruptions.'

If only I'd texted him that quip instead, along with perhaps a carefully chosen emoji, it may have given him time to register the number on the sarcasm-ometer. However, I imagine his confused and slightly fearful look is because I've turned my body to face him. No, he doesn't *look* at me in a confused and fearful way. Oh, heaven forbid.

Tell me, when did eye contact go out of fashion? These people practise their 'Blue Steel' poses for those all-important daily selfies for… what? For 324 people on social media to convey their interest by doing nothing more than clicking the 'like' button? Yet if you put them in front of someone who'll respond without hearts and hashtags, they want to melt into their pre-loved bro sacks.

'I was only trying to offer you my opinion,' he mutters.

'Are you sure it wasn't Google's?' Since he won't look at my pleasant smile, I'm hoping he might hear it in my voice. 'If it was, I bet you're *dying* to cut me off again with some reference to his fondness for egomaniacs and After Eights. Yeah, the first page of search results for him also likes to throw those up.'

He disappears around the corner. Maybe he is looking for a book on quick-witted comebacks.

I return my attention to the author, who wouldn't have graded my shot at satire with even a raised eyebrow. How do I know this? Google, of course. After slogging through his mammoth monologue, I only read the first page of search results, too.

Chapter Two

When the lift doors open on the sixth floor of my apartment building, two people bewitched by their smartphones are waiting to get in. Thankfully, the doors are wide enough for us to pass without needless niceties. I've no idea if they're visitors or residents. Well, what do you expect? I've only lived here for a couple of...

No, it's...

Hang on. It can't be.

Is it nearly three years?

The best thing about my rented nine hundred square feet is the solid front door that locks out everything. A close second is, twice a week, the sweet smell inside of nothing. Today, there aren't any haunting aromas from my morning toast or last night's takeaway. Bless Jana and her proficient use of environmentally safe cleaning products.

My apartment is nothing more than an upscale hotel suite that I don't check out of by eleven on a Friday morning. Its décor is solid and sexless, and it's no different from how it looked when Cal and I first viewed it. It came as shown, which included the furniture and the decorative unisex touches, aimed at those with no desire or time to do anything other than move in the essentials. My contributions are the computer and a smattering of unnecessary giftware. If *Through the Keyhole* visited, they wouldn't have a Scooby.

I turn on the shower and grab the first Molton Brown bottle that comes to hand. I call it a shower because I use it to, that's right, shower in. The leasing agent was eager to stress it was a 'two-person steam shower cabin with hydromassage jets'. Well, it's never been for two while I've lived here, nor has any steam therapy been used to get my pores to open up. I also haven't wanted to holiday in it, which scraps the 'cabin' bit. And as for the fancy jets, those who don't appreciate being aroused at a spa resort by someone with a massage diploma would be in heaven. Personally, the only ones that give me any relief are those below waist height.

Once I have vowed again to apply body lotion after my shower one of these days, I slip into a linen smock dress and my oversized writing cardigan. Sitting at the oak desk near the balcony doors, I turn on my computer.

Outside, a staggered array of buildings as diverse as London's culture splits my view fifty-fifty with an expanse of sky. It's a postcard image. For this reason, it's never mentioned in conversation. I don't want anyone asking to come over and see it. But as wonderful as it is, it cannot distract me when I'm in work mode.

Around eleven o'clock, I take one of my new paperbacks to bed with me and surrender to sleep an hour later. When I wake up, it's still dark outside, or as dark as London will allow. It doesn't hurt to blink, though. I check the time on my phone: 04:37. That's good enough. There's no point in lying here conjuring up fence-jumping woolly livestock to get back to sleep.

I put my coffee mug on the desk, moving aside an abandoned glass of water. At least it's missing a third of its contents. I open a Word document on my computer and return to Estelia's next quest. Now that Greyhougerie Castle has escaped the evil clutches of Yurdinraa, she needs to track down the Wise.

I don't necessarily need caffeine when I'm N.R. Magnusson, not when I'm visiting my world of warriors, dragons and witchcraft. I don't need gimmicks or even deadlines to transport me there. Although I've finished the 'much-anticipated' concluding book in the *Caerli°°ani* series, the next adventure wasn't happy merely brewing in my creative space.

I could've sent Cal the final version of the fourth book sooner – a month early – but he doesn't need further proof that I don't have a life. Unless you include the mythical one, where I spend many an evening.

When I sit back to ponder over an adverb-heavy sentence, I notice the outline of the buildings across the way as the morning gently creeps up. I make another drink and take a moment on my balcony to appreciate the view that I pay a fair bit of rent to temporarily own.

The roads below are buzzing; busy working people with busy lives are juggling extended families and parental responsibilities. I wonder if they're too busy to appreciate what they have. Or do they keep busy to avoid acknowledging what they believe is lacking?

I sometimes let my memory journey back to its own demanding white-collar past. I was fortunate in my day, and not only because you got an entire hour for lunch: if the list of qualities and skills required for a job was extensive, it showed in the pay bracket. You then counterbalanced your increased use of antacids with regular pay rises.

I hear that's not the case these days. When companies advertise now for new team members, they seem to want it all: the ability to work well under pressure, self-motivation, oral and written communication skills, strong interpersonal skills, mind-reading skills, reliability, positivity, your spare kidney, attention to detail, *and* the ability to work independently (always preferable) or as part of a team (if you must).

In return, you'll get a standard holiday entitlement to dip into for any required surgical procedures (at least that's what you'll do if you want career progression) and a wage that equates to pitiful per annum. That's before you deduct tax and National Insurance. You shouldn't forget your recommended workplace pension contributions, too, since you'll be lucky if the state one still exists when you reach retirement.

Oh, but remember the benefits of working for such a prestigious company. Not everywhere has casual Fridays.

It's hardly surprising that people confident in using things like Microsoft 365 are opting to stack shelves for German supermarket chains. They get paid more by being on an hourly rate, and they leave at the end of their shift with a pocketful of fucks that others try to price match.

I remember when I wasn't self-employed. Companies had just started putting on big West End productions to show how the welfare and happiness of their employees were paramount (Eyeroll, that's your cue). These were regularly monitored via anonymous feedback forms. Anonymous, but you had to note the department you worked in, your gender, age bracket and how long you had worked there – in years *and* months.

The last time I worked for someone else, I was the only one who did all the overtime. I didn't have a family, so I had no excuse. Working overtime also stopped me from thinking about the family I didn't want for any other reason than *as* an excuse. Although I was terrible at relationships, I was brilliant at handling customer enquiries. One out of two isn't bad.

Then my job became a relationship.

I started to wonder whether there could be a life for me outside of an office. When I had time to think about anything other than manufacture dates, I also asked myself whether I was being made a fool of. It wouldn't have been the first time. Fortunately, February the fourteenth served as a yearly reminder. It ensured I didn't forget.

Sitting at my desk one day, I made a decision. If nobody else would start work early, take work home, come in on their days off, input orders correctly to prevent the wrong materials from going out, or get up off their arses to change the fucking cyan ink cartridge instead of sending their prints to the copier next door... well, guess what?

I'll never forget that afternoon when I shut my computer down when everyone else did. After three days, they questioned my dedication to the role. It resulted in a chat with my office manager, who knew the quality of my work well. After all, who do you think tidied up her sloppiness?

I listened to what she had to say before reminding her how many customers would only deal with me. I also highlighted my punctuality and my unparalleled level of accuracy. I didn't mention my zero number of duvet days taken, which were crucial to the rest of the team every few weeks. Present company included.

None of my qualities seemed to count, though. She explained to her spider plant that if I only did what they paid me to do, the work would pile up, and (her) errors would slip through unnoticed. They couldn't have that. She said to me that there was no 'i' in 'team'.

I said to myself that there was no 'u' either.

Colleagues expressed outrage on my behalf since

I am rubbish at it. Plus, everybody relishes drama at work – as long as it doesn't involve them.

The memory of handing in my notice stays with me. *Please accept this letter as a formal notification that I am resigning from my position. I am grateful for the opportunity to work for an outstanding company. It's been a pleasure. It's not you.* Blah, blah, reference, reference, lose the grenade pin.

I had three weeks' holiday entitlement owed to me, but I said I'd work a month to give them time to find a replacement. My manager emailed me from her adjoining desk and said there was no need; I could finish that day. Thanks for all my *efforts*. Sorry, no time for a whip-round and a farewell cake.

Oh, but did I mind filling in a feedback form before I left?

I fished out all my twenty-pence coins for the coffee machine from my paperclip pot. I took down my photo of Brad Pitt in *Fight Club*. I threw out the cheap, two-minute meals from my desk drawers.

'But who's going to run the office?' one colleague asked me.

'Your office manager.'

Her tapered eyebrows shot up. 'We have an office manager?'

I handed over the training manuals I had created over the years. I started them on my second day at the company. Back then, you were shown how to do something just once. I gave them to a girl who'd been at the company for six months – the longest-serving after me – who was pleasant and didn't call in sick every fortnight. She also wouldn't spot the manager's mistakes before they went out the door.

There were no grudges or regrets, nor was there any looking back. Within a week, I was sleeping beyond five hours; after a fortnight, I'd forgotten the key code for the door. The trickle of text messages from colleagues wanting to know r u ok? had dried up a month later, which was a relief. I never mixed with any of them outside of work. They only had my number to let me know before seven if they didn't feel like coming in that day.

To the people I worked with, I was merely someone who would quietly listen as they poured out their domestic disharmony between the hours of eight and six, Monday to Friday. Until companies gave in and allowed employees to flaunt their mobile phones.

However, I'll forever be grateful to everyone at that company – not just those who, when they brought in cakes to work, brought in bowls of jelly for me and my anxious stomach. Yes, everyone. Without them, I wouldn't be where I am today.

And soon afterwards, when I stopped feeling stressed, I spelt that word backwards and started enjoying 'desserts' in all their wheat-filled, dairy-laden glory again.

Horns blare six floors down. Not a great start to the day. Either somebody didn't get their morning coffee, or their service provider isn't providing.

Ah well, I suppose I'd better put the past back in its shoebox. With the goblin in my new story unable to decide whether to trade the golden mirror for a faerie king's tears, I also have another problem to figure out.

I don't know who's more excited now that N.R. Magnusson has completed the *Caerli°°ani* series. I'm hoping it's the readers, particularly those who queued for hours to buy the third one upon its release at midnight. Some were already on chapter two when they had to hold it aloft for the assistant to scan the barcode.

Or it might be the production companies salivating for the film rights. Before the first book had even made it to paperback, more than one company wanted to buy them. But my argument was, What if I die before I've written the conclusion? And I still believe it was a solid reason to turn them all down. Cal's response was to ask his tailor to hold off on making any cuts to the material he had selected for his dinner suit.

Could *he* be the one who's most excited? No, I think it would take more than a tasty bank transfer. If they lined his new suit for the film premiere with never-before-seen sonnets by Shakespeare, then maybe.

But Cal's thoughts will be on more than remeasuring and renegotiating now that I've written *The End*. He probably thinks N.R. Magnusson is swapping seats and watching Olivia J. Lawrence crack on with another one-way journey to Loveville.

Only, there won't be any more trips for her.

Should I send a rom-com resignation letter to Cal?

Chapter Three

Getting to do a book tour these days – to stand in front of your readers, your audience – is as rare as someone dying on their birthday. Therefore, I'm grateful for every minute, including the occasional opportunities to sit in green rooms with the most eclectic mix of people, talking to television hosts about my little tale. Can you believe I get the same length of time as everyone else? That I get the same seven minutes as those promoting 300-million-dollar blockbusters?

Honestly, it still blows my mind.

It's quite something for the girl who was always in the background at school, the quiet mouse who hung about with the girl whose name everybody remembered. That said, I never wanted her popularity; the envy she gained from it took too many forms. I never wanted people to be jealous of me, especially if it meant others would equally loathe my presence on earth.

'Unremarkable' is the best way to describe the first two-thirds of my life, and writing a book didn't change that. Neither did getting it published and having a few people buy it.

Having a lot of people buy it, though...

When I quit my last ever 'proper job' (my three sisters' words, not mine), I took my Aunt Izzie's advice and gave up my house in West Yorkshire. I then moved into her unoccupied flat in Cleethorpes, the seaside town where I grew up.

I no longer had any close family or friends there, which was fine. I imagined people I'd been acquainted with before I moved counties still lived locally – lingerers from my schooldays, perhaps, and retail adventures. However, I had no desire to contact them and pick up where we... Nope, nothing.

If there was one thing my dad hoped his kids would learn from him, it was to be frugal. Forget about making high-priced memories to cherish in your twilight years. Therefore, surviving for years on fifty-hour working weeks and a saggy social life meant I had savings he would be proud of. And thanks to Izzie's pitiful rent request, I could get off the stress express. For a while, at least.

I doubt it will surprise anyone that I've written stories for most of my life. Don't many introverts like me do that, so we can live our alter-ego lives on paper – the ones we like to dream up but wouldn't dream of actually having? They stopped when I outgrew shop assistant roles and moved to an office job in the next county. There was no time for words then. Not when my spare evenings were dedicated to someone I hadn't been looking for.

But when your waking hours no longer belong to

either a limited company or a man who achieved what he'd set out to do, Fate puts its foot down. Armed with no excuses and a broken heart that I didn't plan on mending, there was only one thing to do – start writing again.

For two weeks, I scribbled down ideas. As soon as I abandoned those, I wrote two chapters in five days. A month later, when Izzie was in the country on one of her routine visits to see her baffling number of friends, I gave her ten chapters.

'I'll read them tonight, Bee,' she said, flinging her ruby-red pashmina shawl over one shoulder and wafting a wave of Yves Saint Laurent Paris my way. 'As soon as I get back from the party. I promise.'

For the first time, I was letting go of my words. She was the only person I trusted. The only person whose opinion I cared about.

The sweet scent of powdery rose and violet still clung to her hair and clothes some eight hours later, laced with cigarette smoke and a good time. But at three in the morning, my sense of smell was the only one of the five I was letting her have with full permission.

Crouched next to my bed, she didn't blink when she said, 'I want lots more pages, please, you bitch.'

Not only is my foul-mouthed aunt generous with her compliments, but she is also liberal with her honesty. If your arse looks good in those jeans, you'll hear about it; if it doesn't, you'll hear about it. She isn't mean. She is merely a speedy remover of sticking plasters. Hence, I knew there would be no airbag when she told me what she thought of it.

I thought what I'd written was good, but I was still mourning the recent loss of my twenties. It wasn't just that, though. Whether it's applying highlighter correctly or buying the freshest grapes trapped in those clear plastic trays, I always doubt myself. Trust me, when you don't share a bathroom mirror or need a trolley to do your weekly food shop, making all your own decisions gets you like that.

Izzie, however, thought it was *great* – and that upgrade was all I needed.

I was suddenly getting out of bed before my alarm went off, eager to put more words on paper. And I finished it. More than that, I finished *something*. This was a big deal for someone who had yet to complete even a knit-every-row scarf in a single colour. It was my proudest achievement.

During my aunt's next visit, the triumphant coffee cup I held aloft and clinked against hers matched my grin. Behind my smile, though, I was terrified. Finishing something meant one thing: being open to criticism.

Without her encouragement, I would have stockpiled my pages and made a stylish table. But when I completed the manuscript – or should I say, when I finally stopped tweaking and amending and worrying and highlighting and thesaurusing and doubting and swapping – I handed it over. I didn't know what she could do with it, but I knew it was a damn sight more than anything I was capable of. I only took a job in administration because I was hopeless at retail. This was my sales patter:

'Good morning. Would you be interested in—?'

'No thanks.'

'Okay.'

Izzie is the opposite. She can sell chocolate fountains to bridal boutiques. And if it's a market she's unfamiliar with, you can bet your last penny she knows someone – which is why I always believed she was the next best thing to Checkatrade.

So imagine the look on my face when she handed me a thick book listing hundreds of literary agents and publishers. What the hell was I meant to do with it? Carve out a book safe? Go into the book-folding business? Take up origami to make use of all those pages?

'You know I can't sell myself, Izzie.'

'Then sell your fucking book instead,' she instructed.

Easier said than done. 'I read it with interest' cropped up more than once in the polite rejections I received from agents. 'We enjoyed your writing' did too. A few noted that 'as this is a subjective industry, we would encourage you to send your work to other agencies'.

They would *encourage* me.

Suddenly, their words were anything but negative responses, and I knew somebody would be interested. My tale wasn't radical or life-affirming – it wasn't the newly discovered eighth wonder of the world of story types – but I felt it was something people might enjoy. And sometimes, all we need from our reading material is a few fun pages away from troubles and trolls. It really is.

But after twenty-two rejections, I started to think I should put this childhood dream to bed. I had given it my best shot, but it wasn't good enough. 'There will be other opportunities in life' was what I needed as my new mantra – not that I would ever believe it. I couldn't. How could I? I had zero desire to balance on another career ladder. It was impossible to envisage some man sharing my pillow again. Hell, I'd never have a small hand needing mine.

It's a ruddy good job number twenty-three didn't say no then, eh?

And the rest is history, as they say. Well, the story of my being a contemporary romance novelist is almost history, with my last book tour nearly at an end.

But for N.R. Magnusson, there'll never be a last, or even a first. Under this pen name, I'm nothing more than a font type. No gender, no age, no nationality.

The readers of these books didn't care that Olivia won the Romantic Novel of the Year Award a couple of years ago. It mattered nothing to them that a reading recommendation from an Oscar winner made her book sales soar on the other side of the Atlantic. They also missed the Golden Globes, so they didn't see if the former *Emmerdale* star won the best actress award for playing a character Olivia invented.

No, all these readers care about is paddling in a fantasy world that N.R. Magnusson put on paper after I opened the envelope.

The sales of the *Caerli°°ani* books surpass anything Olivia has written by a gro-*tesque* margin, but that isn't my driving force. Fine, having completed four books now, it's not my *only* driving force. With these stories, I get lost in my pretend world as much as the readers do.

Oh, and they do.

Do you ever have one of those days when you can't figure out how the mermaids will overthrow the king of the unicorns? Do you ever not know how your heroine will escape the chains of Créalthador? Do they ever get you to wait in bay one at the drive-thru?

When these things happen to me, I open one of my unread emails from Cal (I have a folder of them; they're the ones *not* entitled 'THIS NEEDS A RESPONSE AND I HAVE READ RECEIPT') and, in the snippets that he copies and pastes from *Caerli°°ani* fan sites, forums and blogs, I read for a while about how safe an environment my followers of make-believe have built for themselves. Within minutes, I'm reminded that I was put on this earth for something worthwhile.

And to think, I used to believe it was only for my ability to solve the *Countdown* conundrums.

Chapter Four

Remember what I do for a living, okay? Therefore, of the fourteen scenarios I imagined, I didn't see Cal's blood pressure rise above normal when he heard my news. In business situations, the man always remains as calm as a meditating white dove sitting on a lavender pillow.

On the outside, anyway.

Beneath that well-dressed exterior, maybe there's another side to him: a chaotic side. A dark side. As I've said before, there's not much I know about him beyond his accent. Maybe he enjoys naked wrestling with his local funeral home's temporary residents on his days off.

No, Cal might like weird shit when he's not getting me a good time slot at the Hay Festival, but I doubt he engages in necrophilia. However, could this be when he lets loose everything those tailored three-piece suits have held in all these years?

I could've told him five days ago, during our wait in the departure lounge at Heathrow Airport. Or during the flight itself to New York. But I had a window seat and a new paperback, and Cal had a pocketful of red Biros. We also both wanted the privacy window up between our seating pods.

I had an opportunity to drop it into the conversation during the subsequent drive to East Hampton. After I fell asleep, though, and had another of those disturbing, vivid dreams, I was just relieved to wake up and find myself still on my side of the back seat and not on... Anyway, after that, I had to leave it for a bit.

Until now, it would seem, in a restaurant overlooking San Francisco Bay. We were told by more than one person at my reading this evening that the crab dishes here are a big deal.

Can you guess who ordered the filet fucking mignon that came with a sharp knife, then?

I watch Cal slowly rest his cutlery on either side of his plate. He lifts his wineglass by the stem and gives it a little swirl to check the flow of the wine legs. He sniffs it. A slow sip. After I've mentally decorated my Christmas tree, he swallows. His glass goes down. A dab of the lips with his napkin.

'Fine,' he answers.

'Really?'

'After all, who wouldn't want to bow out when their career continues to go from strength to strength?'

Hmmm, I'd better just check. 'Is that a rhetorical question or sarcasm?'

Cal picks up his fork and steak knife again. I rest my elbow casually on the table and put a protective hand over my neck. I really should have waited until we were on dessert to tell him.

Or at a finger buffet.

'Does it matter what I think?' he asks.

'Does a NASA scientist know pi to ten decimal places?'

'You've told me your plan. I know you'll have thought long and hard about it first.' The millisecond glimpse Cal threatens me with says that I better have. 'Therefore, what I think is irrelevant.'

'No, Thomas Edison's fear of the dark is irrelevant. What *you* think isn't.'

And Cal does something he has never done in all the years I've professionally trusted him: he shrugs. It's terrifying. It's fight or flight. With very little upper body strength, I'm considering whether to slip off my yellow satin Manolo Blahniks under the table.

'Cal, I need to be honest with my readers.'

He narrows his eyes. 'You write fiction.'

'I write about a subject I don't like pretending I'm an expert on.'

'And J.K. Rowling is an expert on wizards? Stephen King is an expert on mad clowns?'

'You know what I mean.'

'You write stories about women finding love in funny ways,' Cal reminds me.

'But are they believable?'

'I think they often give people hope.'

I'm at a loss. 'Why?'

'Jo, people fall in love every day. Dragons don't… crawl out of volcanoes every day. But you don't question that side of your writing.'

'That's because I'm fooling no one with dragons and witches.'

'You're fooling no one with any of your books,' he says. 'People read them for escapism. For enjoyment.'

'But I get no enjoyment from love.'

Cal sits back and rests his fingers on the flat base of his glass. 'Interesting.'

'From… writing about love.' I quickly search for my copy of *A Dummies Guide to Thinking Before Speaking*, which I've left open somewhere in the back of my eyes. 'I bet people think I write these books and pray it'll happen to me one day. When you know as well as I do, I don't want some man to come along again and, what, temporarily rescue me from my keyboard? Supply me with a short commercial break to take advantage of two-for-one meal offers for a month? No, thank you.'

When the waiter removes our plates, Cal asks for one dessert menu. I may be busy choosing something from it, but he has no excuse for not taking this opportunity to offer his thoughts. Especially since the spectacular view of the Golden Gate Bridge to his left barely even registered with him when we arrived.

He takes his phone out and taps away.

'Do you believe in love, Cal?'

Never before has such a personal question been asked. When we were introduced, the brusque way he shook my hand and never returned my smile said it all; it stopped dead the lively rendition of 'El Jarabe Tapatío' that had weirdly started playing in my head.

My ovaries had been tossing their sombreros and lifting their frilly skirts to it after they clocked him across the terrace.

But within those initial seven seconds, it became apparent Cal had put a bid in for charisma and was auction sniped. With nothing but a shrug, my reproductive organs returned to their cosy hibernation, and the mariachi band moved to another table.

A man with a resting face that depicts a middle finger negotiated a fantasy book deal for N.R. Magnusson that made headlines. It also paved the way for an efficient alliance that has stood the test of time. And even though this question is only at base camp, it still might test the strength of our perfect, dispassionate relationship. It's one that Cal's not at liberty to answer if he doesn't—

'I hope so,' he says.

'*Really*?'

I should learn to hide my shock sometimes.

'During those rare moments when I'm not saying your name in every other sentence, I do have a personal life.'

'You *do*?'

Again, Jo?

'Why does that surprise you?' he asks.

'Because you're bloody good at what you do.'

Cal tugs on his waistcoat and checks where the waiter is. 'That's… kind of you to say.'

As you can tell, the man doesn't do compliments. He's neither the big spoon nor the little spoon where they're concerned. Take Ridley Scott's *The Martian* as an example. Word has it that Cal gave the film only four out of five stars. I mean…

I'm baffled. 'If you're good at your job, why do you need anything else?'

'Even those who enjoy what they do for a living need something more every so often,' he says. 'And maybe I'm… good at what I do because I'm happy with my work-life balance.'

Happy? Cal? That's way beyond my level of imagination.

'Just because you don't need anything else,' he remarks. 'That makes you—'

'Lucky,' I finish for him.

'I was going to say… that makes you an exception. You love what you do. You also get paid well to do it.' Cal's impressive left eyebrow barges into the lines on his forehead. Better than a lot of writers out there, it implies.

'Which I'm grateful for,' I insist, in case anyone who forfeits the second 'i' in aluminium has forgotten.

'You have a gift, Jo.'

Is it a compliment when Cal says it with the same tone he'd use to tell me I have a massive eye bogey?

'But it came in a heart-shaped box,' I point out to him. 'Which is funny, seeing as my heart's not in it.'

Not everyone thinks it's funny, his deadpan expression informs me.

'Look how long it took me to write the last two books,' I say. 'I haven't been that miserable since I worked in an office where half the staff had sad cow's disease. They were *hard work*. It felt like the words were being dragged out of me. If that's the case, how long before my readers notice?'

'I wouldn't let it get to that.'

And Cal wouldn't. Of course he wouldn't. It's in his interests as well as mine, after all. But still.

'I've made up my mind,' I announce.

'Then you are retiring Olivia J. Lawrence and, what?'

'I'll just be N.R. Magnusson from now on.'

He rests on his elbows, his fingers steepled. 'And what about Jo?'

Rarely am I laid open to this level of scrutiny from him.

'Cal, I'm not heavily medicated, so I know you're staring at me.'

'When was the last time you were Josephine Washington?'

I force out a smile that I hope distracts him from the quick retort I don't have to hand. It's wishful thinking, I know, but they say nothing is impossible – other than eating a Rowntree's Fruit Pastille without chewing.

'Here's a thought,' Cal says.

'I thought thinking was what *I* am paid well to do.'

'Why don't you go find the old Jo again? Just for a while.'

The rim of my glass of sparkling water is sporting an outstanding smear of my lip lacquer.

'Did you know Winston Churchill wouldn't allow

lipstick to be rationed?' I offer.

'I… did not know that.'

'And did you know they only rationed bread and potatoes in Britain *after* the war?'

'And did *you* know you always use trivia as a diversionary tactic?' Cal queries.

'Interesting facts might help save someone's lifelines for the million-pound question.'

But the bloody things won't save my attempts today to evade capture.

'Look, I'm sure the… not-as-young-as-she-was Jo is content wherever she is,' I utter.

'Or maybe she'd like a little company.'

'Yeah,' I snort. 'About as much as she'd like to spend an evening reading the terms and conditions.'

I don't need to look at Cal to interpret his thoughts. The 'why don't' and the 'maybe' are mere suggestions, that's all. They're certainly not strong recommendations; he wouldn't *dare* make those to—

'Define "a while", sir.'

'There's no clear-cut definition,' he says.

'A month? Two months? And you said "*just* for a while". That must keep it snug in the "one season or less" category if we're ticking boxes.'

'Why don't we leave it open?'

I needlessly study my dessert menu again. When there's chocolate lava cake, no other dessert exists.

'You know me, Cal. I work better with a deadline. Tell me how long I've got to find Jo. You're the boss, after all.'

'Technically, I'm not your boss,' he states.

'You boss me about.'

'You pay me to boss you—'

I turn on an Oral-B smile and a flirty head tilt for the waiter as I give him my order. The woman at the table next to ours didn't get much ice cream with her dessert – I'd like to make sure I do.

'What are you afraid of?' I hear Cal ask.

Since the waiter is halfway to the kitchen, I doubt that question is for him. Oh, no. Just because I delved into the notion of love, I hope he doesn't think that's opened the floodgates for a rendition of 'Getting to Know You' from *The King and I*.

I don't even have to think about my answer. 'Sweet popcorn, neck massages, and puppies.'

Cal's expression is one that many people on my island adopt when someone says their weight in kilos.

'Just in case I fall on hard times and sign up for *I'm a Celebrity*,' I clarify.

Not even a smirk from the protein-rich, low-carb terminator sitting across from me. I swear you'd have more success betting on an uneventful afternoon as Jessica Fletcher's plus one at Miss Marple's barbecue in Midsomer.

I cross my arms. 'Why do you want to know?'

'I'm curious.'

'After eight years?'

'After eight years, you asked if I believe in love,' Cal says.

'That was work related.'

'So is this.'

'Hmm. Okay.' Pinching my bottom lip, I ponder.

'What am I afraid of? What… am I…? Ooh, I know. Crowds. And wasps. Oh, and asymmetrical houses. They scare the shi-*hit* out of me.'

I think that's an excellent answer. Cal's unblinking gaze thinks otherwise.

'I don't know,' I admit. 'Perhaps… only being known as this small-town writer who lacked ulterior motives. Someone who's happily buried beneath years and years of words from autumns past.' If at first you can't escape, metaphor. And always use your hands, a dreamy look, and a casual air to make it about someone else. 'In an impenetrable paper forest that she's built around herself.'

'Jo's not dead.'

My smile can't be kept alive just by the prospect of chocolate. 'But what if I find her and there's nothing left?'

There's no quiver in my voice, no apprehension in asking something that many people may be afraid to hear the answer to. I ask it matter-of-factly. Yes, it's a question that has raised its head more than once during the twenty-four hours every day when I'm on my own. The first time it was asked, I searched for punctures in the inflatable life jacket. This many years on, just knowing the location of the emergency exits will suffice.

Cal leans forward over the table. For a scary moment, I think he's about to take my hand.

'But what if there is?' he disputes.

I shake my head. 'Writing is what I am.'

'No, writing is what you do.'

'My writing helps you support Savile Row.'

As Cal sits back, he gives a tiny nod to his tailored shoulder. 'I have enough from Savile Row.'

'What about my apartment?'

'Your three-year lease is almost up. You were due a change.'

Does this man know when my next smear test and six-month dental check-up are due? Sadly...

'There are also my work obligations,' I remind him. 'Didn't I have to sign a diabolical pact in blood a while back?'

'This book we're promoting is the last one in the latest deal you signed up for.'

'Then why haven't you signed me up for a new deal?'

Cal shrugs. 'Maybe I knew this was coming.'

'Or maybe *I* need a change of... of...' Really, I need him to write down his official job title one of these days.

'Or maybe,' he says, 'you just need a change of scenery.'

Chapter Five

After three weeks of different time zones, it's back to Greenwich Mean Time. This is where the promotion of my book started last October. These final readings, though, are more intimate.

Usually, the first one takes place where the story is based. Sometimes, it's where the main character originates from. This latest tale is set in York, and the heroine is a Brightonian.

'So why the chuff are we in the Lake District?' I want to know, waking up when the smell of coffee tickles my senses through the open car door.

Cal isn't sure whether to be suspicious or amazed. 'You actually looked at the new itinerary I sent over yesterday?'

I stretch as I sit up. 'What, and spoil the surprise?' I tuck my fleecy blanket under my chin with one hand while the other accepts the proffered large latte. 'No. We're at Ings Services. Windermere town is about five minutes –' I tilt my head and raise my chin '– thataway.'

'How the hell do you know where we are?' Cal

asks, frowning. Actually, no, his frown frowns. It's a double frown. 'This is the first time you've opened your eyes since we got on the M40.'

'I've been here before.'

'If you can identify where we are from a few trees and a slim view of a divided highway, you've been here more than once.'

Ignoring what wasn't a question from Cal but underlyingly was, I make a start on the chicken and avocado salad bowl he hands me. There's no way this came from the refrigerated meal options available inside.

'What's happening in Windermere, then?' I finally ask.

'Bowness-on-Windermere. You have a book reading at The Romford.'

'Oh, The *Romford.*' Ditching the Lincolnshire twang, I adopt my best posh accent. 'I say, Lord Shaggington, we *are* going upmarket. Tell me, will the Earl and Countess of Bumnapper be joining us?'

'You've stayed there?'

'No. I couldn't afford anything above three stars back then.'

'Back then?' probes Cal.

I use my fork as a pointer. 'This may be *the* tastiest chicken and avocado salad I've ever had. Is this cress? You know, the stuff kids grow on a piece of kitchen roll on the windowsill?'

'They're microgreens. How long has it been since you were last here?'

'Even these grainy bits are good.'

'Quinoa.'

'Or kwin-o-a, if you're not posh,' I quip. 'And after you've eaten it, it's kwin... oh, ah, you have half of it stuck in your teeth.'

'Have you not been back here since you had a book published?'

I spear a light green chunk. 'Nope.'

Cal rests against the side of the car. 'Thirteen years is a long time.'

'I always said I hated avocado, but the funny thing is, I can't remember ever trying it until I met you. I gave it a go, and guess what?' My teeth rip it off the fork with gusto. 'I *love* it!'

'I know.'

'Just checking.'

I hold up the bowl while fitting perhaps one of the largest forkfuls of food in history into my mouth. I quickly start loading up the next mighty bite, which means this conversation – I'm sorry to say – is over and done with.

***

The following morning, with the car not due to collect us until eleven o'clock to take us on to York (better late than...), it's a bonus when I wake up early. By the time it's light outside, I'm halfway towards today's word count goal. As I take a brief writing break to enjoy my third coffee, it's impossible not to enjoy something else too.

Thanks to the arched white windows in my four-poster room, the view is panoramic, with England's largest natural lake and its haunting surroundings included in the room rate. Hardy pines and pale, wispy tree skeletons crowd the slopes on the far shore of Windermere, with cascading velvety fells towering around them in subdued beiges and whispers of green. The snowy peaks in the distance are hazy in the morning light, almost blending in with the pale sky. You get to appreciate the view twice this morning, the mirrored image on the mere's surface rippled only by the odd water bird and the faintest breeze.

It's meteorological spring, but the season has yet to reach this far north; the promise of what's coming is still on its way. But I know what to expect, mentally mapping the changes ahead from memories stored in a keepsake box.

When I lived and worked in Halifax, I started driving here on my own every fortnight, just for the day. Every fortnight, for about three years. I became reacquainted with forest walks carpeted in wild garlic and luscious ferns, which thrived out of the spotlight. I revisited waterfalls that sang in the summer and shouted curses at you after the rains.

Or at least that's how I recall them sounding to my adolescent ears.

That was when the woods and waters were our childhood playground for a few years. A time when a secluded house near one of the region's lakes was our base for three weeks during the summer holidays, a fortnight at Easter, and whatever our parents could agree on at Christmas.

After my fifteenth birthday, it would be over a

decade before I ventured across the border into Cumbria again. Once I did, though, that was it. Even if the weather wasn't great (the Lakes average two hundred days of rain a year), I was content to drive around for hours and hours.

When the rest of the traffic went straight on, I turned off the road. Residents would stare at a strange car as I drove through backstreets and tiny hamlets, some of which were only a row of houses and a letterbox. And when many of the watery perimeters on my map were covered in kisses, I extended my search.

I never worried about my car breaking down, despite my green Ford Fiesta getting through its MOT every year on the proverbial rusty wing and a prayer. Nor did I worry about getting lost, whether on foot or behind the wheel. Maybe it was my invincibility cape that made me brave. Most of us temporarily own one, don't we? You know, just until our twenties are taken from us. It's the same one that deflects putting things in perspective and pessimism.

Or maybe it was because of something else. My natural abilities as a map reader and co-pilot, perhaps. They were titles I earned in my youth when I walked ahead of everyone and sat in the passenger seat – granted to me in the absence of a son.

When I moved back to Cleethorpes, there were still areas on my map that weren't crossed out. But I'd tried my best. It was in my glove compartment for years until it... until it wasn't. And finding the house where a little girl shared her imagination became less of a need.

With the views permanently etched in my mind, I had all the inspiration that N.R. Magnusson required. The rest of the world was Olivia's oyster. She could drop her three generations of bakers anywhere in the Cotswolds she fancied. She was allowed to plant her widowed teacher and the ghost of her dead husband in whichever *arrondissement* of Paris she liked.

Just not the Lakes.

***

Apart from Costa Coffee making itself a surprising but (especially for me) welcome two-storey resident since my last visit to Bowness-on-Windermere, this small town with an immense pull has hardly changed.

The wooden rowing boats on the pebble shore have been revarnished a few times instead of renewed; the gentle tide rocks them as they pose seductively on their sides. They must exercise tourists' thumbs on their phones these days more than their arms on the oars. The swans still waddle among them, awaiting their daily handouts. No doubt they continue to terrify children at their eye level.

Moored up at the landing stage are the familiar Miss Cumbria and Miss Lakeland II, still visions in white and swimming-pool blue, with subdued waves slapping noisily against their bows. The booking office and the coffee shop on the pier look like they've had generous coats of racing-green paint reapplied. The river cruise maps next to them show the same excursions. Only the prices have changed since I was here last.

I'm still amazed at how easily I walked away from my Lakeland addiction, unlike guidebook author A. Wainwright. His love affair with the silent fells—

'The lake is beautiful at this time of day, isn't it?'

Where did the elderly couple sitting on the bench next to me come from?

I find my voice. 'It truly is.'

When the wife brings out a paper bag, I gratefully accept a sherbet lemon.

'Where have you come from?' the husband asks.

'London.'

'That's not a city accent.'

'It certainly isn't. I'm a Lincolnshire lass.'

'Lovely part of the country.'

'Especially if you're averse to hills,' I claim.

'This isn't your first time here, though.'

I face them more directly, revealing my pleasant surprise at his deduction. Unless I'm promoting something, it feels strange to be the observed and not always the observer – the only role left when it was my turn to choose. It didn't bother me. I was happy to run with it and make it my own.

I ask him, 'Would you be related to Sherlock Holmes, by any chance?'

He answers me by tapping the side of his nose.

'Steve, honestly,' his wife affectionately faux-scolds. 'He keeps saying he'll be the next great detective novelist. Silly old sod.'

'Why shouldn't I be? You're never too old to dream.' Steve looks at me. 'Don't you agree, lass?'

'Oh, absolutely. And when you give your dream a pen, you're not alone when you write.'

'When you give your dream a pen.' He nods. 'I like that saying. May I steal it?'

I point to my bulging cheek. 'Payment for the sweet.'

'How old do you think I am?'

Isn't it a question anyone over a certain age loves to ask? I often wonder: do they ask it because they're proud of how young they appear? Or do they wish to promote how lucky they are, making it past the age of many of their friends?

The liver spots on Steve's hands are a clue, as is the style of his shoe, chosen for comfort and slip resistance. Then there are the neat hems on his trousers, with his crossed leg revealing a hairless shin above a brown sock. Last but not least, the half Windsor knot in his tie, tucked neatly down the front of a burgundy Damart sweater.

'Thirty... four?' I hazard a guess. 'Thirty-five?'

Steve squeezes my wrist. His grip is full of gratitude. 'Seventy-seven.'

'Never!'

'I didn't give up work until two years ago,' he tells me. 'And I'd still be working if my hip hadn't given out. But then I wouldn't be able to come here every morning to enjoy this.'

'Have you always lived locally?'

'I was born and bred here. I've also bought my plot in the cemetery over there, haven't I, Annie?'

She pouts her lips. 'I'm not discussing that.'

'I've had a full life,' he states, 'and I can die tomorrow with no regrets.'

'I hope it isn't tomorrow,' I remark. 'I want to read this book.'

He winks. 'Steve Tilburn. Keep an eye out in a few years.'

'And when I buy a copy…'

He nudges his wife. 'Hear that? When.'

'… I'll be back and asking for it to be signed.'

'We have authors up here doing that all the time,' Steve says. 'Well-known ones, too. One was here just last night. At the place behind us.'

'Is that so?'

'The son's wife was there.' He turns to Annie. 'Who did Sara say the author was?'

'I don't know. I try not to listen when my daughter-in-law is speaking.'

'But I think you'll be back here well before my book is finished,' Steve tells me.

'You—?'

'Ready to go, Jo?'

Cal is standing a few feet away, hands in the pockets of his navy tailored trousers, his single-breasted jacket pushed back on either side. The chauffeur-driven car is waiting at the kerb behind him.

I know what Steve and Annie are thinking, and they're right – Cal's impressing nobody by showing off his *full* Windsor tie knot.

'Time's up,' I declare, getting to my feet. 'It's been a pleasure meeting you both.'

'You too,' they chorus.

I halt in front of Cal, my hand reaching into his inside breast pocket. It has everything. Including tampons, since that evening in Seattle in 2018. We don't talk about that, though.

From behind, I touch Steve's shoulder and hand him Cal's business card. 'I'll let this chap know you'll be contacting him.'

When I glance back at them, Steve has taken his glasses off and passed them to Annie, who is reading the card now that she can see the words.

'Hey, don't you worry, lass.'

I stop with one Crocs clog in the car's rear footwell, where a latte is waiting along with my two-tone SJP pumps. The Max Mara trouser suit I'm wearing underneath my cashmere coat breathes a sigh of relief.

Steve pats the empty bench seat beside him. 'I'll save this spot for you.'

Chapter Six

'Here she is.'

It is said with the same enthusiasm that a woman would muster up to welcome her ex-husband's twenty-one-year-old girlfriend to the Boxing Day family dinner.

There's no halfhearted stampede from any of my three sisters, despite it being months since my last visit. No warm welcome for me to the home that Ma unintentionally made for them all near Cornwall's St Ives. She permanently left Cleethorpes shortly after I moved to West Yorkshire, hoping to say goodbye to more than just her place of birth and one daughter.

I leave my small suitcase and laptop bag near the door and cross the kitchen. My older sister slowly gets off her stool to give me a hug that feels twenty per cent genuine. The other eighty is what TV believes is the only way to greet people nowadays, regardless of how long you've known them. Forty-four years or forty-four seconds. Who cares? And it doesn't matter if you like them.

'Hey, Keren.'

'You look tired,' she says.

My skin is glowing from a BIOTEC facial. I'm still relaxed after two days at a spa where they rebalanced my chakra with crystals and put the zing back into my Zen. And thanks to all the happy hormones I produce from walking every day and clocking up fifteen miles each morning on my exercise bike, the joy and positivity I radiate could light up a street. But if all she can comment on is how I've fared after six hours behind a steering wheel, that's fine.

I just hope there's a power cut before she finds out who fucking did it.

And... breathe.

'Where is she?' I ask.

'Changing sheets. A member of staff called in sick.'

Leaving my sisters to finish their auditions for the next series of *Gogglebox,* I walk across the courtyard. In the thatched guesthouse, I follow the sound of tuneless singing up the carpeted stairs.

'Hey, Ma.'

Startled during her solo musical, a busty woman with a white pixie cut flings a crumpled pillowcase in the air. With her hands freed up, Ma slaps them over her heart and provides a clip for this year's nominations at the Overacting Awards. By the end of this very long weekend, they'll have a few to choose from.

From faux surprise to faux joy in a nanosecond, she hugs me longer than either of us is truly comfortable with. She releases me after kissing my cheek close to my ear. It always hurts. Ma knows it does too.

'Have you lost some weight, Milly, erm, Jo?'

Knowing she would ask me this, I purposely weighed myself this morning – I'm a pound heavier than last time. 'Nope.'

'You look like you have.'

'Well, I haven't.'

'You look like you have.'

I wait until Ma turns round to pick up some clean bed linen before mouthing behind her, 'Well, I haven't.'

I change a pillowcase and lay the finished product at the head of the fitted sheet.

'What's the goss then?' I ask. 'Where've you been? What's been happening?'

'Nothing much.' Ma rearranges my pillow. Yep, it looks no different. 'Izzie has finally sold her apartment in Spain.'

'Yeah, she emailed me this week.'

'She had to drop the asking price and what have you.'

'Yeah, she… told me everything in her email.'

'She has to be out in four weeks.'

I give up.

'Yes, Ma, and she would've liked you to go over for a week or two while she still has it.'

'She wanted me to go over for a week or two…'

Am I a ghost? Can only those who communicate with spirits hear me?

'… but I'm too busy with this place and what have you.'

'Your manager is more than capable,' I remind her. 'And your receptionist won't mind some overtime now that her son's gone travelling. You also have three daughters who… Your manager and receptionist could run this place without you for a fortnight.'

'It would've been nice. Who knows, Milly, erm, Jo, if I'll ever go away again?'

Ma always talks like she has months to live, yet she doesn't even take blood pressure tablets. Oh, and the 'Milly, erm, Jo' thing? No, it's not dementia. She remembers the name of our current prime minister, but remembering her daughters' names is impossible.

'Then go,' I urge.

'No, I can't.'

'Why? What could go wrong?'

We both know what could go wrong: very little. But this woman wrote the book on being a control freak – without help.

'I should have gone over last September and what have you.'

And Ma will say this many times before Izzie swaps her view of the cathedral in Barcelona for the one in Lincoln. And many times after that.

'Did you book a table for this afternoon?' I ask.

'One o'clock. Is that all right?'

I couldn't have timed my arrival any better. It's half past twelve now and a fifteen-minute drive to the restaurant. 'Perfect.'

'Are you sure?'

'I'm sure.'

'I didn't know if you'd want it for one or two.'

'Either, Ma. I'm not fussed.'

'Are you *sure*?'

'As death and taxes.'

She gives me one end of the bed runner, and we lay it across the quilt together. Once she is happy with how her side looks, Ma bustles over to mine to correct my grave velvet error.

'I should've booked it for two,' she says.

'One is good.'

'I knew I'd get it wrong and what have you.'

'You didn't, honestly. In fact, one is better; I'm absolutely starving.'

'Are you sure? Maybe we can still make it later.'

'Really, *really* sure.'

Ma is flattening and flattening and flattening the top of the quilt. The fold marks will eventually get bored and give up because she never will.

'I wish I'd booked it for two now and what have you,' she mumbles.

God, give me strength – or at least a good alibi.

***

Keren says the lobster has given her indigestion. Milly, twin number one, has been talking to her on-and-off boyfriend on the phone since we got here. Judging by her tone when she ends the call, I assume it's off. However, just as she finishes her rump steak, he shows up. We then witness enough PDA to warrant a visit from the second-base police, forcing me to amend my earlier assumption.

Twin number two, Aine, is with us in body, but her spirit is plugged into Graham Anstell Limited. She flicks through emails and documents on her tablet, picking at her sea bass and hardly touching her dessert. The guilt of taking half of today as a holiday is getting the better of her.

I don't know what she does at the wealth management firm where she works – something to do with financial planning. Whatever it is, she gets paid well and is proud to have a senior-level position at her age, which she achieved by being a hard worker and hard-nosed. Ma is worried her colleagues don't like her. Aine couldn't care less.

I watch her hold a spoonful of rose-petal panna cotta aloft while she reads something on the propped-up screen. It's been there for ages now. If Aine falls on hard times, at least she can spray herself silver and become a street performer – one of those living statues.

'Jo, erm, Aine?'

No reaction.

Ma tries again. 'Aine.'

Nothing.

It's quarter past two, and I'm entering my PIN into the portable card machine. Everyone at the table – bar one – is preparing to leave. Today, I'm more eager than usual to go, seeing as my family aren't following the Washington rules. They clearly state that backhanded compliments are for immediate family *only*.

The woman sitting at a nearby table was the innocent victim. We were both in the bathroom earlier, and I asked her what perfume she was wearing because she smelt heavenly. Black Opium, she said. I told her she was a good advert for it. When she left the restaurant with her husband/fella/lucky man, she said goodbye to me.

And that was when they all started.

'A pretty girl for her size.'

'Coming out wearing hardly any makeup. That takes confidence.'

'Did you see her bloke? I bet she can't believe her luck.'

The waitress is now clearing the plates away around Aine. I would have happily left without her if we'd come in my car, but we didn't. We couldn't.

'Not enough room for three in the back of that thing,' Keren had declared earlier, walking past my Jaguar F-Pace and unlocking her Renault Clio.

I've had this car – my biggest purchase to date – for nearly a year. It's the first time any sister has acknowledged it, even though I've driven it here four times. Perhaps the colour, Carpathian Grey, is too subtle. Maybe I should have got it in Jealous as Hello Yellow. Or Bitter Bitch Blue.

***

'Nothing like some hearty nosh to bring my girls together,' Ma remarks – not quips – as we sneak out of the house to walk her golden retrievers.

Keren is searching for antacid tablets in the kitchen. Milly is in her lodgings above the garage, arguing with her boyfriend. Aine will be somewhere doing something on one of her many modes of communication.

With Leo DiCaprio, David Beckham and Patrick Swayze snuffling in the undergrowth, we stroll through the village and enjoy the surprising warmth from the late March sun.

We admire the front gardens, stopping to look when we are unseen. At least, that's the only time I stop. We backtrack when we smell the beautiful scent of an evergreen viburnum, resplendent with clusters of white flowers. The bush is halted in its attempt to take over the world by a vintage red telephone box, loved equally by tourists and those caught short.

We exhaust discussions about my sisters' love lives. Every time I come over, there's always some drama. None are married, although Keren almost bagged a husband – she claims – when she got pregnant on board the *Pacific Sapphire*. But that relationship only lasted the length of the holiday. Now she puts every failed relationship down to a lack of proper closure with Mr Ocean Cruise.

I think the closure came when she contacted him two months later to give him the good news. The only response Keren got was to wish her good luck. If that wasn't closure, the twenty years of silence are a whopping great billboard in Times Square sign.

There's been a spluttering stream of boyfriends over the years, except none of them will give her what she desperately craves: the opportunity to quit her exhausting job as a part-time purchase ledger clerk. Her dream is to become a stay-at-home wife – as long as her husband works away a lot.

Everyone always said Keren *would* have made someone an ideal trophy wife. Note the emphasis on 'would'. In fact, when she was young, people compared her to Grace Kelly. Sadly, any comparison stopped when she started picking up her son at the school gates. That was when she should've written a book herself. *How to Always Look Miserable* would've been a bestseller.

She still wouldn't have been happy, though.

Then there's Milly. Ah, Milly. Tall, willowy. Absolutely stunning. She could've ridden a glamorous career wave with her looks. But behind the façade, there's still the seventeen-year-old whom her teacher described as an 'aimless underachiever'. She's never set a goal or made a plan; she cares for nothing, not even her jumbled pile of red-soled shoes and designer trainers.

Because Milly lacks arrogance and scores a neutral seven on the pH scale, most of Cornwall's residents are oblivious to her. Despite this, she calls herself an 'it girl', even though she'll soon hit the big four-oh.

We call her a wishful thinker.

Usually, she prefers to sleep with men beyond her postcode who can, at the very least, get into a members-only nightclub. This means Milly can keep her earnings from promoting fashion and beauty brands on social media, which she spends on stuff that doesn't make her happy. It does delay her getting a council tax bill anytime soon, though, that displays her name and address.

Last but not least, there's Aine. If you put Milly and Aine in a line-up and asked anyone to pick out the twins, they would never pick out these two. Never. Five foot two, fabulous curves, and only she knows whether she's beautiful, as she is never seen without full face crayoning. Is she beautiful *with* makeup? That would depend on who you're asking. If you're attracted to women who hone their cosmetic skills by spending time in theatre dressing rooms during panto season, then...

But what Aine lacks in subtle contouring, she makes up for in brains. She has posed in a black gown and mortarboard. She has earned letters after her name. There are even men in her office who earn less than her.

Therefore, the fact she can't find a knight in shining armour who will love her like a fairy-tale princess frustrates the hell out of her.

Aine's current prickly mood is because of her lack of success at a singles mixer, which she attended after an equally unprofitable afternoon prowling yet another menswear department. An article she read claimed that searching for the last remaining white crewneck on the rail was a great way to bag a man. Not great for her, though: starting in Sloane Street's Prada, she's now down to Plymouth's Primark.

Ma thought she was being helpful by reminding Aine about the fabulous Asda at Hayle Harbour that sells menswear. She would even go with her if she wanted.

A supportive mother, some might think.

Beef and lamb joints are on offer this month, and what have you, some might know.

'Now Jo, erm, Aine is joining some of those online dating things,' Ma informs me. 'That eHarmony and Tender and what have you.'

'Tinder.'

'She said it was Tender.'

I shrug. 'Perhaps she did.'

'No, she did.'

'It's Tinder.'

Ma is doubtful. 'Are you sure?'

'I'm positive.'

'She said Tender, though.'

'Yes, but it's *Tinder*.'

'Well, she said it's Tender and what have you.'

I wish those cliffs were a little closer.

'I think Aine, erm, Keren is going to join up with her,' Ma says. 'It would be nice to see the pair of them find love. It isn't easy for them when Keren, erm, Milly is turning men down left, right and what have you.'

Milly has been many things, but right isn't…

'But then she did get her looks from me,' Ma adds. 'Aine, erm, Keren did too, but she lost them, poor thing. Sadly, you and Jo, erm, Aine got your looks from your father and what have you.'

Ma only sugarcoats strawberries. Does it hurt when she says things like this? Remember the old saying: What doesn't kill you...

... means it needs more arsenic.

Well, we've dissected and passed judgement on my sisters' love lives, as we always do, which only leaves...

'How's the writing?' Ma asks.

'Good.'

I don't need to go into detail. As long as it's good, that's enough.

Unless there's a sorrowful-looking woman on the cover with a factory behind her, Ma won't read it. She started to read my first book, *This is Just a Love Story*, but she gave up after a few pages, saying she didn't get it. I didn't take offence. After all, this is the woman who watched the first four minutes of *The Polar Express* and claimed it wasn't very Christmassy.

Ma would never attempt to read one of my *Caerli°°ani* novels, even if she knew about my fantasy sideline. None of them know about it. She eloquently describes all films in that genre as 'bunches of weirdos and ugly people making lots of noise and what have you'. Nope, she's never watched even one. But they keep showing bloody trailers for them in the ad breaks when she's watching *Coronation Street*.

Our pleasant chatter this afternoon brings us to Ma's local pub, where a group of her fellow B&B owners are relishing a couple of hours off. Talk soon turns to tomorrow and her seventieth birthday.

Aine was far too busy with work to organise a

surprise party. Milly has rarely remembered our mother's birthday since her pocket money stopped. Keren always uses the same excuse for everything: her child. Her get-out-of-doing-anything-for-anyone-else card. She still uses it, even though her son lives and works in Manchester.

This meant it was all left to one person to arrange a *Downton Abbey*-themed extravaganza in Ma's adopted county, which required:

- Finding her address book to copy all her contacts – she's been using the same one for twenty-three years. There are quite a few names crossed out now (may they rest in peace)
- Choosing a suitably grand venue
- Posting invitations, ticking off RSVPs and arranging suitable accommodation – taking budgets and stubborn-old-fart special requirements into account
- Booking a Rolls-Royce Phantom and a double-decker bus from the 1920s
- Hiring costumes
- Hiring hair and makeup people
- Paying a florist to buy up the southwest's quota of calla lilies, dusky roses, tulips and enough drapey foliage to cover the Eden Project
- Finding a catering company that can recreate a 1920s feast
- Tracking down a firm to provide a cocktail

bar with a piercing/tattoo/beard-free mixologist
- Hiring a black-tie orchestra
- Hiring waltzing dancers
- Ordering a show-stopping eight-tiered cake
- Organising fireworks to dazzle the guests and to call time on the evening

Finding the address book was something I did during my stay at Christmas. A bit of forward planning, a pat on the back for me. *Well done, Jo.* However, the rest of it needed organising before and during my busy book tour.

I'm telling you, in between my TV, radio and bookshop appearances – not to mention my numerous readings – I don't know how I did it. Somehow, though, I spared Cal enough for him to put all this together. The man is a genius.

The man also likes his handmade leather lace-ups from Italy.

'What I would really like for my birthday this year...' Ma starts to say to her friendly rivals.

'Yes?' five of them ask.

'No. What I would *really* like...'

They all lean forward. 'Yes?'

It's time for Ma to add even more suspense by taking a sip of her drink and savouring it, her head slightly tilted to one side, eyes closed. Her friends can't be sure whether she's about to answer or break into song. They don't know we also have this little performance when we ask whether the local Co-op was busy. I'm not the only artist in my family.

'… is for just *one* of my girls to get married. Just one. Just so I can go wedding dress shopping with them and choose the flowers, the cake, the carriage and what have you. Imagine how I must feel having all these single daughters.'

I may put my mother's little quirks into my stories, but Jane Austen should know her Mrs Bennet is alive and well today – and far more dramatic.

'Did you hear that, Jo?' one of her friends asks.

Ma waves her glass of brandy in my direction. 'Not this one. She doesn't need a husband. Why would she? She has it all. Don't you, Milly, erm, Jo?'

Chapter Seven

I bustle into my apartment and turn on some table lamps. It's only just gone five, and the clocks went forward this past weekend. Usually, that's too early in the afternoon to need artificial lighting. But the glorious weather we've had these past few days has peaked, with the air feeling noticeably heavier each time I stopped on my way back from Cornwall. It looks like the promise of a storm has earned the weather people their bonuses.

Once I'm at my happiest again – bathrobed and braless – I step out onto my balcony to watch the sky getting broodier by the minute. Above the traffic noise, distant rumbles can be heard. On the other side of England's capital, lightning flashes like a silent white explosion below the horizon, briefly silhouetting the skyline.

There's another rumble, more baritone this time. The darkening sky is gradually marching ahead of the storm. When the lightning forks from left to right, my reaction is drowned out by the pursuing thunder that rattles the foundations of the surrounding counties.

The lights flicker. They go out for a second before popping back on. Thunder now cracks loud and close enough to upset dogs and set off car alarms. Other spectators are enjoying the free show, I see. One baby isn't, I hear.

The sky is now awash with loaded purple tones. Yes, this is more like it! It's alive with electricity. Branches of brilliant white slice the sky in two, one after another, their ghostly images hovering in the sky. Flashes on the horizon and high above are cheered on by thunderclaps and booms. They don't pause for breath, providing the soundtrack and building tension. I go back inside just as the heavens open, bringing down a muslin curtain of rain and hail onto London.

The lights could go off again and stay off, giving me an excuse to light some of the candles that people have bought me. They are dotted on the shelves and sideboard, displaying their white wicks. There are more of them on the mantelpiece.

I've always believed there are three reasons for lighting candles: having friends over for dinner, having one friend come over for more than dinner, and power cuts. In which case, I've had no reason to light any of them in nearly three years.

No reason whatsoever.

None.

In nearly three years.

When was the last time you were Josephine Washington?

I look at the gold band on my right ring finger. It's

a leaf pattern dotted with turquoise, my birthstone. I bought it eighteen years ago at a craft fair in Haworth. If fork lightning hit it – if it hit the only ring I own – I wonder who would find my charred remains.

I have no drafts to send or interviews to prepare for, and there are no book covers to sign off on or chapters to fight to keep in, which means Cal won't bother me. Ma won't ring anytime soon, either. Not unless they take ITV3 off the air. Or the price of double-knit yarn skyrockets.

Jana is spending her Christmas bonus on a trip to see her sister in… I don't know where. Bath, Biķernieki, Buenos Aires? She'd most likely be the one to find me when she returns next week. The image would probably stay with my cleaning lady forever, but the stench and the stains left on the rug wouldn't.

The room briefly lights up, and a crack of thunder makes me start. It felt like it was directed my way. Is nature singling me out?

When was the last time you were Josephine Washington?

Right. Olivia J. Lawrence and Josephine Washington. Let me fill you in.

They have both legally been my names, if not my full names. I was christened Olivia and given two middle names: Josephine and Lawrence. No, Lawrence wasn't my surname, and yes, that's how much my parents wanted a son.

After watching the 1949 movie version of *Little Women*, Ma wanted to call me Amy, after one of the March sisters. She wasn't a massive fan of that character. No, she was a massive fan of Elizabeth Taylor, the beautiful actress who played her.

I know what you're thinking. Why not just call me Elizabeth, then? Well, Ma had an aunt called Elizabeth, and Ma's grandmother told everyone God didn't bless her with beauty for a reason: she was convinced her eldest daughter's great mind would make her successful. She would still meet a wealthy man, but she would be admired for her intellect.

Elizabeth never married, and she died a year before she was due to retire – a heart attack while packing frozen fish fingers on a production line.

Dad wanted to name me after his mother. However, Ma despised the name Olivia – *and* his mother – and wouldn't even consider it. Thirty-six hours in labour, though, took their toll on Ma's body (it's something she loves to remind me about every year. Can you guess when?), which meant Dad was tasked with registering the birth.

After Ma argued *at* him the previous evening, he was adamant about what my first name would be. Her tirade couldn't have been that bad, though, as Dad decided to go with her choice for one of my middle names. Except he couldn't remember which sister it was.

Dad asked the lady filling out the form who she thought was most people's favourite character in *Little Women*. Actually, a gold star for remembering the film. As a result, Ma didn't get the first name she wanted for me, and I ended up with a middle name that meant nothing to anyone. Only when I became a writer did being named after Josephine March, a woman with a passion for words, have any significance.

While Dad was working or commuting (or simply hiding away), Ma and Keren would call me Jo. Ma never really warmed to it, but it was preferable to Olivia; I was only called that at school. When the twins came along, they only knew me as Jo. Not knowing any different, I got used to answering to both names.

After my parents separated, it was eight years before they made it official. Ma celebrated by marrying Glynn Scott the following Christmas. Thirteen years later, she caught Glynn with another woman in their stables. Fortunately, his sudden death that same year saved her from having to file for another divorce.

Ma was then free to marry the man she said was her destiny, and she enjoyed ten blissful years with her Swede until he died, too. Within a month, she had given away everything that had belonged to Anders Swettinbedde – including his surname – reverting to her maiden name, Washington.

Although I was already established as Olivia J. Lawrence in the writing world by then, all four daughters showed a rare mark of solidarity by following Ma down the deed poll route. I also used the opportunity to do a little juggling to make my name Josephine Olivia Lawrence Washington. Only those who need to see my ID know the name change is official.

And Cal. Obviously.

When was the last time you were Josephine Washington?

I don't even know what he meant by that. Jo hasn't been anywhere. She's been too busy building up her magical world finale and praying it won't be a *wah-waah* conclusion. And when her witches haven't been defeating evil, she's been putting on paper those romantic scenarios she made up or dreamt or (quite often) rehashed to always – yes, always – meet her deadlines.

He forgets that this is the woman who, in her ninth novel, spun the sad reality of her one-and-only blind date misadventure into slapstick comedy. This was *after* her literary sentimentality had begun perimenopause, too. Few people could do that.

And fewer still will have an Emmy-winning actress bring the main character to life on the big screen next year.

Yes, that was all Jo's doing.

Believe me when I say she's not complaining. Nor does she ever forget how lucky she is to do a job she loves – one that allows her to live a relatively simple life while sleeping on bloody good sheets.

When was the last time you were Josephine Washington?

Cal should know better than anyone that writing is a lifestyle choice. It's also not for the fainthearted. Jo adores what she does for ten of the twelve hours that make up her working day. The other two hours are spent doubting everything she's just written.

When she isn't writing, she is rewriting or researching. Or she's reading what the competition has put out there. Or she is trying to avoid the reviews. And when Jo isn't doing any of those things, she is *thinking* about writing.

It wasn't N.R. Magnusson who thought up the backstories for all thirty-seven characters in the *Caerli°°ani* books. It wasn't Olivia who, while having sex with a data analyst, thought of a clever plot twist for her seventh novel.

No, it was Josephine Washington.

I mean, it was me. I'm… Jo. I'm the one who—

The tring-tring of a bicycle bell drifts from my bag. I retrieve my archaic phone from where it's buried underneath my purse, my Kindle, a – ooh, nice! – fruit scone, a backup book and an empty Squashies bag.

+447708639227: Shame

Even though it's a text from an unsaved number, sadly, it's not from a stranger who sent it in error. Something like that would usually prompt a story from me. If I were still in the romance business, that is.

Are you now wondering why it's from an unsaved number? If you are, you've never had the one who got away not *go* away.

It follows on from one I received this morning when I was saddling up Ken Barlow, Ma's black Trakehner gelding.

+447708639227: What are you up to tonight

Oh, that text definitely triggered something.

Memories, mainly, of the times I've shown him where to find the question mark on his phone's bloody keyboard.

I finally replied to it from a booth in Burger King at the Exeter Services, following a Chicken Royale lunch – and six discarded responses.

Me: I'm busy

Go on, say it. Why did it take me ages to come up with two words? I'm a writer, aren't I? If I take that long to conjure up such a carefully worded response, how long does it take me to write an effing novel?

First, you need to understand who I'm dealing with.

As one company says in their food ads, this isn't just any ex. I have known him for almost as long as it takes to make an overnight success, according to Eddie Cantor (twenty years. Saves you looking it up). Since he has my number, though, and we occasionally correspond – i.e., when desperate times call – he has been labelled a friend in these lean times.

He is, however, first and foremost, an ex. Sorry, The Ex. You know the one: he who lingers on your careful shoulder and stops you from building your hopes up again, lest you have a moment of weakness and forget what's to come.

We've tried the 'friends' thing many, many times over the years. We've tried the 'friends-who-sometimes-aggressively-cuddle' thing, too. Again, many times. And… yes, he was my 'last time'.

Anyway, back to my carefully worded lunchtime response. The issue was that, had I said I was free tonight, the man would have waited however long it had taken for me to text him back. Then he would have said *he* had something on, but he 'could be free later'. Not '*will* be free'. No, he '*could* be'. 'Could' guarantees that I *won't* make any plans.

Yes, okay. I'll step away from the aggressive italics and the air quotes. My apologies.

After I sent my response at lunchtime and deleted the text thread, I put my phone away and continued my journey. I didn't prop it up on the dashboard with the volume on ten. Nor did I check it every three miles, as I knew I hadn't put it on mute. I didn't forget to charge it last night, either. When I stopped for a coffee two hours later, I didn't bother looking. No point.

I stare at the new text again.

+447708639227: Shame

Hardly. If we never get together again, I'm sure life will carry on as usual. I can't imagine it will speed up global warming. Or change how many points Cyprus gives Greece at the next Eurovision.

Before I abandon my phone for the evening, I delete the text. I don't want to leave that convenient apple in the fruit bowl. Someone might resort to making an ill-advised crumble out of it.

As I wait for my computer to—

Tring-tring.

Chapter Eight

When I arrive at the coffee shop, there's no queue at the counter. I hop forward and give the man behind the till a warm smile. He doesn't give me one in return. I order my latte and move along, defogging my specs at the waiting end.

I'm certainly not the sort of clientele this place hopes to attract. Its interior is a clash of industrial meets rustic meets the tailor shop used in the *Kingsman* movie series. It welcomes those who wear glasses to look fashionable, who aren't successful but look it. Those people who need to be seen.

A bang BANG *BANG* click shhhhh bang BANG later, and my drink is presented to me without so much as a 'Ta-daaaa!'. I leave the saucer on the tray, along with all hopes of a tip.

I don't need to search for him. Nor do I need the help of whereishe.com. After all these years, I can sense The Ex. I follow my inner radar to where he's sitting, looking like the place hired him for promo shots, the requirements calling for a slender redhead. It's a pity they couldn't afford a well-known one –

such as the actor N.R. Magnusson hired to narrate the audiobooks.

He has hogged a table surrounded by four semi-comfy chairs, choosing the seat opposite the window. You might think The Ex picked that one because he loves people-watching. Until you see him run a hand over his slicked-back undercut and return the gaze of the person who means the most to him.

I knew he would already have his drink, just like I knew there wouldn't be one for me. It's like last September at Highgate Wood. I thought we were meeting up for a brisk walk and a catch-up. The Ex was twenty-five minutes late, bringing the rain and only one takeaway cup.

'I didn't know what you'd want,' was his excuse that afternoon.

And how long has my drink order remained unaltered? Oh, just the whole time he's known me.

Since he didn't even bring a coat that day, we had to sit in his BMW for eighty-six minutes while he dribbled out his gripes. I was presumably only there to estimate how much cheddar he wanted with all that whine. I finally escaped by instigating an argument.

Over the coffee?

Nnnnnot directly.

Today, The Ex's overpriced drink sits on the low table in front of him: tea with no milk. It could never have worked between us.

I take the chair to his left, shedding my olive Barbour Wray gilet before sitting down. I'm wearing the outfit I just drove back from Cornwall in, which I salvaged from the laundry bin.

'Thanks for making an effort,' The Ex utters.

My pink vest sporting Jane Austen's portrait, brown hiking tights and blue plaid shirt are unworthy of a second look.

'Well,' I say, 'when it comes to a woman with a high hemline and low expectations, I know you can't help yourself.'

'You didn't tip,' he remarks, my sarcasm no longer registering with him.

'They expect a tip before you taste your order. If I can't even get a smile, then I ain't a-tippin'.'

'You are loaded.' The Ex's tone suggests my gratitude could do with a highly toxic dry clean.

'Not really. I have enough to get by. Maybe that's down to not tipping needlessly.'

'These people rely on tips,' he tells his reflection.

'Oh, please! The man had a Baume & Mercier watch on his wrist. He'd also doused himself in Oud Wood.'

He slowly shakes his head. 'How do you sleep at night?'

'With the light off,' I disclose – to myself, it would seem.

A pair of four-inch heels has caught his attention. In fact, there are two pairs among the group who have just walked in, but one of the women is a brunette. I think I was a similar shade when we dated. As far as The Ex is concerned, she might as well have stayed home and played with her cats.

Although the arrival of 'something blonde and

something new' can't banish the hangdog look he is modelling this season, his eyes dig up the remnants of a twinkle from somewhere. As the woman walks past, he sits up straighter, tugging on the collar of the navy and white pinstripe shirt underneath his camel blazer.

Maybe he thinks she's a buyer for Tommy Hilfiger. That would be his ideal irregular stopover. Perhaps such a woman would dare to tell The Ex that his cuffed jeans display too much mustard-coloured sock with a tan brogue. Or at least they do on someone who didn't attend an Ivy League school.

I taste my drink through the foam and try to place it in my top ten. Okay, top twenty. However, given what this place charges for a medium latte, I may ask for the coffee grounds to make insect spray.

Speaking of repelling unwanted pests...

'Anyway.' The sooner I get this out of the way, the better. 'How are things?'

The Ex sips his tea. 'My sex life is virtually non-existent.'

'Then I'm amazed you can sit with your legs crossed.'

'I don't suppose I could pay you for some infrequent action?'

To think I once hoped for a happy ending with this man. Now he doesn't even trigger a happily ever hard-on in me.

I consider my rates. 'As Julia Roberts said to Richard Gere in *Pretty Woman*, I can't take less than a hundred.'

'But you're no Julia Roberts,' The Ex points out.

Oh, I'd love to reach over and stroke his face – I didn't say what with.

I must keep this moving along. 'How's life treating you otherwise?'

'Money's pretty tight.'

'Right. An empty wallet in a Ralph Lauren jacket pocket – I may have to check my calendar for a convenient time to weep.'

'Go ahead,' says The Ex. 'Mock me when I'm down.'

I'm not lacking a conscience. This man has been crying 'woe' for so long that the villagers have blocked him.

'I've got a new apartment,' he laments. 'And a new job.'

At last, the actual reasons for his look of defeat. I'm then forced to hear about the misfortune of an office on the penultimate floor. I must listen to the problems with an EC3 London postcode and a dual-aspect lounge. Finally, I take The Ex's word on the hardships encountered when you own three cars and your new place only has parking for two.

Despite everything, he still can't forego the humblebragging, slipping in the news of the five-figure recognition he got following a deal he instigated, plus the fortnight he recently spent in St Barts on a client's yacht. Unfortunately, neither can be heard without hearing a chorus of Travis's 'Why Does it Always Rain on Me' in my head. It almost drowns out the coffee shop's neo-soul.

'And that's my life in a nutshell,' The Ex says with

a sigh.

I think he's getting his idioms mixed up. Does he believe that tedious fifty-minute grumble, lavishly interspersed with his signature drawn-out *uhs*, was him cutting a long story short? Yeah, right. I probably said something similar in N.R. Magnusson's second book – on page 898.

'Better pay at this new place?' I ask. 'With a higher ratio of women to men?'

Since banging work colleagues is one of his hobbies, The Ex expects that quip. 'Much better pay. It requires commitment, though, and for me, you know what that means?'

Should I call my memory to the witness stand? Or should I select a smart-arse response from my bulging Rolodex?

He beats me to it. 'Stress.'

'Since you don't handle stress very well, wouldn't it have been easier to stay where you were?'

A gentle chime drifts from The Ex's inside pocket. He takes out his phone and looks at a new message.

'And didn't you complain only most of the time and not *all* the time about your old job?' I enquire.

He's typing a response.

'Or had your colleagues noticed your receding hairline?'

He's checking his spelling.

'Or did your monotone kill off one too many in the corridor?'

Once his message has gone, The Ex slides his phone away again and leans forward. There's a smile playing on his lips now that his sorrows are in his Sent items. A whiff of a wink hovers around his left eye. 'I was joking about paying you for sex.'

I lean forward too. 'And I was joking about doing it even if you paid me.'

The Ex sits back, adjusting the Union Jack handkerchief in his top pocket. He gives me a slightly curious look. 'Our sex life wasn't that bad.'

I offer an if-you-say-so shrug.

'The last time was all right,' he says.

'You can remember that far back?'

'It wasn't that long ago.'

'Was Michael Jackson still alive?'

'It was two years ago, Jo.'

'Wow. Was it really?'

Yes, I know when it was. The reason I'm surprised is that The Ex remembers. For me, it's easy: I can count my casual close encounters on two hands. From what I've heard, his number would need to be totted up using tally marks – on not one but two of those four-by-six whiteboards.

'Obviously, it wasn't memorable for you,' he says.

I guarantee it wasn't memorable for him either, because our post-breakup fuck-ups rarely differed. There would be no dinner, no flirting, no foreplay, just sex. If romance with The Ex were a food item, it would be those skinny heel bits you often get on cheap medium-sliced loaves.

I backtrack. 'Wait, I *do* remember that time. And yes, it… certainly was memorable.'

At least that's taken a little of his attention away

from his phone. It hasn't chimed again, but he keeps taking it out and checking, just in case.

I start the story ball rolling. 'I was at a literary festival in Cambridge for three days.'

'I was staying over in Birmingham for a conference.'

'It was about nine o'clock at night, and I received a random text from you.'

'I'd been thinking about you for ages.'

The Ex has repeated what he said that night, although I'd not heard from him in three years.

I summon a smile. 'You recalled all those great times we had together.'

'We had some amazing times, Jo.'

'You have a wonderful memory.' The exception is what I drink. 'We couldn't have a proper catch-up over text, was what you said.'

A corner of his mouth lifts. 'So I suggested we meet up.'

'Almost. You suggested I drive over.'

'I wanted to see you. That was the main thing.'

'You suggested I drive over *that night*.'

'Aren't you glad you did? Because we had a...' The Ex nods slowly. You'd think he was picturing an unforgettable evening. '... a nice time.'

'A brief time,' I gently correct him. 'In a car park. But I don't recall much catching up.'

'Yeah, well.' He frowns at his phone again. 'It was late when you got there.'

'It was late when you asked me – but I chose to make the journey,' I'm the first to insist.

'And it was a good job you didn't hang around afterwards. The amount of snow that fell when you left!'

'Afterwards? You mean, after a thirty-minute chat and a five-minute boning on my back seat?' I'm grinning, and not just because it is ancient history. I made money fictionalising it in my last book. 'Seriously, are you still trying to make out that it was brief because you were concerned about my safety?'

The Ex's exasperation is simmering. 'Look, I've told you before. If you'd asked, you could've stayed in my hotel room.'

'When? When could I have asked? Once you were done –' I wasn't done that night; I wasn't even wet '– you told me you needed to be off as you had work to do.'

He shakes his head like he did the last two times we disputed our versions of events. At the same time, he's admiring the owner of some shapely calves as she hops over the puddles on the pavement. The Ex isn't my property; he may look wherever he likes. It doesn't bother me now.

But when we dated...

I remember him saying that looks weren't essential in a woman he went out with. No, just in the women he admired when out with his stopgap average Jo.

When I briefly hope Miss Legs Eleven will slip on a smear of oil and go arse over perky tit, karma sends my swallowed drink down the wrong pipe. The Ex watches as I try to choke quietly. He showed similar concern when he suddenly ended things between us after two years. 'Don't make a scene,' was his response that day to my shocked tears, sitting in the middle of a busy café – on Valentine's Day.

God love him.

I cough one last time, sneaking a tissue up to the corner of my eye.

'There's no need for tears, Jo. Your performance wasn't that good.'

If I won a British Book Award for every one of my daydreams that involved two bricks and his knackers, I'd require two fireplaces.

The Ex finishes his typed response to another new message. 'I didn't mention work. But if it makes you feel better to keep saying I did…'

'You know what?' I say, smiling. 'After all this time, it doesn't matter.'

'Of course it does, or you wouldn't bring it up.'

I sit back and present my palms to him, although he won't see them unless I send him a photo. 'It's in the past. A lifetime ago. A previous era.'

'Except you gave me the usual silent treatment afterwards,' mumbles The Ex audibly. 'Until I passed the olive branch. Again.'

My attempt to keep up an act of indifference fails miserably. 'I messaged you when I got back to Cambridge. At three o'clock in the morning.'

He's scrolling on his phone now. He's not replying to anything, just… scrolling, scrolling, scrolling.

'I thought even you would want to know I got back safely.'

He is still scrolling.

'Three days it took you to respond.'

The Ex clicks on something.

'Three days,' I reaffirm.

He is reading.

'The same length of time it takes to travel to the moon.'

'Honestly, Jo.' He shakes his head. 'I'm sure you love nothing more than making me out to be a prize cunt.'

'What was it you...? Ah, I remember. You texted me back the word "Good".'

'I was busy,' he says with a half shrug.

'And I was a way to kill an evening when you had nobody else to do?'

The Ex performs one of his legendary slow breath intakes with an eyeroll. It was something he perfected after our relationship peaked for him. 'If that's what you still want to believe.'

Yes. Yes, I do. The only thing I didn't want to believe that night was where I could've ended up while driving back along A-roads that were rapidly being blanketed. The temperature outside was minus two. I relied on the ribbed edge line to tell me I was still on the road, feeling for it under my left tyres.

My caution, however, wasn't the only thing on high alert that night, thanks to the loud spring hinge on my hotel room door. If the hardness of Cal's knock wasn't enough to bring me to my senses, the look on his face did the job. It was one I hoped never to encounter again. Once was enough.

Pointing a loaded finger at my face, Cal struggled

to control his anger and keep the volume down. 'The next time you decide to take off in the middle of the fucking night without telling me – when it's below freezing and heavy snowfall is forecast – and you ignore every single one of my fucking calls and text messages, you and I are through. *Got that*?'

He didn't wait for a response. He couldn't. Had I said anything – had I even mouthed the word *sorry* – he may have punched the wall.

Never in my life had anyone spoken to me like that. No parent or best friend, not even a teacher. Oddly enough, I wasn't hurt or even uncomfortable by Cal's reaction. I couldn't be, not when it was justified. Six calls and four texts that night from the man whose date of birth escapes me.

Not one from the man who left me to dispose of the condom.

The Ex certainly isn't too busy to look at his phone this evening.

'Well,' I announce, getting to my feet, 'I'll be off.'

'Hang on a sec,' he says to his screen.

I zip up my gilet. I dab on some lip gloss. In one pocket, I count how many pieces of chewing gum are left in the packet. In the other, I discern how much tip I withheld: there may be enough for a couple of items from the McCafé range, methinks.

I'm about to ask how long The Ex thinks 'a sec' is when I notice he is no longer scrolling up on the screen; his thumb is moving across. It's also not scrolling. It's…

'You're having me wait while you swipe on a

bloody dating app?'

Unaware I am standing over him and watching the brunettes go left by the wayside, the speed he puts his phone back into his pocket speaks volumes.

'Jo, wait!'

As I step out into the street, I open my umbrella. The Ex stays beneath the coffee shop's awning in his absorbent wool blend.

He opens his arms. 'Can I at least have a hug before you go?'

I can't help laughing. I mean, in the top ten list of absurd questions, this one must sit up there with *Are there any photos of Jesus?*

'Why?' I ask.

'I need one.'

'Well, I don't; I'm fine.' I turn on my hiking boots' heels and shout over the top of the New York skyline printed on my tilted umbrella, 'But thanks for asking.'

'You're welcome?'

I wonder which is more annoying. Is it an ego that's massive enough to require a PA? Or is it an Olymprick who won't type a question mark when it's called for but will use one when it isn't?

I'll let you decide.

Chapter Nine

A fortnight ago, I pulled out of my apartment's underground car park for the last time, acknowledging the van driver who finally let me out. While the London traffic went nowhere, I couldn't be bothered to look over my shoulder at the building where I'd just spent three years of my life. No point, really. I was taking all the happy memories with me. They were on USB sticks.

As I idled behind a black cab, I set the milometer on the car to zero. I then noticed that the cumulative mileage on my second-hand car was only eight thousand. No, the Jaguar and I haven't consciously uncoupled. We are on a break, that's all. It is lodging with my agent. I've tried to imagine the fun they'll have, but… nothing yet.

Cal seemed mildly pleased to be making use of his redundant assigned parking spot for a while. According to his assistant, it pisses off those in the apartment below his. They like to straddle their Porsche over the demarcation line.

I now also own a little French number, which is

like the Jag in many ways. Well, they both have steering wheels. Who cares that it has the boot capacity of a tissue box? Its sunny disposition does shine through, though, with its monetary savings: no road tax and a good number of miles to the gallon, so I've been told. They said how many, but it meant nothing to me. If they'd just said it costs less than fifty quid to fill up the petrol tank, I would've slapped the SOLD sign on myself.

If I was briefly ditching the car, the pseudonyms, and the three-year tenancy agreement, I decided it was time to ditch the look, too. When I told my hairstylist I wanted to return to my original dark brown, Maynard put his hands on my shoulders and met my gaze in the mirror.

'Honey, we're aiming for a new and improved you. Not a trip down Dreary Lane.'

When I could put my glasses back on, I thought the mirror had disappeared and seated across from me was another makeover challenge. Gone was the blonde *Here I Am* shade. In its place was a chocolate brown with gentle caramel highlights, with the length more than halved into a choppy, chin-length bob.

I watched Maynard shake his fingers through the tonged-in curls to loosen them and create a beachy wave vibe. He flicked my hair over to a left parting. A right parting. No, left again. He tugged the ends forward, framing my face. He plumped up the already plumpy lift on my crown. There was yet more tugging, plumping, flicking – more stalling for time. Nobody rushes forward with an *et voilà* when anyone goes from long blonde to short brunette.

No, it's usually a *Right, love. Brace yourself.*

But all I saw in that mirror was a short-haired version of the Jo I said goodbye to many paperbacks ago. And apart from missing the boxed hair-dye colour and the fattest fringe outside of a Cleopatra fan club, she's not changed that much. She has aged a bit, but maybe not by all the candles on her cake. Also, seeing as there aren't many photos of me before I had any bestsellers, only a few people might bother to 'then and now' me.

Despite choosing a new look for myself all those years ago, it was nice to see the old Jo again. Yes, she looked curious and slightly wary, and rightly so. She got dumped for a blonde. She wasn't going to welcome me back with her luxury biscuits.

With my brown waves and budget wheels, I finally got out of London and headed north, following the signs for the M6. I then had only one concern.

Had Steve saved my spot on the bench?

***

It was the reading at The Romford. After that, I couldn't get the Lake District out of my mind again. I suddenly found myself staring at half a page of words on my computer screen for more than forty minutes at a time. I had to turn on the TV before I convinced myself I would never finish another story.

That didn't help. One evening, I had to watch nature photographers in their wellies trailing around the lesser-known (to some people) Lakeland tarns and woodlands. The next night, I had Julia Bradbury in her hiking boots at the top of Helvellyn. Then I had half an hour of B&B owners checking under the toilet rims in Keswick. It was followed by a programme highlighting a harsh winter in the Cumbrian hills and mountains.

I had always told myself that the Lakes was somewhere I didn't need to revisit, neither in person nor on a screen – not even to write the four *Caerli°°ani* books. Unlike Olivia J. Lawrence's romantic travels around the globe to create believable settings, N.R. Magnusson didn't have to lift an arse cheek to put creative pen to paper. And with no *Caerli°°ani* book tours, there's been no reason to return to the place that inspired them.

That was until *someone* suggested I go somewhere different and look for a certain forty-four-year-old who's been missing for a while. How easy would it have been for me to just book a cruise? I could've sailed around the world and searched for her from my cabin's balcony.

I didn't, though. I got in touch with my aunt instead.

As is always the case, Izzie knows this bloke whose nephew's ex-civil partner is taking eight months out in Peru to collect rare... Let's just say she found me somewhere to rent. And now I'm living in a small, one-bedroom, mid-terrace house in one of Britain's National Parks.

In Bowness-on-Windermere.

Quite close to The Romford.

I'll mention it again: the house is small. That wouldn't usually be an issue. There's only me, after all. Over the last week, though, following day after day of relentless rain, cabin fever was only just held at bay by a brilliant discovery I made.

And now I have an idea. A great idea, in fact. One that I emailed just ten minutes ago to—

Wow, that was quick. But why isn't Cal typing his response?

'You're looking to *buy* up there?'

Don't worry. It was a joint decision to forego phone etiquette years ago. Between us, it's as pointless as extended warranties.

'You told me to go away and find myself again,' I remind him.

'By rereading *Eat Pray Love* at the top of a mountain, yes. After two weeks, I didn't think you would announce plans to settle down up there.'

'Cal, I'm asking if you'll look on Rightmove for a renovation project for me, that's all. Not bloody... EMarryMeAlready.'

There's a brief silence on the other end of the line. 'Have you been watching *Homes Under the Hammer*?'

'It was that or *A New Life in the Sun*,' I confess.

'But you'll be looking at places on your own.'

I still regret once telling Cal that, on a list of a hundred things women should be able to do, all I had mastered was changing the subject.

'I'm in New York,' he informs me.

'For fuck's sake, I can look at a few tired houses

by myself. I'm not tackling Everest without a sherpa.'

Chapter Ten

Despite being across the pond for reasons I couldn't care less about, Cal dismissed my protests and arranged property viewings for me. Luckily, my schedule today allows for essential toasted fruit teacake breaks and latte pit stops. These I appreciate.

Unfortunately, these are all I'll be thanking him for.

Five bedrooms in one house that I just looked at. Eight rooms for paying guests in another. One of them had six bathrooms over three floors. The house I'm currently hiking through has three lounges, a steam room, a dressing room *off* the walk-in closet, a wine cellar and a boathouse. Oh, and not forgetting the four-car fucking garage.

These places will blow everyone's socks off when they're done, and hats off to the *experienced* people who take them on. Was there enough stress on that adjective merely with italics? Surely only someone whose online profile includes the words 'property' and 'specialist' should tackle them. Certainly not someone who garnered most of their renovation knowledge from episode build-ups of *Fixer to Fabulous*.

After I have viewed every house for sale in the area that is beyond my capabilities, it's time to consult an expert. And if Phil Spencer hasn't yet recovered from helping his *Location, Location, Location* co-presenter, Kirstie Allsopp, handmake Christmas, I'll need the next best thing.

***

There are three desks in the Ambleside estate agency; only two of them are staffed, and neither is free. Not being in a hurry, I browse some properties displayed on one wall and wait my turn.

A woman emerges from the back office with her phone and a cup. 'Looking for anything in particular?'

'A shattered house with two bedrooms and a view would be nice.' I squeeze my hands together. I'm hoping a little begging might get her to magic one out of a drawer.

She manages a half-smile as she sits down. 'I'm sure it would.'

I give her a minute to enjoy a few sips of her drink and check her phone.

And another minute.

And another.

I'm sorry, but is my appearance too casual for her? Is it my novelty Primark T-shirt? Or does she think I look better in mine than she does in hers? Perhaps it's not my attire. It could be the small coffee stain I am also modelling. Did I say 'small'? Yeah, it's about the size of Australia on a thirty-centimetre globe. Or maybe she just thinks I'm a sassy bitch for walking in off the street. After all, today's preferred method of estranged communication is via a website's *Contact Us* button.

She frowns at her phone screen. Oh dear. I hope our brief exchange hasn't made her miss anything important. I'd feel awful if she was no longer the first to comment on a photo of some homemade veggie pittas.

I gently close the door behind me, my property-searching bubble blown. With my reusable cup struggling to cover the stain, I fantasise about returning later and 'raining' my book advances and royalties onto her desk.

There are many things I'll never do, though, partly because I'm not one of those try-anything-once people (not after I went on a drop tower ride at Hull Fair in 2000), and displaying what I've achieved tops that list, thanks to my dad and his hefty catalogue of no-nos. Therefore, my swaggering threats will only ever be daydreams.

***

Following my house-hunting humiliation, I'm driving back to Bowness-on-Windermere when I'm stopped by temporary traffic lights. Oh, and there's a Volvo further ahead that must've been in a hurry to make it through. For what reason, we will never know. Perhaps there's a box of Magnum Double Gold Caramel Billionaire ice creams in the boot.

The problem looks like it arose when the Range Rover at the front of the queue may have decided there was no hurry, and it pulled up in the left lane behind the red sign when the lights changed to amber. The driver, however, may have panicked when she realised her phone charger wasn't there, and with her Android lifeline about to die, what if her little Elijah gets to his music lesson and discovers he didn't pack his French horn's mouthpiece?

With that first-world problem in mind, she obviously went for it – straight into the side of the overtaking Volvo.

Dairy treats will defrost, a ten-year-old will have to practise buzzing with just his lips for an hour, and everyone waiting on both sides of the lights will have their patience tested. Unless, of course, you're happy to lose a wing mirror by taking the dodgy detour. Otherwise, you've had it.

With nowhere to go, even those who probably binge-watch entire TV series in one sitting turn off their engines. Lucky for me, I bought my lunch from the Co-op before I left Ambleside.

With my bare feet poking out the window and my toes enjoying the spring sunshine, I tuck into my tray of chicken pasta and my packet of crisps. It's just a shame I can't turn the volume up on the two angry women competing in *Roadworks Wars*; I'm three cars back.

There's only one thing better than a catfight, and it's making its way towards the hoo-ha with a head of dark, curly hair after appearing from Eros knows where. The running action smooths out the front of our hero's T-shirt, highlighting the lack of belly fat and spotlighting some divine... I mean, defined pecs. The hemline bounces above the waistband of his flippy-flappy-pocketed work trousers, awarding his keen audience glimpses of a mouth-watering couple of inches of skin.

I'm telling you, all we need now is a can of Diet Coke, Etta James's 'I Just Want to Make Love to You' on the radio, and the clock to read eleven-thirty – which is when they finish counting how many wish lists this man tops today.

The woman in the car in front is leaning to the right for a better look. In my mirror, I see the one behind me has got out. And she's let her hair down. *And* she's touching up her lip gloss. Who cares if the chap was perhaps only a toddler when most of us queued to watch *Bridget Jones's Diary* on the big screen?

He's not a toddler now.

Without giving his own safety a second thought, he places himself between the warring women. It's a while before they realise somebody is trying to break them up. The next minute, they're both looking up at him as if to say, 'Who the hell made you?'

He turns his attention equally from one to the other, back and forth. And what will female opportunists do when confronted with something they know shouldn't be touched? They play their diminished responsibility card, of course. As Ms Volvo sobs loudly on his shoulder, her hands help themselves.

With the man of the moment's physical attributes briefly obscured, I decide to get my drink. While reaching through the gap between the front seats, I spot two men through my rear passenger window. One is wearing a two-piece suit, whereas the other looks like he used to wear something similar until he retired from banking. He now wears whatever he unwraps on Christmas morning.

'I still need some time to think it over,' I overhear the ex-banker say.

'This is a decent offer,' the suit stresses to him. 'It's cash, too, and they want to exchange contracts quickly. Don't forget that the Tree Preservation Order will put people off. There's also the matter of whether it's within the curtilage of your house; your place is a listed building. As well, hardly anyone wants to buy a small, rundown cottage nowadays, not if they can't pull it down and start again. It doesn't make financial sense.'

Small. Rundown. Am I dreaming? There was the fight, and then the Adonis – and now this? If it starts hailing chocolate raisins, I never want to wake up.

'Don't take too long to decide,' the suit warns.

They shake hands, and the ex-banker heads back down his driveway. The suit is heading towards his car.

As am I.

'Excuse me,' I say sheepishly. 'Hi. Sorry, did I hear the two of you mention a small place nearby that requires a fair bit of work?'

He lays his jacket on his back seat. Even behind

his sunglasses, I know he is eyeing my coffee stain. 'It's almost a done deal now,' he mutters.

'Jeff,' a voice calls out. 'You forgot this.'

The ex-banker glances my way as he strides towards us with a document wallet.

'I overheard your conversation,' I confess. 'My apologies. Rude, I know. But I'm looking for somewhere small here in the Lakes. Somewhere that would benefit from TLC and not a JCB.'

The ex-banker chuckles. 'My word, what are the odds?'

This could turn out very well. For two of us, anyway.

'There is someone currently making a reasonable cash offer,' Jeff pipes up.

'Mine would be cash,' I say. 'And I'm not in a chain.'

And I bet your buyer doesn't also have a disarming smile, Jeff-o.

'Well, I think the young lady should be allowed to take a look.' At least the ex-banker values a friendly face. 'I'm just about to take the wife shopping, but I'll be back about three. I'm Clive.'

'I'm Jo. And I'll be here at three,' I tell him, clasping my hands together and bouncing on my toes like Lindt's head product tester. 'In a clean T-shirt.'

If he hadn't mentioned a wife, I would've offered to be here at three in *no* T-shirt.

Chapter Eleven

It is ten to three, and there's no evidence of the clash of the sirens at the roadworks. A grey Transit van is parked across the road, advertising Hart and Hart Building Contractors on the side. I hop down the driveway to where a stereo is blaring out in the woody skeleton of a house extension.

'Hello?' I call.

Combine the stereo with a power saw and a couple of nail guns.

'Hellooooo?'

When a familiar head of dark curls wearing a dust mask appears through a hole in the sheet of plywood above me, the contents of my underwear break through the cobwebs.

I hold my hand up. 'Hi.'

He descends the ladder and stops in front of me, lowering his mask. He's taller than I first thought – and horribly better looking up close. God help the shallow-minded.

'I'm sorry to trouble you.' A drill attempting to get through to the earth's core starts up. 'The van on the front,' I shout.

'Yes?' he shouts back.

'Is one of the Harts available?'

'You're looking at one.'

My imagination is doing more than looking.

'If possible –' the drill stops, but my raised voice doesn't '– may I pay you for fifteen minutes of your time, please…? Oh!'

Deep cheek dimples are the by-product of a toothy grin. His expressive eyebrows display both amusement and curiosity. 'What can I do for you?'

Perhaps the low neckline on my top has made my question very open. Fingers crossed, it provides a happy mix of respectability and intrigue – thanks, in part, to a well-fitting bra. Remember, I'm getting desperate for a dilapidated distraction. If I must adopt the personality of a female character from a *Carry On* film to get one, so be it.

'I'm looking at a property across the road,' I explain. 'All I know is that it needs work, and… I need somebody who might know whether it needs reviving or a buffet at the funeral. If you know what I mean.'

'I would be happy to…?'

'Jo.'

He wipes his hand on his dusty trousers before shaking mine. 'I'm Nyx.'

Very formal, I know. Internally, I'm throwing my arms around him and uttering over his shoulder, 'And they lived happily ever after.'

As we're crossing the road, I say to him, 'I'm sorry

if this seems quite random. I only heard about this place two hours ago, and I know nobody around here.'

'Are you new to the area?'

'Yyyyes and no. I've recently moved up here – temporarily – but we have a long history.'

The owner is heading our way.

'I hope you don't mind, Clive,' I quickly get out there, 'but I've brought someone with me to have a look.'

Clive is smiling. 'Afternoon, Nyx. I saw your mum today in the shop.'

'My mum works for Mr Jackson,' Nyx explains.

With the waist-high weeds having reclaimed much of the driveway, we must walk in single file. Clive leads the way while Nyx walks behind me, bringing up the rear (sorry, it's too warm for me to make a rude quip. If you want to, go ahead. I lined it up).

Clive looks back at me. 'I hope you're ready for this.'

When we round the corner, it takes a moment to figure out where the bushes and trees end and the house begins. It's a good job that Clive almost knows where he's going as he feels his way across the ivy curtains. Eventually, he finds the opening. Nyx holds it to the side and indicates that I should go next.

'It needs doing up inside.'

Why Clive says this while he's unlocking the door, I don't know. I hardly think a house covered in abandonment would hide an interior that *Your Home Made Perfect* created.

We step into a dark hallway, where the sudden

drop in temperature gives me sleeves of goosebumps. The air is cold and stale, making it difficult to take deep breaths.

'We've owned the main house for over twenty years,' Clive tells us, heading for the stairs. 'Then this adjoining land came on the market a few years ago. The wife likes to grow her own, so it was ideal for her polytunnels. This house just happened to be included. I often thought about doing it up and having somewhere for visitors. The idea never went away, but you know how it is.'

Off the landing are two decent-sized bedrooms. Clive tugs open the brown drapes in the first one to reveal single glazing in a rotted window frame. A spectacular view of the dense ivy waterfall outside teases us with mere speckles of sunlight.

'And the bathroom is on the other side of the landing.'

Nyx and I go through, taking a moment to 'admire' the décor.

'Somebody loved peach,' he comments.

'I bet that somebody also loved double denim.'

The suite, the tiles, the walls, the ceiling, the woodwork, the carpet – yes, a carpet – all of it is peach.

I tap my foot. 'Oh, this takes me back.'

Nyx looks puzzled. 'Why would anyone think that a carpet in a bathroom was a good idea?'

'In the seventies and eighties, if it didn't move, you carpeted it: bathrooms, garages, dog kennels. People back then were more worried about the world running out of underlay than antibacterial wipes.'

Back downstairs, the only door off the hallway leads us into a sizeable lounge with a high ceiling. The focal point is an ugly brick fireplace. A two-seater sofa has been left behind; it sits in front of the two-bar electric fire. Only one of the seat cushions is heavily sunken. In front of it on the carpet, a small patch of the swirl pattern is faded and worn.

'The kitchen is through here.'

The room is almost a dark afterthought, designed years before kitchen diners invaded our shores – and way before everyone had stylish splashbacks. In the corner, there's a free-standing cooker with an eye-level grill. A sink unit with sliding wood-effect doors and false drawers sits under the window. A glass-fronted wall cupboard has Olympic ring-shaped rust scars on its painted shelves. A tired Maid Marion kitchen larder with blue doors looks to be the only thing worth salvaging. The word 'vintage' might help it sell on eBay.

Then there's the glaring elephant in the room. It is so inappropriate that it should be covered up: a deluxe front-loading washing machine. Unused by the looks of it. It would have suited a utility room in a bustling Victorian terrace house in South Kensington. It didn't belong in a quiet cottage that had no room for a nanny.

At the back door, Clive is struggling with three different locks. I wonder if the last occupant insisted on them to maintain their independence. Or did somebody else make that decision for them? The laundry-cleaning gifter, perhaps?

'Ah! Here we go.'

When Clive opens the door, I'm ready to be disappointed, and the military line-up of imposing conifers doesn't fill me with hope. They rear up like green ghosts outside the door.

But beyond them, I can hear something.

Nyx stays behind in the kitchen with Clive. I step outside and turn left, following the path alongside the house, which is narrowed to almost a shoulder width by the hardy giants. A shadow up ahead on the wall shows a break in the green army. Another path leads off it. Broken slabs have nettles and brambles attacking from both sides, intertwining at knee height to trip up the nosy. I stamp my way over them in my lace-up boots.

My path is obstructed by a peeling wooden gate that sits between equally high breeze-block walls. A last-century addition, I reckon, to keep out undesirables. Now it is a perfect climbing frame for evergreens, with a wiry maidenhair vine and a glossy tangle of winter-flowering clematis fighting for dominance.

Through the crowded leaves and hardened stems, I find a wrought-iron lock. Sadly, the handle isn't yielding to anyone who doesn't work at Fort Knox.

Spurred on by the sound on the other side, I spot something built against the wall under a carpet of vegetation. An upturned dustbin allows me to get high enough to test whether it will bear my weight. Some hefty thuds on the slanted roof with my boot confirm it should.

And this is where Nyx finds me, gazing across more of the garden beyond the wall. A rippling sea of faded hydrangea flower heads dominates the plot. They'd steal the scene if it wasn't for the surprise a few feet beyond. Cast into shadow by mature trees, it measures perhaps only twenty paces across, but that hardly matters.

Not when Cumbria's most famous lake, Windermere, is part of the property's natural boundary.

Nyx joins me on my makeshift balcony, resting his elbows on top of the wall. 'Wow. Who wouldn't wish to wake up to that every morning?'

He read my mind. I only hope he didn't read it earlier.

We turn to face the mountain of ivy, watching where we step.

'What do you think, Nyx?'

'Nobody builds places like these nowadays. Not in settings like this. If I had the money, I'd love the challenge.'

A challenge.

I put a question to him. 'Would I be crazy to take this on as a flip?'

'Do you know much about renovations?'

When I wrote *Firm Foundations,* I spent a morning with a contractor. Surely…?

'No, not really. But I might know a man now who does.'

***

Back inside the lounge, Nyx lifts a picture frame off the floor. It contains a slightly faded photo of a beautiful stone cottage. A man and a woman are standing in the doorway, smiling at the camera. She is wearing a simple but pretty dress. He has the top button of his shirt done up. Neither quite knows what to do with their hands.

'When do you think this was taken?' he asks.

'Based on what she's wearing, I'd say the forties – the early to mid-forties.'

'Why then?'

'Women in the 1930s wore longer dresses. Clothes rationing from 1941 meant they had to be simpler. It also brought up the hemlines.'

'You know your stuff,' Nyx commends.

'No, it's a fondness for trivia and deduction. Nothing more.'

Their garden was a glorious explosion of summer, which even a black-and-white shot couldn't tone down, with the foliage and profusion of blooms creating a natural frame. Was that why they looked so happy? Were they proud of their green fingers? Or perhaps they were pretending. Pretending to be happy for somebody they loved. For somebody who might need this photo to get them through the dark days ahead.

Did the previous owner take it? Was this a framed memory they hung on to, something they had to look back on during those lonely evenings on that sofa? It was clearly a priceless item to the occupant. Then it was nothing but a worthless relic to those packing up.

I wipe it clean with my fingers and gently prop it up on the fireplace mantel, where it belongs. Nyx holds the hem of his T-shirt out to me, and I rub years of forgotten dirt off my hands. I also get a cheeky flash of the hairs below his navel. Bonus.

'How expensive do you think it would be to do this up?' I ask him.

'We did one last year, which wasn't quite as bad, and the renovations cost almost as much as they paid for the house.'

'Yikes.'

'But that one didn't have this location,' Nyx quickly adds. 'Also, it depends on the spec you'd want.'

'But if the asking price is right?'

He gives me a tight-lipped smile. 'I... doubt it will be.'

My eyes can't help going to the photo again; my imagination is popping a fresh sheet of Microsoft paper into the Apple typewriter. But just before I put on my linen smock dress and oversized writing cardigan...

'Sorry, Nyx.' I put my hand in my trouser pocket. 'Thanks for your time today. How much do I owe you?'

'Nothing.' He pulls out a dog-eared business card. 'Buy me a drink sometime.'

'You're on,' I answer without hesitation, knowing I won't.

We like to be polite, though, don't we?

***

Nyx heads back to his job, leaving me to mourn the loss of the father to the children I never wanted. I join Clive to discuss money.

'What are your thoughts, Jo?'

I can't help grinning. 'Do you need to ask?'

When Clive tells me how much he wants for it, I silently congratulate myself for not reacting with a cartoon jaw drop.

'It's a lot of money,' he says kindly. He obviously recalls the coffee stain from earlier. My little economical car won't fill him with hope, either. 'It may be wise to go home and discuss it with your other half. Or your parents.'

Bless him.

'Thank you, Clive.'

Nyx is hovering near the open back doors of his van. He makes his way across when I get to my car. When he hears the asking price, he slowly nods.

'Does that sound reasonable to you?' I ask.

'For this area – and that view – you'll be paying way over the odds anyway. And after it failed to reach the reserve price at auction, he hasn't put it on the market. If he does, he'll get inundated with silly offers.'

'Then why was he talking to an estate agent earlier?'

'They sniff about for land like this all the time,' Nyx says. 'But Clive's had a lot to deal with lately, what with his daughter's divorce and his elderly mum. They'll keep badgering him until he thinks they're doing him a favour.'

'I don't want to hound him if things are tough.'

'Don't worry, my mum knows the situation. And if this can be sorted out, it will be one less thing he'll be hassled about all the time. Look, later this afternoon, I'll make some calls.'

'But I've already taken up too much of your time.'

'Then buy me two drinks.' Nyx takes his phone out of his pocket. 'If I call you later?'

'I can't remember my number.'

'That's why I prefer to transfer my old one over whenever I get a new contract and... phone.' He's staring at the antique BlackBerry I retrieved from my car.

'I've had this for ten years,' I confess. 'The same number for five.'

'How often do you ring yourself?' he argues for me.

'About as often as I give my number out.'

Rather than move away from me in case what I have is contagious, Nyx takes my robust mobile and looks it over. 'This was by far the best model.'

'You're just being polite.'

'No, I'm serious. And you've really looked after yours.'

'I haven't. It's because it's hardly ever used. I charge it once a week, if that.'

'You're not a mobile phone addict?' he asks.

'I like to tell people I prefer face-to-face communication. But, truthfully? I just don't understand the appeal of weapons of mass distraction.'

Neither do I understand Nyx's intense stare. Is *he* even aware of it? Does he know that when he gives you his full attention, his eyes look like they want to give it to you on the bonnet of your car?

I quickly recall my name and what day it is.

'I totally agree,' he says. 'I don't get what all the fuss is about with social media. Who actually wants to read about all the drama between your ex and their new partner?'

'Precisely. If all you want to do is whine about how bad life is treating you, tell it to someone who wants to listen: your diary.'

Nyx nods. 'Diaries should make a comeback.'

'For sure. Do you have one?'

'No.'

My gaze quickly drops to his hands. 'Me neither.'

He holds my phone up. 'Mind if I...?'

I signal for him to proceed. Nyx scrolls and taps away with one thumb. The next minute, his phone is ringing in his other hand.

'I swear I wasn't tilling the earth when the Vikings seized York,' I clarify.

'Hey, phones aren't your thing.' He hands me back my limited access to the outside world with a dimply display. 'I won't hold it against you.'

I'm suddenly imagining what Nyx *could* hold against me.

My name is Josephine Washington. It's Wednesday.

Chapter Twelve

Nyx telephones while I'm warming up some soup for my tea. I quickly figured out how to use the microwave in my rented house. The washer-dryer, too. I haven't touched the oven or the hob yet, and if I'm only here for a few months, I hope I won't have to.

'Clive's had a few investors make silly offers,' Nyx explains. 'But he's being cautious. He's not keen on seeing the house demolished and a mansion built on it so close to his.'

'He was with an agent today. A chap called Jeff.'

'Ah. The esteemed Jeff Collins, eh?'

'You know him?'

Nyx chuckles. 'I know *of* him.'

'I'm guessing he doesn't go round to the Dalai Lama's to knit warm clothing for bumblebees.'

'Correct.'

'He was trying to persuade Clive to accept an offer he's had,' I tell him. 'He said there's little interest because it can't be knocked down. Something to do with tree protections and cartilage or... umbrage.'

'Curtilage.'

'That's it.'

'His client probably knows how to get around those things,' Nyx says. '*If* there are any actual issues. I'm not convinced. Jeff will also get a tasty backhander if he secures the sale, plus a bit more when his client gets approval to tear it down.'

'Do you think they'll get approval?'

'Maybe. You know the old saying: It's not *what* you know...'

I finish it for him. '... it's who you blow.'

'Sorry?'

Oh, crapping hell. 'Know! Who you... It's who you *know*. Not... Not what you know. And it's certainly not who you... No, it's... it's *who* you know.'

'Right.'

Nyx isn't convinced. I'm the same whenever I see *Best Regards* in an email.

'Just to be clear, Jo, how badly do you want it?'

Wait, are we still talking about the house?

Washington, you daft twat, concentrate. This is serious money.

'I know it's madness,' I respond, 'but I want to offer Clive the full asking price.'

'In which case, you'd have to renovate it on a tight budget.'

'I wouldn't. That wouldn't work for me. I'd want to do it right.'

'Then you might not make much profit,' Nyx warns.

111

'I realise that.'

I can almost hear him trying to figure me out.

'Something happened to you today,' he remarks.

'That photo you found and the looks on their faces. It moved me more than anything has in… in a while.' That's an understatement. It may be going back to when cars had cassette tape players. 'At that moment, my gut told me I should give that little house a second chance, and I think… I think bringing it back to life is the kindest thing to do; it's the only thing to do. It's a part of history. Okay, it won't have a bank holiday named after it or a… or a gathering of world leaders on special anniversaries, but dreams were made there once.'

'And dreams can come true,' Nyx adds.

'Yyyyeeeaahhhnnnnn… Do they?' asks my pragmatism. 'Do they come true, or is perseverance rewarded?'

Oh, no. Dead air. Quick, before I get a—

'I'm sorry, Nyx. Ignore me.'

'Don't apologise.'

'I must. I often prattle into a dull alley. What a snore!'

'Not at all. And it's okay. I get it.'

'You, erm… You do?'

'Yeah,' Nyx says. 'I was watching you the whole time…'

Creepy or hot?

'… and I saw you fall in love.'

He saw me fall in… what?

'Do I have your word, Jo, that you won't tear it

down?'

'Cross my heart.'

'Then ring Clive and offer him twenty thousand less,' Nyx instructs.

'But I got the impression he really wants something close to the full asking price.'

'Which he'll never get. He knows that. But I know what Clive *will* accept if someone can be trusted.'

'How do you know?' I whisper. Whenever anything sounds slightly suspect, I immediately think my phone is tapped, and I'll be the only one who goes to jail.

He responds with, 'Do you want the house where more memories can be made?'

I mentally work out where they might incarcerate me. Would I be allowed to take in my *Sex and the City* boxset?

'I do, Nyx. But what if—?'

'Twenty thousand below the asking price.' And don't ask any more questions, his tone conveys.

I feel a little uneasy when I come off the phone. When it comes to doing things by the book, I'm the queen of squeaky clean. Returning to my car once after being in a supermarket with Ma, I found a packet of sausage casserole mix wedged down the side of her trolley. Because she hadn't paid for it, I insisted on taking the trolley back with it still in there.

I struggle to enter Clive's phone number, something I usually only fumble to do in dreams. The line is now taking ages to ring, giving panic time to rise. I don't want to haggle. It's Cal's area of expertise, not mine; it's what he gets off on. I only tried it when I was too young to know what 'haggle' meant. 'We're locals, so my dad wants to know whether we get a discount,' I had to say to ice-cream vendors wherever we went. We never got them cheaper, not even locally, but I had to ask every—

'Hello?'

'Hi, Clive. It's Jo. Thanks again for showing me the house today.'

'You're welcome.'

I take a deep breath. 'I'd like to make an offer, please.'

After I've offered twenty thousand below the asking price, I check my screen to see if Clive is still there.

'And that's your very best offer?' he eventually asks.

'Yes.' I hope my scrunched-up expression isn't apparent in my voice. If I lose out, I'm going to put a curse on every biscuit that Nyx dunks.

'I see.'

What does he see?

'Would you mind if I get back to you, Jo?'

I can't very well ask when that will be, can I? It could be ten minutes. Then again, it could be next week. I said something similar to a schoolteacher I met up with for coffee. It was the best date I'd been on in ages. He asked if I was up for a picnic the following weekend. That was four years ago. I hope he's not still waiting for an answer.

I want to ring Nyx, but Clive might call back. I

decide to text him instead. Shit, do I put an 'x' at the end? And if so, should it be in uppercase or lowercase?

My to 'x' or not to 'x' dilemma vanishes from the screen.

'Hi, Clive.'

'Hello, Jo.'

Was that a weighty hello? I think it was. It's not good news. My shoulders droop, but not out of a sense of relief. Damn it. That's the last time I trust anyone good-looking enough to get a second interview when they're unsuitable for the job.

'You're going to be very busy for the next few months,' Clive says. 'I hope you don't mind getting your hands dirty.'

'Mind? I love nothing more.' Except for coffee and Christmas tree ornaments. 'Thank you, Clive. Thank you *so* much.'

'You should also thank someone else.'

And that's my next phone call.

'How can I ever thank you enough, Nyx?'

Whoa. Easy, tiger. It's before the watershed.

'If I recall,' he says, 'we agreed – well, sort of – that you'd buy me *two* drinks.'

'But that hardly covers it. Maybe I could name a star after you.'

'Actually, I would really like that.'

I know I'm imagining it, but Nyx sounds sincere.

'Can I get a quote from you for the work, please?'

'No problem, Jo. Do you have some other contractors to call?'

'Ah. I should have. Right?'
'Yes. I insist.'

Chapter Thirteen

Three weeks later, I have the keys to the derelict cottage. That's bloody quick, people tell me. No, that's bloody Cal, is something I *don't* tell them. But he knows how grateful I am when he must sign for a parcel – one that couldn't be left behind a plant pot if nobody was home.

I collect them upon my return from a business trip to the States – in California. Fine, I was in Hollywood. Just… discussing another romance novel being optioned, that's all. No biggie.

No, really, it's not that big of a deal. When a book is optioned by a production company, it doesn't mean it's guaranteed to be made into a movie. Far from it. Far – far – from it. And you are warned early in your career not to get too excited.

Despite the advice, you're putting together your own cast list before the money is even in your account. The next minute, you're pairing up the off-screen romances. After that, you're wondering who to wear on the red carpet. Usually, that's a week before I find an excuse not to attend the premiere.

But you learn.

I've been optioned on a handful of my romance novels, and I've seen something come about on a few of them, which is nice. It's money in the bank. Book sales increase, too, meaning the taxman's rubbing his hands.

Cal is quietly optimistic about this one. Optimistic, not excited. No, my agent wouldn't recognise excitement. Not even if it met him at Manchester Airport with a dramatic hair makeover.

The first contractor arrives at the house and spends most of his time sucking in his breath and checking his phone. He says he'll get back to me with a price, but it won't be cheap.

The second one doesn't show up.

I wait while contractor number three paces up and down the recently weeded driveway and has a heated phone conversation. When I do eventually get his attention, he is charming. However, five minutes into our property tour, he tells me his daily rate (despite not seeing the inside of the house yet) and halts my list of questions by answering one of his three phones. With it pressed to his ear, he heads to his car. I assume he's getting something he forgot: a writing pad, perhaps, or a brochure. Or some Arial-font evidence of his five-star reviews.

I watch him start the engine, close the car door, and drive away.

The fourth contractor is here before me, which is a rarity. If I'm due anywhere, I'm ten minutes early; anything less, I apologise for being late.

An older gentleman, sporting a neat head of white hair and well-worn loose jeans, is making notes on a spiral notepad and casting an eye over the roof. Or what he can see of it through the plant camouflage.

His colleague exits their van, tucking a pen behind his ear. His cheeks and chin are sporting a previously unseen stubble that's possibly a few days old. But I recognise his beautifully messy curls.

'Joanne, is it?' asks the older gentleman.

'It's *Jo*, Grandad.' Nyx shakes his head. 'I told you her name a dozen times.'

'Sorry. I thought Jo was short for Joanne.'

I give him a reassuring smile. 'It is, but it's also short for Josephine – my extended version. You must be Mr Hart.'

'Colin.' His handshake is gentle, despite his paws being rough enough to sand planks. They're also big enough to stop goals. 'You know this young trouble, I hear.'

'Hey, Jo.'

After I viewed the house with Nyx, my mental image of him quickly went from vivid to fuzzy. I soon believed I'd only imagined his tastiness. Nobody could be as yummy as my memory was trying to make them out to be. I put it down to the amount of spinach I've been eating and the fresh Cumbrian air.

I thought I'd struggle to recognise him three weeks later. But within three seconds of seeing him and those autumn-hazel eyes again, I could still pick Nyx out in a line-up of the top one hundred luscious locals – on my first attempt.

'How was your trip?' Colin asks me.

'Ah. I stared at loads of words and did lots of listening.' Mainly to the ocean, in between meetings.

'Whatever it takes to pay the bills, eh?'

I had told Nyx I would be gone for a few days 'with work'.

Nyx: Don't think you're getting out of buying me those two drinks x

Me: When I get back. I promise x

That was the text response I finally went with. No, I'm not telling you how many it was out of.

After Nyx and Colin have finished their house inspection, we meet in the lounge.

'You have a solid little place here,' Colin remarks.

I feel a rush of love for the house. It always knew it would play second fiddle to the view, but it was okay with it. Besides, I'm a massive cheerleader for runners-up.

'What would you like to see, Jo?' Nyx asks.

You have no idea how hard it is for me. Like I said, three seconds.

'I'd like to see more of the porch. Perhaps extend it and have it on two sides of the house. If that's possible?'

'Okay.'

'I also think open-plan living spaces work.'

'Definitely.' Nyx pats the wall dividing the kitchen and the lounge. 'If you get rid of this, you'll have room for a formal dining area *and* a separate utility room off the kitchen. That's if you want it.'

I nod. 'I want it.'

Don't say anything.

Nyx is rubbing his chin as he steps back, drawing a plan with his eyes. 'I'm thinking... two sets of double doors on this outer wall, one at each end. It's long, so it can take it. Or we could centre multi-slide doors – two left, two right – and bring the outside in.'

'That sounds exciting,' I say.

'Doable, Grandad?'

'Yep.'

'In the kitchen, put units across these two walls,' Nyx proposes. 'And, personally, I'd go for an island.'

'I'm with you on the island.' I wish.

'Have your dining area on that side. Then all of this –' Nyx strides across to the ugly fireplace '– would be your lounge. Have a nice feature wall. Perhaps put in a wood-burning stove.'

'That would be perfect.'

'Great.' Nyx makes a note in his book. 'Would you like to take me upstairs?'

All I would like more is to inherit Coca-Cola's secret ingredient.

In the main bedroom, Nyx considers things for a moment. 'If we move this partition wall back, you'd still have a decent-sized spare room, but it would give you six by... ten, an extra sixty square feet in here.'

An idea pops into my head. 'Or sixty square feet for an en suite. If that's enough room for one?'

'More than enough.' Nyx stops in front of the wall. 'Maybe a double basin vanity unit on the back wall. A shower here.' He steps sideways, spreading his arms. 'Add another door here for the toilet to be separate.'

'Ooh, that would be sexy.'

Wait, what word did I use to describe a possible crap-in-privacy room?

Nyx smiles at me over his shoulder.

'I mean, splendid.' I briefly stop jotting things down to push my glasses back up. The layer of glow is making them slide. 'Great idea.'

He stands in front of the window, hands on his hips. 'When that ivy comes down, you'll have one hell of a view from here.'

I'm thinking the same thing from the other side of the room, but I vow to avoid any saucy adjectives this time. 'I will. Or, should I say, whoever buys it will.'

'I imagine you'd like to take full advantage of it from the bedroom windows.' Nyx pulls out his phone. 'What are we here? North-west?'

I don't care. I only know what I would like to take full advantage of.

Do I feel any guilt for these thoughts? No. I'm forty-four and harmless; I'm not forty-four and dead from the waist down. Could I have a son as tall as Nyx? Yes, I could. Do I have a son as tall as Nyx? No, I don't. What I *do* have, though, is a well-paid, overactive imagination. Therefore, not only can I afford to fix up a rundown house with a view that potential buyers will admire, but I can also afford to hire a pert view that *I* will admire. Everyone's a winner.

We say our goodbyes over an hour later, and Colin promises to work out a price by Friday.

The final contractor arrives at three thirty, although we'd agreed to three o'clock. Evidently, no apology or explanation is necessary. I meet his Mitsubishi four-by-four in the driveway. No, I won't call it an SUV – just like the fourth Friday in November is not Black Friday. Not on my side of the pond.

According to Cal, this one has the most experience. He emailed me a list of contractors he had selected, contacted and quizzed. And, knowing him, vetted. I'm paying close attention to what they say, as he will test me afterwards.

'You're the one who bought this pile, then,' is how Mr Mitsubishi introduces himself. It's also his idea of a handshake.

But his line of sight, hidden behind aviator sunglasses, isn't on 'this pile'. If he thinks an indiscreet up and down will intimidate me, he hasn't witnessed how long I can stare at some arsehole who parks next to my car when there are umpteen spaces.

Once his assessment of the owner is finished and mentally scored out of ten, the man's lack of interest turns to the house. 'What are you thinking of doing to it?'

I consult my notes. 'I can walk you through some of my ideas, and then I'd appreciate any advice that—'

'Darling, my advice is simple,' Mr Mitsubishi says. 'This here? Nothing but a money pit. Don't waste your time. Sell it on to someone who can get planning to knock it down and start again.'

I don't need to cast my eyes over what I've paid over the odds for. I know it's a cash sinkhole hiding behind an evergreen shroud, a cover that potentially conceals problem after problem. After problem. After problem. Agreed, the number of 'after problems' goes up between midnight and four a.m., but I've noted a mean average.

Mr Mitsubishi's sigh tells me how bored he is. 'Look, I know these programmes make fixing up houses look like *fun*, but it's not – it's hard work. You need to know what you're doing. So, come on. Stop being silly.'

Stop being silly.

I said the same thing many years ago after I'd saved enough money to buy a red second-hand Ford Escort Cabriolet. It was impractical, but it looked like fun. Something I was lacking.

Stop being silly.

After that, I continued to drive around in my 1985 beige Nissan Sunny for another five years. Now, that car would be retro.

Back then, it was bloody awful.

So how do I tell this walking foreskin that I have hours to spare? How do I explain to him that I also have money to play with?

'I'm sorry you've had a wasted journey. But thank you for your time.'

It's more polite than pelting him with a handful of middle fingers, wouldn't you say?

Chapter Fourteen

After a walk there and back to Stock Ghyll Force, a seventy-foot waterfall near Ambleside, I relax in a pub booth after enjoying one of their hearty roast dinners and a generous wedge (25,000 steps today, all right?) of their triple chocolate cheesecake.

With a fire glowing in the grate, I sit back with a nice beverage and read a few chapters of *Sense and Sensibility*. I'm using a piece of paper that the breath-sucking contractor shoved through my rental's letterbox yesterday evening as a makeshift bookmark. I was standing on the other side of the door when he posted it.

A half-glazed door.

Cost for standard work to be carried out
at Lake View Cottage
£75,000 (excl. VAT)

There was no breakdown showing how he came up with that figure. No hourly rate. There wasn't even a price for a sheet of plasterboard. And what was 'standard'? For all I knew, that was magnolia paint and brown cord carpet in every room. There wasn't even a cheery *Hi Jo* or a – if our business wouldn't be a pleasure – *Dear Jo*.

When did high price tags become undeserving of an explanation? Yes, I know I can afford a starter and a dessert these days, and I don't have to worry now about NHS waiting lists for a dentist, but I still shop around for the best price on my car insurance.

Okay, when I say that *I* shop around...

Remember, it's not me who insists on flying business class. I asked once why we don't fly economy. Once. I was then subjected to my American's bore-me report about frequent flyer benefits, credit card rewards, and sign-up bonuses. Instead of simply saying it's because Cal would eat a Big Mac with a knife and fork.

Hence, when The Ex jokes that I—

One sec, that's my phone. It's the first time in weeks that I've thought about The Ex, and now my phone is ringing?

My fingers tidy my windblown waves when I see who's calling. 'Hey, Nyx.'

'Hey, Jo. I have that quote.'

'Wonderful.'

'Mind if I pop it over now?'

Jeans just slim enough (not the craze currently sweeping the nation for ones that are tight enough to show if they're circumcised) have replaced Nyx's work trousers. A semi-fitted shirt graces his broad shoulders, with the back of the collar providing a resting place for his curls. The ones on top of his head must have been repeatedly swept back to downgrade them into soft waves.

The jacket over his arm tells me he's going somewhere after this – somewhere with one lucky girl. Yes, it'll probably end in tears, but she can worry about that when she starts to sign birthday cards from both of them.

Nyx's charming smile distracts me from what he's saying, but I get the gist from the envelope he proffers.

'Grandad's quicker at writing with a pen.'

I take out the ten pages adorned with Colin's loopy lettering.

'I've also brought along a few catalogues.' Nyx lifts his jacket. 'Just, you know, some ideas.'

'Lovely. Thank you.'

'I've highlighted some pages and referenced them in the quote. Unless you… have half an hour?'

'Of course.' I gesture towards a chair. 'Please, sit down. Would you like a drink?'

'I'd love a coffee.'

'They do lattes and cappuccinos that come highly recommended on thatswhatidrink.com.'

'Well, in that case, I'll have a latte, please.'

After we've ordered our drinks from a passing staff member, I cast an eye over the quote. Everything is listed and priced individually in understandable terminology.

'Your grandad's handwriting is lovely. I might use this for a feature wall somewhere.'

Nyx's smile shows the perfect number of upper

teeth. 'If you do, the greedy bugger will start charging for quotes.'

I can't help mirroring his facial expression. His hypnotic handsomeness is just—

Jo, this isn't one of Olivia's rom-coms. Eyes down.

'And these windows you have noted on page two?' I ask.

Sitting forward, Nyx pulls out one of the catalogues. He flips to the right page and lays it on the table between us, explaining the options available. I've sniffed out this young man's passion, it would seem, as he rakes his hair back. Now I'm sniffing clean skin and fruity top notes in his cologne, which the woody middle note isn't overpowering. Yeah, like he needs any scented help! If he merely asked a woman to pass the salt, she would happily bury her self-control in his neck.

'... and they're A-rated windows too,' Nyx is saying, 'which would look good when you're selling it. They would also fit in with the cottage's character, don't you think?'

Sorry, was he going beyond making the world a more attractive place to live?

'Erm, yes.' I adjust my glasses. 'Absolutely.'

'They're a bit more expensive, but we've fitted them before; they're worth every penny. If you have room in your budget for them.'

'Well, I definitely have a budget.'

Cal kept drumming those words into me. He said I needed to repeat them often and firmly when talking to contractors. In the end, I threatened to harvest his eyes if he mentioned them again.

'But I'd like it done right the first time,' I add. 'I wouldn't want to appeal to starter marriage types.'

'You don't.'

Nyx's gaze jumps back to the brochures. What was he staring at? Are my grey roots showing?

When we sit back to let the waitress unload her drinks tray, I look up to thank her and waste a smile. I have my purse out, but Nyx is already handing money over and telling her to keep the change.

'But I asked if *you* would like a coffee,' I protest.

'Does it matter?'

'Yes. I owe you two drinks as well.'

'Do you?'

An eyebrow war plays out in silence for a few moments. I don't think now is the time to admit I never handle disagreements like an adult.

I am shown more pictures of items included in their quote, plus other available options. I'm amazed these two have put all this together in such a short space of time.

There is something else on the seat next to him.

'Oh. Oh, yeah. I, erm... I did some quick sketches.' Nyx fiddles with the drawing pad. 'Just... using the photos that I took the other day. I hope you don't mind.'

'Not at all.' I look at the first one. 'Sorry, this is your idea of a *quick* sketch?'

'I was pushed for time, so the detailing isn't great.'

'I can see that – a peony is missing not one but *two* petals.'

Nyx dimples his cheeks again, tucking his hands beneath his thighs and biting his bottom lip.

The drawing looks like it has been done from a position on a fireside chair, capturing the entire room bathed in sunlight. The must-have island welcomes you to the kitchen area on the right. An elegant dining table sits in front of a wall of glass doors, with glimpses of a bordered lawn beyond. A deep sofa is scattered with just enough mismatched cushions to make you want to spend the night on it. In front of the log burner, a low table is artfully buried underneath the accumulated clutter that must come from creating a home. Beside the fireplace, he has drawn a desk. There's just one item on it.

'That old photo we found in the lounge,' Nyx remarks. 'It wasn't there the other day.'

'I took it home. For safekeeping.'

The second drawing is of the main bedroom, with the lake showing through the bars of a Juliet balcony. A sumptuous bed is on the wall to the right, and the restored cast iron fireplace is opposite.

I point at all the photo frames drawn on top of a chest of drawers. They are vying for space with vases of flowers. 'You think the house will be good for more memories?'

'Definitely.'

'Then I'm sure I can use that as a selling point.'

I turn to the third drawing.

'I took a bit of a risk with the main bathroom,' Nyx warns.

One width wall has a shower big enough to fit a

string quartet. A stone countertop basin has been drawn on a simple shelf. A free-standing oval tub sits in front of a wide window, which looks out into the leafy branches of the contentious oak. I love that tree more every time I see it.

I hug the drawing pad. 'Sir, you did well.'

I can tell I just brightened up this young man's late afternoon.

Another of Cal's bloody mantras leaves my mouth. 'I need to sit down and look closely at these figures.'

'Of course. It's a lot of money.' Nyx nods towards my froth-lined cup. 'Same again?'

'May I please pay this time?'

He quickly picks up the empty cups. 'You get the next ones.'

As Nyx waits at the bar, I can alternate my admiration between his sketches and the view of him from the back. The man has an eye for design. I bet his spank mag pile must consist purely of interior design magazines.

Professionalism aside, get a load of his even more amazing—

When Nyx gets his change (pocketing the notes and returning most of the coins), I quickly turn my attention back to his use of shading.

'How come you're texturing walls and not canvasses for a living?' I ask as he sits down again.

Nyx shrugs. 'Drawing can't pay the bills.'

'How long have you been a contractor?'

'It's almost nine years now. I left school and

started an intermediate apprenticeship at my uncle's building firm the day after my sixteenth birthday. It was mostly learning on the job...'

Sixteen plus nine – sorry, almost nine. Bugger.

Ah, well. It's not like I'm disappointed. I'm not stupid, either; I know Nyx's interest is purely winning-the-job-related. Still, if we forty-something, flying-solo fillies ever grow tired of watching Ryan Gosling in *Crazy, Stupid, Love* (I doubt it), we will need alternative fuel for our imaginations.

'... Then, two years ago, I set up with Grandad. This suited us both, seeing as he didn't want to fully retire.'

'And how is business?'

Nyx nods. 'It's good. We've been lucky: work has come to us almost from day one, mostly by word of mouth, from the years he's been in the trade.'

As well as from the lonely wives living across the road from where they're working, I imagine. One look at Nyx, and they're convincing their husbands they need a fourth bedroom *and* an office – only after they've lost a couple of pounds and had fresh highlights.

'Did you choose the job?' I ask. 'Or did the job choose you?'

'I'm not sure. I got roped into it during the school holidays. It was probably to stop me from hanging with the wrong crowd. But, by the time I was fifteen, I knew it was what I'd do for a living. Mum likes to think that's why I didn't do great at school.'

'Study isn't the only place where learning lives.'

'Right.' Nyx smiles. 'What about you? I bet you went all the way.'

Don't you dare, I warn my horny right eyebrow.

'No. No, I didn't. I did well in my GCSEs, scraped a couple of A-Level passes in art and English literature, and that's it. I didn't go down the university path. I might have if the national curriculum had included lessons in overcoming failure and forming emotional relationships. Instead, I worked my way up from retail to office, consuming shelves of books on the way.' Not one word of which is a lie.

'And now you're flying across the ocean with your job,' Nyx comments.

'Oh, that isn't something I do very often; in fact, hardly ever. No, my commute to work is usually five paces from the sofa to my desk.'

'What is it you do?'

'I'm a book editor,' I tell him without hesitation.

No, it's not an answer I've just invented for this beautiful man who scrubs up well. It's the one I initially give to anyone outside of a literary festival if they ask me what I do. And technically, it *is* what I do for a living. Well, partly. But if you tell people you're a writer, they assume at least two of the following:

- You're a hermit
- You're minted
- You work when you feel like it
- You don't own a vacuum cleaner

'Which means I usually only need a computer and internet connection to do my job.' And before anyone who takes manuscripts in the shower with them will tell you, I know that's not all book editors need. But is Nyx going to know that? 'Therefore, I can work from home ninety-five per cent of the time.'

'Lucky you. So, what's with the renovation sideline?'

'I'm on holiday.' It's better than saying I'm searching for the old me.

Nyx's eyebrows draw together. 'It's an expensive and dirty holiday.'

I lean forward in case someone (whose paper currency is all one size) is listening; I wouldn't put it past Cal. 'The thing is,' I whisper, 'I don't do holidays.'

'Why are you taking one, then?' Nyx whispers back.

'My boss... Well, sort of. The bossy one who runs things thinks I need one.' My shrug and eyeroll say how much I agree with him.

'Maybe he was thinking you'd spend two weeks on a beach somewhere.'

'No, he knows that's not my style. Neither is buying a house, if I'm honest. But I need to keep my mind occupied.'

'Why?' Nyx asks. 'What happens if you don't?'

I am poised to answer, but seconds pass before any words come out. 'You know, I'm not entirely sure.'

'How long has it been since you last took a break from work, Jo?'

'I believe David Cameron was Prime Minister.'

'You must love what you do.'

I think about my response. 'Most of the time, yes.'

'Well, I've always thought the whole point of a holiday is to empty your mind. Or is that yoga?'

'Hmm, I think it is.'

'Then a holiday is for…' Nyx is searching for the right words.

'You don't take many either, do you?'

'I have an excuse. If I don't work, I don't get paid.'

'And when *I* come up with an excuse…' I point at who'll be the first to hear.

'At least you're doing something with your downtime – something that may not see you out of pocket.'

'That's true. And if it has happy new owners by the end of this summer, that would be delightful.'

'But if it doesn't sell straight away, might you be tempted to stay a while longer?' Nyx asks.

I do one of those non-committal head shakes/nods. They have served me well over the years, especially when someone asks if I'm going for a drink with everyone later.

'I think it's great what you're doing,' he says. 'We should all do it: make the time to step away from our busy jobs and concentrate on something else – something we're interested in.'

'Exactly.'

I may as well humour him. When Nyx has two kids under ten wanting iPhones for Easter and Gucci for school, we'll see what he's concentrating on then.

I also know what he's going to say next.

'And money isn't everything.'

Bingo! Those exact words often accompany thirty-carat diamond rings and a matching age gap. Especially when, in the absence of a prenup, they know 'everything' is what they'll get when they marry rich and wrinkled instead of hard-up and hot.

'As long as you save a little every month for those rainy days,' Nyx adds. 'Which I'm guessing you have done.'

'Since I work all the time, saving is... Well, my hobby, I suppose. I only have eight pairs of fancy shoes because that's all I need. The most expensive thing I've purchased until now is a car. I take four-minute showers and turn off the lights when I leave a room. I drink tap water, and I swear by the sniff test. So...'

So, what? Is my thriftiness something to be proud of? Or something that deserves sympathy? A sad epitaph, perhaps, which may one day grace the outside of my single-crypt mausoleum.

'Good for you, Jo.'

With a tight-lipped smile, I allow the judges time to consider that compliment. Mercifully, our coffees arrive before I find out whether I've made it to pity camp.

Nyx warms his hands around his cup. 'If it's not too personal a question, is there a Mr Washington or, you know, a... potential Mr Washington? Or any little Washingtons?'

With a mouthful of latte, I shake my head and hold up my thumb. My index and middle fingers will join in soon. 'No to the first,' I answer when I can. 'Not in the foreseeable future to the second. And hell, *never* to the third.'

'I may have missed the subtlety, but would I be right in thinking that you're not a fan of kids?'

'I like them even less than paper cuts.'

Why does my chest flutter when Nyx laughs at the silly lines I occasionally come out with?

'You can't hate them all,' he tells me.

'Well, I'm yet to meet one that doesn't make my train journeys unbearable.'

'What is it about them that annoys you?'

'If you want a short answer, ask me what it is about them I *like*.'

'Hit me with the long one,' Nyx challenges.

'Right. Here goes.' I lace my fingers and gently bend them backwards. 'I hate the noise, the histrionics, the lack of interesting conversation, the monotone voice. I cannot tolerate the silly sounds, the triviality, the neediness, the inability to work out the uses of a tissue.' I take a breath. 'They're ungrateful, nasty, smelly. They also have short attention spans. And they get the best parking spots at supermarkets. *And* they will eventually replace us.'

'You were little yourself once,' he reminds me.

'Only in stature.'

'I would love to have met this two-year-old you.' He chuckles. 'I'm sure there are some two-year-olds out there you might like.'

'And I'll happily meet them. As soon as parents realise the idolisation they lavish on them won't be returned in kind.'

137

His head tilts to one side. 'I don't think that's... why people have children. Is it?'

'I'll tell you why they do. These days, it's for social media. They know a photo of their kid asleep on a rug wearing a massive bow headband will get the most "likes".'

As Nyx struggles to respond, I sit back with my drink and cross my legs.

'Anything... else?' he dares to ask.

'If you purchase my first book of reasons for hating emotionally manipulating infants, I'll let you have the sequel at half price.'

Nyx smiles and nods. 'Got it. But just in case you decide not to sell, do you want me to keep hold of the sketch of the spare room with a princess bed?'

My deadpan look makes him quickly hide behind his cup.

Obviously, I can't ask him now if he has a girlfriend. What do you mean, why is it...? Because it would sound like I'm interested in him, and he might think I interpreted his asking me about my circumstances as some... some... preposterous notion that he is interested in me. Which, of course, he isn't.

Yes, I know I'm the queen of risk-free flirting, but a twenty-four-year-old sober man of Nyx's calibre? There's more chance of me winning a gold medal or going into space. Or even appearing on *Too Hot to Handle*.

It's okay. Don't worry, I'm fine. Facts are facts, simple as that. If parents were this honest, they would save a fortune on university costs. Then they wouldn't have to watch their kid fail to find a job where a degree in media studies is handy.

Nyx's phone, forgotten on the table underneath a catalogue, starts ringing. He picks it up and glances at the screen. 'Do you mind if I...?'

'Not at all.'

He drops his elbows onto his knees. 'Hi... Look in the cupboard under the stairs... Then try the basket in the lounge... No, I won't be long... Yeah, as soon as I get back... Okay... I love you too. Bye.' Nyx checks that the call has ended. 'Sorry about that.'

'Was it science asking where you've hidden the answer to the meaning of life?'

'No,' he says. 'Actually, it was... my daughter.'

I don't mean to make half the people sitting near us jump, but I can't stop the raucous laughter bursting out of my mouth. I have no control over my stomping boot, either. Nor do I want to stop slapping my leg. Not when it's the funniest joke that I've heard all year.

I'm the only one who's laughing, though.

'Oh.' My stupid merriment morphs into a faux-delighted smile. 'Well, I'm sure your...' I don't know the right word, but I hope it's written on my upturned palm. '... is the one exception to my long list of... of just, just... silly reasons.'

The corners of Nyx's mouth lift. 'It was my little brother.'

My relief must be visible from Mars. 'That was about as funny as someone saying chocolate is their favourite c-word.'

'Oh, it was funny.'

'Just the one sibling?' I ask, fanning my cheeks with a brochure.

'No, I have five-year-old twin brothers and three sisters: they are fifteen, nineteen and… twenty-two.'

I cringe. 'Ooh, menstrual synchrony. Would you like my condolences, or shall I ask God to consider you for sainthood?'

'Leniency from the judge might help. We all still live at home with Mum, too.'

Not Dad.

'Either you have more than one bathroom, or you're all very close.'

'We're very close.' Nyx's beaming smile could toast bread. 'I will also hold my hands up to being a mummy's boy.'

'Are you serious?' I blurt out.

His happy expression falters. 'My… My mum's my hero. She's the most… She's the most amazing person alive. She is doing an amazing job raising us, and I'm… I'm *proud* to—'

'No, no. I'm sorry,' I quickly interject. 'I was reacting to the one-bathroom situation.'

The temperature goes back up, and Nyx's dazzling disarmer of a grin makes me crave a T-shirt. But when the weather this morning threatened to harden every nipple in Cumbria, I had to dig out a polo-neck sweater.

'Well,' he says, 'when you don't know any different…'

'Hands down, having your own bathroom is better than seeing an ex fail to find anyone better than you.'

'No way. I thought nothing could top that.'

Clearly, Nyx hasn't written any books that are still on the *New York Times* bestseller list three years after their release.

I return to his earlier comment. 'So you and your brothers and sisters all get along?'

'We do now. Which is probably why Mum never wants us to leave.' Nyx tilts his cup in my direction. 'What about you? Any siblings?'

'Allegedly. Twins, like yourself. Sisters, though, who will be forty sometime this year. But unlike your mum, mine likes children only marginally more than I do.'

'But she had three of them?'

'She did. No, she had four – I forgot about my older sister, their honeymoon baby. Then I came along eleven months later, proving that not everyone can use breastfeeding as a method of birth control. I was four when she had the twins, and – that's right – I'm forty-four.' I grin at him. 'I could see you working it out.'

Nyx hesitates. 'You're forty-four?'

'In human years, yes. In goldfish years, I'm dead.'

'I don't believe you.'

I sip my coffee as he scrutinises me.

'You can't be,' he decides.

'Unless Hollywood is willing to pay big bucks, Nyx, would any woman lie if she's actually younger?'

'But you only look about twenty-eight.'

Whenever someone says I don't look my age, I rarely believe them. We all say it, don't we?

Sometimes we mean it; other times, we say it to be kind; often, we're just wheedling for a compliment in return. However, when it comes from someone who's popped into your head during a little private browsing time, you want to grab the monarch's crown as you shuffle them off the throne.

'You're far too kind,' I tell him. 'But it's all down to my dark limbal rings.'

'Which rings?'

I make a circular motion with my finger in front of my eye. 'Those around my irises.'

Nyx rises from his chair for a closer look.

A much closer look.

'Dark limbal rings can, erm... can resent you,' I explain. 'No, they don't resent you. They can represent you – represent *youth*. Youth and, and good health.' Oh, God. My coffee breath. 'It's because babies have ones – dark ones – dark... rings.'

'Fascinating.'

When someone's phone starts to ring, Nyx sits back down.

It's still ringing.

Still ring—

Oh, it's mine.

I check who the caller is before offering him an apologetic face. 'Hey, Ma. Can I call you back shortly?'

'Why, what's wrong, Milly, erm, Jo?'

'Nothing.'

'Are you—?'

'Yes, I'm sure. Listen, Ma, it's really going to

sound like I'm cutting you off now.'

Nyx watches me pocket my phone. 'Did you really just…?'

'Cut my Ma off? Oh, I wish!'

When we stand up, the pub's dark windows tell us daylight went home some time ago.

'Sorry, Jo. I've taken up too much of your evening.'

I wave his apology aside. 'Don't worry. The most exciting thing I'm likely to do on a Friday night is eat a ready meal on its best before date.'

'We can swap,' Nyx says. 'If you'd rather spend it on a PlayStation with two small boys.'

The outfit wasn't to impress a hot date. What a waste. Well, maybe not. This dinosaur appreciated it.

I clench my fists. 'If only I didn't have *The Lives and Loves of a Drone Ant* waiting for me at home on video cassette.'

'Next time.'

'I promise to keep open never the thirty-first. I will also get back to you soon about the quote.'

'Hm? Oh, yeah. Right.' Nyx flashes his sparkling teeth at me. They're easy to keep clean when they're that nice and straight. I love him.

I mean, I love a man with teeth – with *good* teeth.

As I lead the way out, I notice that the mirrors behind the bar reflect our empty table.

'Nyx. Is that short for Nicholas?'

'No, just Nyx, the name of the Greek goddess of the night, who scared Zeus. Yeah, that's right, a god*dess*.' He shakes his head. 'No points for guessing

I was the only boy named Nyx at my school.'

'I like it. Originality these days is refreshing – something I wish the moviemakers would invest in.' I hold my hand out. 'Well, thank you so far for all your work: the quote, the brochures, the *fabulous* drawings.'

Nyx's grip matches mine. 'You're very welcome.'

'And thank you for your... excellent company,' I'm surprised to hear myself say.

'What is it, Jo?'

'Please don't take this the wrong way.' How to put it without sounding like I buy his music and have him as a screensaver. Oh, sod it. 'But you may be the finest-looking man I have ever seen in the flesh.'

Thank goodness Nyx laughs. 'Really?'

'Yes. Therefore, there is little need for you to be as engaging as you are, since most women would be happy to sit and watch your mouth as you explain how grass grows.' I bite my bottom lip. 'I'm sorry if that's offensive.'

'Not at all.'

'Phew.' I pump his hand once more for luck. 'Thank you again.'

'No, thank *you*.' Nyx tips an imaginary cap. 'You've made my day.'

I won't say what he's made me.

He points towards his car. 'Can I give you a lift?'

'It's kind of you to offer, but I must work off some of that cheesecake. And my place is only two streets away.'

'Okay. Well, I hope to see you again – and soon.'

Nyx walks backwards. 'You still owe me two drinks, remember?'

'Only because you wouldn't let me pay in there.'

He gives me a playful wink. 'That's right.' Turning away, he calls over his shoulder, 'Are you looking at my bum again, Josephine?'

'N-No! I'm... I'm merely a-admiring the... the stitching on your, erm... your b-back pockets.'

My embarrassment and I wave as Nyx's car goes by and drives off up the hill. I then spot a woman's reflection in the shop window: she's walking with her phone to her ear, her pace bouncy enough to sway her bobbed hair. A huge smile lights up her face.

'Is something wrong with your BlueBerry, Milly, erm, Jo?' Ma asks when she answers her phone. 'It cut me off earlier.'

'That was my fault, Ma.'

'Are you sure?'

Chapter Fifteen

I'm standing on step ladders in front of the wall that divides the cottage's kitchen and the lounge. Nyx is behind me, holding the ladders steady.

Do I care that his face has a close-up view of my arse? No. Am I worried that, when I exert myself, my capacity to control my flatulence is slowly seeping away with each passing year? I'll give you two guesses.

'Ready, Jo?'

'Ready.'

'Goggles on.'

I lower the plastic goggles over my glasses and pick up my hardware of choice. After we removed a skinny layer of plaster (the easy bit), I declined the scary heavy-duty drill Nyx offered me for this next stage. Instead, I'm sticking with the tools that most horror movies would think are too PG.

I put the bolster between the bricks and hit it with the hammer.

Tap, tap, tap, tap.

'Nothing's happening,' I tell him.

'Hit it harder.'

Tap, tap, tap, tap.

'Bloody hell! Convincing me reality shows are real wouldn't be this hard.'

'Shall I get you started?' Nyx offers.

'Yes, please.'

We swap places.

Bang! Bang! Bang!

Five bricks hit the floor.

'I think I loosened those,' I utter.

'You did.'

We swap places again.

Tap, tap, tap, tap.

I try wiggling the brick out like a milk tooth.

'Chip a bit more of the mortar out,' Nyx suggests.

Tap, tap, wiggle. *Tap, tap, wiggle.*

'Jo, if you—'

'I've got it.'

I put the tools down and wiggle the damn brick with both—

Saying nothing, I climb down the ladder.

While Nyx knocks the bricks out, I grab a flexible bucket and – keeping a keen eye on where he drops them – fill it only half full, as per his advice, before taking it to the skip.

Soon, however, he's knocking them out quicker than I can clear them away. As I trot back and forth with my weight limit, Nyx stops when the pile gets too big, and he fills up and empties the wheelbarrow before knocking out a few more.

'You're doing an amazing job there, Jo.'

I want to tell him I prefer chocolates to having smoke blown up my arse, but all my energy – including that for speaking – has been redeployed to my weak arms. Those things usually do nothing more strenuous than sweep across the view when my legs reach the top of Skiddaw.

But working on tiny loads allows me time to admire the workman. Especially when I follow Nyx to the skip and watch him sprint up the thin gangplank to tip the barrow. The action causes his bum to jiggle and my mouth to drool.

Nyx destroys the wall in no time, leaving the ceiling held up by the props he had positioned before we started. He's not even out of breath. Imagine what he's like after a good—

'We did it,' he says. 'We've made a start.'

'*You* did it.' I force a tired arm to return his high-five. Why couldn't he have made it a low one instead?

'Hey. Team effort.'

I resist folding my arms. 'Should I stick to what I'm good at going forward: supplying the coffee and the cash?'

'Nope. Now, upstairs,' Nyx orders. 'I want you in the bedroom.'

And there is the fantasy I'll forever play out when put on hold.

'You're doing the wall in there on your own,' he informs me. 'It's just a stud.'

'What does that mean? That it's good for making baby walls?'

Nyx nods towards the dog, who's still not bored

with pouncing on the same bit of wood. 'It means even Bacon could knock it down.'

Have I not mentioned the dog? My apologies. She's just a... I don't know, a... short-haired Heinz 57, about the size of a cairn terrier. Her coat is almost every colour in the canine rainbow: her nose, both ears, one eye and a saddle across her back are black; a large area of her body, tail and legs are salt-and-pepper; her paws and chest are sand; and her belly and the other eye are pops of white.

No, she's not Nyx's. Five evenings ago, I had a date with a supermarket's vegan range of heat-and-eat meals on my rented patio. I was about to tuck into my spaghetti and veggie balls when it became apparent I had unwanted company.

I know. Is there any other type for me?

I was twirling my third forkful when the animal took a tentative step forward. Then another. It sat down again, an equal distance from me and the slightly open gate. Despite my death glare, it continued to creep forward.

'Nothing to see here.'

It took another step forward. I kept twirling and eating. By my fifth mouthful, the dog's head was resting on my knee on its front paws, its mournful eyes trying to melt me. Their sense of smell may be over 10,000 times better than ours, but their mind-reading skills are poo.

I noticed it was wearing a tattered, rainbow-coloured collar. There was no ID tag, just a word embroidered on it. 'Someone named you Bacon? Let me guess: did their vegan girlfriend leave the gate open on purpose?'

I let go of the collar, and the dog jumped straight onto my lap.

'Whoa, what are you doing? No, you need to go. It's late. Well, it will be somewhere. Go on now. Go on!'

It wagged its tail and stomped its front legs harder on my thighs. Its eyes flicked to my makeshift plate, the brightest pink tongue licking one side of its muzzle and then the other.

'You wouldn't like this: it counts towards your five-a-day. And if I feed you, you'll think I like you and want to get to know you better. Newsflash: I don't. You're not my type. I'm not into facial hair.' I looked between the dog's legs. 'Or women. You'll outstay your welcome, and everything you do will start to annoy me. Before long, it'll be tomay-to tomah-to and... In fact, let's call it off now, the whole thing.'

More pawing.

'I have pepper spray inside – and yes, I'm afraid to use it.'

The dog let out the tiniest squeak, its floppy lips vibrating.

Now, unlike kids, I don't hate animals. I don't love all of them; I'm not keen on caged rodents or anything you keep in a vivarium. However, I confess to getting mushy whenever I see baby orangutans going to nursery in a wheelbarrow. I also got 'something in my eye' every time I watched *Paul O'Grady: For the*

Love of Dogs.

The many golden retrievers my family has owned over the years have belonged to everyone registered at our address, watering down my level of ownership enough. Since then, I've never wanted a dog of my own. Not only do they need you, but they also offer far too much unconditional love for my liking.

The dog scrambled off my lap when I put the plastic dish on the floor.

'Enjoy.'

An impossibility, given the speed at which it was eating.

'And when you're done, see yourself out. If you can close the gate behind you as well, I'll... Yeah, goodnight.'

I went back inside the house, shutting the patio doors and drawing the curtains, even though it was only six o'clock. I took a mug of coffee and a bowl of cereal upstairs.

The cool air that often accompanies a heavy shower woke me up. I was upright on the bed, my laptop on my outstretched legs. My head had dropped to the side against one of the angled pillows, tilting my glasses. At first, I thought I'd regained clear vision in one eye.

I turned off the light and lay down. The rain upped a gear, drumming loudly on the tilted glass of the open window. It was a wonder it never banged shut. I could hear the gutters overflowing and water surging down the drainpipes. Anyone caught in it would be drenched.

Or any*thing*.

My eyes flew open.

I tiptoed across the living room (yes, I know the patio doors are double-glazed) and peeped through a tiny side gap in the curtain. The empty food tray was filling with boisterous raindrops, sitting alone in the middle of the patio with just the chairs for company. Sighing with relief, I flung back the curtains and—

'Damn it!'

My eyes darted to the dancing washing line – and away from the soggy animal sitting sideways to the glass, water dripping from one of its drooping ears. It was trying to get any shelter it could from the narrow overhang.

I banged the hall door shut and grabbed the first towel that came to hand from the wash basket, shaking it open and tossing it onto the floor in front of the unlit fire. I yanked open the patio door.

But it was only the rain on the strengthening wind that rushed in.

'What, do you want a handwritten invitation posted out?'

No, it didn't.

'On the—'

But the dog was already there, shaking off its wet topcoat. It then circled a spot on the towel five times before folding its little legs beneath it, shrinking to about the size of one of those fluffy bear paw slippers.

Its eyes were back on me.

'You rip anything, scratch anything, or shit on anything,' I warned, heading for the hallway, 'and those animals at the RSPCA will miss out on my monthly donations. Got that?' I stopped with the door open and the light behind me. 'One night. One. If you so much as chew a cushion tassel, I'm taking you to court. One night.'

Bacon has taken on the role of supervisor today. Before I start on the stud wall, she watches me and Nyx cut up the bedroom carpet and compacted underlay. We then roll it into manageable pieces and carry them over our shoulders to the skip.

This type of wall is better for me. Even with my inability to get the sledgehammer above waist height, I still bash it all the way through to the other side. In less than an hour, it's nothing more than a pile of broken laths and chunks of plaster.

Once everything is cleared away, we can gauge how big the main bedroom will be. Nyx measures where the new walls will go for the en suite, stealing areas from both bedrooms and spraying lines on the hardboard he left down. He seems to appreciate the help from my four-legged squatter.

'Or this could be one huge bedroom instead of two,' I think aloud.

Nyx stops spraying. 'It... could. But what happens if the new owners have a baby? Or they'd like company over?'

'Oh, it would certainly discourage both.'

He narrows his eyes. 'I'm not entirely certain you're joking.'

I smile and nod my head. 'I am.'

'Really?'

Still smiling, I shake my head. 'No.'

**

Nyx carries the wares I bought this morning from the newly discovered farmers' market to the pebbly water's edge. Thanks to him, it is now accessible through the gate. Lunch is the only payment he will accept for giving up his Saturday morning.

After I have spread my new, waterproof picnic blanket (made from recycled wool, by the way) on a dry patch of shoreline, we empty my new basket (made from sustainably produced willow grown here in Cumbria) of its contents: girthy sausage rolls, hand-cooked crisps, crusty bread to enjoy with the locally made brie, and homemade chutney. For dessert, there are elaborate key lime cupcakes. There's also a bottle of sparkling apple and blackberry juice to wash it all down.

There's a jar of honey in the car, too. And six fresh eggs.

And ten wax melts.

And a wind chime, a bag of apples, an apron, some cooked beetroot, and two bottles of pale ale.

No, I don't drink beer. But how could I leave out one stall?

'Thanks again for your patience today, Nyx.'

'No problem. I've enjoyed it.' He slices off another generous chunk of brie, balancing it on the torn-off piece of bread. 'And it's your project, so you should be the one to get the ball rolling.'

'I hope I haven't ruined your weekend plans.'

'Nah. My mate got a replacement best man at the last minute.'

Nyx nudges my shoulder to reassure me that it *is* a joke. I'm guessing he does this because he remembers how easily he pulled my leg about having a child. Another thing it does is make me aware of how close we are sitting on this blanket. His arm was already gently pressed against mine before the nudge, but it didn't register after we had sat down. Maybe that's because, without trumpets and highlights on teatime news, it is easy to jump into a comfortable alliance with a man when the chemistry is right – with one as tasty as him, too. Who would have thought it?

'To tell you the truth,' Nyx says, nudging my shoulder again, 'I would've probably still been in bed, watching sport.'

'Hey, if that's your thing.' I swig from the bottle and then pass it to him. He doesn't bother wiping the top before taking a swig himself. 'When you've worked hard all week, you can do as much or as little as you want on your days off – and don't let anyone tell you otherwise.'

Nyx's expression asks whether he heard me correctly. My confirmation prompts him to put his lunch aside. He drops to one knee and takes my hand. 'Marry me, Jo Washington.'

'Hmm.' I give it careful thought while munching on my doughy mouthful of brie and chutney.

'Say yes, sweetheart.'

Six people on a dayboat clearly know what the one knee signifies.

'If she won't, I will,' shouts a deep voice.

My heavy sigh makes it sound like it's not the worst thing in the world, but it is a slight inconvenience. 'Oh, all right. I'll marry you.'

Holding his arms aloft, Nyx looks across at our audience. 'She said yes!'

There is cheering and the tooting of a horn. My own horn is resisting the urge to tickle the expanse of exposed skin above his waistband that's torturing me at eye level. As is his—

'Give her a snog then,' somebody commands.

I give Nyx the green light when I open my arms, and we hide our faces in each other's necks. But the pebbly surface digs into his knee, and repeated apologies from him exceed his curses when he stumbles forward and falls on top of me.

The applause and whistles our 'kiss' receives can hardly be heard above our giggles. Bacon bounces around us and nuzzles our ears and cheeks with her juicy nose, encouraging the betrothed as much as the non-paying public.

A splash of nervousness creeps over us with the fading of the boat's engine. We sit up again, tugging down hemlines and straightening headbands. I welcome Bacon filling the gap between us, wishing she'd done it sooner.

Nyx looks at the time on his phone. 'Wow. I really need to get going.'

He probably doesn't 'really' need to, but he obviously wants out of here now. I can feel mortification rising from the steel toes in my dusty boots.

As Nyx helps me to my feet, I say to the print on the front of his T-shirt, 'Thanks again for today.'

'My pleasure, Jo. What are your plans for the rest of the day?'

'Don't tell anyone, but I intend to do some work.'

'I thought you were taking a break?'

'Oh, writers don't know the meaning of the word.'

At least I'm walking ahead of him when this slips out. Buggering hell. I blame that off-putting skin contact. What moisturiser is Nyx wearing: Nivea Men Hydrating *Truth* Serum?

'Do you still have to be on call for your authors?'

Phew. That was close.

'Always. Particularly when publishing deadlines loom. Authors make their editors and agents earn their money.' As Cal knows all too well.

'I bet.'

'But they're very nice people,' I quickly add.

Nyx walks with me to my car and opens the passenger door. Bacon doesn't need any encouragement to jump in and scramble into her new booster seat. She sits still so Nyx can click her collar to the harness. He rewards her good behaviour with a loud kiss between her eyes. Honestly, that animal gets more action than I do.

'Have you had any calls about our pretty girl?' he asks.

After she made herself too comfortable on one of my fluffy Egyptian cotton towels, a trip to the vet showed her microchip details weren't up to date. I

157

informed the district council and some local rescue centres. One of them kindly showed me where to get a 'found dog' poster template online. Her mugshot is now adorning shop windows and public notice boards as far afield as Ambleside.

'I've only had responses from Storm Models,' I tell him while opening the car boot.

Nyx says to Bacon, 'Well, let's keep our fingers crossed that nobody comes forward.'

I scowl at him over the boot shelf. 'I heard that.'

'Good. It saves me having to repeat it.'

I hand Nyx the spare set of house keys. 'Work your magic for me, please.'

'I sure will. I'll see you Monday?'

'Why? Is there more I can do right now?'

There is one thing I can do: I can look on Amazon for a replacement making-a-complete-twat-of-myself detector. Mine failed me earlier on the shoreline.

'No, but it would be nice if you just... popped in for a chat.' Nyx pulls his headband off and rakes back his dusty waves. 'And we can show you what's going to happen. It's your house.'

'Yes, but it's your job. I don't want to get in the way.'

'You won't.'

I twirl my keys on my finger. 'Okay.'

'I'll see you Monday, then?' he prompts.

'Erm...' Still twirling. 'Yeah. Yeah, okay.'

Nyx's smile displays teeth that are twenty years younger than mine. 'Promise?'

'Okay.'

***

For twenty-five hours, I… Wait, should I include my four hours of *in*terrupted sleep? Okay. For twenty-*nine* hours, I wanted to rewind time and accept Nyx's proposal by creating a pleasant playlist on my laptop. Or perhaps by making a beautiful mood board on Pinterest.

Anything rather than that tragic hug job.

Why was I worrying, you might ask. Others may chime in with, Why was I *still* worrying?

One answer for both crowds: I live alone.

The benefits of being permasingle would fill the pages of a redundant encyclopaedia. The shortcomings, meanwhile, would need just a few lines; a subheading would do. Starting with the word 'scrutinise'.

As a writer, I can usually turn that solo frown upside down and smash my daily word count goal. It's a different story, though, when I shouldn't have a keyboard or pen to hand. It could drive an author to think.

Which is what happened, and thinking I had messed up with my contractor by crossing the plumb line wouldn't go away.

That was until three hours ago. When I received a text.

Nyx: Hey future wife. How's your Sunday been? Have you picked out a dress yet? x

Consequently, I missed the end of *Miss Marple*. I didn't see the first episode of that new drama series

159

on ITV1, either. I'd also meant to set the satellite thing to record the nine o'clock film, but I kept forgetting. I've missed most of it now because I'm carting my phone everywhere, with my text count probably exceeding the number I sent during the first quarter of this year.

We decide on autumn for our wedding; it's my favourite season and Nyx's second favourite. It takes a while to settle on the actual date, finally plumping for the twenty-sixth of October to guarantee maximum pumpkin availability. Without them, it wouldn't be a wedding.

After that, I almost call it off when Nyx says he wants to wear a brown suit for the ceremony. As for my outfit, an agreement is eventually reached: understated and a shade of cream. I'll be almost forty-five when we get married. I'm not going near tulle or a veil.

The topics then hit some wild rapids, from what we would choose for our last meal on death row to our favourite baby names. He likes Betty for a girl; I like Ichabod. For a boy, though, I like Bruce.

Wonderfully irrelevant silliness, the SMSing likes of which I haven't enjoyed since...

Wow, I almost went two days without being reminded of The Ex. He's cropping up more and more just lately.

When our eyes had locked over a photocopier, I was worried that I might finally have to believe in kismet. Two months later, The Ex asked me out. And tucked away one Monday evening in a village pub bordering the next county, I listened to him talk about himself in his unvarying tone for three hours.

Three – long – hours.

I couldn't believe it. The man was nothing more than an eye-catching cover that disguised a boring novel, one you can't bring yourself to finish. Much to my relief, kismet returned to being just a popular name for Indian restaurants.

The sound of a bicycle bell has me pressing pause on the past.

Nyx: I was thinking. If you love autumn, maybe we could honeymoon in New England? X

It was through a few silly texts – like these that I'm having with Nyx – that everything changed with the handsome hardback that was difficult to read.

The Ex: Your celebrity crush just got married x

Me: Noooooo x

The Ex: You could fancy me instead if you like x

Yes, back when mobile phones still whiffed of novelty (and the term 'cyberbullying' hadn't been invented), I thought his texts were charming. Admittedly, he could still be duller than an accountant talking about accounting. There were moments, though, when he was belly-laugh funny, and I eventually liked him enough. Not enough to fall in love with him, I had safely convinced myself.

Sadly, he had other plans.

Whenever anyone gave him a challenge, he accepted it. He loved them, and I loved cheering him on as he went at them like a ten-year-old with a piñata the day after Lent.

It's incredible that I didn't realise I was one too. A challenge.

Before long, all he had to text was I miss u shithead x, and I was abandoning a rare evening out with the few friends I had dared to make in my new county. When will u be back x had me telling those at a much-loved colleague's retirement party that I didn't feel well.

It took him a while, but he got there. Then, almost overnight, the spell he liked to claim I held over him was broken.

The same couldn't be said for me.

Tring-tring.

Nyx: Are you still awake? x

I stare at his message.

No, it's not *his* message.

But all the same…

I adjust the sound profile on my phone to 'calls only' before leaving it on the dressing table. I go back and turn off the LED notification and vibrate mode.

I climb into bed and settle back with a dog on my lap and a classic, heartwarming book. I've read it several times; the last time was December 2021 (according to its bookmark, a Tesco receipt).

The story's ending is predictable: there's an 'I do'. That being said, with public and publishing pressure, the author would have had little choice. Still, I'll bet she often wondered how readers would have reacted if the headstrong heroine had walked off into the sunset holding no one's hand.

For what it's worth, this reader believes she would've done fine on her own.

Chapter Sixteen

Nyx pushes up his protective eyewear and returns my smile with one that should've been immortalised on a chapel's ceiling in Vatican City.

I hover in the doorway as he makes his way across. The minefield of wires and piping covering what's left of the floor is too daunting for me to tackle. Two men seem to have a handle on what they're doing with them, though. Two more are working on something in the timber-framed walls.

'I was starting to worry that I wouldn't see you today,' Nyx says.

I mentally chastise myself for feeling a flutter.

No, it's not the first Monday of the job. After a night of self-doubt following our textathon, I woke up with a clear head, and in the early morning sunshine with a coffee, I re-read our exchanges. Instantly, I appreciated them for what they were – mere light relief, nothing more – and brushed off any depth I may have tried to find in them. After all, the hour had been late. Let's not forget my flare-up of 'The Ex' memories, too.

Since I'd promised to be at the house that first Monday, I reminded Second Thoughts that this was business. I won't tell you how long I deliberated over what time to go – put it this way: in the song, there weren't many bottles of beer left on the wall – but I did. I was glad that I did as well.

Monday catch-ups now have Wednesday and Friday ones, too. My presence on site in a hard hat and gloves is also in double figures. Admittedly, I always need to share a bath with Epsom salts afterwards, but hey-ho.

As well as detailed updates throughout the week, Nyx and I regularly swap texts. They're always about the project. Okay, the first ones are, but going off topic is fine; it's friendly banter between contractor and contractee.

I wave Nyx out of sight of the other men before retrieving two large Costa lattes. 'I didn't know who else would be here today.'

'They'll be nipping out for bacon butties soon,' he assures me.

Stepping outside with him to get some fresh air, I try not to look at the front of the house. It looks very different from how it did.

In fact, worryingly different.

The draping evergreen climbers have had more than a trim. The death trap of a front porch is also gone, with a replacement going up later this week. But without the vegetation and the joinery, the extent of the neglect takes centre stage.

Patchy rendering cannot hide the ugly repairs

made to the front using bricks and breeze blocks. They were used when 'It's all right, just cover it up. Nobody will be any the wiser' was cheaper than the cost of stone. However, they guarantee that all of this will be hidden by cladding, whereas the back and one side of the house will keep the beautiful stonework. On a positive note, this is cleaning up nicely.

We're into summer now and three weeks into The Reinvention. That was the name I gave it on the fifth day, when I arrived to find little more than four outer walls and floor beams above my head. I also had an open view of the sky through holes in my roof. Hardly anything was left of the house I had paid a premium for. It was minimalism gone mad.

Nyx and Colin, however, didn't seem remotely fazed as they walked me through what was happening. When I left, I didn't feel as bad about being influenced by someone's good looks. And in just weeks, I have seen it go from a wreck to a shell to a mess of cables.

'The plumbing and the electrics will be in place hopefully by the start of next week,' Nyx tells me. 'The subflooring can then be finished. After that, the plasterers can come in and start boarding up.'

'That's terrific news.'

'So we need to look at kitchens, in case there's a lead time. The place we like to use is open late tonight. Are you available?'

'What time?' I ask.

'If I pick you up at six?'

'I'll be ready.'

'And if you have no other plans after that,' Nyx says, 'I know a nice little Italian.'

***

I must go to the farmers' market tomorrow, as my cupboards are almost bare. Therefore, I would have only cooked a packet of mac and cheese for tea tonight. Hey, if I need to add hot water, a knob of butter, *and* milk to something before putting it in the microwave – and stir it not once but *twice* during the heating process – *that* is cooking.

The major downside to eating out is having to change out of my pyjama bottoms. Even worse than that, it means putting a bra back on.

I flick through my staple clothing diet of wide-leg trousers and novelty T-shirts, which I've built quite a collection of since my twenties. Amazingly, they still fit. I know a middle-aged waistline will happen eventually, as will a remake of *Back to the Future*. But I'll worry about both another day.

I rummage in the side of my wardrobe where some dresses and stylish pieces are hidden. I didn't go out and buy these myself – the woman responsible for packing my touring clothes did. Katrina may have just saved the date.

Day! Saved the *day*. It's a day, not a...

I opt for a belted, knee-length navy dress that has a full skirt and cap sleeves. It's a neat balance of conservative and pretty, I hope. Nude-coloured leather ballet flats keep it on this side of daywear.

Doubting the mirror's honesty and my earlier

confidence, I ask Bacon, 'It doesn't look like I'm trying too hard. Does it?'

The dog lying on the end of my bed lowers her chin onto her paws and wags her tail.

'I'm not trying to woo him. Hell, no. Nor am I trying to look like I want him to woo me, either. Wooing is out of the question. His generation probably doesn't even call it wooing now. *His* generation, not mine. This –' I indicate my torso with a pointy finger '– is a woo-free zone.'

She wags her tail.

'I know you're very much in love with him, but don't go getting ideas. Yes, he's cute, and I think I can safely say I have a cute ally now, but that is as far as it will ever go. Got that?'

She wags her tail.

'Right, this outfit. Bark once if it's a safe option.'

She wags her tail.

'Bark once if I need a reality check.'

She wags her tail.

'Bark once if I'm never going to win the Booker Prize.'

Woof!

I snatch up my bag. 'I must remember to cry when you're gone.'

***

'You look lovely, Jo.'

'Thank you.'

Nyx's compliment makes me part bounce/part skip down my garden path.

168

'I know we're only going to look at kitchen stuff,' I say, 'but I needed an excuse to air my legs.'

He opens the passenger door for me. 'Then I'll find more excuses.'

My contractor is on first-name terms with the people in the showroom. Do you think it's because he's a regular or because they're all women? There's no need to phone a friend for the answer.

After we've done a circuit of solid wood and gloss finishes – and I have said 'That one's nice' three times and 'That one's very nice' twice – I must tell him the truth.

'Kitchens aren't my thing.' I'm whispering because I don't want the assistants to hear: they love everything they sell. 'I don't even own a saucepan.'

Nyx raises his eyebrows. 'You're kidding.'

'Don't judge me.'

'At least we know what to put on our wedding gift list.'

'Along with a guide on how to use them,' I add.

'What happens when we're married?'

'I was counting on you being more than just a pretty face.'

Moving his lips close to my ear, he murmurs, 'My talent lies elsewhere.'

I beg the mint ingredient in my brilliant powder foundation to hide my blushes. After all, Nyx's talent could be that he knows every keyboard shortcut.

Our double act is gooseberried by the lovely Sherrie, who pretends she wants to know how we're getting on. We follow her to a computer where the dimensions for my kitchen have already been input.

As she establishes with Nyx the best places for the major appliances and the sink to go, I'm happy to sit back and watch. However, when those things have been sorted, it's not range cookers they're now looking at.

Nyx turns the pages of the catalogue in front of me. 'Let's start with a style you said was very nice.'

But once it's on the big screen, I know my expression isn't fooling anyone. I'm sorry, I don't care about wood versus laminate veneer. I don't enjoy shopping at the best of times. Therefore, deciding whether someone will get more pleasure from a high gloss rather than a matt finish...

'Shall I?' Nyx offers.

My inward sigh has 'relief' written all over it. 'Please do.'

He flips through the catalogue to another one I liked: a shaker design. It turns out he has fitted this one a few times. He then shows me the seven colour options. Anything over three would usually see me pinching my bottom lip for a fortnight before skipping the country. I am therefore surprised when, without hesitation, I point to the darkest shade: a lead colour. A grey with attitude.

Nyx grins. 'That's my favourite too.'

And the element of doubt I always like to carry around with me ain't pissing on my Pradas today.

I watch the glass door cabinets go up, the open countertop cupboards go into place, and the veined granite top slide onto the impressive island.

'Open plate racks along the top.' Nyx moves the mouse pointer and drops shapes onto the screen. 'Basket drawers underneath. Different handles on the top cabinets will give it some character. Which ones do you like?'

'Am I crazy for liking these two styles in brushed brass?'

'Not at all.'

I watch the warm metal contrast with the cool grey. 'They look amazing.'

Nyx's knee touches mine. He thinks they do as well.

'May I have one of those fancy taps with the spray thingy on it, please?' I request.

'No problem.'

'Should it be in—?'

But a brushed brass pull-out spray tap has already appeared between the two farmhouse sinks.

I sit forward. 'Do you think I could also have one of these spice storage drawer cabinets at the end?'

'Of course,' Nyx says.

'And what about one of these snazzy roll-out pantries for the tall cabinet?'

'Jo, you can have anything you want.'

Would that stand up in court, do you think?

When we're walking back to his car, I remark, 'I hope Sherrie splits her commission with you.'

Nyx's smile broadens. 'Aw, she'll look after us. Grandad and I shop here a lot, so she always gives us a good deal.'

'Yep, I'm sure that's why!'

He returns my sidelong glance. 'What are you inferring, Miss Washington?'

'Why, nothing at all, Mr Hart.'

Chapter Seventeen

When Nyx mentioned 'a nice little Italian', I visualised a cosy establishment with red-and-white gingham tablecloths. However, when I see the sign saying 'GRASMERE – Please drive carefully', that image is gone.

For anyone unfamiliar with the Lake District, this place is special. William Wordsworth, the English Romantic poet, seemed to agree. Grasmere is a lake *and* a small village. To some tourists, the latter is little more than a few narrow streets surrounded by big-brother hills, neatly scattered with hotels, cafés and art galleries. This is the place to be spotted in your best hiking gear, which you'll need to wear to work off their famous gingerbread.

Nyx turns off the main road onto a gravel driveway leading to a car park.

A five-star hotel's car park.

One with a bloody Michelin-starred restaurant.

As soon as we exit the car, I tell him, 'Before we go any further, I'd like this to be my treat.'

'No.'

'Nyx, let's not be one of those couples who fight in public.'

'Even better. Let's not be one of those couples who fight in public *over who is paying*. I invited you out, remember?'

'Yes, you, erm… you did.' I look around again at the establishment. 'But the way you described this place, I thought it would involve Parmesan from a plastic container.' There is rustling overhead in the leaves. 'I bet they even have red squirrels.'

'If they do,' Nyx says, 'this place doesn't own them.'

'I think those things are pretty fussy about where they'll strut their stuff.'

'They're squirrels, Jo. Not supermodels.'

I cross my arms. 'Unless you let me pay at least half, I'm not going in.'

Nyx shrugs. 'Fine.'

'Good. I'm glad that's settled.'

Seconds later, I realise I am the only one making their way towards the hotel entrance. When I turn round, Nyx holds up his key fob and unlocks his car. He opens the passenger door.

'Are you serious?' I ask.

'Very.'

'But… I will owe you at least a meal out, anyway.'

Nyx looks perplexed. 'What for?'

'The great kitchen deal you're getting me because of your *loyalty*.'

'One, I don't have the deal yet. Two, there *is* more to me than just these dimples. And three, you won't owe me anything once I get it.'

That's me told.

He leans against his car. 'Now, do you want me to take you home? Or are you going to let me pay for dinner?'

***

When we're shown to our table, Nyx steals the maître d's job by getting my chair for me.

'We came here for Grandad's birthday last year,' he informs me.

'It's very nice.'

Too nice.

I open the menu and do an excellent job of pretending not to—

'Stop looking at the prices,' Nyx says, scanning the separate list of today's specials.

The experienced waiter knows when to approach our table. 'You look like you're ready to order.'

Nyx goes first. 'I'll start with the grilled peach and burrata salad.'

'Excellent choice, sir. And for madam?'

'May I have the... garlic bread, please?'

'And for your main course, madam?'

Two pairs of eyes are on me.

'From the starter's menu, can I possibly have the ravioli—?'

'Would you mind if we have a couple more minutes?' Nyx quietly asks him.

As soon as the waiter has gone, we almost bump our foreheads when we lean in together.

'You're ordering the cheapest things on the menu,' Nyx hisses.

'No, I'm not,' I hiss back. 'They're not the most expensive items on it. That's all.'

'You said on the way over that you were hungry.'

I nod towards the table next to ours. 'Have you seen the size of the portions?'

'You ate a bloody twelve-inch pizza the other day.'

'Hey, I'd done a full-body workout at the house – *and* I took two slices home.'

'Do you want to run around the car park a few times?' Nyx suggests. 'Work up a bit more of an appetite?'

'Right then, Bosszilla, let's get something straight: *if* there's a next time, *I* am paying.'

Nyx nods. 'Definitely…'

'I'm glad that's settled.'

'… *never* happening in this marriage,' he scoffs.

I casually shrug. 'Then we never eat out again after this.'

'That's a shame.'

'It certainly is.'

When the waiter reappears, we spring apart.

'I'll have the soup, please,' I say.

'You won't,' Nyx quietly tells his menu.

'The… bruschetta?'

'Nope.'

'The stuffed peppers, please.'

Nyx sticks with the grilled peaches and orders a medium-rare fillet steak with green peppercorn sauce for his main course. Then he asks me, 'How would you like *your* fillet cooked?'

'I might go for the cannelloni.'

'I think not,' he murmurs.

I grin at the waiter. 'Medium rare as well, please.'

Once another staff member has served me my elderflower cordial and Nyx his Coke, I touch a petal on the rose in the silver vase.

'Real,' I mouth.

'I should have saved the proposal for tonight.'

'Yeah, you peaked too soon.'

Nyx rests his forearms on the table. 'Tell me, Josephine Washington. Why are you single?'

'Why are *you* single?' Oh shit. 'Sorry, *are* you single? How rude of me to presume.'

Despite looking somewhat puzzled, he smiles. 'Of course I am.'

Of course he is. Silly me. Nyx wouldn't resort to asking the wage payer out to dinner otherwise, not if he had choices. Sometimes I forget my status as the woman who fills in the gap between past and future relationships.

Sometimes.

Not often.

'When was the last time you had a girlfriend, Nyx?'

As soon as I say 'girl', I realise I don't in fact *know* whether he's an XX or an XY lover. Why would I? I've hired him to fix up my house. That's all. I might get a bill at the end for the playful marriage banter.

'I've only ever had one you'd call a proper

girlfriend, and it was…' Nyx thinks back. 'Blimey, it was two years ago.'

Phew, what a relief! I mean, relief that I didn't… faux pas.

'How long were you together?'

'About four months,' he answers.

'And why did you break up?'

'Hmm, how do I put this…?'

'Was it because she chewed with her mouth open?' I enquire.

'No.'

'Because she had curly back hair?'

Nyx tries to keep a straight face.

'She took her teeth out to whistle?'

He can't suppress his chuckle any longer. 'No. Claire… Claire was great. She was kind, she was good company and… *very* pretty. She was a director of… something – a successful one, too – at a big tech company. I admired her for that. I did.'

'Wow. The woman sounds like a complete monster.' I offer Nyx the expression I usually reserve for those who say sarcasm is the lowest form of wit. 'Did you break up because she spent too much time saving sea turtles and doing charity runs?'

'The thing was, she couldn't turn her success off. And I don't want to sound whiny, but I didn't feel… necessary.' A line appears between Nyx's eyebrows. 'If that makes sense? Because this woman could do it all herself. She even did the chasing. She said men nowadays are too scared. Or they're too lazy.'

I press my lips together.

He continues. 'That's fine, but when women are on top of everything, what can we offer in a relationship?'

There's a question mark. Damn it.

'When you word it like that, Nyx, I suppose… not much. I understand why men want to feel needed somehow. Women's magazines often ask whether men are necessary nowadays, which begs the question: How can men *enjoy* being men?'

'Exactly.' Nyx leans forward. 'I needed to know I could be more than just a… just a…'

I help him out. '… naked friend?'

'Yes. Thank you. Contrary to popular belief, not all men are threatened by successful women.'

I finish buttering my piece of bread. 'Just the successful ones who earn more than them?'

When I look up, at least Nyx has the grace to acknowledge with a sheepish smile that he's been rumbled. Fortunately, he's at an age where tiny imperfections can still be delicately highlighted; he doesn't need to react like it's a personal attack on his whole character. Not yet, anyway.

And not like those from my generation.

While we were sitting around a dining table with four of his work colleagues and their partners, The Ex didn't appreciate my discreet mime alerting him to the mayonnaise around his mouth. When we broke up a year later, he played the 'You made me look stupid in front of my best friends' card. He shuffled it in with the many others he'd made up. In the end, few believed he was to blame.

But this isn't about *him*.

'How old was your director of something?' I ask.

'Thirty-seven.'

I raise my eyebrows and dip my chin in congratulations.

'Age doesn't matter, though,' Nyx says with a shrug. 'Age is nothing but numbers.'

'Isn't money nothing but numbers?'

'No, money is nothing but power.' The humour in his eyes has dissolved slightly.

'Did you feel she had power over you?'

'I didn't like people thinking I was dating my meal ticket, because I wasn't,' Nyx states.

'She must've known that. I imagine your family knew too.'

'Yeah, but some people didn't.'

Can I blame Nyx for focusing on the naysayers? He's dining with the woman whose method of self-harm was filtering the reviews and only reading the ones below three stars. I stopped punishing myself when my books had been translated into over thirty languages.

Nyx gazes at me. 'You think I'm too proud?'

'Is that a question or a concern?'

'It wasn't about pride. It was about self-respect.'

'I see.' Let's pretend I don't, though. 'And you broke up with her because she could afford to buy *you* nice things. Is... that right? Or was it because she could afford to buy nice things for herself?'

'She earned almost double what I took home,' is Nyx's answer. 'I couldn't compete with that.'

Smiling, I tilt my head to one side. 'Relationships should never be about competition.'

'I know,' he mumbles.

I divulge some of Izzie's wordy wisdom. 'My mad aunt claims that when you truly love someone, it's easy to show pride the door.'

Nyx wipes the condensation off his glass. 'That actually makes sense because... I didn't love Claire. Not really. And maybe when someone special does come along, how well she's done for herself won't matter.'

I wish he could believe that. I bet Nyx wishes he could, too.

'Just remember,' I say. 'Once you let pride out, don't forget to lock the bloody door afterwards.'

A smile creeps across his face. 'That's sound advice.'

'Talking of pride.' I rest my chin on my hand. 'When I offered to pay at least half the bill tonight...?'

'I appreciated the offer,' Nyx is quick to say, 'but I asked *you* out.'

'And if it had been the other way round?'

He bites his lip while rearranging the salt and pepper pots.

'Nnnnyyyyx?'

'I would *hate* it if you paid.'

'Why?'

'Blame my mum,' he says.

'From what you've told me about her, she sounds like a very independent lady.'

'Oh, she is. But she thinks all men are only after

181

one thing, so she only goes out for a meal with them if they're paying.'

I grin and nod slowly. 'Your mum is a smart woman.'

Nyx's eyes widen. 'Do you agree with her?'

'Well, those men aren't paying to get her thoughts on last night's dreams.'

I thought my response had a nice whiff of comedy about it. But judging by the look of mortification on Nyx's face…

'Is that what you think… my intentions are tonight?' he asks.

Bugger me blind!

'Of course not,' I quickly assure him. 'Please, Nyx, don't worry. I never, not for one moment, thought this was anything other than friendly business.'

'You didn't?'

'No.' I playfully slap his arm. 'Don't be daft.'

I take my glasses off and slowly wipe the lenses with my napkin. Slow enough, I hope, for any hint of misunderstanding to exit the building before I put them back on.

'Truth be told,' Nyx confesses, 'I haven't taken many women to fancy restaurants.'

'Breaking news: women don't watch their weight by abstaining. Gyms were invented for those who wear a size ten and love a sweet trolley.'

'No, what I mean is… most of my, erm… my dates haven't… they haven't cared about, you know, interesting conversations over dinner.' Nyx fiddles with his collar. 'Like what… we're having.'

'Then you should start asking out the interesting girls.'

'That's what I'm—'

Our waiter is back. 'The stuffed peppers for madam…'

Never have I grumbled about when my meal arrives until now, when it interrupts our relaxed tête-à-tête. I'm surprised by how much I enjoy our chats. I never thought I could get such pleasure from something so easy.

Which, sadly, is what Nyx continues to be on the eye.

Oh, I wish I could get past how he looks. But when he fixes me with that intense stare, it's as if nobody else in the bedroom matters.

Wait, where did I…?

I meant in the room. Nobody else in the *room* matters.

Just as our starters arrive, we are joined by a burly chap who looks moderately comfortable in a formal shirt. If someone asked him to wear a tie, though, there's a good chance they'd be buried in concrete footings.

He gives Nyx a friendly chokehold from behind. 'Does your mother know you're out this late?'

'Yes, Uncle Frank,' Nyx forces out. 'But I have to ring her on the hour, so she knows child traffickers haven't taken me.'

His uncle playfully throttles him once more for luck. 'How the devil are you, boy? Keeping busy?'

'Yeah, work keeps me out of trouble.' Nyx smiles at the woman who has joined his uncle. 'Hey, Auntie Jane.'

Pleasantries that members of the same family apparently like to exchange pass between them. Meanwhile, I wonder if I should start eating. Or should I check the quality of the toilet paper in—?

'Uncle Frank, Auntie Jane, this is Jo.'

Although I don't understand why Nyx isn't trying to make me disappear, I always remember my manners. 'Nice to meet you.'

Uncle Frank is making his way over. Even when he plants a kiss on my cheek, I keep smiling.

'Any excuse,' he says, squeezing my shoulders. At least I'm spared the police hold. 'Is our Nyx being a gentleman?'

'A perfect one,' I assure him.

'If he misbehaves, you call Uncle Frank.' In a loud whisper, he adds, 'Would you like my number, just in case?'

Auntie Jane rolls her eyes. 'No, she wouldn't. Come on, you. Leave them alone.' She touches Nyx's arm. 'Tell your mum I'll call her this week.'

As they make their way to their table, Nyx grins after them. When I glance across, Uncle Frank drops his thumbs up.

I offer my contractor some advice. 'You'd better fill your mum in on the situation before Auntie Jane does.'

'Mum already knows all about you.' Nyx loads up his fork. 'You must try my starter.'

He takes advantage of my open mouth.

'Oh, wow!' I savour the delicious sample. 'That is worthy of a wash *and* wax.'

'Don't you wish now you hadn't been such a cheapskate?'

'How do you know mine isn't as good?'

Nyx points to his expression. Either he is enjoying his mouthful of cheese and peach, or someone is enjoying him under the table. The last time I saw someone enjoying food that much was in an advert back in the day for flaky chocolate. Yes, *back in the day*. Nowadays, everyone is terrified that such ads might upset some people.

Oh, but all the ads reminding older adults to put money aside for their funerals *aren't* upsetting?

Nyx takes the forkful of food I offer him from my plate, committing the deadly sin of looking me in the eye during the exchange. No, I won't cover him in fire and brimstone for it.

But I can think of something else I'd like to cover him in.

'Not bad,' Nyx says. 'Not as good as mine, though. Next time we come, you'll know what to order.'

'You mean when I've rung ahead and paid in advance?'

He threatens me with his fork. 'If you ever do that, I'll be fighting you for custody of the kids.'

Forget the kids, chirps up my lacy Brazilian knickers. *Let's have a go at making one!*

'Is this how our marriage is going to be?' I demand to know.

'If you're lucky.'

'Well then, since we'll never eat here again, any gentleman would split such a tasty dish.'

'Yeah, right,' Nyx says with a snigger. 'Tell it to Uncle Frank.'

Once we finish our starters, we are forced to sit back so the waiter can take our plates. I didn't realise until then how close we were sitting. Our elbows could've shared trade secrets.

'Since the pretty director, Nyx, hasn't there been anyone?'

'No. Well, nothing you'd call a serious relationship. That hasn't been by choice, though.'

'*You* struggle to find a girlfriend?' Smiling, I shake my head in disbelief. 'Sorry, no. I'm not buying that.'

He shrugs. 'It's true.'

'Do you think it's because you immediately come across as a good guy?'

Nyx raises his eyes heavenward. 'Mum says that too. But women don't want the good ones, do they?'

'Oh, they do. As long as that's not what a man puts in his own advert.'

'But bad boys always seem to do better,' he remarks.

'Hmm, I think that's debatable. Maybe some do, yes. But only when women know what they're letting themselves in for.'

'Then why have I been unlucky in love?'

'I don't think it's because you're too good to be true,' I assure him. 'I think it could be that devilish curse of being too good-*looking*.'

'Really, Jo, I'm nothing special.' And if this isn't the first time Nyx has said that, then he's rehearsed that line with the top five per cent of his class at RADA.

'Nyx, Nyx, Nyx.' I cover his hand with mine. 'You can try to deny climate change. You can wear blinkers to see who's parading their nuclear weapons. You can't, however, pretend you're not extremely good-looking, because it's right *there*.'

'Says somebody as beautiful as you who's single,' he challenges.

'I'm not beautiful,' I say without a hint of sadness. 'I'm charming and flirty, which comes across as attractive.'

Nyx's wide grin highlights his dimples. 'Those weren't the first things about you that stood out. But yes, you are charming and flirty. *And* you're beautiful.'

I smile and place my hand over my heart, which is concealed behind my dress's modest neckline this evening. Unlike when we first met. 'Sorry, what were the first things about me—?'

'Yeah, back to my question, which you are cleverly avoiding.' Nyx sits forward, his elbows on the table, his fingers loosely interlaced. 'Why are you single, Miss Washington?'

'Women in their forties will get chatted up by two age groups,' I explain. 'There are those chaps in their fifties who can no longer pull the hot thirty-somethings. Then there are those in their twenties: they think forty-something women are more skilled, more confident, and *much* more grateful.'

'Aaaaand you still didn't answer the question.'

'I did.'

'You told me who chats up women your age,' Nyx says. 'You never said why you don't accept any offers.'

I narrow my eyes. 'Fine. I just… never had much luck with relationships.' My admission doesn't cause me any embarrassment.

'You mean you've attracted the wrong types?'

'Not really. I think it was more a case of… I wasn't anyone's right type.' I offer a light-hearted shrug. 'Honestly, Nyx, my tale wouldn't last a Eurotunnel train ride.'

'But you don't seem that bothered about it.'

'Oh, I accepted my lot in life years ago.'

Nyx shakes his head. 'You can't say that.'

'Yes, I can.'

'You're too young to be talking in the past tense.'

I give him a wry smile. 'But I'm too old to keep talking about *when*.'

'Do you think maybe you're just overly cautious?'

'I don't know.' My answer is honest. 'If I used to be a social butterfly, that might've been the case. But I wasn't.'

'Stop past tensing!'

'Sorry. *These* days, I don't put myself in situations where I can meet anyone. I rarely get home after eight o'clock. In truth, I find greater enjoyment in my own thoughts than I ever could in a room full of people afraid of missing a YouTube moment. Therefore, happily RSVPing a "no thanks" could explain why I'm slightly cautious if someone—'

'When someone,' Nyx corrects.

'If.'

'*When.*'

'Okay.' I resist pulling a face. '*When* someone comes along. Who knows?'

Nyx looks at me with a thoughtful expression. 'I can't believe you don't have your pick of men.'

'And I can't believe Barry Manilow has written over 400 songs, but he *didn't* write "I Write the Songs".'

'I'm serious.'

I accept defeat. 'Well, maybe it's not that I'm cautious any more. Maybe I'm merely beyond the realms of out of practice.'

'How many times has your heart been broken?'

Our main courses arrive, giving me a minute to think. Oddly enough, I don't feel like giving Nyx the ambiguous response that I rehearse with Cal prior to giving interviews.

Before I enjoy the greatest edible wonder of the world – triple-cooked chips – I give an answer. 'Once.'

'And that's why you prefer to stay single?'

'Oh, that was *more* than enough for me.'

'I imagine everyone goes through it at least once,' Nyx says.

'But the majority don't take it so personally.'

'Whereas the minority…?'

'Hey, even when another motorist doesn't

acknowledge me when I let them through, it hits a nerve.'

I dribble some green peppercorn sauce over my steak.

'Anybody stupid enough to hurt you, Jo, is a fool.'

I can't help smiling. 'If someone stops loving you, you can't do anything about it.'

'At least you're not bitter,' Nyx remarks.

'After all this time? What would be the point?'

'Then maybe you haven't entirely given up on finding love again.'

Keep your mouth shut, Jo. Don't say anything. Don't—

'Love is a weakness, Nyx. A let-down. Maintained by poets and the church until moving pictures came along and kept it afloat. Now it's barely kept alive by chick lit, white dresses, and power ballads.'

The only sound at our table is crunching as I savour a crispy chip.

'I wrote that for my internal monologue,' I confess. 'But I said it out loud, didn't I?'

With raised eyebrows, Nyx nods. 'Yyyyeah.'

Chapter Eighteen

It's a damp, warm lunchtime in July, and my aunt's train is on time. She sees my homemade sign on the platform at Windermere station before figuring out who is holding it up. Izzie may spearhead incontinence pads, but she still must stop and hold between her legs as a comet-halting laugh beats the humidity.

'Where did you get that sodding photo?'

I raise one eyebrow. 'I have many risqué snaps of you, woman, which I may use if the royalties dry up.'

This one's not that risqué: a slim blonde in a bikini posing on the bonnet of a car. The way Izzie is looking into the camera, though, probably had the developer in 1975 deliberating over an extra copy for Friday night alone time.

'If you didn't have this picture of a hot chick, I would have walked straight past.' Izzie's hands cup my bobbed hair. 'Fucking hell, I'd forgotten how good you look as a brunette.'

'It passes?'

'It's sexier than the blonde.'

I guffaw loudly. 'Liar! You have five seconds to name one movie where the leading lady went from blonde to brunette. Fivefourthreetwoone. Told you.'

'It looks wonderful, Bee, so shut your flapping shithole. Is this your natural colour?'

'If only. No, every six weeks, my parting resembles the bloody lane dividers on the M1. Yet underneath, there's hardly a grey hair in sight.'

Izzie kisses me on both cheeks. I allow her to greet me this way because she has lived in countries where English isn't the official language; otherwise, it should be outlawed. And don't get me started on those who do it when they first meet. Although I do howl when I see someone on television pull away after one kiss, leaving the other person pucker-hanging. It's comedy gold.

'I was a hottie back then,' Izzie states when we're in the car, the sign propped up on her knees. Her memories only ever produce smiles.

'You still are. Few sixty-seven-year-olds get chatted up by—'

'How old?' she asks.

'Fifty-seven.'

'How old?'

'Forty-seven.'

'*How* old?'

'Fifty-seven. You should've quit while you were ahead, Nelly Narcissist.'

'Fuck off. It helps when you have fabulous tits like mine.' Izzie runs her hands over them. 'Did you notice how good they looked when I walked up?'

'Notice them? You wheeled that bloke's suitcase with them.'

'I don't think I'll ever get bored with them. They're still the best investment I've ever made.'

I keep glancing over, and every time...

'Izzie, you're not a fifteen-year-old boy. Leave them alone.'

'Sorry. Ooh, I can't wait to see this cottage.'

'Don't you want to see where you're staying first and settle in?'

'What for? To change my support stockings and soak my false teeth? I'm not that fucking old, you cheeky twat.'

'I see the medication is helping to curb the profanities,' I mumble.

'And where's my bastard coffee?'

'Costa needed extra time to monogram it. Here's the money: two large lattes and whatever you want. I can't stop outside, but if I slow down, you can roll out.'

'Up yours!' my aunt exclaims. 'At my age, I'll break more than just the world record for the most rotations. And why am I getting three?'

'One for the contractor.'

'I hope he's doing a good job to warrant good coffee.'

'He is.'

I sense Izzie admiring my jawline. I mean, what else would she be examining so closely?

'New hair,' she remarks, 'new sideline, new... *Please* tell me your gorgeous car is in for repairs, and this is just a… Well, maybe not a "courtesy" car. What model is it? Matchbox?'

'The Jaguar and I are taking some time apart.'

'And this is the best rebound you could come up with?' Izzie asks with a chuckle.

'Do you mind? It has feelings.'

'Was that one of the selling points the salesman used?'

'It's very economical.'

'You fly sodding first class,' she points out.

'No, I fly *business* class, and only because…' There's no point in repeating it. 'Why do I need a car like that, anyway?'

'Because you don't have breasts like mine.'

'If you like it that much, you can use it. Cal won't go anywhere in it.'

'It isn't my style,' Izzie says. 'It is yours, though. Hot single author zipping about town.'

'Happy single woman who works in publishing, remember?'

'Are we *still* playing that game?'

'It's not a game, Izzie.'

'No, it's not. Shall I tell you again what it is?'

'Go ahead. But it'll be the last thing you ever do.'

***

And they say *I* am a flirt.

'Izzie, this is Nyx.'

Izzie floats towards him, shedding her recently applied hair clip. In slow motion, she shakes back her white bob. All she needs now is a wind machine.

And a tissue.

'Well, hello.' She grasps Nyx's hand. 'I'm Izabella. Izabella Washington. But you can call me Izzie. *How* do you do?'

'Nice to meet you.' Nyx flashes a charming smile. 'Jo has told me a lot about you.'

'Did my niece mention I can still get both feet behind my head?'

His raised eyebrows almost touch his hairline. 'No, she didn't, but... y-yeah, it's... it's good to know.'

Izzie doesn't laugh like that usually.

'You can let go of his hand now, Izzie.'

'I know.'

I take the lid off Nyx's coffee cup before passing it across, what with his horny handicap.

'Remember why you're here,' I tell her.

'Will *you* give me the tour, Nyx?'

Because Izzie is still holding one of his hands, Nyx uses his cup to point out the sliding doors and the stunning sash windows. It's so bright in the house now that no actress over fifty would allow herself to be interviewed at this address.

'You will *love* this kitchen,' I say, hurrying over to the island and caressing the granite countertop. Next, I showcase the built-in coffee machine like a model on *The Price is Right*. 'This was Nyx's idea.'

'Was it now?' It doesn't take much for Izzie to give Nyx her undivided attention, but any excuse is better than gawking. 'My, you certainly know how to get inside my niece's knickers.'

There go Nyx's eyebrows again.

I shake my head. 'I tried to warn you.'

'Just be aware,' Izzie informs him. 'If she makes you dinner, the only thing you'll be eager to tell everyone is not to use the bathroom after you.'

My smile is of the smug variety. 'Nyx already knows that.'

I follow the pair of them upstairs. Izzie's grip on Nyx's hand isn't loosening, so I'm relieved her other hand is holding her drink; otherwise, she'd be feeling more than just the heat.

My aunt feels oppressed by anything that isn't airy, but even she falls in love with the bathroom. The exposed stone and the varying shades of the dark slate tile highlight the white free-standing bath. It's a big bath; it's big enough for two. We tested it in the showroom. Nyx's idea, before you say anything.

Izzie spots the walk-in shower and nudges him in front of her. There's no escape for him.

'Plenty of room for lovers, Nyx,' she observes. 'Two showerheads. Was that your idea, too?'

'It was, actually.'

'I like it.' Izzie winks at him. 'But I think I like you more.'

Turning on my heel, I say to her, 'When you're done with him, meet me across the hall.'

In the main bedroom, Izzie's gaze takes in all the space. 'Now, this is my style.' She drags my contractor across to the French doors. 'Oh, Nyx.'

He smiles at me while she admires the outside from this vantage point. The height difference means her head is almost on his shoulder.

'You approve?' I ask her.

Izzie grins. 'Absolutely.'

Her eyes, however, are no longer taking in the view.

'The *house*. Izzie.'

'Oh. Oh, yes.' She waves a dismissive hand. 'The house is lovely too.'

'I knew you'd like it.'

Izzie blinks up at Nyx. 'I could teach you everything you need to know about the female orgasm – and I mean *everything*.'

I head for the stairs with a resigned sigh. 'Unbelievable. Nyx, thank you for the enforced tour, and please accept my profound apologies. Blood, we're leaving. Now!'

They walk outside to find me holding the passenger door open.

'I think you're in trouble, Izzie,' Nyx says.

She gives him a knowing look as she gets into the car. 'It's *well* over two years, Nyx.'

Izzie had better be talking about her last eye test.

'I've invited him out for dinner with us tomorrow evening,' she announces.

'If that's all right with you, Jo?' Nyx asks.

'Of course it is,' says someone who hasn't won a British Fantasy Award.

Izzie waves to Nyx out the car window until he's out of sight, then whips her head round. '*Why* have you never mentioned him?'

'I have. I told you I had a contractor doing the

work.'

'You never told me you had a contractor who looked like *that*.'

'Then it's not just me who thinks, on a scale of what's worth doing, I'd give him one?'

'He is mag-*nificent*,' Izzie growls. 'How *dare* you keep that quiet?'

I lean away from her. 'All right, Doctor Dreadful, bring it down a notch. Do you want an apology from me or a restraining order?'

'You seem on friendly terms with him: you buy him good coffee and exchange llllingering looks.'

'Nyx likes nice coffee, and no looks we exchanged llllingered,' I clarify. 'However, yes, we're on friendly terms.'

'How friendly are we talking?'

'We both enjoy walking.' That was something I discovered. 'So we walk together. Sometimes.'

'Did he enjoy walking before he heard how much *you* enjoy it?'

'Yes.'

At least, he said he did. Nyx did say he did. Didn't he? I mean, why would he...?

'And you walk together only *sometimes*?' Izzie checks.

'That's right.'

'I see. Anything else?'

I pretend to give it some thought. 'Nnnnno, not really.'

'There have been no Friday nights at the cinema, then?'

The minute my bloody back was turned...

'Once,' I say. 'We'd arranged a walk, but it rained.'

'It's been more than once.'

'Maybe twice. It rains here a lot. The annual rainfall—'

'It's been more than twice, Bee.'

'It's someone to go with, all right? And I hate to waste all that popcorn.'

'There hasn't been any dining out together?' is Izzie's next question.

'Not... very often.'

'How often is "not... very"?'

'A couple of times,' I lie.

'A *couple*, eh? That's an interesting word choice.'

'Stop reading, Izzie.'

'There's no need to read, not when you're each supplying the audio versions for me.' A hefty slurp of her cold coffee is followed by a satisfied *ahhh*. 'Have you seen him naked?'

I count on my fingers. 'Walking, cinema, eating: explain to me which of those situations calls for Nyx to lose all his clothes. Go on. I will buy you lunch tomorrow in Paris if you can come up with just one.'

'I'm only asking. "Friends" can mean a lot of things these days. There's all this Netflix and chill going about.'

'I don't have Netflix.'

'Maybe you should get it,' Izzie suggests.

'I don't want it.'

'From what I was seeing—'

'We are just friends,' I state.

'You rarely bother with friends, though.'

'Hence my non-scientific experiment, as I'm still certain they're unnecessary. But I'll warn you now: *if* I am wrong, whatever you say will make your nose bleed. However, *when* I am proven right, I'll be smug until a politician gives a straight answer.'

'And you decide to test the theory with that specimen?' Izzie's question is laced with scepticism.

'Why not?'

'Have you got an hour?'

'Did you notice anything about him, Izzie?'

'Oh, yes,' she says in a breathy voice. 'The man smelt delicious. He spritzed before we arrived. I doubt he did it for the hairy-arsed electrician, though, or for your amazing aunt.'

'His age?'

'Mid-twenties?' Izzie guesses.

'No, he's not quite in the middle yet.'

'But you don't look a day over thirty, Bee.'

'But I am many days over thirty,' I remind her.

'Does he know that?'

'Yes.'

'Well, there you go. A gorgeous young man is sweet on you, and—'

'Whoa.' I swing into a parking spot in the hotel car park and turn to face her. 'Why do you say he is sweet on me?'

'Is this where I'm staying?' Izzie's nose is almost pushed against the passenger door window. 'It looks fucking posh.'

'Izzie?'

But she is already swinging her legs out of the car. 'You didn't have to book me into a hotel. I could have bunked in with you. We could've had movie nights in our PJs and binged on snacks.'

'That would've been nice. On par with getting stuck at the top of the London Eye on a windy day – after eating a ten-day-old chicken sandwich and drinking the world's strongest coffee.'

My aunt looks back inside the car at me. 'Whatever your problem is, I'm sure it's hard to spell.'

I open the boot to get her things out and ask her again. 'Why do you say Nyx is sweet on me?'

I've known Izzie too long to believe those wide eyes have any innocence left in them. 'I said I *think* he is sweet on you.'

'No, you didn't.'

'I'm old,' she declares. 'I'm also hungry. So grab my bags, knob gobbler, and we'll see if the hotel's fucking seafood is anything to write home about.'

***

I prong a bit of battered fish.

'Mae West,' Izzie says.

I add a chunky chip to my fork.

'Queen Mary the First.'

I squeeze on some mushy peas.

'George Eliot had one,' she adds to her list. 'And I'm certain Anaïs Nin had more than one, but not at the same time.'

I briefly stop munching my way to heart disease. 'Izzie, did any of these women have *long*-term relationships with younger men?'

'If you want to know that, I'll need Google. I'm only giving you some examples.'

'Which I didn't ask for. Remember, I'm qualified to put my own bins out and remove hair from the plughole. I've also been told I don't need a man, as I already have it all.'

Izzie points a menacing finger at me. 'Those are your mother's words.'

'But it's true – and what have you.'

'When do you listen to her? My sister's always talking shit. She would say that too – the woman married three times because she wasn't wealthy or successful. And don't sit there shrugging your shoulders. You're the product of emotionally unavailable parents, but you turned out okay. You struggle with relationships, as do your sisters, but so what? And you've had some crappy luck,' Izzie adds offhandedly. 'That doesn't mean you aren't deserving of love, though.'

Wow, this is an excellent piece of haddock. It's almost as good as a piece from my favourite chippy back in Cleethorpes.

Izzie leans her head to one side. 'Speaking of love, Bee, don't you ever wonder why you let your imagination run wild on paper, but you won't allow yourself that freedom?'

We both smile at the waitress as she replenishes our water glasses. I wait until she's gone before returning Izzie's lovingly challenging look.

'Come on, big author. Aren't you going to pick up that pen and fight me?'

I rearrange my napkin. 'I'm happy on my own.'

'That doesn't mean you couldn't be happi-*er* with someone.'

I start my bit-of-everything-on-my-fork routine again, focusing half my concentration on getting the perfect balance. The other half is attempting to master the art of invisibility.

'Auntie, if you're waiting for an answer, it won't be today. Tomorrow's looking sketchy too.'

Izzie could take patience to a new level. If only that level was inside a tall building with a dodgy lift.

Since there's no point in testing it, I try to impress her by holding up my loaded fork. 'Did you know…'

'Probably not,' Izzie says. 'And at my age, I probably don't need to know.'

'… that Charles Dickens mentions chips in *A Tale of Two Cities*?'

'Really? How boring.'

'He referred to them as—'

The hand that reaches over the table and adjusts my collar makes me drop my juggling nonsense. I shoot across a cursory 'I love you, but fuck off' glance. But it's wasted on this woman.

'Why couldn't you be happy with someone after all this time?' Izzie gently asks.

My mouth and shoulders shrug. 'Perhaps you should ask Ma. That woman loves telling me what's going on with my sisters' love lives, or lack thereof, but she never – she *never* – asks about mine. Yes, I know I don't have one any more, and I'm good with that. But still.'

'Don't take it personally, Bee. Remember, your mother has fuck-all else to discuss. All she does is make beds and imagine ways she can shake off your sisters, which she thinks can only happen if men come along and drag them away. Your mum is proud you got out into the world,' she assures me.

'Pleased, more like.'

'She loves you – in her own way.'

'Whereas my sisters hate me in every way.'

'No. Your sisters are jealous of what you have achieved.'

I sit back. 'Are you going to bill me for this session?'

'I hung up my notepad and couch five years ago,' Izzie reminds me.

As the waitress clears away our plates, we praise the food and service enough to compensate for the arsehole sitting near the window. He even complained to her about the rain.

'You asked Nyx if he is sweet on me.'

Izzie quirks an eyebrow. 'Do you think I needed to?'

I look back at the dessert board.

'Would you like to know what he said, Bee?' she enquires.

'No.'

'Ooh, this is where it gets good.' She rubs her hands together. 'Whenever there are signs that a guy likes you…'

'*Likes* me.'

'… that is when you tell him what you really do for a living. Then, that's it. You're convinced he can't possibly like you for the right reasons.'

'And *like* is all it will ever be.'

'But you still haven't told this chap everything.' Izzie's grey matter is working overtime. 'Fascinating.'

'To be honest, I only did this to give you something to think about. I don't want you going down that route of pottery classes and tai chi.'

'Yeah, right,' she scoffs. 'When you first saw Nyx, I'm sure your thoughts were on keeping your favourite old dear from a care home.'

I must carefully bring down this bubbly fun. 'He is one of only a few new friends I've made in a while.'

'But if you plan on keeping it just friends, you need to tell him.'

'I don't need to tell him anything, Izzie. He knows that's all we'll ever be.'

'And you truly believe that?'

I frown at the curtains. 'Yes, I do.'

'If that's the case, Bee, you'll soon need to give him up.'

I resist the urge to push my bottom lip out.

'I know it's not what you want to hear,' Izzie says.

'He'll move on soon, anyway.'

'If that's what you're hoping…'

'He will,' I assure everyone at our table. 'He will.'

Chapter Nineteen

Once the rest of the downstairs flooring is installed later this week, I've said there will be no more greasy takeaway lounge picnics in the renovated cottage. Therefore, I'm making the most of this one with Nyx.

Yes, we're on our own this evening. Izzie and Bacon are in Hawkshead. My aunt is visiting another group of her Cumbrian friends. The third group. Just two more to go.

With our selection of silver trays on the floor, Nyx and I temporarily fill up on empty calories as we enjoy the outside flowing in through the open sliding doors. Admittedly, the current view isn't the best. My back garden is divided into two areas: one side is an expanse of flattened and cracked mud where the builders have marched and wheelbarrowed; the other would only excite those aiming to keep Britain's insect population thriving. I'm not a fan of the wild look, which is partly why Izzie the ivy tamer is here.

By the time we get down to the noodly dregs of our meal, we're lying on our backs to prevent the necessity of unbuttoning waistbands.

Nyx groans. 'I'm so full.'

'Same here.' I reach across and pick up the two fortune cookies. 'Left or right?'

'Left.'

'Damn!'

'Right, then.'

I toss one over to him. 'You give in far too easily, mate.'

Nyx mumbles something inaudible.

'What did you say?' I ask.

'Nothing.'

The only sound to be heard is the cracking of sweet pastries.

He reads his first. '*Don't try to predict the future. Just enjoy the surprises.* That's what I do anyway.'

'Wait until you wake up and your fortieth birthday is straddling you with balloons and a receding hairline,' I warn.

'Yeah, I'll probably start thinking differently then.'

I pull out the fortune from my cookie. '*Let sarcasm be just one of the great services you—*'

Nobody claiming they were fit to burst a minute ago can bounce up onto their knees as quickly as Nyx does. He snatches the piece of paper away and leans over me, resting on one hand.

Oh, shit. I don't think he realises how close his head is to mine now.

But I'm a-fucking-ware.

'*Don't wallow in the what-ifs,*' Nyx reads. '*Let life shrug off the oh-wells.*'

He folds it in half and slides it into my breast pocket. My heart starts to throw out a loud hip-hop beat when his gaze shifts.

Wait, what is that look he's giving me? I haven't seen that one before. Yes, I may have seen something similar, but I've always been able to abscond in time, saving us both from embarrassment. And I know those looks don't really mean anything, no matter what Izzie says. I know they don't.

They don't.

I'm sure they don't.

I can't escape from this one, though, not while Nyx is hovering above me.

Don't wallow in the what-ifs.

What if.

A conversation plays out on a showreel in my head, taking my mind temporarily off entering the last four digits that make up the nuclear launch code.

'But what if I find her and there's nothing left?' I remember asking Cal when he suggested I go find Jo again.

And he leaned forward over the table and said to me—

'Anyone home?'

No, that wasn't what he said. No, Cal said...

Cal?

I dig my heels in and slide my body out mechanic-style (minus the creeper seat) from under Nyx. I clamber to my feet a tad too energetically and hasten into the hallway.

'Did you take a wrong turn out of Knightsbridge?'

Now that Cal knows he isn't standing in someone else's hallway, he closes the front door. 'I was in the neighborhood.'

'Why, has your corner shop run out of flax milk?'

'Something like that,' he utters. 'I also haven't heard from you in a while.'

I score a perfect ten with my eyeroll. 'It's been, what, a week?'

'It's been longer than that, Jo.'

'A fortnight at the most.'

Cal touches his tie knot. 'It's closer to three weeks.'

His usual murderous expression is suddenly directed at my messy topknot. It's not that bad. I'm sure my hair has looked worse after a long-haul...

Hang on. It's not my hair that's getting Cal's death stare.

Nyx hovers just inside the open living area. His curiosity is doing a shit job of hiding behind nothing but a tight smile. There's only one excuse he can have for following the sound of another man's voice: he needs to know whether he can beat him at wrestling.

My focus bats from one to the other. To the other. To the oth—

'Hey.' A calloused hand is held out.

'Sorry!' I wake up. 'Nyx, this is my Cal.'

Eyebrows narrowly avoid the flight paths as their hands come together.

'I mean, this is my boss.'

'I'm not your boss,' Cal murmurs.

'This is my co-worker, Cal. Not... Not *my* Cal.'

My cackling laughter is accompanied by rapid blinking. 'We work for the same company on a… a… semi-self-employed basis. A book company. A book-editing company. We're… We're editors-in-arms, aren't we?'

'That's right.' There's not even a moment's hesitation from the American.

'And this is Nyx Hart. He's a contractor.'

'Yours?' Cal checks.

'No, we're just good fr—Oh. You mean, is he my…? Yes. Yes, he's my contractor. He's doing a great job, too.' I turn round. 'Aren't you, Nyx?'

'I hope so.'

'You are,' I assure him.

To the one wearing cufflinks, I state, 'He is.'

Maybe everyone's quiet because we're all keeping an ear out for the same thing. A dripping sound, perhaps, which could help us find any leaking pipes. Or sonar pings, alerting us to enemy submarines. I'm sorry, those are the only excuses I can come up with.

'Well,' Nyx says, breaking the awkward silence, 'I promised my brothers they could try to hammer me at *Rocket League* before bed.' He points his thumb over his shoulder. 'Did you need a hand clearing up, Jo?'

'No, it'll take me two minutes.'

As Nyx heads towards his Astra, I stand at the top of the porch steps. With exaggerated strokes, I show off the beautifully painted (by me) handrail to the person standing behind me in the doorway.

Nyx walks past Cal's mode of transport as it gleams in the glow of the setting sun. 'Nice Jag.'

'Thanks,' both Cal and I say.

Wait, we *both*…? Oh, for fu—

'Jo chose the color for me.'

Nyx nods. 'She chose well.'

Once my contractor's tail lights have disappeared down the driveway, I turn round to ask Cal how my car is running, which will be after I've heard his thoughts on my wood spindles.

However, I appear to be minus one agent.

***

I watch Cal give the kitchen a thorough examination. 'Why are you here?'

'I drove up this morning to see a client in Manchester,' he tells the inside of the oven.

'Seeing them professionally or fictionally?'

'And since I'm up this way, I thought I'd stop by.'

The utility room is now getting a score out of ten.

'Well, as you can see, everything's peachy,' I'm more than pleased to tell him.

'I also wanted to discuss a few things before the meeting.'

His sidelong glance is all too familiar.

'I haven't forgotten.' It's imminent. I know that much, at least.

Cal wafts past me. He must have been driving for over six hours today, yet he still smells like a basket of freshly laundered towels.

'Couldn't we have discussed them via email?' I ask.

He scrutinises the wood burner, checking that the

plinth underneath extends far enough out and on either side to meet building regulations.

'Shall I even respond to that?' he retorts, checking the seal on the stove pipe.

'Nah.'

The multi-slide doors are being closed now. And opened again. Closed. I'm waiting for the PAT testing labels to come out next.

'Was he one of the contractors I found you?'

'Nope.' I lead the way upstairs. 'Yours were all shit.'

I stand back as Cal walks the perimeter of the main bedroom, his hand checking the plaster finish.

I can't help but grin. 'It's smooth, right?'

His eyes travel up to the cornice.

'I went with the classic style, not too big,' I quickly explain. 'The rooms aren't massive, and I didn't want to—'

'Plaster?'

'No, hardened polyurethane.' I'm pleased Cal has been fooled by it, too. 'It's great because it won't crack over time. But everyone thinks it looks like plaster.'

He crouches in front of the cast iron fireplace.

'This had about eight coats of paint on it.' I crouch next to him. 'And this stuff I found online peeled it straight off and…' The shift in Cal's knee when mine nudges it is barely perceptible, but it's there. '… it showed all this, erm… this detail… under… underneath.' *Don't get hung up on the knee thing, Jo.* 'Then I used this, erm… this brass-coloured brushy thing on a spinny bit that you put in your drill.'

'A wire brush drill bit,' he clarifies.

'That's the fella. It took me a while, but look at the results. A bit of black grate polish and, hey presto! Gorgeous, don't you think?'

Cal is looking at the three-metre lengths of skirting board. They're waiting to be fitted once the flooring is laid. 'You've gone with oak?'

'It matches the doors and the flooring. It's also more durable. *And* it's sustainably sourced.' No, I'm not on commission, before you ask. 'From your country, in fact.'

I'm not following Cal into the en suite. It may be big enough for two, but not for us two. I'm sure the detailed results will come in his report anyway, which he'll probably type up after his carbless, glutonless, passionless dinner. One that any Michelin-starred chef would only rustle up if you threatened to cut his butter supply in half.

After his visual inspection of the other rooms, I ask, 'Well?'

'The standard of work is…' Cal finishes his sentence with a slow nod.

'Do you like it?'

He shrugs. 'It has character.'

'Do you like it?'

I just know the tosser is itching to comment on my choice of brushed antique brass instead of polished chrome for the sockets and light switches. I hope he does. No, I can't give him all twelve reasons right now…

But I know what I would like to give him.

'I think people will be interested,' is Cal's answer.

I block his escape from the second bedroom when he's less than an arm's length away. 'Do you like it?'

His hands slide into his trouser pockets.

I fix my eyes on him. 'A yes or no. That's all I'm asking for.'

Even if a closing-down sale is declared at Hotel Chocolat, my arm isn't moving off the frigging door jamb.

Cal looks around one last time. You can be sure it *will* be the last time, or else—

'Yes. I like it.'

I don't think I've ever felt such relief, and I have no qualms about showing it. When I clasp my hands together under my chin, it releases him from his enforced incarceration.

'And you're keeping within budget?'

'Yyyyyeeeessss.' I drag the word out while traipsing behind him down the stairs. Hopefully, my stroppy stomp doesn't go unnoticed. I'm also praying it cloaks that slight bending of the truth. Cal doesn't need to see all the receipts when it's done. Especially those for the en-suite fixtures.

'I'm only looking out for your interests.'

'I know,' I mumble.

'It's easy to let your heart rule your head.'

'What the hell are you inferring?'

Cal halts his descent. 'People get emotionally caught up in these house flips and stop thinking about profit margins.'

'I swear no hearts will be harmed during the making of this home.'

Did I say that in Arabic? Is Cal looking at me and waiting for Siri to translate it through his invisible AirPods? Otherwise, why is he taking forever to acknowledge what I said?

Acknowledge it.

Just fucking acknow—!

'All right, Jo.'

Outside, Cal hovers behind me as I lock the front door.

'Have you found somewhere to stay tonight?'

Why have I asked this? I should've just recommended some clean motorway services between here and London. Cal is going to say he hasn't – it's summer and the Lakes – and then I'll be forced to share my bed with the one person I love beyond words, even though I'll never be able to tell her.

'I have found somewhere,' he says.

'That's lucky.'

Lucky for us both – me more than him – because Izzie would've given Cal her hotel room without hesitation. Then I would've had to sleep with her snoring. I tried it once. By two in the morning, I'd written enough murder scenarios to one-up Agatha Christie.

'It must've been slim pickings,' I remark. 'Getting a hotel room here in July is harder than cutting open an avocado on the one day it's ripe.'

'I'm not staying in a hotel. Or a guesthouse.'

'You're in a dorm in a hostel?' I'd rest a concerned hand on their arm if it were anyone else. 'Did you pack your waterproof socks for the shared shower?'

'I've rented a villa close to here,' Cal informs me.

'In *July*? When you can't walk to your recycling bin without twatting your face against a swinging "No Vacancies" sign, you're telling me you snagged a last-minute villa?'

'That's right.'

I believe him as much as I entrust a married person with a secret that can't be shared.

'And because it was available for more than one night,' Cal adds, 'I figured why not see if you could do with some cheap labor.'

I wish I had bags in my hands for a dramatic drop. It would match my expression.

'Which shocks you the most?' he asks. 'My knowing how to wire an electrical outlet, or that I come cheap?'

'Actually, it's the thought of you wearing something that's washed at forty degrees.'

I think I'm funny. I don't care what Cal thinks. But as he gets into the Jaguar, the tiny shake of his head says I won't be laughing when he puts in his bill.

Chapter Twenty

'Good morning, handsome,' Izzie sings, announcing our arrival at the cottage.

Nyx stops painting the kitchen ceiling and climbs down the stepladder. 'Morning, Jo. Morning, Izzie.'

It's good he's a hugger; otherwise, he would be by the time the hospital tracks my aunt down.

She hands him a takeaway cup. 'A hot, sexy latte for one of my favourite men, and...'

Nyx looks inside the bag she gives him. 'How did you know sausage and cheese toasties are my favourite?'

'Intuition,' Izzie claims while doing a runway walk towards the hallway with her four-cup carry tray. 'Tell me, Nyx, do I rock these work dungarees or what?'

'You're looking good from this angle.'

Once she and her swaying hips have sashayed out of sight, Nyx notices I'm holding only a latte. 'Hey, Intuition, where's your tasty treat?'

'I don't get one, as it's not my Cumberland banger she dreams about.'

I listen to Izzie's footsteps on the bare stairs. She's on her way to deposit the spare drink to the person who, moments ago, stopped with the flooring nailer when the pitter-patter of tiny paws introduced herself.

I heard Bacon go in there, but…

Two sets of boots are now echoing on the stairs, and Izzie's loud laughter means they'll need to stop for a second. I don't care about her lady-dribbles, but if she's laughing, that hopefully means Cal's angry resting face didn't cause my dog to freeze in fear when she set eyes on him.

Izzie walks in first with a beaming grin. 'Somebody is smitten.'

One of Cal's hands is holding his takeaway cup. The other is cradling the little, multicoloured canine that would appear to be his emotional kryptonite (if the high-pitched baby talk tumbling from his mouth is anything to go by).

Cal's lips do this rare thing where they curl up at the edges and show his front teeth. 'I adore dogs.' He shifts his smile down to Bacon. 'And I wuv you. Yes, I do.' His voice sounds like Scooby-Doo on helium. 'I do. I wuv you *very* much.'

Bacon responds by trying to lick the skin off his chin.

Izzie thinks this is adorable. I think Nyx is even fighting back a manly *Aww* face. I'm thinking about selling a kidney to raise the ransom money to get my agent back, as this stand-in ain't cuttin' the mustard.

'Bacon is Jo's baby,' Izzie tells him.

'She's not my baby,' I clarify. 'She's my dog. No,

she's not... *my* dog. She is somebody's, but she wandered into my yard and... Anyway, I've put up posters.'

'But nobody's come forward yet,' Izzie adds as she joins the lovefest. She'll use any excuse to get close to a man. I think she's hoping Cal won't notice two tongues.

'It's only a matter of time,' I tell everyone.

Cal remarks, 'Social media might be a good place to—'

Izzie rests her hand on his forearm. 'It's fine, Cal. The posters are fine for now.'

I pick up my gardening gloves. 'Right, Auntie Cray-Cray. Do you want to walk us through your grand plans for the outside?'

Although Cal can't do much while he's holding a dog like a newborn, nothing can stop those pesky lines between his eyebrows from making a comeback.

'She knows the budget,' I toss back at him.

Behind my house in the land that time forgot, Izzie sums up what needs doing. I wanted to see my aunt – that goes without saying – but her becoming a landscape gardener during her transition from a clinical psychologist to a banging pensioner was a horticultural bonus. I also knew she wouldn't want to come over and be bored.

Nyx, Bacon and I trail after her as she points out what needs to go. Even before she arrived, the conifers blocking the view knew their time was up. As soon as the cash went from my account to Clive's, Nyx helped me cut them down and dig up their creeping roots.

'I'll make a start on that buddleia,' Izzie says. 'It's not the best time to cut it back, but needs must. Nyx, Bee, can you take out these shrubs? They're past their best. The soil can go too.'

While the three of us are cutting and digging, Nyx asks Izzie, 'Why do you call her Bee?'

'When she was little, her dad would play peek-a-boo with her. That was when she said her first word, but she said "bee", not "boo". It was the only word she said until she was nearly two. She then went from one word to dozens of tiny sentences overnight. It scared her mum, but we thought it was hilarious. From then on, her dad and I called her Bee.'

'That's a cute story,' Nyx says. 'And it suits you. Bee.'

I keep digging. Izzie is under the buddleia again, pruning and talking to herself. Bacon is chasing butterflies.

'It's sweet that you still have a nickname your dad gave you,' he comments.

I love this shovel that's been loaned to me.

'I don't think I've ever heard you mention him.'

Its actual name is a grafter, but I keep asking to borrow the 'gaffer'. It always makes Colin chuckle.

'What does your dad do?' Nyx asks.

The 'gaffer' is slicing into this hard mud like a knife through butter.

'Jo?'

I ram the shovel down, making Bacon jump. 'He was in the same line of work as me.'

'Was?'

'He died.'

'Oh shit. I'm sorry, Jo—'

'Izzie, I don't think I'm really levelling this patch of ground,' I grumble. 'It now just looks like a miniature version of the Alps.'

***

Nyx and I always work well as a team, and today we maintain that winning streak. He fills the wheelbarrow two-thirds to my third, usually whisking it away before I get a chance. All the same, I won't let him do all the heavy wheeling. When I insist on taking a turn, though, I know he's only filling it up to a point. But as lunchtime approaches and the midday sun peaks, even these loads feel heavy.

'I've got it,' I say through gritted teeth, picking up speed and getting the wheelbarrow onto the wooden plank.

Although my head thinks it's still in its twenties, my body no longer laughs at the stairlift adverts, and I am halfway up the plank when my energy hears the nursing home's dinner bell.

Luckily, Nyx appears like Superman on my left and gets his hands under the side of the wheelbarrow before it topples, straightening it up again. Between us, we push it the rest of the way. All I need to do now is tip its contents over the lip of the skip.

Sounds easy, right?

Following my disappearance into the waste abyss with the wheelbarrow, someone who can't stifle their giggles asks, 'Are you okay?'

I sit upright on the heap of mud, chunky roots, and tangled branches. My head is just above the rim of the skip. 'Couldn't you wait until we know whether I've sustained any permanent damage before laughing your socks off?'

'You're fine.' Nyx wipes away tears. 'I wish I'd had my phone to hand. *You've Been Framed* would've bought that.'

I swing my legs over the side and perch on the rim. I hitch up one leg of my combat trousers to reveal a slight scrape on my kneecap. Nyx caresses the... Sorry, he *assesses* the damage first before kissing it. On... On Bacon's behalf, of course, because she... she can't... she can't reach to kiss it herself, can she?

Nyx holds out his hand to me. I take it, and he hauls me over his shoulder in a fireman's lift. Sadly, I don't have the energy to fight him or to protest. I'm about to remind him that gravity and middle age go together like nuts and chewing gum when I notice Bacon's ears are pricked up.

A woman is walking towards us. Even from my strange angle, I know Elite Model Management must ask to hire her womb.

'Hey, Mum,' Nyx says.

Please, driveway, open up and swallow me whole!

After I've been lowered back onto my feet, my blood takes the slowest train away from my face. Not that it needs additional colour. No, the heat and mortification already have it covered. The rest of me isn't ready for its closeup, either. Everything is skew-whiff: my vest, my combats (one leg is still pushed up), my hairstyle, my glasses. My good name.

I am now standing in front of a woman who, even in flat espadrilles, towers above me. She's wearing a floaty summer dress that perfectly highlights her tiny waist and truly incredible boobs. Her hair, falling in long, silky waves around her shoulders, only adds to the image of a brunette Sofía Vergara.

Her gaze flickers between us. Her almond-shaped eyes are the same hazel colour as her son's. 'I hope my coming over is all right.'

Nyx slaps his forehead. 'Hell, I should have mentioned it.'

That may earn him a Worst Actor nomination at the Golden Raspberry Awards next year.

'Mum has made lunch for us, and I meant to tell you she was coming over. Jo, I'm sorry. I totally forgot.'

If you believe that, you also think the local authorities used to add a chemical to public swimming pools to turn the water blue if you peed in them.

I conjure up a smile. 'No problem. That's great.'

Discreetly, I try to correct my physical appearance, but I know my effort is like the proverbial turd being polished. There's an embedded stain across my vest from carrying lumps of mud. I have leaves and twigs nestled in my hair. My back is wetter than Derwentwater.

I take my gloves off. 'Hmm. I would usually shake hands, but...' I display my dirty fingers.

'That's okay.' Her radiant smile matches the rest

of her. 'I'm Maria, and it's lovely to meet you.'

Behind me, I hear Cal utter, 'Ah, there you are. Jo, Izzie wants to…'

After looking round to check Cal hasn't fallen down an uncovered maintenance hole, I follow his eye line to see why he didn't finish his sentence.

And it's standing in front of me, wearing Dior Dune.

Once Nyx has made the introductions, Maria looks down at Cal's outstretched hand. She needs a second to remember what to do.

'I'm blown away by your son's handiwork,' Cal tells her. 'You must be proud.'

Who the fuck is this smooth operator, I want to know, looking up at a side that's been kept in Pandora's box all this time. What will the man who suddenly has smiles for miles say next? Kiss me if I'm wrong, but unicorns are real? Wouldn't we look cute together on a wedding invitation?

Wait a minute.

Stop. Everything.

As I watch Cal surrender to Maria's enchanting forty-inch spell, the answer to the sexual orientation question becomes clear.

'My aunt,' I hear myself say. 'She's, erm… She's… working. In the… In the back.'

Maria points down the driveway beyond the row of vans. 'I have some things in the car.'

'I'll get them,' I quickly offer.

Nyx steps forward. 'I'll help you, Jo—'

'No!' My sharp response takes him by surprise. 'I

mean, no, you're all right: Cal will help me. You show your mum the…'

Cal, however, has scooped Bacon up and is saying to Maria, 'Let me show you the way.'

He has finished with the smiling stage; ear to ear has been overtaken. It's almost a continuous path now around his enormous head. I also see his forehead lines are enjoying a *vacation* lower down on his face. They've turned ninety degrees during the flight and deeply tucked themselves in on either side of his dental display.

Cal's hand extends forward and hovers close to Maria's back, not quite touching it but showing a *ladies first* action. There's nothing wrong with that. He always lets me go first.

But that's where the similarity with this gesture would appear to end.

I head towards Maria's car with a stride I usually reserve for modes of transport I'm about to miss. Nyx puts a swinging distance between us, which he is wise to do.

'I genuinely forgot she was coming,' he blurts out.

'Yeah, right! Just like all items that are refunded were damaged when they bought them.'

He holds his hands up. 'Fine. I kept quiet because I didn't want to freak you out.'

'Look at the state of me!'

'You look great.'

'I do not, and next to your mum, I look like a… bad bout of diarrhoea.'

'Jo—'

Having used up my daily quota of pissed-off snaps, I must cut him off with a limp objection. 'No, Nyx. This is… This is mean of you.'

I grab a tray of food and a cool bag from her Hyundai's boot and take them into the kitchen. On my next trip, I spot my reflection in Maria's rear-view mirror.

Noooooooooooo!

I shove the covered bowls onto the island with the rest before dashing upstairs into the bathroom, hoping her car mirror was only playing tricks.

It turns out it was being kind.

It looks like someone rescued me from a rugby scrum and then shoved me into bed underneath a twenty-tog duvet – with the electric blanket on tropical.

While the washbasin fills up, I splash my face, neck and cleavage. I dip my arms into the lukewarm water and scrub off the caked mud. My deodorant is downstairs in my bag, along with my shirt. At least I can throw that on and hide the dirty vest.

I remove my claw clip and gather up the escaped hair. Risking another look, I now only resemble an unfit runner. My sunglasses would hide a multitude of under-eye wrinkle sins, but guess where they are?

I rinse my filthy glasses under the tap, drying them on some toilet tissue before putting them back on. That's better. I glance at my reflection again. No, it's not. Perhaps I should've left them as they were. If only I had some equally dirty pairs to hand out.

Everyone is gathered in the kitchen. Thank

heavens for Izzie: she's chatting with Maria like they're old friends and gushing over the food. I can imagine what Cal is gushing over, which is why I don't bother looking. I don't want confirmation or a bloody trophy for guessing—

Yep, I was right. Five points to Team Jo.

I prop up my smile while taking in the dishes of colourful lettuce leaves, seasoned rice, buttered new potatoes, herby croutons, creamy chicken pasta, marinated olives and feta, roasted tomatoes, and watermelon chunks with basil. Never have I seen salad look so tasty this far east of LA. I should tell her, really.

The tiler and the decorator take their hearty portions to eat near their vans. With the sun threatening to curdle the mayonnaise, the rest of us hover around the island. Nyx fills his plate and stands next to me, probably to avoid the death stares he would get if he stood opposite me.

Between mouthfuls, I say to Maria, 'This is extremely kind of you.'

'Oh, it's nothing.'

Nothing? She could give Nigella Lawson a good run for her money – in more ways than one.

Hang on, why haven't I said that out loud? I love to dish out compliments. I pride myself on being like an elf with a Santa hat full of candy canes.

'Are you a chef by trade?' Cal coos. Well, it sounded like cooing to me.

'No,' Maria replies. 'I love any excuse to cook, that's all. And any excuse to come over.'

227

'Has our lovely Nyx not given you a peek before now?' Izzie asks her.

'He didn't like to without asking.'

I bite back a retort to the person on my right. 'Well, Maria, let me show you the upstairs—'

Izzie jumps in. 'Let me, Jo. I don't like to be left alone with Nyx without a chaperone. Cal, did you want to…?'

Of course he wants to. I bet he'd like to show Maria the upstairs too.

Cal puts down the plate he can't fill just yet, not when his eyes are helping themselves to dessert.

As Bacon tucks into her bowl of food, I sit with my plate on the shaded doorstep overlooking the back garden. Just as I'm eating my last potato, I hear size ten boots approaching from behind. Nyx takes a seat next to me.

'Your mum seems nice,' I remark.

'She's the best.' I don't need to see the proud look on his face. 'She's wanted to meet you for ages now. I've… wanted you to meet her too.'

'Well, I'd probably be just as curious if I had a son hanging around with a woman twice his age.'

I listen to the breeze above us in the tops of the trees.

Nyx murmurs, 'You're not twice my age.'

'I was four years ago.'

When friendly voices return to the kitchen, I leave Nyx to eat in peace.

'This is an amazing house,' Maria comments.

'Thanks to your family,' I remind her. 'I'm very

grateful for what Nyx and Colin have done. And it's almost finished, so you'll soon get your son back.'

I can feel the heat of Izzie's gaze on me.

'I also wanted to invite all of you over for dinner one night next week,' Maria says. 'Nothing special – just chicken.'

'I would love nothing more,' Izzie declares.

'Just chicken beats my ready-in-two-minutes vegetable rice any day,' I respond. 'Thank you.'

Maria fiddles with her little bottle of sparkling water and looks at my agent.

A smile accompanies his answer. 'I would like that very much.'

No, Cal doesn't smile *when* he says that: he hasn't stopped smiling since he saw those tits come in.

'Bee, why don't you show Maria that wonderful view?' Izzie suggests.

I fill up my plate again first. Since I'm sweating like a pig and the colour of a cooked one, I should complete the image.

Maria and I exit via the patio doors.

'You'd better walk in front,' I advise, 'because I must smell as savoury as I look.'

Maria chuckles. 'Don't worry. It's simply nice to put a face to the name. I feel like I know you already – and you're just as Nyx described you.'

Great. I couldn't look any worse, and I'm *just* as Nyx described me? Only reading one of my books and telling everyone it's not worth the paper it's printed on would be a bigger kick in the fanny.

'I couldn't have done this renovation without

Nyx,' I tell her when we stop near the colourful terrain of dome-shaped hydrangea flower heads. 'You have a good lad there.'

I've often wondered what a proud parent looks like. Now I know.

'You haven't mentioned how handsome he is,' Maria remarks with a friendly wink.

'How long have you got?'

'Is it creepy to say I'd be after him if we weren't related?'

'Only if you hadn't said "Is it creepy" at the beginning.'

It's obvious where Nyx got his smile.

'He talks about you a lot,' she confides. 'And he hasn't done that before.'

'What, talk about one of his friends a lot?'

'About anyone.'

'Well, that's… nice.' They must have heard my hard swallow in New Zealand.

Maria's hand gently squeezes my forearm. 'If my son's happy, I'm happy.'

'Good. Me, too. If your son's happy, so am I. I'm his friend, after all.' Well, I was.

'Friends. More than friends. A lot more than friends.' She shrugs. 'I don't mind.'

'Yeah, if it's multiple choice, it's most definitely a big, *big* tick next to option A.'

Maria nods while gazing beyond the hardy shrubs and across the shimmering mere. 'The house is beautiful, Jo. But this is…'

'It's something, isn't it?'

We watch the Miss Ambleside rock by, the top deck full on this perfect, cloudless day. I wish I was on there, enjoying that cooling breeze. Instead, I'm portraying 'the morning after' while standing next to 'the night before'.

'Would you like to meet for a drink sometime?' Maria asks.

'Sure.'

No, I'm not sure. I never am. I thought I was once – I regretted it until it grew out.

Phones are retrieved from pockets. Nyx showed me how to find my number, but I don't need to look any more. Who knew I'd be giving it out willy-nilly these days?

Watching Maria tap her screen, I'm pleased to note her short nails are devoid of colour or shine. There may be just a hint of dirt under one of them, too. It's a little thing, but I'm straw-grasping, okay?

***

Once Nyx and I have watched Maria's car make it onto the main road, I'm about to return to the house when he gently takes my wrist.

'Jo—?'

I snatch my hand away. 'I had to meet your mum looking like this. Thanks a lot.'

'What's wrong with how you look?'

'There are only two things that don't lie: kids and leggings. Nice try.'

'I didn't know you would want to get *glammed up* just to meet my mum.'

'I wouldn't. But I would've appreciated a little advanced notice. Just enough time to make myself look presentable, that's all.'

Nyx shakes his head. 'I don't get why you're making such a big deal out of it.'

'One minute before she arrived, I was in a bloody skip.'

He can't keep the dimples at bay. He's as good as laughing at me.

'I'll bet you a fiver, Jo, you're going to look back on this—'

'What, and laugh? Maybe.' I head back up the driveway. 'But not today.'

He follows behind me. 'Wow.'

I roll my eyes. 'Wow, what?'

'I'm… surprised, that's all. I think you're overreacting. Today wasn't—'

When I spin round, my expression stops him in his tracks. 'I didn't know you had permission to judge me, Nyx. Is God advertising on Indeed?'

'I'm just saying.'

'I am not overreacting.' I keep my composure. 'The thing is, I don't know what you've told your mum about me – maybe you've said I'm nothing special, and that's fine – but I would've appreciated just five minutes to make myself look almost as good as "nothing special". And if that makes me a drama queen in your eyes, so be it. Ask your mum first, though, how she would feel if the roles were reversed before you judge me.'

I've always struggled to raise my voice in anger;

hence, the tummy issues in the past and the absence of italics and exclamation marks during my present rant. A doctor once recommended standing in the middle of a field and screaming. I chose the less embarrassing route: I try to avoid situations like the one I'm walking away from today.

Chapter Twenty-One

After making a soak in the bath drag out for the longest six minutes in history, I'm forced to lie on my stomach in only my pyjama shorts. That's because the gardening workout has given me more than just tight calves.

I felt fine when I was working. Well, physically, I was fine. My mood... Yeah, that was a different matter. I felt the same at four-thirty, too. That was when I'd had enough of the house and everyone in it. I then drove around for an hour, taking my annoyance out on the ozone layer.

The problem only came to my attention when I was getting dry. My back felt like I'd made love on a nettle bed! I looked over my shoulder in the mirror and was horrified. My back and shoulders were a flaming red, enhanced by the pale areas where my vest had been. This was despite the factor thirty I slathered on every couple of hours or... thereabouts.

Knock, knock-knock, knock.

When will that woman take 'no' for an answer? Izzie offered to come over, and I said no, *please* don't, as I can't handle that type of retired medical intervention right now.

I cover my naked chest with the first towel I find and stagger onto the landing.

'It's unlocked,' I shout.

Knock knock.

I pad down four stairs. 'It's *unlocked.*'

I hear the front door open and close as I trundle back up.

'And before you piss your crotchless knickers, you gutter slag,' I say, 'I'm dressed like this because my bastard back and shoulders are sunburnt.'

'Have you put anything on them?'

I spin round, pulling the towel a little higher.

It's not my loopy aunt.

Bacon is behaving as though she hasn't seen him before. Nyx is looking up the stairs like he has never seen *me* before – in what are basically frilly pants and a fingertip towel. That's right, not a hand towel; it is one for dinner guests to use. In inches, it is eleven by eighteen. In centimetres, it's a fucking small one.

'I thought I had some aloe vera gel.' It turned out to be a three-minute, cleansing cucumber face mask.

'I'll nipple—I mean, *nip.* I will nip to the, erm… to the… to the shop then and get something for…' Nyx does some sort of pointing/not pointing action. 'I'll be back in a blink.'

Which is something he is struggling to do.

It's a ten-minute blink, during which my attempts to put on a light pyjama top are abandoned. At least the shorts have been replaced with pyjama bottoms.

235

More than just my nipples are covered too, with a hand towel now tucked under my arms.

I perch on the edge of the bed, and Nyx kneels behind me. He kneels *on my bed*. He's never been in here before, I don't think. Unless he sneaks a peek en route to the loo.

I hear the cap on the bottle click open. Within seconds of the lotion dribbling onto my skin, there's a worry that it may start sizzling. Yes, that's how much heat my back is radiating!

Nyx is trying his hardest to be gentle, but it still feels like it's being applied by two digits wrapped in the softest grit sandpaper.

'I won't rub it all in,' he says.

'I don't care if you leave me looking like I'm about to swim the Channel in January.'

'How does that feel?'

'A little better. I don't suppose you have any liquid nitrogen? Or an ice sculpture you could rest me against?'

Areas on my back suddenly feel cooler. Nyx is gently blowing on me, sweeping back and forth. I relish the feeling, moving my shoulders. If this wasn't a medical emergency, I'd be dusting off my sex playlist.

'That is heavenly,' I utter.

'I'm going to have to keep stopping.'

'Please don't.'

'So we can talk.'

'Text and blow,' I suggest.

Nyx picks up a magazine off the bedside table. A

fifty-page breeze then starts to fan my shoulders and back.

'I spoke to my mum,' he says.

'Oh yeah?'

'And Izzie.'

My shoulders slump. 'Oh no.'

'I spoke to Cal, too.'

'Eh?'

'And I'm really, really sorry, Jo.'

A few more wafts fill the silence that I can't politely pack. When did Cal find the time to become an expert on women? Unless he bought the audiobook version of *1,001 Things Not to Say When a Woman Says, 'What?'*.

'I guess there's a lot I need to learn about the opposite sex,' Nyx admits.

'Well, you still have time.'

His head appears from the side.

'Am I forgiv—?'

'Ow ow ow *ow*!'

The merest lock of his hair brushing my shoulder feels like razor blades slicing through my skin. I slide off the edge of the bed and rotate 180 degrees as I drop onto my knees. Torvill and Dean performed a similar move at the end of their Olympic routine to Ravel's 'Boléro'. They, however, got a faceful of ice. I get white cotton percale.

'It's that painful?' Nyx checks.

'Yes,' I squeak into my bed linen.

He opens the large side window and drags the padded ottoman in front of it for me. I sit down and raise my knees to rest my cheek. A tender breeze caresses my inflamed skin.

Over the next hour or so, we wonder which natural disaster movies might come true during our lifetimes. We discuss our three wishes. We debate bread versus potatoes. After we've decided what would win in a fight between a pig and a sheep, the lull gives Nyx a moment to notice what he's sprawled out on.

'I've never shared a bed,' he confesses.

'Really?' For being able to keep the level of shock at bay, I should commend myse—

'No, I'm not a virgin.'

'Right. If you were, there'd be nothing wrong with that,' I quickly add.

'I know.'

I tuck my towel a little higher, lowering my knees to sit cross-legged. 'So, when you're... where do you...?'

'Yeah, I've done it *in* one.'

Of course he has. Look at him. Who wouldn't want Nyx making up the numbers in their double bed, even if only for a brief interlude? Hell, I'd do it with him on a baggage carousel.

'With the woman that you dated a couple of years ago, I imagine.'

'Among others. Quite a few others, in fact. No, what I mean is, there haven't been... there haven't been *loads*. Certainly not recently,' he insists. 'It's a... It's a reasonable number, I'd say. Probably somewhere close to the average. Maybe slightly... No, I don't think it would be much higher than the

238

average number. I don't... think.'

Aw, bless him. Is he applying to be a member of the backpedalling party?

'Nyx, your number is your business,' I gently remind him.

'But I don't want you to think I'm... I'm a...'

'A fan of musical beds?'

'Exactly!'

I tilt my head to one side. 'What does it matter what I think?'

'It matters a great deal.'

'I understand why a few generations are now into casual sex in a big internet way...'

Nyx sits up. 'And that's what you think I'm like?'

'I never said that.'

'Why? Because of my age?'

'I don't think it's an age thing. Many now seem to think the same, which is good. But it *could* mean the number of people who want more than just... casual internal decorating is shrinking. Perhaps relationships are becoming a three-tiered relic; only time will tell. I swear, I'm not judging you. It's your life. If it works for you, enjoy it, my friend. Our time on earth is short,' I point out. 'And youth is such an undervalued magical power.'

Nyx chuckles while pulling a face. 'Internal decorating?'

I cover my eyes. 'I know. I'm sorry.'

'For the record, I'm not one of those people,' he wants me to know. 'I *am* someone who's looking for a serious relationship. But until one comes along,

I'll… yeah, I'll take what I can get.'

'And you *should*. And fortunately for you, the pond out there – far, *far* out there – is *huge*.'

Whereas my body of water is the opposite. Two clownfish would fight in mine.

'Got it,' Nyx acknowledges.

'Good. Now, back to you never having shared a bed. Trust me, you're not missing anything. You'll see. It's *very* overrated.'

'You like sleeping alone?'

'It's in my top ten,' I own up. 'Between sausage and egg McMuffins and *The Golden Girls*.'

After a brief staring contest with his socks, Nyx swings his legs off the bed and slaps his thighs. The loud noise startles the small dog sleeping on my lap.

'I should go.'

'Oh.' And I thought mistimed ad breaks were the only things that surprised me nowadays. 'Right. Okay. Well… thank you for… coming over and… helping with my back.'

'No problem.'

Nyx pulls his trainers on with Bacon's enthusiastic support. She wriggles onto his knees, her rapid tail bashing him in the face as he tries to tie his laces. But nobody can get annoyed with her.

'Today's been full of firsts,' he remarks.

'I'll say! I fell into a skip. Then I beat the record for looking terrible, which meant I would, of course, meet your mum.'

'You didn't look terrible to me, Jo,' Nyx says, getting to his feet.

I make sure my towel is securely in place before standing up. I briefly turn my back to the room, adjusting the angle of the ottoman by not a fraction.

'I have also invented a new shade of burnt that *won't* be all the rage at Paris Fashion Week, and you have seen me...' I glance down at my fluffy front. 'You've seen me. Is there anything else I can fail at today? Any doors I can push that should be pulled?'

'I think you're done for a while.'

'Oh, I don't know. I'm sure I'm one step away from a fall on a treadmill.'

Nyx stands in front of me, just outside my dance space. 'We also had our first fight.'

'We, erm... We did.'

He waits until I meet his gaze. 'Let's make it our last one as well, yeah?'

With a tight-lipped smile, I nod my head. 'Yeah.'

Chapter Twenty-Two

Izzie is pleased with the progress made yesterday in the garden. Colin is with us today, and he helps Nyx shift the last of the soil and thorny plants.

I try not to be jealous of all the golden skin on display. Izzie gets a tan just by booking a holiday. Nyx's tool-belt career means his young skin has already had a few years of weathering. He will eventually be like Colin, tanning a mahogany colour when the sun's strong enough to melt the last frosts. I'm sure Cal's is just a T-shirt tan. I don't want proof.

Then there's me, dressed in a polo shirt to hide the shade of red more commonly seen on a stop sign, ordered to work inside between eleven and three.

I have the job today of marking Cal's measurements on the lengths of skirting board. Once he's cut them, I blob on the glue and then hold one end as he nails them to the walls. I tried to use the nail gun, but it required both hands, meaning he had to kneel open-legged directly behind me with his arms on either side to hold the skirting in place. I soon returned to blobbing and holding.

I'm the lunch runner as well. I volunteered, seeing as today is farmers' market day.

'I'll drive,' Cal offers.

Since he's also having to work indoors, I guess he could do with some fresh air too. It's also peak season, meaning the car parks will be chock-a-block, and any miracle spaces on the busy roads will require particular parking skills. Unless you're like me and prefer to drive up and down a dozen times until an end spot becomes available. Failing that, Cal can always drop me off.

***

We have found a parking space. That's the good news. The bad news is that it requires parking of the 'parallel' kind. I wouldn't tackle it even in my little French Fisher-Price. Cal, however, puts the indicator on and pulls forward alongside the car in front. With one hand on the side of my headrest and the other on the wheel, he manoeuvres the Jaguar into the space on his first attempt, with no help from the car's built-in parking aids. It's a skill that would have Simon Cowell banging his Golden Buzzer on *America's Got Talent*.

I close the car door and hook the handle on my wicker basket over my arm. When I hold out Bacon's lead, Cal hesitates.

'Jo, can we lose the dog bandanna first?'

'It's not a fashion accessory; it's her cooling collar.'

'That is disguised as a bad bandanna.'

'She likes it,' I tell him.

'Are those her exact words?'

I give him his options. 'The dog or the basket.'

Since the market is busy today, Bacon doesn't mind Cal carrying her. But before long, he can't move without some stranger's hands tickling behind her velvety ears. It's plain to see she is in her element.

And she's not the only one.

With my precariously balanced strawberry and blueberry punnets, I politely squeeze my way through the people who are waiting to make their fruit purchases. I thought my wingman was just behind me with the basket, which he also insisted on carrying. Instead, he's beyond the fruit fanciers with a crowd of his own. It's a veritable pussy party. They're all stroking Bacon and wishing it was the muscled arm holding my dog they could stroke instead. Either Cal is enjoying the inadvertent attention, or some of those women are stroking something else.

'Sorry if I'm cramping your style,' I say, my presence breaking up the breast bash. 'Maybe I should carry the basket.'

'No, I've got it.'

The bread stall also has a crowd, but the owner spots me. Marjorie exits by the side entrance, holding a cloth bag aloft.

'A cranberry and walnut loaf, a seeded wholemeal and four baguettes,' she reels off, checking the bag's contents. 'Oh, and a mixture of scones. You wanted a mix, right?'

'As long as there's a chocolate and pecan one.'

She smiles. '*Two* chocolate and pecan.'

'Yes!'

'And a lemon and cranberry one.'

'A close second,' I declare.

'And a new one for you to try for me: blackberry and coconut.'

'That, Marjorie, is summer in a bloody scone.'

'Try it and text me what you think.'

'Don't I always?'

'I've put you in a focaccia as well,' she informs me, swapping the bag for payment. I wave aside her habitual attempts to give me my change. Nowadays, she never charges me enough. 'Tomato and rosemary.'

'That won't make it to teatime.'

She walks towards Cal, who has to adjust his hold on the excited puppy in his arms. The way Bacon gently nips the first bone-shaped banana and honey bread snack from Marjorie's fingers, you'd think she hadn't eaten in a week.

'I can't forget my favourite customer now, can I?' she says, the second and third treats quickly following the first.

I don't need to follow her eye line.

'Marjorie, this is Cal.'

'Hello. Are you Jo's new fella?'

'No, I'm a—'

'He's just a colleague.' I try to see over the array of summer hats. 'Is Tony here today?'

'He is, but you'd better hurry. His pies and rolls are flying out.'

I take Cal's elbow. 'Thanks, Marjorie. See you later.'

'Don't forget to text me.'

'I won't.'

Before we get to Tony, I have items to collect from three other stalls. Therefore, I know I'll have three other stallholders to correct.

Annabel says she always thought I was keeping quiet about having a husband. I pay for a jar of orange blossom honey, some soap and a beeswax lotion bar (which I've ordered in bulk for Christmas presents) before telling her I'm not married and, no, this man isn't in the running for the role.

Hattie is next, someone who has expanded my dairy palate beyond brie at her wine and cheese evenings in her beautiful home in Keswick. This afternoon, she supplies me with some sharp white cheddar and a delicious blue cheese that will pair nicely with the honey.

'Would you like to try a sample?' she asks Cal.

'Sure.'

Yes, his arms are full. But why are they both looking at me?

I hold the very edge of the gluten-free cracker, ready to drop it as soon as it's far enough in his mouth.

Please don't look me in the eye, Cal. Please don't look—

He doesn't.

'That's good,' he says.

'You've kept quiet about him, Jo,' Hattie remarks. 'How long have you two been together?'

'Professionally, eight years.' I select a sample of mature cheddar. 'Personally, when life becomes fair.'

The Kiwi chap at the next stall fills my reusable bag with a selection of salad and seasonal vegetables, all grown in his polytunnels and organic field.

'How was the soup?' he asks.

'It was the best I've made so far, Mick.'

Yes, he's speaking in English, not Māori; however, the way Cal looks at me…

'I make vegetable soup from scratch now,' I explain. '*And* I bought a saucepan.'

'Have you not tried any yet?' Mick asks him.

Cal raises his eyebrows. 'No. No, I… No, not… not yet.'

'Mate, when your girlfriend makes you a great bowl of soup—'

'I'm not his girlfriend, Mick,' I am quick to point out.

'Well, once he tries your soup—'

'I still won't be. Thanks again. See you next week.'

The deli stall holder makes a show of looking at his watch when we get there.

'A bear attacked the car,' I offer.

Nope.

'I forgot to put my clocks back.'

A weary sigh escapes him as he picks up a white box and some tongs, flipping the lid open and waiting.

'The road was washed away.'

Tony looks at the man standing behind me. 'You need to be both impressed and worried about how quickly your better half can summon up excuses.'

I scan what's on offer today in the display unit. 'I'll have those last two pork and chorizo sausage rolls, please, and a corned beef and potato slice. No, make that two; they're marriage material. And… two little spinach and mushroom quiches.'

'Anything else?'

'Just one other thing: his better half and mine don't make a whole.'

As we exchange the warm box for payment, I refuse to acknowledge Tony's wink and nod towards the one who only gets paid if I write. And by next week, I'm hoping to have forgotten them, too.

***

I'm sweeping up the sawdust remnants in the main bedroom when I get a text from Nyx's mum, asking whether I'd like to have lunch with her tomorrow at one. Lunch, not a drink. Oh, hell. One o'clock, as well. That would give me only seven hours to make myself look as good as…

Who am I kidding?

Izzie's voice floats up through the bedroom's open French doors. 'What are your plans tonight, Nyx? Jo and I are dining out if you'd like to join us.'

'I wish I could, but I have something on tonight.'

'First Cal tosses us off,' she remarks, 'and now you.'

I don't care why Cal has tossed us off. He can toss off too. Maybe that's his problem: he doesn't—

'You're doing something that will be more

exciting than the company of two extraordinary and beautiful women?' Izzie playfully asks him.

'Oh, not even close.'

'What is it, then?'

'It's just... stuff I do with the family.'

'What kind of stuff?' she presses.

'Boring stuff, really.'

I move onto the stairs with my dustpan and brush, leaving Izzie to her free wheedling and Nyx to his artful dodging.

***

It's four o'clock and a slightly earlier finish for everyone today. I'm checking that everything is turned off upstairs for the second time, as I usually do. Basin taps, in particular.

'Mum says she's disappointed you can't make lunch tomorrow.'

Where did Nyx spring from?

'I'd already made plans with Izzie.' Admittedly, it was fifteen minutes *after* I got Maria's text. Close enough, though. 'But when we eventually do, I doubt you'll crop up in the conversation.'

'If I don't, I'll be having words.' Nyx smiles as he gently adjusts one side of my collar. 'I'm busy tonight and tomorrow night, but I'm free after one on Sunday if you fancy doing something?'

'Ooh, you're "busy" on a Friday night *and* a Saturday night.' I perform a slow wink. 'Please tell me it's because you have a hot date on at least one of them?'

Nyx's dimples disappear. 'Why would you say that?'

'I'm teasing you.' Laughing, I gently touch my fist to his chin. 'Friends can do that, can't they?'

'It's just family stuff, Jo, that's all. I promise.'

'Okey-dokes.' I fidget with the towel on the rail and swipe a finger over a tile. I then check to see if the taps are still turned off. Yes, I know they were checked only moments ago. 'I think we're done up here, aren't we…?'

But Nyx is blocking the doorway to the en suite.

'How's the sunburn?'

'Hm? Oh, that. Yeah, it's still tender, but it's fine.'

'Let me see.'

I turn my back to him so he can pull the neck of my T-shirt open. I jump a little when his fingers brush the loose strands of hair aside.

'How's it looking?' I ask.

'Better.' Nyx's head is *very* close to mine. 'Remember to put on more of that cream.'

'Yes, doctor.'

He is between me and the door. I can either stay where I am or turn to face him. But I don't have to turn round.

'I'm sorry I can't be there again tonight to look after you,' Nyx tells my reflection. He lets go of my T-shirt but doesn't move back. People stand only fractionally further away on the underground during rush hour. 'I wish I could be.'

'That's okay,' I quickly say. 'I'm a big girl all the women who are independent and all that I have very flexible arms just call me Miss Tickle well we'd better be off need to get Bacon some dinner have some editing to do later meeting Izzie for tea looking forward to watching that documentary on Channel Four at ten about bubble wrap...'

And I'm still babbling as I skirt past, keeping my back to him the whole time. Out on the landing, I'm still talking, still not dishing out any commas. Not even when I forget where I'm going and have to double back.

No, not even when I dodge the literary agent standing on the fifth step down.

Chapter Twenty-Three

If I invited you over for dinner and said it was 'just chicken', you would get some pre-cooked, pre-sliced organic white meat from Tony, served on Marjorie's seeded split tin. Oh, and a handful of salad leaves from Mick if you needed to make up the numbers on your five a day. Then it would be *bon appétit.*

I feel that 'just chicken' for Maria will be like the royal household describing the monarch's birthday celebrations as 'just a small gathering'. Don't tell me this woman ever needs to travel via a man's gullet to get to his heart. If I looked like her, I'd simply employ the services of Heinz and Hovis.

Speaking of gullets, when Nyx shows Izzie and me through to their tidy, comfortable lounge, one is already there, standing next to the unlit fire.

I observe Cal's relaxed attire. 'You look very...' Sorry, I do what with words for a living?

Until my agent showed up at my house and volunteered to wield a spirit level, I hadn't seen him in anything that didn't include the word 'tailored'. He even endures a twelve-hour flight in a shirt. He usually carries two in his hand luggage, changing them during the flight and again before we land. You'll see me on planes in breathable fabrics and elasticated waists; then you'll see him, always hot off the professional steam press.

Come to think of it, I'd quite like to see the inside of Cal's walk-in closet. Oh, he'll have a walk-in, without a doubt. Shirts in safe shades – no patterns or stripes – ranging from light to dark, left to right, with three-finger widths between each hanger. Shirts, jackets and waistcoats will be on the top rail, with trousers on the bottom. He'll have a wall of conservative ties and a staggered array of tilted shelves for his footwear.

Cal has good taste in shoes: he loves Paolo Scafora and Gucci. And Armani. Who, I've learnt this evening, makes his jeans of choice. As well as flannel shirts in a check pattern.

Maria walks through, her dark hair Niagara falling in waves about her shoulders. This evening, those terrifyingly perfect boobs are concealed behind the high neckline of a magenta shift dress, one that highlights her curves to bloody perfection. I try not to imagine how I must look standing next to her, wearing a long, loose, bohemian-style dress with lantern sleeves. I couldn't compete, so…

Izzie admires our hostess. 'Maria, look at you!'

'You are stunning,' I say to her with…

Fuck me. Was it… with *difficulty*? But why? When any woman looks stunning, they deserve to hear it. Why should she be any different?

Maria breaks eye contact with Cal when she gently squeezes our shoulders and fibs about the age of her dress. I'll bet the price tag is upstairs.

'I hope you're all hungry,' she warns.

We didn't need a heads-up. When Nyx put those last two dishes down, the ominous creak from the table said it all.

'Ravenous,' Cal declares.

As I've already mentioned, he and I don't 'share'. I don't know whether he prefers boxers to briefs. Nor do I know if he puts flat-pack furniture together without consulting the instructions. I also couldn't give a monkey's hairy nut whether he kisses his *mom* on the lips or the cheek. Nevertheless, I know Cal's eating habits well. It's a skill I've perfected from sitting opposite him for three meals a day in many time zones. In fact, if we were to appear on *All Star Mr & Mrs* and the questions were purely food-related, we would be in the final and playing for the jackpot prize.

However, in all this time, I've never heard Cal say he's ravenous. He usually eats with one hand and emails with the other. I'm then forced to read another few pages of my book while waiting for him to finish what has congealed on his plate.

Which makes me wonder this evening what he has a ravenous appetite for.

Maria's food both smells and looks great. I could happily belly-flop into every steaming bowl and munch my way out. I'd love to paddle in her rich gravy, astride her fluffy Yorkshire puddings. It is

Carb Canaveral at its finest. One heaped plate of cellulite is coming right up!

Unless you're Cal, of course, who enjoys punishing himself mainly with a carb/sugar/dairy-free lifestyle. It's not because his body reacts badly to them. No, I believe it's because he doesn't wank enough.

I must work with a man who hasn't touched gluten in all the years I've known him. I don't imagine any slices of gorgeous white bread and butter have ever made a ménage à trois with his turkey bacon. Not since texting became the most popular form of mobile communication.

Over the breakfast table in countless hotels, Cal has seen me devour pancakes like a blue whale. In return, I've had to listen to him order cauliflower, green beans, spinach and broccoli mixed with egg whites and fried in coconut oil. If I ate that, I'd be farting for gold at the Olympics.

Maria has seated him beside me, thinking I must know him best. Perhaps I do, in the loosest sense of the word. With Maria sitting opposite Cal, I'm stuck with Izzie and her wayward eyebrows in front of me. Nyx is on my right, at the head of the table. All the kids are staying with grandparents and boyfriends tonight.

'Please, tuck in,' Maria orders.

Dishes are lifted and passed around the table like business cards in The Shard.

'Oh, not for me, thanks,' I say to Nyx, just before he lands a spoonful of butter beans on my plate. If nobody else was here, it would have been, 'If those nasty buggers touch down, you'll have three Adam's apples.'

Cal serves me the white chicken meat, taking some dark for himself. I dish out his-and-hers broccoli and carrots before plopping some creamy mashed potato onto my plate, but not Cal's. I'm about to pass the bowl to Izzie when he intercepts it. Our eyes briefly meet as he takes a giant spoonful of mash and drops it next to his...

Wait a minute – he has taken *three* Yorkshire puddings?

'Right then, Cal,' Maria starts. 'Tell us about yourself.'

'Well, my parents settled in Ann Arbor after they graduated from the city's University of Michigan. That's where my two younger sisters and I were born...'

All eyes are on Cal as he gets us up to speed on his personal history. Yes, all. I look down at my plate of happiness. I shouldn't be making it apparent that this is all news to me, too.

'... I grew up in Boston, though, and went to college there. Then I received a job offer in New York, thanks to my dad. He put in a good word.'

'What does he do for a living?'

Maria needs to be careful fluttering those eyelashes when she asks Cal a question – she might knock him off his chair.

'My dad... owns a publishing company,' he answers. 'Among other things.'

My fork drops with a clatter when I cough, my hand covering my mouth. Then I don't know what's worse. Is it having two men pat me on the back or my unattractive sputtering?

No, I think it's the piece of broccoli I spat out that may have landed in the bowl of peas.

'Are you all right?' echoes around the table.

I nod behind my glass of water, the one I snatched off Cal before he held it to my lips.

'How did you and Jo meet?' Nyx asks him.

'Around eight years ago, I requested a transfer to the London office.'

Maria flicks her hair back. 'And did you two hit it off straight away?'

'Do you really want to know?'

Maria sits forward. 'I do.'

'Oh yeah,' encourages Nyx.

Personally, all *I* want to know is whether anyone here can loan me two cheerleader pompoms. Then I can give him an 'N' and an 'O'.

'I'd like to hear it again,' says Izzie.

Again? When did she...?

My aunt ignores my glare.

'Do you *really* want to know?'

Why is Cal playing with them? I thought the only teasing he might do involved a comb and his hair after a rough night's sleep.

I need to intervene. 'Cal, is that your phone ringing in the hall—?'

'I landed in the country two hours before we were due to meet...'

I wish I hadn't been for a wee only five minutes ago.

'… and I arrived at the company's drinks party jet-lagged and hungry; therefore, I was grumpy as hell. And everyone kept telling me about this woman with an amazing voice. Then I heard her. I turned around, and there she was with that… incredible smile of hers, wearing a trouser suit and a gray T-shirt with a photo of Jupiter on it. Finally, we were introduced, and I just wanted everyone to shut up and let her do the talking.'

I force myself to reduce the grip on my knife and fork. It isn't easy.

'Sadly, I know Jo's first impressions of me were less favorable,' Cal recalls. 'Like I said, I wasn't in the greatest of moods – plus this face will never be asked to read a bedtime story on *CBeebies*.'

There are polite protests and titters from *most* of the people at the table.

'Despite that, it was the start of something amazing.'

'*Work* amazing,' I clarify.

I don't know how I get those words out. Truth be told, after that revelation, I'm shocked that my focus isn't on how *I* get out.

'And I can't imagine loving my job as much as I do if it wasn't for her,' Cal adds.

They're all smiling. I sense everyone would like a response from me.

'Maria, this mashed potato is worthy of a George Cross.'

'Thanks, Jo.'

'Are you married or seeing anyone?' Nyx asks him – obviously on someone else's behalf.

'I was married once, a long time ago. I'm currently single.'

'Any children?' Maria checks.

'No. Which is one reason I'm divorced.'

She glances at her lap. It's probably to see what's next on her list of questions. 'How old are you, if you don't mind my asking?'

Cal picks up his wineglass. 'I'm forty-four. I'm a week younger than Jo, actually.'

Izzie looks puzzled. 'I thought you were twenty-two, Bee.'

'He must be talking about another Jo,' I utter.

Maria rests her chin on her hand. 'Do you ever celebrate your birthdays together?'

'No.' My quick response hopefully doesn't sound like I omitted the word 'hell' at the start – and 400 exclamation marks at the end.

After that, it is easy chatter, warm laughter, and humorous anecdotes for the rest of the meal. For the rest of the evening, in fact.

Well, it is for everyone else.

For me, it is hours of fucking torture.

I don't think I have *ever* been this angry with anyone. I just want to... to get away from him. Or rather this, this... other side to him. A side that I wasn't introduced to eight years ago.

Eight years.

Too little too late, anyone?

***

'Interesting.'

It's never a good thing when a former thoughts inspector says that. 'Ooh, how so?' most might ask. Not me. I'm happy walking Izzie back to her hotel in relative silence. Maybe I'll remark on the stars. Or I'll say something when I spot Elliot Eight-Pints slurring his texts.

I dig my hand into my cardigan pocket and pull out a bit of fluff. 'Did you know this stuff has a name?'

'Cal.'

'No, it's called gnurr,' I educate.

'And you.'

'Gnurr.'

'Eight years.'

'It sounds like the noise a bear would make when he's unsure whether you're a threat. Gnurr,' I growl.

'And during all that time, Bee, have you two ever…?'

I return Izzie's curious look. Genuinely, I don't know the ending to that question. Ever fought over the last oxygen mask? Ever shared the bathwater? Ever – I don't know – shown up to an event in the same dress?

She waggles her eyebrows. '… done a little mattress dancing?'

'Christ the Lord and heavens above, no!'

'Doth my niece protest too much?'

'Until he clocked Maria, I had no idea whether he bumped uglies with Waynes or Jaynes.'

Izzie stops and gawps at me. 'You have worked together for *eight years.*'

'Worked,' I emphasise.

'How can you work with someone for that long and not know this about them?'

I shrug. 'Why would I need to know whether Cal owns a Cher album?'

She has that expression I use when someone starts a sentence with 'If I were you...'.

'We work on books, Izzie, not on *Loose Women*.'

'But he oozes sex appeal.'

'Are we still talking about Cal?' I ask.

'Yes! With those vivid blue eyes and smouldering looks and his rugged handsomeness. *Very* Steve McQueen.'

I sniff. 'I always preferred Paul Newman.'

'Not me – give me a bad boy *every* time. I want adventure and turbulence, not ruddy... politeness and predictability.'

'Unless you're getting on a plane.'

'Cal is mysterious in a sort of...'

'... "they'll never find out where the body is buried" way?' I finish for her.

'Speaking of bodies, he has the loveliest bum.' Izzie puckers her lips and makes vertical saucer shapes with her hands. 'The nicest one I've seen in a long time.'

'I'll take your word for it.'

'Oh, come on. You must have noticed it – and in those jeans.' She blows a chef's kiss off the tips of her fingers.

'Regarding anything below Cal's waist, I like to imagine a Ken doll.'

'Why?'

'We have a very harmonious working relationship.'

'That doesn't stop you from enjoying the view,' Izzie argues.

'Yes, it does, because when you're lusting over things like your agent's... I don't know, his... prominent arm veins—'

She grabs my arm. 'You noticed those too?'

'Are we certain about who wanted to go down on him tonight if there hadn't been a roomful of people?'

'Are you referring to Maria?'

'No, Izzie. Catherine the Great.'

'I think she just appreciates a good-looking man as much as the next woman.'

'Yeah,' I say with a snigger. 'That level of appreciation should come with an arrest warrant.'

We are on Lake Road now, passing down the hill and the small gathering of shops. One of them has a sale on women's walking trousers. We stop outside and look through the window.

'How, erm... How did you know?' I ask. 'That... Cal likes...?'

'Pussy? Bee, it's blatantly obvious.'

'To those who are raving in the rafters, maybe.'

'It was after one of your book readings last year,' Izzie reveals. 'We were enjoying a cosy chat when he mentioned some exes.'

'*Some* exes?'

'Only the serious ones.'

Ooh, their quick-drying leggings have twenty per

cent off. Some water-resistant trousers are on offer too.

I point at a rail. 'I knew those bloody navy trekking leggings wouldn't be in the sale. How many did he say were serious?'

'Let me think.'

Three. Yeah, I'm going for three, tops.

No, two.

No, three.

Izzie finally stops counting in her head. 'I think he said there were seven.'

'*Seven*?' My voice suddenly has a high pitch. 'Cal has had *seven* serious relationships?'

'That's what he said.'

'He is *my* age, which means in roughly twenty-eight years of dating, that's… one every four years.'

'Most of them only lasted about two years.'

A thought hits me. 'He's probably had a couple while we've been together.'

Izzie tucks a loose curl of mine behind my ear. 'Do you feel you've been cheated on?'

'Don't be absurd. No, all I feel is the need for speed. Now move it!'

I wait until we've passed two more shops. Well, almost.

'So… what else did you and him talk about?'

'Oh, you know, the usual: mistakes, aspirations, love.'

I quirk an eyebrow. 'Were the two of you listening to Bob Dylan at the time and draped in matching tie-dye?'

Her arm links through mine, which I allow this once. 'Cal has reached that interesting age, and he's getting—'

'Are you sure it was seven, Izzie?'

'Ask him.'

I wave such a ridiculous suggestion away.

'You know, Bee, it might help if you took some time to get to know him.'

'Why? Would it increase my book sales?'

Izzie's hand on my arm stops our steady pace. 'If you did, you might be surprised.'

I spot the turquoise band ring on her third finger. It was bought at a craft fair in Haworth; it was the one where I got mine.

'As surprised as I am by bookshop assistants who *tell* people where the self-help books are?' I ask. 'Surely the whole point of a self-help book is for them to find it... What?' I watch Izzie stride ahead. 'What did I say?'

Chapter Twenty-Four

Bacon hears Izzie approaching before I do. A sleek bob and Jackie O sunglasses soon appear among the tourists heading in our direction to catch the Windermere ferry to the western shore. She is in her pristine leggings and sports top today. Are they pristine because she takes good care of them? Or is it because Santa's ab machine gets more use?

My aunt must stop and grab hold of a bronzed arm when she laughs. Whatever her companion said, I doubt it was that funny. I don't doubt she lost a bit of wee, though.

When they are close, I let go of the dog's lead. Bacon gives her a cursory greeting before wriggling around the third wheel.

Izzie frowns at my one-legged stance. 'What's all this?'

I switch legs and hold the other foot behind me. 'I'm just warming up.'

'What for?'

'Next year's Country Music Awards.'

'It's important to stretch before exercising, Izzie,'

Cal eventually says. He's struggling to avoid the little tongue that's trying its utmost to get between his lips.

My look hopefully conveys my lack of appreciation for his words of wisdom. It's almost equal to how I feel about him gate-crashing our walk.

'He called in for a coffee after his run,' Izzie explains, stroking his shoulder. 'How far had you been?'

'I'm not sure.'

Bollocks. Cal will have a chart, a calorie count, a stopwatch, a pedometer *and* a personal chuffing best.

'I told him I was just on my way out for a gentle stroll with my lovely niece, and if he wasn't too bushed, he was welcome to join us.'

I aim my question at Bacon's sparkly new collar. 'Haven't you done enough exercise for one day?'

Cal gives her belly and back the scratchy attention she believes they deserve. 'Can you ever do enough?' is his response.

My acid tongue is gearing up to melt the nearby ice-cream van's wares.

'The way they talk nowadays,' Izzie jumps in with, 'I think they're trying to encourage us oldies to kill ourselves with exercise rather than live longer.'

Over the next few hours, *I* could be the one who does the encouraging.

There are four things my aunt doesn't like. Top of the list are coffeehouses that don't offer full-fat milk. A close second are people who insist on a window seat on a plane and close the blinds. The colour pink in any shade really gets on her pre-paid tits. And—

'I'm not doing any hills.'

'There are no hills,' I assure her.

'Do you promise?'

My open arms ask whether I would lie.

Izzie snatches the lilac pamphlet off me and holds it at arm's length – she's wearing prescription sunglasses that are only good for distance. No, she won't have bifocals. Nor will she buy face cream for 'mature' skin. Or wear jeans with a comfy waistband.

'I can't fucking read that,' she snaps. 'But that looks like a hill.'

'It's not a hill.'

'If it's a hill, you know I won't be happy.'

'It's not a hill.'

***

Cal and I stop again, looking down the trail we've just climbed. Izzie is searching for oxygen in the trickling streams crossing the pathway and between the cracks in the mossy walls. Aided by the tiny wannabe husky, she can only take a few steps at a time before having to stop – and it's not just to award us a new version of her withering look.

We've already waited several times for her to catch us up. We have to; we need her presence. Fine, *I* need it. While my relationship with Cal happily erred on the side of purely work-based caution, we never suffered from silences of the uncomfortable kind. That is, until today.

Izzie's puffing and panting are way ahead of her. 'You said… there were… no hills,' she shouts up to us.

'Technically, I think Claife Heights is a Marilyn,' I shout back, 'as it's a hill with a prominence of over 150 metres.'

'That just... makes it a... hill with a... thing for... *presidents*.' I get the finger. No, not the middle one. '*You* said... no hills!'

'And *you* told your doctor that you hike with your niece three times a week.'

Izzie stops again and points at the spot where she might very well die. 'This... will count as... a month's worth... of hikes.'

'You're doing great, Izzie,' Cal applauds.

My response is to perform the world's finest eyeroll.

When Izzie tries to smile for him again, it looks even more like she has indigestion. She abandons another attempt and returns her attention to the ankle-twisting pathway.

'Jo?' says a grating voice to my left.

With my eyes fixed on my aunt, I force out an aggressive, 'Yes?'

'Have I done something to upset you?'

Finally!

I'm sure the look I give Cal would ordinarily be enough. 'What the *fuck* was all that about last night?'

He takes my arm and pulls me to the side, out of Izzie's line of sight. 'All what?'

'Oh, when Jo and I met, her incredible voice almost made me come in my pants.' I don't care if my American accent is way off. If he laughs, he'll be swallowing one of his bollocks. 'Her smile dazzled the *ass* off of me.'

Cal looks confused. 'That's not *quite* what I said.'

I have an issue with pointing fingers at people; it's rude and off-putting. But one of mine is suddenly in his face. 'That wasn't the impression you've led *me* to believe all these years.'

'If you recall, Jo, you hardly welcomed me with open arms.'

'When we were introduced, you looked at me like the agency had asked you to lick dog piss off a tree.'

'I was jet-lagged,' Cal says.

'No, you were disappointed!'

'*What*?'

'Don't… give me that face. You got lumbered with me.'

'Oh my God!' He shakes his head. 'You've believed that all this time, haven't you?'

I aim my words at the mossy rocks over his right shoulder. 'You never wanted me, Cal, and *that's* why you're impossible to impress.'

'You don't have to impress me.'

'But if I can't impress my fucking agent, what chance—?'

'Oh, I'm your fucking agent now, am I?' His eyebrows shoot up. 'I'm not your "co-worker"? We're not "editors-in-arms"?'

'You *know* that I rarely tell anyone straight away what I do for a living.'

'Yes, and I also know when you *will*. Usually, it's when anyone gets too close, right?' Cal's grip on my arm stops me from turning away from him. 'Do you want to tell me what's truly bothering you, Jo?'

'I just have!'

'Really?'

I recognise his expression. It's the same one I modelled after Ma said my sisters 'couldn't wait to see' what I planned to wear to the BAFTA Film Awards.

'So it has nothing to do with my finding Maria attractive?' Cal enquires.

'Why the hell would I care who you fancy?'

'I didn't say I fancied her.'

'By the way, I don't know how long it's been since you last fancied somebody…'

'I *don't* fancy her.'

'… but my tip would be, don't be so *bloody* obvious.' Miming Cal's angry resting face, I pretend to dollop spoon after spoon of mashed potato onto a plate.

'Oh, do you think I should play it cool?' he asks. 'Like you're doing with Maria's son?'

I glower at him. 'Nyx is just a friend.'

'Bullshit!'

'*Nothing* is going on between us.'

'Does he know that?'

'Of course he—Wait, who I'm friends with is none of your business.'

'Let's drop it then, shall we?'

'Good idea!' I quickly turn away from him, but only for a second. Damn, I almost pulled it off. 'And why have you never told me your dad owns a sodding publishing company?'

Cal shrugs. 'It's not one of your publishers.'

'Oh, but you decided last night was a great time to suddenly mention it?'

He leans forward. 'I was doing you a *favor*.'

'Me? Finally discovering the dusty button that switches on Mr Chatty was doing *me* a favour?'

'Yes. Because if I hadn't gone on about *my* family most of the night, then Maria might have asked you about *yours*.'

The sound of someone gasping for breath means Izzie has reached us. Either that or an asthmatic has lost their inhaler.

'I... fucking... made it!'

'Well done,' I say from one side of the pathway.

'Great going, Izzie,' Cal says from the other side, clapping loudly.

I love Americans. But right now, I wish one of them would take his sneakers, his fanny pack, and his panties and go 'shoot the breeze' somewhere else.

Izzie's cheer may be a few minutes away, as she must fit her lungs back in first. She flops against a boulder. 'How much...?'

'We're nearly there,' I assure her.

'You've fucking... said that... five fucking... times now.'

'If I'd said we weren't close, you would've turned back.'

'Too... fucking right.' She frowns at us. 'How is it... you two... aren't even... puffing?'

'It's because I do actually hike,' I explain. 'And

271

he…'

He, what? I don't know any more. I don't care.

I've never cared.

Izzie points up the track. 'Go all the way… to the top and… let me know… really… how far.'

'We'll go up and come back down for you,' Cal offers.

'Stop fucking… showing off… unless you're… taking me… to bed.'

I tuck my water bottle away.

'I bet I can beat you,' he says, as though we hadn't swapped heated words moments ago.

'Without a doubt,' I utter with the heftiest pile of shit I don't give.

'You're not going to challenge me?'

'Sorry, I gave up competitive sports when scrunchies were fashionable.'

I watch Izzie reach into Cal's back pocket and ease out the corner of his wallet. When his hand gets there a second too late, it falls out and bounces a short distance down the pathway.

Don't ask me why, but I'm suddenly springing up that path as if there's money riding on the outcome. I keep my eyes on the hazards that oaks and birches have thrown across the pathway, bending forward and using my hands where possible to aid my ascent.

Cal's fingers brush against the back of my boot. He was clearly going to catch me up. Yes, we were both born in the decade when Spielberg made everyone afraid to swim in the ocean, but my form of exercise is walking, whereas his is painful.

I'm slowed down when he grabs the back of my T-shirt by the hem. I dig my toes in, leaning forward, my top stretching. The finish line is almost within my reach. One tug, though, and I'm falling backwards, with one of Cal's arms encircling my ribs and the other behind my knees.

Before I know it, I go from being lifted off my feet to being dangled over the edge at the top of the pathway. The abundance of bracken below might cushion a drop, but not by much.

'You wouldn't dare, Cal!'

'Oh, wouldn't I?'

When he suddenly bends his knees, I experience a brief feeling of weightlessness. I scream, and instinct makes me clutch his neck.

'Please don't,' I beg with a giggling whimper.

'I'm sorry I never told you.'

My nervous laughter trails off. 'It's okay. Maybe I should've... I could've asked what your parents did. It's not like... It's not like there's never been an opportunity.'

'Can we be more than just colleagues, Jo?'

I don't know what pulls me up the most: the gentleness of Cal's voice or the unexpected request. I'm only glad he's the one doing the holding; otherwise, he'd be plucking bramble bush thorns out of his arse tonight.

'Can we try to be friends?' he asks.

Oh, Cal wants to be *friends*. That's a relief! It is a relief. Isn't it? Yeah. Yes, of course it is.

But we're not talking about being friends *again*.

We're not making up after a falling out. We've never been friends. I always thought we were more than that – better than that.

'We can try it,' I whisper. 'The… friends thing. We can try being friends.'

A whiff of a smile reaches up to Cal's eyes. I knew their colour before Izzie gushed about them: a piercing cobalt gaze on a stormy afternoon face. When the agency's managing director introduced us that day, it was the first thing I noticed about him. His look of blatant irritation was a very close second.

Or so I'd always been led to believe.

But only with nowhere to run can I study the striking streaks of gold shooting through his blue irises. Yes, our faces are that close. Cal must be able to smell my cherry lip gloss. Hell, if he stuck out his tongue, he would taste it. If the thought had crossed his mind at any point.

Not that I think for a moment that he would want to. He doesn't want to, and I don't want him to. I've never wanted him to. Why would I? I mean, why would I?

'Ahem.'

Izzie is sitting on a tree stump a few feet away, casually sipping from her water bottle. She lets go of Bacon's lead, but we can't fuss over the little dog when she jumps up at his knees.

'You can… put me down now if you… if you like,' I suggest.

'Right.'

Bacon parks her bum and expresses her

impatience.

Izzie smiles. 'Whenever you're ready, Cal.'

He blinks. 'Yes. Sorry.'

Chapter Twenty-Five

When I answer my rented front door, I find Nyx holding two bulging carrier bags aloft.

'What do you have there?' I ask. 'Meals on Wheels?'

He wipes his feet on the doormat. 'This evening, we are cooking.'

After we've worked at the house together, this isn't how it ever pans out when Nyx comes over. Usually, I fan the leaflets that make up two-thirds of my post and ask him to pick a takeaway menu, any menu.

'I hope this "we" are you and your multiple personalities,' I say.

Nyx takes the apron I bought at the farmers' market off the hook on the back of the kitchen door. 'Nope.'

When he slips both arms about my waist to tie it up, I allow my disgruntlement to be heard. Over his shoulder, I read all the notes scribbled on the chalkboard.

From one bag, Nyx removes various cooking

vessels. I watch as he takes out mainly perishable items from the other one, including a tray of chicken portions.

I lean as far back as I can from them. 'They are *raw*.'

'Please tell me you've cooked chicken at least once.'

I'm offended that he needs to ask me this. 'Yes.'

'Cook it. Not warm it up in a ready meal.'

I'm offended that he needs to ask me this. 'No.'

The look Nyx gives me is one of disbelief. I, however, feel no shame. He punishes me by stealing my bag of honey-roasted nuts.

'These will spoil your dinner,' he says.

'They will if it's going to be ready in five minutes. If it'll take more than half an hour, I'm off out and leaving you to it – *and* I'm taking the nuts.'

As I lack both enthusiasm and skill, I get vegetable duty.

'I know you like your PlayStation,' I remark while Nyx browns the chicken. 'And you enjoy drawing. But is there anything else you like doing when I'm not monopolising you?'

'Well, that doesn't leave much time, if I'm honest.' Nyx ignores my idle threat with the knife. 'Nothing wild, I'm afraid: a pint with the lads, imagining more ways I can get you to monopolise me…'

I put my fist to my heart and then point at him.

'I enjoy reading,' he confesses hesitantly. 'I enjoy reading a lot, actually.'

'You've kept that quiet.'

'Only because you're trying to take a break from books.'

'I had my suspicions,' I admit. 'People who love reading don't use the word "like" as a sentence filler. Or unnecessary upward inflexions at the ends of their sentences.'

Nyx chuckles. 'Do those things annoy you, too?'

'They pip to the post those who can't tell the time on an analogue clock.'

I check that my mushroom quartering meets his standards.

'What genres do you like, then?' I ask.

'My favourite is easily fantasy: the likes of K. Fillingham and Terry Pratchett. I also really love George R.R. Martin and N.R. Magnusson.'

I swear I haven't paid him to say that.

'I love escapism, even at my age.' Nyx moves his eyebrows close together. 'Should I be telling you that?'

'You're confessing this to the right person. I once beat the January blues by rereading Fillingham's *The Chronicles of Imoricus Wibb* books. All ten of them.'

'Those books are amazing. They're almost as good as the *Caerli°°ani* stories.'

Did Nyx back that up by giving all three of them five stars on Amazon? I'll never know.

'If you like those writers, you may enjoy Craig Aguirre's *Heart, Sword and Honour* books,' I tell him. 'I have them somewhere. I'll find them for you.'

'Thanks.'

'Oh, and the *Stravaiger* trilogy by Axelle Wilde. Unless you've read it already?'

'Not yet,' Nyx says.

'And Lysander Rome's *The Hopes of Vanusalla* books – I loved overdosing on those.'

He cocks his head to one side. 'I knew you liked Tolkien, as you have the most well-thumbed copy of *The Return of the King…*'

'But you didn't know I liked fantasy enough to have dog-eared pages well before the movie took all the Oscars?'

Nyx stops rotating the sizzling chicken pieces with the tongs and faces away from me. 'I don't want you to see me like this.'

'I will think no less of you for crying,' I assure him.

'Yeah, the problem's a little more southerly than that.'

To continue evenly cooking the meat, Nyx reverses.

'Don't you think N.R. Magnusson's *Caerli°°ani* stories are even better than the original *Waenaga* tales by Quinn Manning?' he asks.

'You know they're not sequels, don't you?'

'Oh yeah. But some characters have crossed over into them from Manning's books. Why do you think that is?'

'Maybe because some of them hadn't been explored thoroughly enough by their original author.'

I made that sound like a mere observation, wouldn't you agree?

Nyx nods. 'That's what I thought too. Magnusson really delves into their histories, doesn't he? Whereas I felt Manning didn't dig deep enough.'

'Quinn Manning was more in love with the world he created than the stories that lie hidden in them.' Do I sound bitter? 'That's just another theory of mine,' I add.

'No, there are plenty who think that.'

I know there are.

'Were you aware Manning used to live here?' Nyx asks.

I stop chopping. 'In Bowness?'

'No, I'm not sure exactly where, but it was in the Lake District. He based the Bewitching Woods of Ily-something…'

I hate to see anyone struggle. 'Ilyanicia.'

'That's it, on Grizedale Forest. And he used the hollow tree near Grasmere as inspiration for the entrance to Mr Cottonwill's library.'

I smile to myself. 'Did he? That's interesting.'

'You're an editor,' Nyx says, 'so you might know the answer to this one. How has Magnusson got away with using characters that someone else created? Is it because Manning died a few years back, and now anyone can use them?'

'No, the characters are usually under copyright until the author's been dead for seventy years.'

'Does that mean Manning or his estate could've sold the copyright to Magnusson?'

I shrug my shoulders. 'Perhaps.'

'Or maybe Manning left it to him in his will.'

Another shrug. 'Who knows?'

'Many fans think Magnusson might be one of his two stepsons.'

If I shrug again, Nyx will think I'm hearing music in my head. 'It's a theory.'

'One rumour I've heard,' he says, 'and one I lean towards, seeing as his stepsons aren't much older than me, is that N.R. Magnusson is Monty Harding. You know, Manning's former assistant? It makes perfect sense. He worked with him for years, typed up all his stories, helped him with research. Who else would know the characters better?'

I take another onion out of the bag. 'Do these all want chopping up?'

'Yes, please. If you can also make the pieces just a *bit* smaller.'

'Oops. Yes, chef.'

'Did you know, Jo…'

I thought I owned the rights to those three words.

'… that Magnusson is well on his way to selling more books than Manning? And he's only written three so far.'

Don't worry, the baseless pronoun Nyx uses has never made me wonder if my actions will sway the country to bring back the death penalty.

'Manning wrote… Was it five books?' he asks.

'Six.' Shit, I corrected him too quickly. 'Or it could be five.'

'Writers must make a lot of money.'

'Very, very few of them do,' I report. 'Not many can afford a lavish lifestyle just from writing.'

'That's crazy.'

'It surprises a lot of people.'

'Do any of your authors make big bucks?'

'A couple of them do quite well out of it,' I answer.

'Are we talking J.K. Rowling levels?'

'Nyx, unless you're James Patterson, who writes fourteen books a year on average, nobody is on those levels.'

'How much do you think Manning made? From the books, the films, all the merch?'

'Enough to shop at Waitrose, I should think.'

'And enough to allow his wife to give up modelling before he died,' Nyx comments. 'She's in that shitty reality series now. What's it called? *For Better or Worth*?'

'Something like that.'

'I guess when you miss the attention, it doesn't matter how much money your spouse leaves you.'

Nyx cuts the pancetta into stumpy bits before putting it into the pan he used for the chicken, along with my chopped onions and mushrooms. I start slicing up the carrots.

'Is it fantasy authors you work with?' he enquires.

'Mainly. Those and romance. But I'm ditching the latter. I'm... thinking of ditching those.'

'Now, why does that not surprise me?'

That earns Nyx a nudge to the back of his knee.

'Don't you ever think about writing books yourself, Jo?'

I restrain a smile. 'Since I've been doing the house, not as often as I did.'

'Think what it must feel like to have millions of people delving into your imagination.' Nyx spins the spatula in his hand and stares out of the window. 'It must seem surreal. A bit... exposing. But amazing, I bet.'

'After overcoming procrastination ten times per chapter, your headspace vying twenty-four-seven with witty narrative, and beating difficult middles into submission, you *want* it to feel amazing.' Crap! 'That's what my authors tell me.'

Nyx puts the browned ingredients into a casserole pot and mixes in the carrots and some flour, dropping in some fresh thyme leaves from the plant I appear to have in the courtyard. He pours a pint of stock into it a little at a time, stirring with a wooden spoon. Pour and stir. Pour and stir.

'Why did you learn to cook, Nyx?'

He laughs. 'That must be *the* maddest question ever.'

'Why?'

'Because everyone should learn. Cooking is a survival skill.'

'It also puts takeaways and ready-made meal makers out of business.'

Nyx points the spoon at me. 'Remember when I asked *why* you're single?'

'But you live with a woman who loves to cook. Look at all the hours you could have dedicated to teatime soaps and downloading music illegally and... thinking of ways to waste time.'

'If I hadn't learnt, Mum would've had to cut her

hours and rely on handouts. And I discovered early on just how proud she is.'

'Hmmm, who else is proud?' I tap my chin. 'Let me think.'

The 'who else' is grinning.

'How old were you when you learnt?' I ask.

'I was nine or ten. Mum returned to work soon after Jenna, my youngest sister, was born, and Nanna watched the baby. I asked Mum to teach me so I could help when I got home from school. Then I would give my other sisters, Xena and Megan, their baths after tea and help Nanna put them to bed.'

'That's a lot of responsibility for a young chap.'

Nyx shrugs. 'Needs must. It was never forced on me. I knew how tight money was. Mum has always been upfront about it, even when I was young, so it was just my way of contributing. When they were old enough, my sisters mucked in too.'

'How old were you when your mum and dad split up?'

'He fucked off when I was a few months old.'

'Do you have any contact with him now?'

'I've not seen or heard from him in...' Nyx is thinking hard. 'It must be seventeen years. I've seen him a grand total of three times since he left. The last I heard, he was living in Mexico. He could be dead for all I know.'

He puts the rested chicken portions into the pot and adjusts the heat to a simmer.

'Mum then met Xena and Megan's dad. He was a good bloke, but they were always fighting. Then I got home from school one day and found all his stuff in the hallway and my sisters crying on the stairs. I could hear him and Mum yelling at each other in the living room. Apparently, the girls had to be held back so he could leave.

'Then she got pregnant by this married bloke she was working for,' Nyx continues. 'He moved in with us for a few months. His wife and sons lived two streets away. When Mum was about seven months pregnant, he said he missed his proper family. His wife only agreed to take him back if they moved away. They packed up and left before Jenna was born. He makes his payments, though, and sends her money every birthday. Then it was us five on our own for a few years.'

'Then she met the twins' dad?'

Nyx smiles. 'Yeah, *she* met him – we never did – and to this day, she won't let on who the father is.'

'You've basically been the man of the house for over half your life, then?'

'I guess so.'

'That's a lot to take on.'

'I've never known any different,' Nyx states. 'Mum still made sure we all had brilliant childhoods – and I still did my fair share of stuff that got me grounded.'

'With that cheeky face, I bet you got away with plenty.'

His cheeky wink answers for him.

'There's something, Nyx, that doesn't quite add up.'

'How do you mean?'

'You once told me you didn't do well at school.'

'That's right.'

'Which means either you didn't turn up for your exams or you did, *but*... you didn't do well on purpose.'

Nyx gives the casserole one more slow stir, his pursed lips moving from side to side. 'Which do you think?'

'The latter. Only a compassionate person would downplay his intelligence and artistic flair to put his family first. Somebody who, perhaps, couldn't forgive the one man he regarded as a father figure for walking out on him.'

'Why would you think that?' he asks the pot he is now sliding into the oven.

'Your sisters "apparently" had to be held back when their dad left. Except you were there, too; you said you got home from school and saw your sisters on the stairs. Yet when he left, you never saw how they reacted. That suggests you didn't watch him go. Or you couldn't.'

With his arms folded and his hip resting against the kitchen unit, Nyx nods thoughtfully, chewing his lip. He turns on a well-rehearsed smile, one he has used often to get him off the hook, I'll bet.

'You listen,' he observes.

'It's not technically a superpower.'

'But about as rare as one.'

I touch his arm as I walk past. 'How long will dinner be?'

'About an hour.'

'Are you kidding me?' I scan the counters. 'Where are those sodding nuts?'

**

Following an intense game of Trivial Pursuit, we tuck into the world's best chicken casserole, with Bacon taking care of what's left. When we're comfortably seated in the lounge afterwards, she's forced to lie on her back in the crook of my arm.

I sigh, patting my belly. 'Nyx, this is why I agreed to marry you.'

'Well, since I have you all content and – hopefully – with your guard down…'

Uh-oh.

'… can I get you to come to my birthday bash next Sunday?'

I force a smile and mentally flick through my book of diversionary tactics at lightning speed. 'It's your birthday?'

'And Mum's. She's organised a barbecue. Just for family and close friends.'

'Mum and son share a birthday.' I put a hand over my heart. 'That's beautiful.'

'Then you'll come?'

'I'll certainly try.'

And I'm sure Nyx believes m—

'On a scale of one to ten, Jo, where does that "try" sit?'

'It sits mightily high on the try-ometer.'

'How high?'

'It's promising.'

He's waiting.

'Can I text you the number later tonight?'

'No.'

'Okay.' I think for a second, rubbing Bacon's chin. Finally, I raise one of her paws in triumph. 'An extremely strong three.'

But my good score isn't to everyone's liking.

'Out of ten?' Nyx's brow furrows. 'A piffling three?'

'No, an *extremely strong* three.'

'It's still a three.'

'That's a bloody good score for me. I haven't given more than a two in years.'

'Jo...'

'I'm sorry, but... me and crowds? Vampires and daylight? Geminis and Scorpios?'

Nyx bats his eyelids. 'It would mean a lot to me.'

'That expression might get me to sign up for three pounds a month to save retired mayflies, but I'm not changing my score.'

'Please?'

'But I won't know anybody there except you and Colin. And your mum.'

'Cal will be there,' Nyx says.

Oh. Cal's been asked already, eh?

'Mum asked him.'

'Yeah, so?' I mumble.

'So... there'll be someone else there who you know.'

I think quickly. 'That *could* be the day I'm due a

delivery between seven a.m. and eight p.m. that needs a signature.'

'Try another excuse, Jo.'

'May I have twenty-four hours to list them all?'

Nyx sits on my armchair's footstool, his knees wide on either side of mine. 'Please?'

I rest my head back. 'I didn't sign up for this crap when I agreed to be your friend.'

He springs forward and plops a kiss on my forehead. 'But you did when you agreed to marry me.'

Chapter Twenty-Six

If Izzie could've stayed a few more days, I wouldn't be attending this sodding party unaccompanied. Yes, Cal is going. He is Maria's guest, though, something my aunt needed frequent reminders about. But yesterday morning, after heartfelt goodbyes to everyone working on the house – and two people in particular – I dropped her off at the station.

'I hope he'll come and visit me,' Izzie said.

I looked at my watch to see when I could schedule a time next year to ask which one she meant.

'And you can come over sometime too,' she added as an afterthought.

I leaned forward so she could hug me. 'I'm busy that week.'

'Sooner rather than later, Bee.' She pulled me closer. 'I'll let you go if you promise to come over—'

'I promise.'

'Good.' Izzie pulled away and patted the tops of my arms. 'Right, I'm going to get my seat. Don't stand here waving me off. You're not a fucking extra on *The Railway Children*.'

'Suits me. Wanks for coming!'

On the way to my car, I sent her a text.

Me: No talking to naked strangers. No breastfeeding anyone who can't spell 'separately'. Text me when you get home x

Seconds later…

Izzie: Will do. And give one of those hunky men a big kiss – not from me xxxxxxxxxxx

Even if I hadn't been to Nyx's house before, I'd know I was on the right street just by the number of cars parked up on kerbs along either side. Although all the semi-detached houses look similar in the bright sunshine, I don't need to check that I have the correct house number – only one has balloons and a banner wishing Maria and Nyx a happy birthday.

The front door is open. Despite hearing music and voices, I still knock and wait. After seven seconds, I'm considering making a run for it – using the 'there was no answer' excuse – when a tall girl with amazing lilac hair clatters down the stairs. Based on her outfit, I assume she is about to muck out some cows, not eat their flesh in the garden.

'Hello.' I smile. 'I'm a friend of—'

'Nyx!' she hollers, loping off through a doorway.

I'm left second-guessing what my next move should be. I also wonder how many people in Japan with that name just spilt their saké.

The birthday boy appears, raking back his top waves. Clean hair, clean-shaven, clean outfit. At least my thoughts are filthy; otherwise, it would be a Disney production.

'Hey.' Nyx looks me up and down. 'You look gorgeous.'

'Really?' Do blushes spoil an outfit or enhance it? 'Erm, thank you.'

I can usually get ready in ten minutes. Twenty, if it's food with someone who isn't a family member. Today, I took thirty-five.

'You, of course, look as handsome as ever, sir.'

Nyx tugs on the hem of his paisley-patterned shirt. 'I thought I'd better make an effort. Anyway, come in. You didn't have to knock.'

I close my embroidered lace parasol and step inside the hallway. 'Who's the beautiful girl with the lilac hair?'

'My youngest sister, Jenna.'

'Please, *please* tell me there's someone in your family who isn't Rimmel perfect?'

'My sisters very much get their looks from Mum,' Nyx says, chuckling, 'which causes me a lot of headaches.'

'I may be way behind on the latest teen fashion trends, but…?'

'She works on a farm at weekends.'

'And she's just finished?' I ask.

'No, she's been home a while, but that one will do anything to avoid socialising.'

'I like her more by the second.'

Nyx grins. 'I thought you would.'

I hold out a cotton tote bag by its long handles.

'Jo, you didn't have to get me anything.'

Although it's to be expected, Nyx still surprises me when he looms in for a kiss. Except I don't offer him my cheek quickly enough, and it grazes the corner of my mouth. I somehow maintain my composure, but not as well as he does.

Knowing the answer, I ask it anyway. 'Would you have let me pay for dinner instead?'

'Not a chance.'

'Exactly. Only… will you open this in private?'

Nyx's eyebrows dance. 'Ooh, hello.'

'No, it wasn't delivered to my house in an unmarked box.'

'Intriguing. I'll pop it in this drawer for now and introduce you quickly to a few people.'

'Oh no,' escapes my lips.

'You'll be fine.'

At least my fear of social gatherings is momentarily overshadowed when he takes my hand without permission. It must look like I'm being dragged instead of led through the tiny kitchen.

In the back garden, half the population of Bowness-on-Windermere is chatting and drinking (well, that's how many people it feels like to someone who exhibits more than one trait on the social anxiety scale), and a new arrival attracts subtle interest. Many pairs of sunglasses are not looking our way, meaning many sideways glances are. Fortunately, Maria is weaving through the human obstacle course towards us – with her plus one.

I get my hand back off Nyx in double-quick time,

using them both to delve into my bag and pull out a card. It's a big bag, all right? It needs two hands.

'Happy birthday, lady.'

'Thank you, Jo.'

'Jeez!' I hold my hand in front of my prescription lenses. 'Something has just blinded me.'

'Yes, sorry about that.' Maria smiles as she brushes her fingers across the sparkling object on her left wrist. 'That would be because I'm wearing only the prettiest bracelet in the world.'

I admire it as though I'm seeing it for the first time: a silver chain bearing six charms, each carefully chosen by an offspring. I know how much it cost, and it wasn't cheap. But the way Maria is gazing down at it and stroking it, you would think it was the key to George Clooney's trailer.

The last bit of jewellery I bought Ma came in a distinctive blue box. Knowing she probably wouldn't wear whatever I picked, I opted for the 'wow' factor. I still feel no guilt that it took me only two minutes to choose it, seeing as I've never seen her wear it.

Maria holds my hand to the side. 'I *love* your dress.'

'Thank you. Matalan. Summer sale, last year.'

'No, it wasn't,' says a quiet voice too close to my ear. Which forces my elbow to discreetly strike a Michigan forearm.

'How come you can make anything look good?' Maria gently chastises me. 'Like those jeans you wore the other day when you came into the shop. Why can't I get jeans from a car boot sale to fit me that well?'

I can't get jeans from a car boot sale to fit me that well, either.

'That's because you have big hips,' comments someone behind her.

The pain that a teenage taunt can still inflict flashes in Maria's eyes for the briefest of seconds, and then it's gone – for now.

Her unfaltering smile turns towards the woman who is joining us. 'Sara. What a pleasant surprise! I didn't think you'd be able to make it.'

'It's an in and out for me. Bob will be back soon.'

'Sara, this is Jo, Nyx's friend – and mine,' Maria happily states. 'And this is Cal.'

Oh, it's just 'Cal', eh? Interpret that as you will.

'Sara is my sister.'

'*Younger* sister,' Sara adds.

Since you'd never guess correctly, you can't blame her for pointing that out. I also don't need to ask her what she does for a living. Sara is clearly a lemon sucker by day and a miserable fucker at night.

Cal shakes her hand. 'It's a pleasure to meet you, Sara.'

Fiddling with her necklace, she smiles up at him. 'No, the… pleasure is all mine.'

My toothy grin and I are next. 'Hi!'

'Hello.' Sara's lukewarm response perfectly matches her limp handshake.

Today, I promised Izzie that I would make it look like I enjoy irrelevant small talk with people I'll never meet again. The problem is, I didn't expect a tsunami this early on. Sara looks at me as if I could jeopardise vibrator production.

'Have we met before?' she asks me.

'I don't… think so.'

Sara narrows her eyes. 'Your face is *very* familiar.'

Fuckity McFuck!

'I do walk a lot.' I don't know why I demonstrate a walking action. 'Maybe you've seen me pounding the pavements.'

'No.'

Oh.

'It might come to me,' Sara says with a dismissive shrug.

People claim you can't say 'bubbles' in an angry way. I think this woman can.

'Let's get you a drink, Jo,' Maria suggests.

Before I can put my hand to better use, she grabs hold of it and leads the way. This family and holding hands – there's a theme.

Nyx walks behind me, one hand on my shoulder. I hear Sara chatting with the person who lost to her in the pleasure stakes. Hopefully, Cal can distract her sketchy memory for long enough.

In the kitchen, Maria opens the door to her well-stocked fridge. There's more food in it than my one back in London saw in three years.

She holds up a bottle. 'Is sparkling elderflower water okay?'

'Perfect.' I give Nyx a thank-you nudge for remembering.

'Mum, did you invite your sister?'

'I hadn't planned to, but your grandad mentioned

it to her. Then she was on the phone, wanting to know why she hadn't been asked. I lied and said I was going to, but I didn't think she'd come. Anyway, Bob will be back in a minute.'

'Bob's her long-suffering spouse,' Nyx tells me.

'Unhappily married for twenty-two years now,' Maria says.

'Why don't they divorce?' I ask her.

'He doesn't want one, and Sara won't divorce him because he'll get custody of the kids. She'll also lose the nice car, the generous pocket money, and the three holidays abroad every year. Which is why she can sometimes come across as a...'

'Fucking nasty bitch,' Nyx sneers.

I blink at him. I rarely hear him say anything harsh about anyone. Or any*thing*. At a Chinese restaurant in Kendal once, his second steamed dumpling was only mediocre. He blamed it on expectations being too high after the first one.

'I'm sure it's nothing that carbs and a good balling couldn't cure,' I casually remark.

When Maria laughs loud enough for people outside to think she's pissing feathers, the recently formed rows of tension on her forehead disappear. Still wiping away tears, she opens the envelope I gave her earlier. Vouchers for various pampering treatments at a local spa resort are inside the card. She politely reads each one.

'You don't know how much I need these, Jo.' When she swarms in for a hug, her sweet perfume surrounds me in a not-too-unpleasant way. 'Thank you.'

I tap her twice on the back with three fingertips. 'You're welcome.'

'Can I steal her away for a bit, Mum?'

'Why?' she asks.

'My friends want to meet her. And she is my guest.'

'She's mine too.'

Maria forgets that she already has one.

Nyx gives her a loud kiss on the cheek. 'But I got here first.'

A car horn sounds. It's not a beep-beep; it's a BEEEEEEEEEEEEP.

'Bob's here.' Maria looks at her son. 'You two, go mingle. Quick, before Sara comes through!'

And I am more than happy to be swiftly exiting via the back door as his agonising aunt makes her way towards it.

The celebrations for Nyx's birthday actually started last night. No, not a stretch limousine to enjoy some city nightlife and bottles of Moët. He went to his local and watched the match on the big-screen television.

'And then?' I ask, opening my parasol.

'Then we went for a curry.'

'And then?'

'Then I came home.'

'To get dressed up to go clubbing?'

'No.'

'What did you do?' I sound like a tired parent when they're videoing mummy's empty makeup box and their five-year-old clown.

'My sisters bought me a new game, so I was on my PlayStation until about two... What?' Nyx says, laughing and grabbing my hand again.

Seriously, are those pockets of his sewn up?

'When you get to my age, Nyx, you'll never be able to start a sentence with "When I was your age". Not if that's the best you can do.'

'And how often do *you* start a sentence with "When I was your age"?'

I slap his arm. 'Never. That's my point. Let my boring past be a lesson to you.'

Apart from Nyx's twin brothers and one other boy, this is (thankfully) a grownup's soirée. He attempts to introduce them while I'm listening to some of Colin's anecdotes, which all begin with, 'Let me just tell you this one...'. Fortunately, they always wriggle free and continue their laps of the garden. They must have done fifty since I've been here.

After I've met somewhere between eight and eighty of his friends (their names went over my head after the fourth handshake), Nyx says to me, 'I think that's enough for now. I don't want to spook you.'

He keeps reassuring me that I'm doing great as he leads us back through the kitchen. In the hallway, he retrieves the tote bag I gave him earlier.

'Let's go upstairs for a bit,' he suggests.

If only.

***

Being the only grown male in the house, Nyx gets his

own room. His brothers get the converted attic, and his three sisters share the large main bedroom. I spot Maria's neatly made-up single bed in the next room.

Nyx closes the door to afford us some privacy. Within a minute, I am jolted into reality. I'm in a boy's bedroom. Okay, he doesn't have a Spider-Man duvet cover, but it's still his bedroom in his mum's house.

Once I get over how small the room is, I quickly realise it is a man's space. A low, bowed clothes rail is crowded with a colourful assortment of shirts and T-shirts. There are three floating shelves above it: one holds a collection of aftershave bottles, along with some other *things* – expensive works of art, perhaps, or his brothers' classroom creations. I don't know the difference. Two shelves are given over entirely to books. A wall-mounted cupboard is only accessible by standing on the single bed. A massive telly dominates the adjacent wall, with every form of games console – past and present – fighting for attention on a shelf below it.

And that's basically it. These mismatched items crowding a tiny area make up Nyx's entire world.

Well, almost.

There is one wall in his bedroom that has been saved for last. I stand back as far as I can (which isn't far) to admire what covers nearly every inch, with the light from the window adding contrast to some of his clever use of shading.

Nyx points to one sketch. 'That's Ullswater. The mountains make it something else to draw.'

'I love that lake. It's so eerie.'

'Then I'll take you up Sheffield Pike sometime.'

I plump up my waves and blink slowly at him. 'That's an offer I haven't had in a while!'

The kiss Nyx drops onto my bare shoulder shows how relaxed we are now with each other. And I know that a pretty face will eventually come along and nudge me out of this comfortable friendship. I also know my number will be the second thing to go; it will be deleted from his phone but noted down somewhere. You know, just in case. However, it's not something for me to worry about today.

Then I remember.

It's not something for me to worry about after the summer.

I crouch down to look at a small group of drawings highlighting his love of fantasy.

'That one's from *Morratalio's Shadow*,' Nyx explains. 'That one's the Hope.'

'From Quinn Manning's *Search for Emerald Reef*.'

'Bloody hell. You've done it to me again.' He does some adjusting in his jeans. 'And this one's Greyhougerie. Or at least how I imagine the castle to look.'

That's because N.R. Magnusson likes readers to put in the work too.

My attention is captivated by a drawing of Pyrredira, the king of the faeries. A pencil has brought to life every adjective I used to create him.

'Your attention to detail is amazing, Nyx. You're

wasted on a building site.'

'Coming from you, that means a lot to me.'

It would also come from some other people I know.

Nyx bounces down onto the bed and tucks his leg under him. 'Sit,' he urges, patting the spot directly in front of him, an area I would reserve for cereal bowls or laundry folding.

I take a seat a pillow's length away and watch him delve into the tote bag.

He grins as he pulls out what looks like a distressed leather-bound journal. 'This is fancy.' Nyx undoes the leather thong and opens the front cover. He stops when he sees what it is. 'How…?'

I keep my eyes fixed on his fingers as they fumble with the pages.

'*Nyx*,' he reads. '*Promise me you will never share your dreams with anyone who says the cherry blossom is all too fleeting. Happy Birthday…*' He swallows. '*… N.R. Magnusson.*'

'I know a friend of a friend in their office.' I wave a dismissive hand. 'Story, boring, long. Anyway, they owed me a favour from way back.'

He holds the book up in both hands like an airport pickup sign. 'This is the last book in the *Caerli°°ani* series.'

I nod slowly.

'It's not due out until Christmas,' Nyx stresses.

More slow nodding.

Flicking through the pages, he looks at the words that go on and on. And on. N.R. Magnusson gives you your money's worth. When Nyx holds it to his chest, he looks at me with such sincerity that I'm worried he'll ask if we can get matching tribal ink tattoos.

I look again at the wall of drawings.

'Jo—'

'Okay then.' I pat his bended knee in a 'jolly good show' way before jumping to my feet. 'Happy Birthday, handsome.'

I step over to the shelves to sniff the aftershave bottle tops and to brace myself. Fortunately, I tense up only a little when Nyx's arms encircle my shoulders from behind.

He presses his cheek against mine. 'It's the best gift ever. I'll treasure it. Thank you.'

I briefly squeeze his forearm. 'You're welcome.'

Nyx continues to hug me. In case you haven't noticed, I'm not big on this hugging, snuggling, cuddling craze. They're all just cute words for what it actually is: holding on. However, it's his birthday. Besides that, when it's coming from someone who embodies forbidden fruit, it's bloody hard not to execute a wrestling move to get him onto the bed.

You can probably imagine my relief when I hear multiple feet hammering up the stairs. Three small boys burst in, almost toppling over each other when they see someone who needs a bra – and who, more intriguingly, isn't from the same gene pool as two of them – in their brother's room. At least Nyx and I are now standing apart. They look at us quickly in turn before the giggles take over.

'Mum says the barbecue's hotted enough now,'

one of the matching pair manages to blurt out.

'Yeah, we'll be down in a minute.'

They're still hovering, joined together in a tight huddle by an invisible rope.

'Anything else?' Nyx asks them.

With much shouting and whooping, the boys turn around and scramble across the landing and down the stairs.

'Nyx is in lurve,' floats up, followed by kissing sounds and more giggles.

***

I help Nyx carry the plates of raw meat outside and then decline his spare apron with tact, referring to the dry-clean label on my dress. And the necessity to 'mingle', of course.

I know what you're thinking: I'd rather blowtorch my chin whiskers off than make polite shitchat. I'm a guest, though, and I'm here today for my friend.

Friends. Maria's a... a friend too.

Strangely enough, I don't zigzag among the groups like a PR specialist, but I enjoy a few conversations with friendly faces who stop to speak, including Nyx's sassy eldest sister, Xena. I am also briefly joined by two of his friends from earlier (no, I can't recall their names), and I discuss Jason Momoa's attributes with the middle sister, Megan, who is – you guessed it – butt-ugly. I'm kidding. With her mum's eyes and mane of dark hair, she'll struggle to get a job if every interviewer has low self-esteem.

Once everyone's barbecue and salad needs are

met, the volume in the garden reduces to less than half. Nyx and I pile up our plates and escape to the swings; they are tucked back and offer a safe, free-of-polite-conversation vantage point. Under the shade of a mature oak, we can enjoy the party and nosy in on everyone else.

Well, almost everyone. I'm not bothered, but… someone isn't outside enjoying themselves.

And neither is Maria.

'Holy hangovers!' I exclaim. 'Your mum's food is something else.'

Honestly, it is. It's delicious. Yes, it tasted better a minute ago, but I blame the heat.

'Can I move in?' I ask between mouthfuls.

'Yeah, my little brothers come with the food,' Nyx warns.

'Hmm. Maybe I'll bring some Tupperware round instead.'

Not caring if I look greedy, I go back for more. It's only (mostly) salad, and if I eat another portion, I don't have to drink the pond scum in my fridge – sorry, the kale and kiwi blend. It is nestled next to one of Tony's curried vegetable pasties, which will be devoured later. As will the slice of blood orange and thyme yoghurt cake, which Marjorie has asked me to test and score out of five. Both will be guilt-free after this green, lean cuisine.

As well, if I use a teaspoon to fill my plate instead of a serving spoon, it gives me ample opportunity to nose beyond the buffet table. A few of those missing from the garden are in the lounge, enjoying a brief respite from the sun.

A few. Not all.

I drop back down onto the swing and attack my Greek salad.

'Well, Mr Hart, twenty-five. Do you feel any different?'

'I'm not joking when I say I woke up this morning with a stiff hip.'

'With a stiff what?'

Nyx laughs. 'Hip.'

'You know what they say: hips today, groin tomorrow.'

We resume our non-participant observations from this safe distance. The small boys are running and shouting and running and bouncing and running and... Shit, I'm exhausted just watching them.

Maria is back from wherever she and... Anyway, she's floating here and there, ensuring everyone is having a good time on her day. She's laughing at people's jokes and cracking some of her own. She is unaware of those women who are only pretending to find her hilarious; they aren't listening to a word she says. How can they, when they're busy gauging how funny their husbands find her gags?

Somebody who I thought would be there appreciating her comedic talent is instead chatting with her daughters. How cosy.

Sorry, *cozy*.

I cram the last bite of hot dog bun into my mouth and put my empty plate down. I push myself back and forth on the swing with my feet until Nyx takes over.

Every push creates a breeze that strokes my face and blows away unwanted thoughts.

'What are you doing tonight?' he asks.

'I'm rigging myself up one of these.'

'In your bedroom?'

'Excuse me!' I love pretending to be affronted. 'I'm practically middle-aged.'

'There's nothing middle-aged about you.'

'Except for the amount of experience I've racked up.'

'There's nothing wrong with plenty of experience,' Nyx comments.

'I'm talking about *life* experience.'

'Oh.'

I cast him a look. 'How many beers have you had?'

'Two, m'lady.'

I pump my legs to gain height, straightening my arms on the chains and leaning back slightly. How long has it been since I got to play on a swing? Not since I started paying National Insurance, that's for sure.

'I still don't believe you're as—' Oops, Nyx nearly slipped. 'That... you're the age you say you are.'

'Ha! You were about to say "as old".'

'I was not,' he insists.

'It's fine. Don't worry. I never play for the easily offended team. As for my age, I'm certain I'm getting younger as I get older. At least I am in my head.'

'I still think you can only be in your twenties.'

I drop my head back and give him an upside-down smile. 'Keep saying it, and even *I* might start believing it.'

'You should.'

'The perks of never having children or a husband. If there's nobody there to make you grow up and feel old, why bother?'

At my request, Nyx pushes me higher on the swing.

'Have you ever been close to getting married, Jo?'

'I thought I was once. But deep down, I've probably always known it would never happen. That doesn't stop me from enjoying a happy ending for others, though.'

'How can anyone know whether it will happen to them?'

'No one can,' I say. 'But you can have a feeling. And maybe there *is* someone out there for me. Except, at my age, could I change? Or would I even want to?'

'Do you think that's why you shy away from relationships?'

'I don't shy away.'

'Oh, come on.'

'What?'

'I've seen how blokes look at you,' Nyx says.

'Then I must need my eyes tested because I don't see them.'

'There's someone over there looking at you right now.'

I slowly shake my head. 'There is not.'

'Believe me, I'm getting daggers.'

I don't bother looking – what's the point? – but I play along. 'You mean you've been cramping my style?'

'Yeah.'

'Well, seeing as I tell girls that slimming clubs use your todger in the "after" photos, that must make us even.'

Nyx pinches my side.

'Tell me, sir, when are these damn cakes being cut? My dog is looking forward to me taking home two *huge* slices.'

'Soon. Would you mind if I came back with you?'

'Yes, I would.' At first, Nyx thinks I'm joking. 'It's your birthday. Half of these people are here for you.'

'No, they're not. Most of them are Mum's friends.'

'Most, not all,' I remind him. 'You can't leave your own party.'

'I was with that lot over there last night. And I haven't seen you all weekend.'

'Well, come over tomorrow night.'

'Don't *I* get to decide what I want to do on my birthday?'

And I hate myself a little for thinking it, but I wish he didn't.

'You do, Nyx. I'm sorry.'

'Good. What I *want* to do this afternoon is walk Bacon with you and work off some of those burgers.'

'That's probably not a bad idea,' I murmur. 'When you wolfed down that third one, I thought you would give that shirt stretchmarks.'

Everyone remains outside after the happy birthdays have been sung, enjoying their slices of either chocolate torte or lemon drizzle cake. The harsh sun is creeping behind the house, creating more pockets of shade. It's still warm, but the air is starting to feel muggy.

'You're going?' Maria asks when we politely interrupt her storytelling.

'Yeah, Jo's got to get back for the dog,' Nyx explains.

'Oh, that's a shame.'

I let Maria hug me again. It *is* her birthday.

'Enjoy the rest of your day, lady. By the way, the food was amazing.'

'You are more than welcome,' she tells me. 'Any time.'

'Happy birthday, bud,' utters a member of her rapt audience.

'Cheers, Cal,' Nyx says.

When Maria and I pull apart, her hands briefly cup my face. She is smiling. Maybe she's looking forward to returning most of her presents and getting something she likes.

Or maybe she's looking forward to getting something else entirely.

I quickly wave a hand above my head to the person behind me. 'See you whenever, Cal.'

'Bye, Jo.'

When we've said goodbye to everyone at least twice, we finally manage to leave.

Nyx chuckles. 'You know what they'll be saying now.'

'Yeah, they'll be saying that was the greedy sod

who ate all the burgers.'

Chapter Twenty-Seven

Bacon behaves as though Nyx and I have just returned from a holiday on Neptune, her tail whipping across her face as she twists between us.

I've missed you. Get my lead. Where's my ball? I've missed you. Let's go, let's go. Forget the lead. Let's GO!

At Cockshott Point, a stroll from Bowness Bay, we watch her paddling at the water's edge. She jumps back when the tiniest ripple takes her by surprise. She trots ahead, stopping every now and again to make sure we're still following.

'Do you think it's time to give her a proper name?' Nyx asks.

'It's not my place to name her; she's not mine. Somebody will come forward for her, eventually.'

'Well, you are currently her foster mum.'

'Click on the link and see how much off you can fuck,' I tell him.

'Would it hurt to give her a better name for now?'

'What for?'

'She's too pretty to be called Bacon.'

I observe the patchwork quilt on four legs. 'Are we looking at the same animal?'

Nyx nudges me with his elbow. 'You would miss her.'

'I wouldn't. That dog's a pain. I can't remember the last time I ate a biscuit without someone offering to help.'

We see the dark clouds gathering. Hearing the first low rumbles, we aren't sure if they are thunder or a plane. A flash in the distance answers our question. We pick up our pace along Glebe Road, heading back to my little rental.

The first giant raindrops start when we're at the corner and are soon bombarding us. I pull my long dress up to my knees, and we run the short distance up the hill. Under the weight of the watery onslaught, cheery flowers in tubs and hanging baskets take a battering. The road is quickly becoming a river, rushing past my gate.

As I unlock the door, a lightning flash directly above the house lights up the sky. A loud clap almost rattles the roof as we fall into the hallway.

In the lounge, we turn on some lamps. The room looks cosy for barely a minute before they go off. I'm reminded of another thunderstorm, but one that played with more than just the lights in my London apartment.

Was that really only a season ago?

My thumb moves my ring around my finger as the sky booms and cracks. I watch the fork lightning pop across the sky from east to west, west to north. Nyx is behind me, lighting some of my farmers' market candles. I have more if he needs them. I've already bought replacements for those that have almost burnt to the bottom.

'Jo?'

Thunder starts low and builds. A flash hovers across the sky. And another.

Nyx's hands on my damp shoulders jolt me more than the forces of nature. 'Come away from the window.'

He carries out the instruction himself, turning me and my thoughts away from storms past and present.

An explosion of thunder sends Bacon under the six inches of wet hem on my dress. I crouch down and tickle her neck until she emerges. When I pick her up, she is shaking.

I give her a vigorous rub with the towel while speaking gently to her. 'It's all right, baby girl.'

Passing her to Nyx, I assure her little whimpers that I'll be quick. I nip upstairs and change into comfy striped pyjama bottoms and a faded *Labyrinth* vest.

I return with an oversized grey T-shirt. 'If you want to hang your shirt up to dry, you can borrow this.'

Nyx slaps a towel over his shoulder and brushes his damp hair back with his free hand. 'Why? Are you worried the sight of me topless will get you hot under the collar?'

I roll my eyes. 'Oh, please!'

No, really. Please.

I hurry towards the kitchen to generate a breeze on

314

my cheeks. 'Do you fancy a coff...?' I grip the door frame on either side. 'No!'

'How long has it been since you had caffeine?' Nyx asks.

'I daren't think.' I take some deep breaths. 'Jesus, Mary, Mungo and Midge, I'll never make it.' I stagger over to the fridge and peer into its dark innards. 'There is orange juice.' I don't even mention the kale and kiwi catastrophe. I look in the cupboard. 'Elderflower cordial. Lemonade. Peach schnapps... Peach schnapps? When did I buy this?'

The answer is: I didn't. It was a housewarming gift from Izzie, which has moved with me twice now.

He comes through with Bacon still in his arms. 'Crack open the schnapps, woman. It's my birthday.'

Izzie and I hardly ever drink, which is why the only tipple found in my house can be dulled with a gallon of lemonade. Nyx deals out the alcohol while I pour the softness. I opt for one part schnapps and four parts lemonade. He goes fifty-fifty.

I realise something once we're sitting in front of the blank TV screen. 'I'm going to miss *Countryfile*.'

'I like that programme.'

'I have a big crush on one of the presenters.'

'I don't like it any more,' Nyx murmurs. 'And the one you like is probably gay.'

'He is not.'

As I suck slowly on my straw, I notice he's almost finished his drink.

'Who else do you fancy?' he wants to know.

'Before I even bother listing them, will you claim

everyone on my to-do list is a friend of Dorothy?'

'Yeah, duh!'

Nyx goes into the kitchen and returns with the schnapps bottle. He pours some into my glass while I'm sucking on my straw, ignoring my high-pitched protests. He sits back down and tops up his own drink. When I put mine on the table, he tops it up again.

'Are you trying to get me drunk?' I ask.

'No. Just tipsy.'

The lemonade bottle I bring through is quickly taken off me. Nyx swaps it for an empty glass one that adorns the sideboard, an ornament that merely collects dust during my stay. He clears the coffee table and kneels on the opposite side. Laying the bottle flat, he gives it a gentle spin.

The thunder lets out another low growl.

'Truth or dare,' Nyx says. 'And you must take a drink when it lands on you. Ladies first.'

I spin the bottle, and we both watch it come to a stop.

I need to think of a question fast. 'Who is your male celebrity crush?'

'Tom Hardy,' Nyx answers without thinking. He starts the bottle off on another spin cycle while taking a slug of his drink without his straw.

It points at him again.

'Have you ever used self-tanning lotion?' I ask.

I don't think I have ever seen anyone look so confused.

'Seriously, Jo?'

'Isn't that something a lot of men would rather

take a dare for than own up to?'

'It's not that,' Nyx grumbles. 'It's the sort of question your nanna would ask.'

He is waiting for another one. When he shows Bacon the time on his watch, it appears he has been waiting too long.

Pinching my bottom lip, I journey into my inner library. Wait, didn't I include a similar game to this in *Every Witch Way*?

I remember one. 'Which would you rather do with someone who looks like your mum: go down on her or get a blowjob from her?'

Nyx almost disguises his expression by using his tongue to dislodge some imaginary morsel of food stuck between his teeth and cheek. His gaze drops to the bottle. Eventually, he shakes his head and flops onto his back, covering his eyes and emitting a low groan. Bacon seizes the opportunity to give him the kiss of life.

'Dare me,' he orders.

I remember the dare, too. 'Dance quickly for thirty seconds, moving only your legs and head.'

Getting to his feet, Nyx tugs his borrowed T-shirt down. 'Be warned. My dares won't all be PG-rated.'

Bacon's squeaky barks and my laughter drown out the thunder. My stomach hurts watching him give it his 'dancing' all with a limb restriction. Still, his expressive head wobbles and tongue-showing more than make up for the limitations.

Nyx knocks his drink back while the spinning bottle slows down.

Shit!

'Who's the most bizarre person you've had a sex dream about?' he asks.

'Charlie Chaplin.'

'Wow. You answered with no hesitation.'

'That's because it was good enough to make my top five *actual* encounters.'

I suck on my straw until I get the thumbs up. Already, I feel a little louder.

My spin of the bottle eventually stops.

'Nyx, if I'd known in advance, I could've researched some funny questions.'

'What's wrong with spontaneity?'

'That's how you wake up with no teeth sleeping next to you.'

He bangs the table. 'Come on, truth me.'

'All right. Would you rather... I don't know... dominate in the bedroom or *be* dominated?'

'Ooh, good one.' Nyx's fingers play with Bacon's ear as he thinks, his straw in the side of his mouth. 'I quite like the idea of being dominated.'

I brush a teeny bit of fluff off my pyjama leg. 'Then you've never, erm... you've never been...?'

'No, I'm always the dominator.'

Nyx clamps the straw between his teeth and grins. I quickly stare out the spinning bottle.

Then it's my turn to worry.

'If you had to suck off one animal—'

'I'll take a dare,' I rush to say.

He holds out his hand. 'I send one text to a random person on your phone.'

'But what if—?'

'Ah-ah, you chose a dare. Hand it over.'

I watch him scroll through the names in my contacts.

'Nyx, you said a random person.'

His thumbs are warp-speeding over the tiny keyboard. Before I can ask what safe word we agreed on when we started this game, he places my phone face down on the table and nods towards my drink.

'Can I please at least read what you sent?'

'I deleted it,' he says.

'At least tell me who you sent it to.'

'No.'

I already have my question ready when my bottle spin points at him. 'Fuck, marry, kill.'

'I have a horrible feeling that I know where—'

'Your three sisters.'

Leaning back on his hands, Nyx glowers at me. 'You're sick.'

'How is that any worse than you asking me what animal I'd blow?'

'Right, I couldn't marry Xena – she'd be too much for me. Megan is quite sweet. I couldn't fuck Jenna, not my little sister. So I'd have to fuck Xena, marry Megan, and kill Jenna.' He holds a hand up towards the door. 'Sorry, Jenna.'

'After how easily you answered that question, shouldn't you be apologising to all three?'

Nyx tops up his drink and takes a large mouthful as we wait. The spinning bottle almost looks like it is stopping in the middle. Sadly…

'What's your dirtiest fantasy, Jo?'

'I'm sitting next to a campfire with Simon Reeve and Professor Brian Cox, who are politely battling for my affections using only interesting facts... What?' I ask when I see his expression. 'Stop looking at me like that. Nyx, I'm forty-four. If I haven't done it in the bedroom by now, it probably means I can't be bothered.'

He grudgingly holds his glass up. When I tap mine against it, the clink is loud. Uh-oh. I think my coordination is starting to dance the rumba with seventeen per cent alcohol content.

When the bottle stops spinning, there's no question about who it's pointing at.

'Similar question to you, Mr Hart. What's your dirtiest *secret*?'

Nyx watches his finger wipe off the last remnants of dust from the bottle, a nervous smile twitching his lips. A decision is made, and he takes his phone out of his pocket. After some tapping and scrolling, he shows me a photo. It's of himself, looking simply spectacular, as usual. But he also looks...

There's something else. Something... Something more.

Because Nyx is not alone in the photo.

'That's Esmé,' he explains. 'She was a happy accident three years ago after a one-night stand. And she's the... family stuff I do when I'm... when I'm not with you.'

Although I sense Nyx's desperate stare, I keep looking at the photo because I don't know what else to do. I don't know how I should respond.

'You, erm…' I scrabble around for words. 'You have a… a…'

'I have a daughter, Jo.'

'Okay.'

This is uncharted territory for me. The fact that I don't like kids has never been a secret. But besides their pointless noises spoiling it when I'm eating in and not taking away, my dislike of them has been purely from observation.

'Even though she wasn't planned,' Nyx says, 'she is everything to me.'

'And she… she should be.'

That's the correct response, right? Isn't that what people should say? At least I avoid using a rising intonation. That's hard to do. Well, it's hard for someone who doesn't understand what it's like to put somebody at the centre of their universe – somebody who will, I imagine, ask if they can have their inheritance in advance.

I think the polite thing would be to stare at the photo until the next ice age, telling Nyx how pretty his little girl is and how lucky *he* is, and… and… Look, I don't pissing know, do I?

I remember when people I worked with returned from maternity leave. They gathered the entire office to look at a hundred photos of a baby doing nothing. All it made me want to ask was whether they were taking this time off their lunch breaks. I never took part in the cooing. Unless the photo showed a Hollywood A-lister caught in a compromising position, they knew I wouldn't care.

I can see Nyx wants me to comment further.

Say something, Jo.

Anything.

'Congratulations.'

It's the best of a bad bunch, I promise you. I nearly said, 'Well done.' Even worse, I almost added a question mark.

'I've waited to tell you about her,' Nyx says with a hesitant smile. 'Seeing as you're not really a... fan of kids.'

That's putting it mildly. It's like saying I'm not a fan of internal examinations in front of a paying audience.

'I'm not, no. But I dislike pineapple on pizza even more.'

That's not true. Yes, I loathe pineapple on pizza. However, if given a choice, I would opt for a fruity violation once every twenty-ninth of February.

'Whenever I meet a woman, I never let on that I have a kid, not straight away. But with you...' Nyx fidgets on his knees, looking at the photo. 'When I brought the quote over, I quickly learnt your views about them. I mean, talk about a strong opinion!'

At least he's laughing, and he isn't recalling what happened that afternoon in the pub after he pretended—

'Your reaction as well when I made out it was my daughter on the phone.'

I spoke too soon.

'Nyx, surely that told you everything you needed

to know about me.'

His gaze shifts from the photo to Bacon. 'You would've thought so, yeah? But it didn't. It... couldn't. And I wanted to tell you when the time was right, but it's never...' He shakes his head and shrugs. 'Mum has been getting on at me, saying I was making things worse by putting it off. I've done that before, and it doesn't always end well. Actually, when you tell someone you have a kid, it rarely... So I promised to do it this evening. It... It had to be this evening. Which meant I needed to make sure nobody else told you first.'

'And, erm... at the party today?' I hate to ask.

'Everyone had promised not to mention her. Well, almost everyone. Sara didn't know.'

'But why go to all that trouble?'

The smile Nyx gives me isn't confident enough to reach his eyes. 'I think by now, Jo, even you must have a pretty good idea why.'

For the first time in ages, I examine my nails. I really should devote the odd half an hour to their welfare.

'Nyx, we're... we're just friends.'

Izzie predicted I would have to say this one day, but I didn't believe her. Now I wish I had. I also wish I had looked at him when I said it instead of waiting until afterwards.

Nyx is studying the photo again while he digests those words, a rueful smile tugging at one corner of his mouth. 'Perhaps I should've taken a dare instead.'

'Perhaps.'

The table lamps come back on. It's as though they timed it just right. Just as the end credits are rolling.

'I'd better get going.'

Nyx changes into his damp shirt. I don't pretend to avert my gaze – after all, it's my last chance.

I shut Bacon in the lounge and follow him to the front door. He hesitates after opening it.

'I must ask, Jo. Was it just me who felt something between us?'

'Of course not. I mean –' I highlight the six-foot handsome package standing on the doormat '– this wasn't wasted on me.'

'But nothing more than that?'

I look Nyx directly in the eye. 'There is a *lot* more to you than that. And if things had been different, I might not be holding back. But I have to. For both of us.'

He twists his lips and surveys the clearing sky. 'Give me one good reason.'

If I were to downplay it, I could give him twelve. Reluctantly hauling in N.R. Magnusson's contributions would give me fifteen reasons. And when Nyx had tallied up the results of my success, I know what would've happened, and it wouldn't have been fair to him. Because he's a good man. He is everything a woman could want and more – just not a woman with monetary numbers. And no matter how much he might someday truly love me, he could never believe I didn't crave power over him.

It's not just that, though. Nyx isn't…

He just isn't…

'It's because I have a daughter,' Nyx states.

I wish that was the reason, and if that had been a question instead, I may have struggled to respond.

'I'm truly sorry, Nyx.'

And I am. I'm sorry I refused to see this coming. I'm sorry Nyx didn't want me only in my wildest dreams, where I would have been happy to let him stay. I'm sorry that the fantasy isn't the reality I want.

And I am sorry to let him go.

I watch him walk down the short garden path. The gate squeaks when he gently shuts it. Without a backward glance, he turns right and heads down the hill, disappearing out of sight behind the hedgerow that my neighbours use to shut out nosy passers-by.

Steam rises off the tarmac as the water evaporates in the muggy heat. Car tyres *shhhhhh* on the wet roads at the bottom of the hill. A video game's vicious gunfire escapes through my other neighbour's open window. At least, I hope it's a video game.

After returning the offending bottles to the sideboard and the pantry, I slip a latte pod into the coffee machine and rattle a bag of Bacon's favourite beefy treats. I take my drink into the lounge and turn on my computer. While a large Word document is slowly opening, I watch my dog munching happily on her tasty snacks under the coffee table. Which is when I spot my phone. It's where Nyx left it.

Cal: Meet you at midnight with a shovel... where?

Chapter Twenty-Eight

'Hello, duckie.'

'Morning, Colin.' I check my watch. It is still morning. Just. 'I'm sorry I couldn't get here any earlier.' I ditch my lame excuses.

'No worries. It wasn't urgent. You've just missed Nyx.'

I'm grateful to Colin's generation. They would rather pick up a prescription in the nude than offer relationship advice or discuss personal issues.

We do another circuit of the cottage with his shrinking snag list. Finally, I am happy with the timber oil colour being used on the porch flooring. And if anyone asks, *I* chose walnut – not someone who talked the others into the shade he personally would *favor* over rosewood.

When we agree on the height of the pendant lights above the kitchen island, Colin's list shows more crossings out than one of my first drafts in a particular person's newly calloused hands. Maybe that's what Cal's doing today – some angry editing. Seeing as somebody else is giving the walls in the main bedroom one final coat.

Or maybe he's doing some*one* else.

The painters don't need me to tell them when they've missed a spot, plus I know everything is in more than capable hands. With no other reason to stand out like a CEO on the shop floor, I collect my silly dog from the garden, where she's joyfully rubbing her back on the newly turfed lawn.

As we head down the driveway, Bacon's pricked-up ears alert me to where a familiar Astra is now parked. If there were any possibility that I might still be welcomed at Nyx's lowered car window, I would be across there. Even if it's only to say I won't be back again today.

I hold his gaze for a split second before smiling and looking away. And for most of my walk up to Orrest Head, I'm left hoping it wasn't long before he looked away, too.

***

Less than a hundred steps from home, my phone rings. When I find it in one of the deep pockets on my rucksack, my shoulders sag when the screen shows just a number, not a name from my contacts. As always, I only bother checking the last three digits. I don't recognise them, which rules out the Ghost of Sexmas Past. Maybe it's another of those *lovely* automated messages telling me my internet is being disconnected – something to do with illegal activity, or so they keep alleging. Was the call from a landline? I should have checked.

'Is that Jo?'

'Speaking.'

'Hi, Jo. My name's Jenny?'

Let's see. The odds-on favourite now is a supposed tax rebate. Five-to-one, it's a criminal agency saying my assets have been seized.

'We're in a coffee shop in Ambleside, and we've just spotted one of your posters about Bacon?'

The pounding of my heart can be felt in my throat.

'We live in Derby, but my in-laws are in Dumfries? We visited them after Christmas, and my daughter forgot to shut the gate? How she ended up in Cumbria months later, we don't know?'

Fortunately, Jenny only has my first name and phone number. *Un*fortunately, the ends of her sentences only have question marks.

'Is she still with you, Jo?'

Bacon jumps up at me. She is eager for her mum to… for me to take her lead off so she can scamper up the rest of the hill and get home before… get to my rented house before me.

'Jo—?'

'Yes. Yes, she's still… she's still with me.'

After giving her my address ('It's okay, we don't need directions? We have Google Maps?'), I somehow make it to my front door. I put my rucksack down in the hallway before heading up the stairs.

I sit on the bed and close my eyes when I hear four tiny paws approaching. I listen to the dog licking its chops after a well-earned drink. The next minute, it's beside me and forcing my arm up with its nose to get onto my lap.

When I remain impassive to its cuteness, its excitement wanes. Nevertheless, it still leans its little body against my stomach. It tilts its head back at intervals to breathe against the underside of my chin, checking to see when I'll be ready to love it again.

If there isn't much traffic, I have about ten minutes to say goodbye. And I should be doing it with the dog's body held close to mine for our hearts to beat in rhythm, tight enough that it would try to wriggle free.

But I don't.

I can't.

I just can't.

I knew this day would come. It had to. Sadly, this is what happens when you let yourself get comfortable. When you let something in.

Soon, I'll be...

I'll be alone again.

I hear a car pull up outside. There's a cheerful knock at the front door. It's one of those excited raps. You know the ones I mean: knock, knock-knock-knock, knock, knock. The dog springs off my lap and rushes onto the landing to warn all would-be intruders to venture no further without permission.

At the bottom of the stairs, I lift a jacket off one of the coat hooks. Behind it is the tattered, rainbow-coloured collar it was wearing when I found it.

When I found... her.

No. No, it wasn't when *I* found *her*.

There's another knock. For crying out loud, do I need to label the fucking doorbell? I'll stop answering the bloody thing if people don't use it. In fact, I might start now.

Jenny is wearing the prettiest lemon sundress, which I instantly think is too short for her age; she can't be much younger than me. And she really should stay out of the sun. And does she know what damage she's doing to her hair by colouring it *that* many shades lighter?

Bacon's absence is noticed. For one glorious moment, I think this must be merely a case of mistaken identity. Yes, they lost a dog called Bacon. Yes, she's also an adorable mish-mash mutt.

Oh, but that's not our dog? Sorry to trouble you, Jo?

Two little girls are hovering near the gate. Something behind me makes them drop to their knees. The dog flies past me and jumps onto one of them amid a blast of squeals. Then onto the other one. Just as quickly, Bacon runs back to me.

Back to the girls again, and back to me.

Back to the girls again.

'We can't thank you enough?' Jenny says/asks, shaking my hand.

The husband shakes it next. I hope the girls don't follow suit. I'm a writer, not a minor royal.

'No worries,' I murmur.

Go. Please go.

The husband opens his wallet. 'We would like to give you something for looking after her.'

'A small donation to a local animal shelter is fine,' I utter.

Go away. Go away.

Go. Away.

'Girls, let's get Bacon in the car?' Jenny says/asks.

She gets it, and my unwavering expression is thanking her.

'Do you want to say goodbye to her?' asks one of the girls.

'No,' Jenny quickly replies before I can't. 'I think Jo's okay?'

Is it a question or a fact?

I give the tiniest nod.

She smiles. 'Thanks again?'

After shutting the door, I sit on the stairs and listen to the girls' chatter through the partially open top window on the landing. Car doors open and close.

I should have given them its booster seat; it loves that seat. There's also its jumpy pet ball, which keeps it amused when I have to go out for a bit. And the squeaky cord elephant that she likes to travel with.

It likes to travel with.

Liked. *Liked* to travel with.

There's two weeks' worth of dog food in the cupboard, too. Plus the treats, shampoo, brush, nail clippers, toothbrush, toothpaste…

The car's engine starts. Music blares out, with Idina Menzel still telling everyone to let it go. I hear the girls' high-pitched excitement as the car pulls away.

And that's all I hear.

I go upstairs and climb underneath the duvet with the remote control. I don't care that I still have my boots on. I don't care what I might have dragged in from outside. I don't care that I only changed my bedding this morning.

I flick through the TV channels until I hear someone say to Ben Shephard, 'Drop zone three, please'. After that, I compete with Alexander Armstrong's contestants to come up with some pointless answers. Then it's Bradley Walsh's turn to ask the questions, with Frosty Knickers beating the remaining players in the Final Chase.

When I emerge from my white cocoon, I grab my phone and earphones. Tucking some money into the small zip-up pocket on the back of my leggings, I head out.

***

I can now go out whenever I want and not feel guilty for leaving that *bloody dog* at home. I can take a bath without that *bloody dog* trying to join me. I can look forward to the day I get rid of the last of the *bloody dog* hairs. I can leave half a box of Maltesers on the coffee table and not worry about... Who am I kidding? I always finish them.

It's nice walking at my pace again. I'm not stopping all the time to let that *bloody dog* sniff every leaf and cigarette butt. Not to mention all the takeaway cups and empty food wrappers that some motorists and their passengers toss from their windows. Apparently, their cars can't pull over when they see a bin.

It's close to sunset when my walk brings me to

Ambleside. I pass an abandoned former boathouse. At least, I think that's what it is. I'm sure I once spent an afternoon inside it during a school trip, doing a pencil drawing of the ripples in the water.

When the pavements get busier with holidaymakers, I stop bombarding my eardrums with Linkin Park. People in walking shoes are returning to lodgings. They're tired but happy and exhilarated after being entertained all day by mountains and waterfalls. Daylight hours are their preferred time to let their hair down. Others are dressed up and ready for a lively evening in the bars and restaurants, where energetic conversations flow out of open doorways. They're getting louder as the evening progresses and the alcohol impresses.

I stop walking when the road bends to the left. Following the route will take me away from the crowds. I don't want that, though. Not tonight. I head into the pub directly in front of me, not caring that it's their karaoke night.

Their *loud* karaoke night.

'I'll have the burger and chips, please,' I shout to the barman. 'And a soda water. No, make that a Coke – a vodka and Coke. In fact, make it a double. Thank you.'

Since there aren't any empty tables on the patio, I must eat inside. As the protein and carbs soak up some of the alcohol, what's left puts a strange fire in my belly and a pleasant dullness to my overthinking. Oddly enough, it makes the Elvis wannabes and the volume almost bearable.

***

My stretched waistband and I are walking back to my place when I get a call.

'Whatever you're phoning about, Izzie, have you given it serious thought as to whether it was something you could have texted me instead?'

'You sound out of breath,' she comments. 'You'd better be shagging.'

'Would I answer the phone if I were?'

'You're right. It's been so long that you'd be using it to tell the organisers to set off the fireworks!'

'No, I wouldn't, Izzie. I'm saving those for the day when you say something funny.'

'I just thought I'd give you a quick bell,' my aunt says. 'See how you're doing.'

If those on the Titanic had taken as much heed to those iceberg warnings...

'What are you up to this evening, Bee?'

Apart from sweeping this call for explosives?

'I'm walking,' I tell her.

'At this time of night?'

'It's only nine-ish.'

I look at my watch. Oh.

'It's gone ten,' Izzie corrects me. 'A bit late to be out walking far from home, wouldn't you say?'

'I'm not that far from... Hang on, how do you know how far away I am?'

'I don't, but you're out of breath. Since you're quite fit for a greying lady garden, you wouldn't be puffing during a short stroll.'

I still cast a wary eye around me. After all, dressed up as one of the gorilla baddies from *Planet of the*

Apes, this is the woman who jumped out from behind my bedroom door to scare me – when I was six.

'I'm on my way back,' is my answer.

'Have you got your little minder with you?'

I lower my phone.

'Bee?' a voice says from somewhere near my hip.

I resist the urge to throw it and raise it to my ear again. 'No.'

'You've gone out without her? Bless her. She'll sulk when you—'

'The dog's gone, Izzie.'

'What do you mean?'

'The owners showed up this afternoon.'

Annoying silences make me feel uneasy. They feel far too much like lingering fucking hugs.

Izzie sighs. 'Oh, sweetheart.'

'They were clearly happy to have it back.'

'And what about you?'

'The dog seemed happy to be back with them, too,' I state matter-of-factly.

These pauses might have worked with her patients when she wanted to get them to talk, but not with her goddaughter.

'I can be over there tomorrow, Bee, if—'

'What for?' It comes out harsher than I intended, but my grip is slipping.

'Okay. Well, you know where I am.'

'Yes, I know. You're in a field, scaring crows.'

'I stopped listening to you three sentences ago,' Izzie tells me. 'Bye, Four-Eyes.'

Seconds after ending the call, I step under the dark

shade of a chestnut tree and pebbledash the unkempt edge of the pavement with my partially digested, Vodka-tasting supper. I take a minute in case there's still more to come.

A couple of cars pass by. At least nobody witnessed me barking at the ants; that's some consolation. And unless they look carefully, they won't see me under the leafy branches – the ones that like to thrash you if you're texting while walking.

Another car passes. I straighten up, one hand on the mossy wooden fence rail, waiting for the vomiting trembles to pass. Another car. And another. It's after ten! Are they all off to queue outside a furniture retailer for the bloody sale of all sales or something? There isn't this much traffic on a bank fucking holiday.

I can hear a car slowing down. Why? There are no turn-offs along this stretch of the A591, no driveways. Please don't be lost. Please don't ask me how far it is to the holiday park. The way I feel right now, I might direct them to Dante's seventh circle of—

'Jo?'

I can't trust myself to speak. I can't commit to letting go of the rail yet, either. However, hearing Nyx's voice at least allows me to worry about something other than how I'll walk the rest of the way home.

I raise one hand for a second, keeping my attention focused on the path that lies ahead of me. No, the *actual* pathway, not the... Speaking of which, the council needs to level out the ones around here. From where I'm standing (only just), there are blames and claims everywhere.

'Are you all right?' Nyx asks.

One of my hands goes up again. I team it with a vigorous nod.

'Can I give you a lift?'

The dense undergrowth on the other side of the rail – which I'm now holding on to with both hands – won't answer for me, no matter how hard I stare into it.

'No.' I remember my manners. 'But thank—'

The 'you' is there in spirit. Not the alcoholic one in that lumpy puddle I've left for fellow walkers tomorrow. I am sorry.

His engine turns off, and I hear a car door open and close. I look both ways, weighing up my options. I glance behind me: Nyx is standing a good eight feet away. Someone deserves a medal for the wide pavement along this section. If this had been a mile back, we would have been spooning. Yes, that's how narrow it is in places.

'I drove past about twenty minutes ago,' he says. 'I called Izzie because I was worried.'

I force my legs to bear my weight so I can turn round. I soon regret my hasty decision and return one hand to my rickety support. 'Why do you have my aunt's number?'

'She… said I might need it.'

Is it any wonder Olivia J. Lawrence's books are often dedicated to her?

'You're upset about Bacon,' Nyx says.

'That's not what I told Izzie.'

'You didn't need to.'

'I'm not upset.'

Cars are now slowing down as they pass. Rubber-fucking-neckers. And if the one that just *screamed* around the corner slows down any more, they may as well stop and…

Fuck off. The nosy fucker in a flashy Jag *is* stopping.

The nosy fucker in… *my* flashy Jag.

I try to stand up straighter, but it doesn't feel right. I know it can't look very comfortable. Or very convincing.

I scowl at the pair of them. 'What is this? A bloody… intervention?'

Nyx and Cal simultaneously slide their hands into their pockets.

'It was just a dog,' I remind them, like I reminded myself.

'You could have called either of us,' Nyx says.

'Why?' I demand to know, eyeballing them while holding on to the rail with one hand and gesturing with the other. 'If I'd said anything to… to anyone, I would've had to say in the same breath that yes, I'm fine, end of! But *no*, everyone would've presumed the exact *fucking* opposite,' I yell. 'And you'd have been, you'd have been… bombarding me with your shitty concern. When I don't want *anyone* to, to even… to even… give a shit! All right? Therefore, why don't you two get together with Izzie and have your fucking worry pie with, with, with… whipped *fucking* cream, because it's wasted on me. *Wasted!'*

'Is that what you want?' Nyx's question isn't the only thing that sounds quiet after my honking tirade.

I glare at the rail. 'Yes, that's what I *fucking* want!'

Swapping hands allows me to turn round and face the other way, the way I'm heading. I put one foot in front of the other. Even though my knuckles are white and my hand is shaking, I must let go at some point. Except I'm…

No, I'm okay. I can manage. It might not look like it, but I can. I can do this. Of that, I'm… Yeah. A few deep breaths, and I'll be fine. It's fine. Honestly, everything's fine. It's just all that talking. Or rather, all that shouting.

I take another small step, shuffling my hand along. I'll let go in a second – after a couple of those deep breaths again. Yeah, those lovely, deep… shuddery breaths.

My steps are getting smaller – if that last one could even be called a step. I instruct my foot to move, but nothing's happening. I try moving the other one. Same thing.

Wait, it's my legs. It's my legs that aren't working. I can't get them to do anything! Maybe it was that vodka. Or perhaps I'm having an adverse reaction to that relish I'd never tried before. That must be it. I mean, what else can it be?

I squat down, allowing my body to rest sideways against the fence, which doesn't feel up to the challenge. My hand touches my face. The tightness in my cheeks is forcing my eyes closed. My lips are drawn back, but my mouth emits no sound.

I wrap my arms around my legs and grasp my ankles. At least this gives me a shred of comfort. But after a moment, I'm fighting to keep that hold. I mean, *really* fighting. It's as though some unknown force is prising my hands away…

Oh. It's not unknown.

I hear a car door opening as I'm being lifted.

'Thanks, Nyx,' a voice close to my ear says. 'I'll take it from here.'

Chapter Twenty-Nine

As Cal drives in the opposite direction to Bowness-on-Windermere, I stay huddled in the back seat, my forehead resting against the window. Glimpses of life glide by within the varying speed limits and without comment.

I recognise Thirlmere when it appears on our left. I recall the Saturday when Bacon and I walked around it. The ten miles were nothing for her little legs. Cal pulls into a lay-by at the end, where an ice-cream van parks during daylight hours and tempts motorists and walkers alike. The kind owner once gave me a free cone for her.

When Cal climbs into the back with me, I try to move closer to the door, keeping my eyes fixed on the emptiness outside.

I tense up when a hand closes around the top of my arm.

'Don't,' I warn.

I resist Cal's gentle tug and try to twist my arm free. I pull at his fingers.

'You're hurting me,' I tell him through gritted

teeth.

'Then stop struggling.'

'Leave me alone.'

Cal slips his arm behind me and turns me round to face him as he pulls me onto his lap. With one of his arms encircling my shoulders and the other holding me around my waist, I struggle to get my hands between us to free our chests.

'Let – me – *go.*'

I shove against him wherever I can, trying to use my foot against the raised backseat armrest to gain some leverage. All my strength is in my legs. I wish the same could be said for him.

'Get off me!'

Cal's sweater is in danger of having the neck and shoulder seams ripped apart as I grab and push him and strain my head away. I kick the door, the backrest, the back of the passenger seat—

'*Get off me!*'

I cannot keep this up for much longer.

'Please!' I beg.

My anger is diminishing with every weakening shove.

'Please.'

My last attempt is hardly that.

'Please?'

Resigned to my fate, my arms awkwardly find their way around Cal's neck. As he pulls me close, he pulls the trigger, and the first sob bursts out of my mouth. It is followed by another one, then another. They are almost falling over each other in their attempts to escape. When Cal pulls me closer still, I give my grief permission to take what it needs, and the more his arms hold me together, the less scary it is to let go.

I don't know how long it takes – twenty minutes, an hour – but the supply of tears I have built up over many years starts to run dry. When my noisy mourning dribbles to a whimper, I force open my eyes. Foggy windows obscure the outside world. As my body is gently rocked, I watch the condensation trickle down the glass in wonky rivulets.

I wait for my hammering heart to calm and my uneven breaths to peter out. We remain huddled together even when the rise and fall of our chests have synchronised. The quietness only breaks when cars pass by, the sound drifting through the partially open driver's window.

'When Beth sent you my first *Caerli°°ani* story, what did you think of it?' I ask.

The fingers that are gently massaging my neck don't falter.

'I thought it was magical.'

I don't know what it is, but suddenly my mind feels pleasantly fuzzy. Maybe it's the oxytocin that my body is releasing from being held. Either that, or it's what Cal thought of my story. Over the years, I've read similar reviews, but no matter how many I read, they never get old. However, hearing those words come from him...

'I also thought we wouldn't be allowed to publish it,' he adds.

I continue stroking the back of his head. 'What's the name of your father's publishing company?'

Cal must have wondered when this day would come. Sadly, this is the fallout from giving back the object that reawakened my heart. And although I know the answer – I knew it as soon as he said what his father did – it must be asked for the question that will inevitably follow.

'Adams & Chadwick. My mom's dad, Foster Adams, was one of the co-founders. Mom's an only child, and she's never been interested in books. When my grandpa retired, my dad stepped up to the plate.'

Playing with the short hair above the back of his neck soothes me. If Cal didn't like it, he would say, I know he would. He's good like that.

'And you spoke to my dad's former assistant?' I ask.

Cal takes in a long breath, my chest moving with his. 'When I read your manuscript, I knew there was more to it. Monty retired years ago, but he and my dad kept in touch. I drove out to Connecticut and met with him. After your dad's… diagnosis, he confessed everything, telling Monty that most of the characters in the *Waenaga* books weren't even his. He said that leaving them in his will to the rightful owner was the honorable thing to do; it was the only thing to do. Your dad hoped it was a way of… making amends.'

An owl's territorial hoots echo within the forest of towering fir trees across the road from where we are parked.

'When we were made to visit him here,' a voice

from me retells, 'he insisted on these long daily walks. I'm talking miles, and the twins were only small; they quickly got bored. Which is why I made up stories – to keep them entertained. But the more elaborate I made the stories, the longer he made the walks. A Catch-22 for the twins, you might say. He loved them, though.'

'The twins?'

I manage a weak chuckle. 'No, the stories. I started getting invitations to my dad's study. I remember every detail of that room. I can't remember where the house was or what my bedroom was like, just that study. And only I got invited, not my sisters – never my sisters. He would have a little tea party waiting for me: tiny sandwiches and Mr Kipling cakes arranged on one of those tiered cake stands. Do you know the ones I mean, with the different-sized plates on them?'

'I know them.'

'There would be a silver teapot and a porcelain milk jug. There were even those funny little tongs for the sugar lumps. God, I must have drunk pots and pots of tea. Maybe that's why I don't enjoy it now. And I would sit there, stuffing my face and sipping my drink, excited to be doing something with him. Excited to be… to be noticed. When I left that study, I was always on a high – and it wasn't just from the sugar.

'I eventually asked him why he took notes – why he would only listen and never join in. My dad said he wanted to preserve our time together. But when I veered off the subject of faeries and friendly goblins, he would try to steer me back. If he couldn't, the pen would go down, and he'd be looking at his watch. Trust me, my sulks are nothing compared to what his were like!'

Cal senses my sudden need to draw him closer. When my arms tighten about him, he reciprocates. When my hold relaxes again, his does the same. He'll go where I go.

'By the time I was nearly twelve, the tea party invites were business meeting requests,' I recollect. 'It was time to discuss my notes. And while I was building the foundations for a magical realm with pearl dragons, I had his undivided attention. None of my sisters ever came close to getting that. And I used to think… if this was how he showed his love, at least it was something; it was better than nothing. Or so I thought.

'It didn't last long: a few years, that's all. Just until my dad had some ideas of his own – and he found an editor who could help flesh mine out. After that, I never saw him again. I only found out his first *Waenaga* tale had been published when I saw it in WHSmith's window. I was eighteen. Likewise, I only found out he'd remarried when Ma spotted a photo of them in the *Daily Star*.'

'Did you ever meet his second wife or her sons? Your… stepbrothers?'

'No.'

Cal's massaging fingers are reducing any remaining tension in my body to rubber. The pressure he is using is just firm enough. Perfect, in fact.

'Is that why you used to come here often before you were a writer, Jo – to find the house and confront him?'

'I never thought that far ahead. I don't know if I ever really wanted to find it. Obviously not, or I could've just asked Ma for the address. Maybe I just needed to… look for something.'

'Why didn't you try to expose the truth?'

'I had no proof. My dad kept all my notebooks. And what would be the point? People would think I was only after money.'

'Is it true that he left your sisters ten thousand pounds each in his will, and you got only the copyright?'

'My family still thinks he left me nothing, just a letter I've never shown them. Hats off to him, though. Can you think of a better way to provoke a child into building on your legacy? Also…' I lower my voice to a whisper against his ear. '… I never told Quinn Manning the best stories.'

'No.' Cal's chuckling breath warms my skin. 'No, you certainly did not.'

Not enough time has passed before he loosens his arms. When he lifts his face from my neck, it feels… The space he has left feels…

'Your legs must be numb,' I suddenly point out.

'No, no, I'm fine. You don't have to…'

But I'm already halfway into my clumsy dismount.

'Oops.' I'm guessing his chin felt my elbow strike more than I did. 'Sorry.'

347

More apologies are issued from both of us for the awkward hand and knee placements. Eventually, I slump back in the seat and close my eyes. A second later, my fingers tighten when Cal sits forward.

'I didn't mean to wake you,' he says.

'Wake me? Was I asleep?'

'Only for a while. We should make tracks.'

My exit from the back of the car is snagged on something. We both look down at the space on the seat between us.

I'm not sure who is the first to let go of the other person's hand.

It takes a couple of minutes to demist the windows. All of them, it would seem, not just the ones nearest my meltdown. I can imagine what those driving by must have thought.

I have to drag my seatbelt on. Getting out of the back and into the front has taken its toll. 'Why do I feel like I've just finished a triathlon ahead of last year's winner?'

'Because you're completely drained.' Cal turns the steering wheel with the palm of his hand and pulls out onto the road. 'Both emotionally and physically.'

I say nothing when he drives past my street. I watch the road as we travel down the hill and past Bowness Pier. We head out of town and towards the southern end of the lake. We travel through Newby Bridge. It's the village where Bacon and I would start our woodland walks to Finsthwaite Heights. We leave the trunk road at Backbarrow, driving down a street lined with stone homes and rendered terraced houses.

Softly lit residential gives way to moonlit rural again, and we're on a twisting lane I'm unfamiliar with. After five minutes, we turn left off the road and rattle over a cattle grid.

We drive slowly down a slope to a small gathering of buildings surrounding the tail end of a pond. Floor-to-ceiling windows in single-storey, timber-clad accommodations create soft-glow spotlights that highlight the edges of the water.

Cal holds the passenger door open and watches me brace myself for the physical challenge I'm about to tackle. Finally, I accept the hand he offers me. My legs wobble under my weight as I take a few steps. Although the gravel isn't helping, I assure him I can manage.

We enter his villa via the front door and step straight into a lounge with a vaulted ceiling. I sink down onto the U-shaped squidgy sofa.

'Would you like a drink or anything?'

When Cal crouches in front of me, I realise I haven't responded. I shake my head.

'Are you warm enough?' he checks.

A scant nod is as much of an effort.

He gathers up some cushions, piling them on top of each other. I'm not sure if it's him guiding my shoulders down onto them or if I topple over. He takes off my boots and lifts my legs. My eyes close. The weight of a light blanket covers my exposed arms. Sleep has almost claimed me when I feel my glasses gently being removed.

Chapter Thirty

A table lamp has been left on, not that I needed it. When I wake up, I open my eyes to the pale glow that precedes an early August sunrise. A moment of panic quickens my heart at the unfamiliar surroundings. However, strange lounges aside, the sight of Cal asleep on one side of the sofa in his rented villa is security enough.

Another bedroom is behind the third door I open along the corridor off the lounge. But near the window, there's a familiar selection of brown leather Maxwell-Scott bags. There's a partially open door on the other side of the bed. The white tiles on the floor in there are the giveaway.

Bathroom lights will never be remembered in my acceptance speech, especially after today. I think this one has a personal grudge against me. There's little I can do about how I look, though. But the fur coating in my mouth can be fixed.

I take a tentative look inside the open washbag as I gargle with Cal's mouthwash. If you don't touch anything, it's not snooping. There's half a tube of

L'Occitane Cade aftershave balm, a texturising spray for his hair, and some Clinique for Men products. There are also three bottles of aftershave.

I sniff the spray nozzle on the bottle of Creed Aventus. He wore this to a book reading in Edinburgh earlier this year. And to a book fair in Miami last November.

I smell the Dior Sauvage. He wears this in the office sometimes with his light grey suit. He was wearing it when we went to the farmers' market.

Bleu de Chanel is not one of his regulars, but there were remnants of it on him last night: it was lingering behind his ear, on that area of soft skin close to his hairline. I remember thinking it smelt fresh. And sensual. I wonder who got him into it. I sniff the nozzle again. One of his *many* serious girlfriends, no doubt.

In the lounge, Cal is still in the same propped-up position. His legs are sprawled out in front of him, his ankles are crossed, and his arms are folded. His head has dropped back and to the side a little.

This is the first time I've seen him asleep. He must sleep at some point when we travel. After all, look how much time we spend together in a flying metal tube at thirty-odd thousand feet.

But every time we get on a late evening flight, Cal asks a crew member for an extra pillow for me before he has stowed our hand luggage in the overheads, and whenever I wake up, his eyes are open, and he is doing something – usually on an electronic device or with a red pen. I've even caught him engrossed in something that's already a *Sunday Times* bestseller.

As sleep softens Cal's unfathomable expression almost beyond recognition, I wonder if there are nights when he lies awake and frets about the same things as me.

Does his mind ever question last week's decisions? Does he ever stress over what the screening tests might find rather than what they probably won't? Has he ever worried himself into one a.m. about the possibility of sharing a single bed one day with nothing but dementia?

Whatever might be going on in his life, Cal always has room on his shoulders for me and the troubling weight of my words. Yet he can sleep like this, with his eyes unmoving behind their lids, his eyebrows unclenched, and his lips… his lips slightly parted.

I remind myself that studying him at his most vulnerable is an intrusion. It's a privilege reserved for those permitted to do more than merely observe. I push myself up off the coffee table and go in search of liquid refreshment, walking off my pins and needles.

That's strange. I wasn't sitting in front of Cal for *that* long.

Was I?

Glass jars near the kettle contain items that are 'compliments of the owners': espresso coffee bags from an award-winning coffee roaster; rough-cut sugar cubes; homemade shortbread; and a selection of 'local' teabags. Where they grow the tea around here…

I leave some coffee bags in hot water in the thermal coffee carafe and locate the cups and spoons. I panic for a second before opening the fridge door. Cal might stomach grown-up coffee as it comes, but I'm a one-third hot milk gal.

Only after I've poured the dark liquid into two cups does it occur to me that maybe he has tea first thing. He's had tea during his stay, if the level in the jar is anything to go by. It might also explain the open bottle of milk.

And does Cal take sugar in either?

Eight years, and I still don't know this simple thing about him. Eight years of him handing me my drink of choice whenever I woke up during a journey. Eight years of him having my drink of choice waiting for me in the car.

For eight years, Cal has picked restaurants where I always find something I like on the menu. For eight years, nutritious meals have always magically appeared when we're on the road. My favourite biscuits have been stored in the agency's staff kitchen cupboard for eight years. That's almost how long his fruit salads have been too much for one person.

Surely…

No. No, it can't have all been for—

'Morning.'

When I turn round, Cal's sleepy smile disappears. He quickly cups my cheeks and attempts to wiper blade my tears away with his thumbs.

'Jo?'

My face crumples. 'I d-d-don't know what you d-drink in a m-m-morning.'

Cal's worry softens when he realises I haven't just received devastating news, and the relief makes him smile again. His face looks like it's meant to smile. He looks so different when he smiles. He looks...

'I have coffee first thing,' he says.

'And sugar? Do you t-t-take sugar? I don't know,' I sob. 'All this t-t-time, and I d-d-don't even know this about y-y-you.'

His pale blue sweater won't appreciate the two dark patches I'm creating on it. I sniff. Make that three.

'One sugar in coffee,' Cal tells me. 'Milk and no sugar in my tea.'

'O-O-Okay,' comes out muffled when said into a cashmere tissue.

I'm not sure how hot he likes it. The fact he's waiting until my moment of weepy insanity passes doesn't answer that question, either. No, it just makes my tears start afresh. My arms wrap tighter around him. My hold is becoming almost as indisputable as his.

I eventually take a deep breath and gain the strength to remove my face from his chest, inspecting the damp damage. Cal loosens his hold but hovers. But no, I'm in control again. I step back, wiping my eyes and muttering my apologies – which aren't only for the state of his sweater.

I pop a cube into his cup and give it a good stir. 'One sugar.'

'Thanks.' Cal takes a sip. 'Mmm, you make great

coffee.'

'Is it hot enough? Should I pop it in the microwave?'

'It's perfect.'

***

Coffee addicts know the first drink is the fix. We then enjoy the ones drunk for pleasure on the slate-paved terrace. We also tuck into a couple of cooked breakfasts, which he has rustled up from items delivered to his door each morning in a basket.

The sun is above the mountaintops, and the thin mist is disappearing. It's going to be another scorcher. Copious amounts of ice cream will be consumed today, which means people will battle for benches overlooking the lakes to sit down and enjoy them.

We watch the other holiday dwellings come to life. As adults slowly wake up, children show how easily it's done without nicotine and caffeine. One family's two young labradors bounce around them. Their older dog wags his tail, trying to join in. It must be nice not knowing why you can't do something any more.

'How are you feeling?' Cal asks.

'I miss her,' I'm not ashamed to admit. 'But I'm all right.'

I'm actually surprised by how calm I feel. Enough, I notice when comparing plates, to be making light work of my breakfast. The man knows how to make tasty scrambled eggs.

Cal nods. 'Good. You look much better.'

'That's because I slathered my face in your

Clinique stuff.'

'Did you also use my electric razor to trim your beard?'

'I couldn't. I clogged it with my toe hair.'

He disappears inside and re-emerges with his briefcase. 'Some papers to look over for the meeting.'

A day of boardroom boredom and polite conversation for a share of the net profits that the *Caerli°°ani* movies might make. They offered five per cent; Cal wanted fifteen. They eventually met somewhere in the middle.

Before meetings and events, he always asks me to edit my opinions. I don't know why he needs to do this every time now. Only because, at a book launch party four years ago, I gave a lovely journalist a tiny piece of advice. I suggested she watch how very loud-mouthed boyfriends react to massive gaps in a queue of traffic before introducing them to authors. I didn't see an issue.

Cal removes some document wallets. 'There is also next month's speaking engagement in Chichester to discuss, N.R. Magnusson's website redesign to look at, some book cover art…'

I drop my head back. 'Do we *have* to go through all this now?'

'I'm afraid so.'

'But I've only had one and a half coffees. I may make a rash decision.'

'I'm leaving this morning.'

My head springs back up. 'Do you have to?'

Cal studies the blank envelope in his hand. 'My

family is flying in early.'

His reaction is the handshake from eight years ago all over again – but he won't tell me in another eight that I misread this one.

'That'll be nice,' I somehow say.

'Your train tickets and hotel reservation for one night.' Cal places the envelope on top of a novel, which I'll now be taking home sooner rather than later. 'Could you also give Alexandra's new book a brief review?'

'Yeah. Sure.'

***

I fiddle with the car radio as Cal drives me back to Bowness-on-Windermere. One station has too many overused words thrown about during the banal chatter. On another, there's no variation in the guest's tone. There are adverts on the next one, and on the next. Someone, play one chuffing song, please.

Cal stops at temporary traffic lights that have just turned red.

'I'm paid up for two more nights,' he says. 'If you fancy making use of the villa's hot tub.'

I can't refrain from sneering... I mean, saying, 'Maybe Maria would like it.'

Either the traffic light is stuck, or the infrared sensor is broken. It's been red for at least three minutes. There's not even a hole in the road, so why—?

The light turns green, and the car's powerful engine pushes me back into my seat. Further back than usual.

'I won't see her before I leave,' Cal utters.

The road gently bends and brings us into my temporary town. The familiarity and wonderful incompatibility of the residential block opposite Bowness Bay is on our right. It may be an odd welcome to visitors in the eyes of the tourism board, but it's almost an ode to the town too. It's a pork pie on a Michelin-starred restaurant's plate of food.

A friend of mine from the market owns one. A grandparent left it to her, of course, as nobody who creates scented oils in her garage for a living can afford anything around here. Not nowadays.

As the car pulls up outside my rental, I make a decision. 'I'll use the hot tub if nobody else wants to.'

'I will drop the key off once I'm packed.'

I undo my seatbelt. 'I'll be at the house.'

'No problem. I'll call there—'

'Don't bother,' I tell the glove box. 'Just pop it through the letterbox here.'

'Okay.'

I'm about to close the passenger door when I remember my manners. 'Thanks – for last night.'

I don't wait for Cal's response.

Chapter Thirty-One

Nyx's mum is here before me. I *knew* this would happen.

When she asked if we could meet in town for a drink, why didn't I stick with the first outfit I picked: an orange hazmat suit and a contrasting bulletproof vest? Instead, I spent sodding ages deciding on a simple pair of trousers and a plain T-shirt. Now I'm only eight minutes early.

I couldn't have been here any sooner. Even in trainers, it's a brisk five-minute walk from my rented house. I've also just discovered it can be done in five when wearing pink polka-dot pumps with four-inch heels. That deserves a round of applause.

Or at least a full-face crash helmet.

Maria is looking through her phone, sitting a row away from all the occupied window seats. Couples should be banned from sitting in them; they have each other to look at. They don't need distractions or options.

'Can I get you another drink?' I ask.

She looks up and then back at her glass. A

thimbleful of wine is left at the bottom.

'Glass of red,' I answer for her.

Maria slips her phone away when I place her replenished goldfish bowl in front of her. With my cranberry and soda water, I take the seat opposite. This way, she won't need bumpers when she launches her ten-pin bowling ball at me.

'Do you want to tell me what happened?' Maria is somebody else who thinks build-ups to the main conversational event are as overrated as maturity.

'You mean…?'

'My son told me why you turned him down. Now I'd like to hear the truth.'

My rapid blinking is cooling down my eyeballs but not my burning cheeks. 'That was the… the truth, and… and Nyx said other women have rejected him for the same reason.'

'But it wasn't *your* reason.'

I don't have the energy for this. 'It'll have to do, Maria. I'm sorry.'

'He lied to you.'

'He didn't. He… held back the truth.'

'About having a daughter,' she reminds me. 'That's the same as lying. And he kept that lie going.'

'It was a soft lie.'

'A lie is a lie.'

'I'm sure there are worse things people lie about.'

Maria crosses her arms. 'Such as?'

I pick up my drink, but my hand shakes enough to be noticed. I quickly put it down again, sliding it closer.

'Give me some examples, Jo.'

'Okay.' Bouncing my leg helps me think. 'Would you say it's worse when someone claims they never lie?'

Maria's expression says it's probably on par. It also says she wants more than one example. Especially if I want to leave here in one piece. And not in a body bag.

'How about... texting LOL but not actually laughing out loud?'

She nods. 'And what about when your little boys ask what cows they are? Is it terrible to always say they're milk ones and not beef ones?'

'It's no worse than telling kids those big trucks are taking livestock on their holidays.'

'That's a fair point. I don't feel so bad now.'

Maria sips her decent pinot noir. Her nerves are showing since she can't drink it with a straw. On the table, her free hand looks like it's sending a message in Morse code to the sniper across the street. All the same, I still want to reach over and grab her fingers. I want to will all her anger and emotions into me. I'll have them – I deserve them.

'What if he'd lied about something like... Oh, I don't know.' Maria almost looks like she is carefully pondering. 'Writing twelve books and selling millions of copies?'

With my elbows resting on the table and my lips busy around my straw, I can only raise my eyebrows and nod slowly. On the outside, I may appear unruffled. Internally, I'm throwing autographed

Olivia J. Lawrence hardbacks at the other seventy passengers racing to get to the last lifeboat.

Speaking of signed copies of my books…

The son's wife was there, said Steve, who saved me a spot on that bench. *Who did Sara say the author was*?

'Your sister said she recognised my face.'

'It just took her a couple of gins after the barbecue to remember where from,' Maria remarks. 'She said she enjoyed your book reading.'

'And Nyx?' I don't care about favourable reviews right now.

'He won't find out from me. Or my sister.'

'But she looks like someone who enjoys tumble-drying hornets' nests.'

'The thing is, Sara believes texting me details of her infidelities is as good as penance.' Maria raises one eyebrow. 'I told her if she breathes a word to anyone before you, I'll show her husband how often she's enjoying a "wellness retreat" in Bath.'

I daren't voice my immense gratitude.

'You have to hate me, Maria.'

'When Sara told me, my initial thoughts weren't good, and… yes, I did – I hated you. I was angry at you, too. Just the thought of you *lying* to *my son* because you didn't *trust* him.' The faster Maria talks, the louder she gets. 'And thinking he'd be interested in someone based on what they have is *ridiculous*. It's… It's *insulting*. Nyx doesn't give a *shit* about wealth.'

I blink slowly.

'And *especially* someone else's. In fact, he is turned *off* by it.'

I press my lips together.

'He ended a *relationship* because of it.' Maria's scowl softens. 'But you know that already,' she says, her volume and emphasised words dissolving.

'It… came up.'

'And rather than watch his silly pride fail to handle your success, you took the blame.'

'I took it because your son's a good soul.'

'And a good friend?' Maria asks. 'I imagine you often stressed that to him as much as you did to me the first time we met.'

'I tried,' I assure her.

'Despite that, you still let yourself be portrayed as the villain.'

'It was the least I could do.'

I match the speed at which Maria's hand shoots across the table, squeezing equally as tightly.

'Don't leave the Lakes, Jo.'

'I'll have to soon.'

'Why?'

'I only moved up here to see if…' I don't need to tell her everything. 'I moved here for a break, and the house was a pleasant distraction. I've loved doing it. But it's finished. It's going on the market.'

'Why do you have to sell it?'

'What else can I do with it?'

Maria thinks this is a ridiculous question. Either that, or someone's just informed her how much time she'd save by doing the things she said would save her time if she did them. 'You can live in it.'

'Why would I do that?'

'Because you love that house.'

'I don't.'

The corner of her mouth quirks up. 'How much did that fancy waterfall shower in the en suite cost?'

'I wanted it to be just right.'

'Yes, but just right for *whom*?'

'That's… what we'll hopefully find out.'

'This is where you belong,' Maria states firmly. 'I know it. Izzie knows it.'

'That woman barely knows how to work the pedal on a bin.'

'And Cal knows it.'

My head snaps up. 'Cal? Cal said that? When? When did he say that?'

'After the barbecue.'

I hope Maria doesn't elaborate on what she was doing – or what he was doing to her – after that.

'He waited until everyone had gone,' she says, 'and he…'

Lalalalalalalala—

'… stayed another hour to help me clean up.'

Where did I put my guide on how to blink and close my mouth?

My ability to speak eventually returns. 'Yeah, Cal likes… He likes things clean.'

Maria frowns. 'The man has his own recipe for floor cleaner.'

'He also has a keyboard that doesn't sound like a maraca when you shake it. His desk, monitor, everything. Spotless.'

'Perhaps he secretly hides clutter somewhere.'

'You'll never guess what Cal keeps in his office file drawers.' I check that nobody is listening. 'He keeps *files*. Those things aren't for storing Hobnob biscuits and Pot Noodles. The only non-work-related item in them is his pack of disinfectant wipes, which he gets out every time he returns to his desk. The guy has serious trust issues.'

'Aren't you ever tempted, Jo?'

I raise my hands and let them drop. 'Maria, you sound like Izzie. Why is it hard to believe that two people can work well together without things turning sexual?'

She shakes her head. 'That's not what I meant.'

'Oh.'

'Aren't you ever tempted to mess up his desk?'

'No, never. I just lick his computer mouse whenever he leaves the room.'

It's such a relief to hear Maria laughing again.

'Actually,' she says, 'it's partly why he and I would never have worked out.'

Why is it only 'partly'? And why do I feel like my Duracells have just been changed?

'But I thought... I thought there was lots of interest,' I say, 'from, erm... you know, from... both sides.'

'Oh, I think he found me attractive, and vice versa. I mean, how could you not?'

I don't know why Maria is looking at me with raised eyebrows.

365

'Don't you think Cal is attractive?' she asks.

'We work together.'

'That's not an answer.'

'I've used it multiple times and with relative success.'

'Anyway,' she says, shrugging her shoulders, 'he sterilised my dishcloth and then left.'

'I'm really sorry.'

'Don't be.' Maria waves it aside. 'I'm fine. And my kitchen's never been so clean.'

She sips her wine with a steadier hand.

'He thinks a lot of you,' she tells me.

'Of course he does. He's on my payroll.'

'Are you sure that's why?'

'Maria, we—'

'Work together. I get that. But people change. How we feel about people changes.'

'Cal's feelings towards me haven't changed.'

'You're right.' Maria nods slowly. '*His* feelings haven't.'

I sit up a little straighter, taking a deep breath. 'We're trying the "friend" thing. He asked if we could.'

'That's a start.'

'I suppose.'

Maria tilts her head to one side. 'You're very guarded, Jo.'

My smile is one of relief at finally being rumbled.

'My son would never admit it, but…'

'He would have struggled with that,' I end the sentence for her. 'I know my shortcomings very well.'

She raises her glass. 'Luckily for you, so does Cal.'

Chapter Thirty-Two

The fifth estate agent in as many days evaluates my lakeside cottage. He checks the finish on my wooden floors, tests the power in the showers, and turns the dimmer light switches on and off. I don't bother saying much. I learnt that my running commentary was unnecessary after the second agent echoed the first; since then, I've let the craftsmanship and the location do the talking.

The agent takes another photo of the feature fireplace wall in the lounge. 'Who did you say you used?'

I call him 'the agent' when I may as well use his proper name. It's good ol' Jeff, the man who initially alerted me to this place. When I phoned his agency and asked if somebody wouldn't mind coming over, I bet he was out the door faster than someone who gets a Monday morning refund on a party dress.

'I used Colin and Nyx Hart, a grandfather and grandson team.'

He's clicking away on his phone's camera again.

'They do a fair bit of work in this area,' I add.

'Perhaps you've heard of them?'

Jeff grunts. It could be a yes.

'They came up with *loads* of ideas and saved so much stuff,' I tell him. 'Colin used the old floors from upstairs to create that lovely shiplap on some of the walls. Did you get any photos of those? Oh, and these multi-slide doors? Nyx's brilliant suggestion. This entire kitchen was his doing, too. And the turquoise back door? It took him a while to convince me, but I'm glad he did.'

'Nyx is the young bloke, isn't he?'

'That's right. And the one who helped me get this place,' I happily recall.

I doubt that's how Jeff recalls it.

'Was he a friend of yours before?' he asks.

'Not before, no.'

'Well, it sounds to me like you were lucky.'

'Oh, I was. Meeting Nyx was—'

'That's not what I meant. You knew nothing about their company or this line of business. You could've been shafted.'

I stand up straighter. 'I wasn't.'

'How do you know?'

'Because they did their homework to win this job,' I clearly state, 'and I did too.'

Since Jeff is facing away from me, I can only hear the snigger in his slight exhalation of breath.

'You need to be aware,' he says, 'that there are conmen who prey on women like you.'

Women like me? What, short women? Bespectacled women? Sagittarius women? Having someone point out my naivety reminds me of my recurring nightmare: the one where I'm sitting on a public toilet with no door. But when it's raised by a massive oil tanker like—

'You underestimate her, Jeff.' Across the room, Nyx is standing between the lounge and hallway, leaning against the door jamb with his arms crossed. 'Jo knows a rogue when she sees one.'

As my contractor strolls towards me, my desire to reach into my bra cups and perk up my boobs is as strong as ever. After all, Nyx is still a wildly gorgeous man.

He's just not the wildly gorgeous man for me.

'She's pleased with what you've done here,' Jeff says, seeing as it would hurt that massive ego to pass the compliment off as his own.

Nyx's eyes lock with mine. 'As long as Jo's happy, that's all that matters.'

'Hmm.' Jeff is thumbing away on his phone. 'Right, I'll take this information back to the office.'

***

From the porch, Nyx and I watch him drive away. I'm sure the amount of gravel his car wheels kick up would have impressed the girls twenty years ago.

Then we are alone. If I were to guess, I'd say Nyx is here to drop off a certificate for the boiler or the windows, or he forgot some tools in the garage. Whatever the reason, I don't care. I'm merely pleased to get even a few moments with him again. Now all I can hope is that the easy camaraderie stolen from us

370

hasn't been lost forever, as that would be a real shame.

'How have the valuations gone?'

I stop in the doorway. 'Disappointing.'

'I'm sorry, Jo. I did say at the start that you'd be lucky to make much profit.'

'You did. But what you've created is better than *anything* I could've imagined.'

Nyx accepts the glowing praise, although it clearly makes him slightly uncomfortable.

'I'm glad you like it.' He slowly looks around at what he and his team have achieved. 'It's just a shame the estate agents don't think buyers will feel the same way.'

'That's not why the valuations were disappointing, Nyx.'

I have his attention again.

'I'm not selling.'

'You're moving in?'

'I am.' My eyes are desperately asking if that's all right.

Nyx's affable grin slides into place. 'And yet you *still* let that slimeball Jeff in.'

'I couldn't resist.'

He looks up at the wall lanterns on either side of the front door: die-cast aluminium, walnut finish, tinted glass. They cost a small fortune, even with his trade discount. Before I handed over my debit card, Nyx gently reminded me that it was a needless expense for a fixer-upper. But perhaps I knew even then that I wouldn't sell it – that I didn't need to.

That I didn't want to.

Something Izzie said the day before she left springs to mind. 'We often fall in love with things gradually, Bee, but we can convince ourselves for a long time into thinking we haven't.' Only when the estate agents started showing up did I realise she was obviously referring to this house – and not *Peaky Blinders*.

'Admit it, Mr Hart. Those lanterns look amazing.'

And there are those dimples again and that twinkle in his eye. That smile of his must chase away his daughter's fears.

'I take it all back, Jo. They do. And what difference does a few hundred quid make when you've already blown your lighting budget?'

Nyx doesn't avoid my gentle punch to his shoulder. Hopefully, it means he misses what we developed over the season as much as I do. He has to.

It's as if the familiar cloth tote bag he retrieved from his car has spoken to him. 'This is yours.'

I reluctantly accept it. 'It was a birthday gift.'

'Now that I've read it, I want you to have it back.'

I recall the number of bedrooms in his mum's house and the tiny area Nyx had to call his own. Even after paying child maintenance to his daughter's mother (amounts that will be more than the CMS says he must pay), he must take home enough to be able to move out. He won't, though, not anytime soon. Not when his lodge helps Maria balance a stretched weekly budget. I can't imagine there will ever be much spare change for the future.

How many nest eggs could these pages have laid

for them?

'This book just confirms it,' Nyx says. 'N.R. Magnusson is a better storyteller than Quinn Manning ever was.'

It feels wrong when you can't thank someone for a compliment.

'I will let him know.'

He shrugs. 'Or her.'

I put the bag down on the restored Victorian writing desk. It's one we discovered upended and minus its legs in the garage. Something else we found stands on top of it.

'By next year, Jo, your garden will look as good as it did then.'

I touch the frame, my heart filling as it does every time I look at the old photo and those two smiling faces.

'Maybe that could be my next challenge,' I suggest.

Nyx opens his arms, and I step into them and practise a hug. A proper hug. I'm… I'm getting the hang of them.

'Thanks for a great summer, Jo.'

'You too.'

When he steps back, it's reassuring to see that his look of relief is equal to mine.

He stops on the second porch step. 'Let me know if you feel like doing up another house.'

'Careful, Nyx. I may hold you to that.'

He grins. 'Please do.'

Chapter Thirty-Three

I watch the mountainous landscape through the train window as it scales down to hills and an equal share of blue sky. When the ratio of rural to urban sways in the latter's favour, I open my laptop and the Word document I've been working on. While other passengers audibly tut about occasionally slow Wi-Fi ruining their lives, I finish the last chapter.

With each passing station, the number of people boarding the train creeps up. Clothing changes from stylish holiday outfits to comfortable workwear. Enthusiasm levels are hovering around a three by the time we pick up at Crewe, reflected by some and disguised by others in their attire.

I'm suddenly conscious of what I am wearing. I've dressed up, seizing the opportunity to scrub clean the build-up of matt paint and garden soil from under my fingernails. The weather report last night also influenced me. When it said the Lakes would be hot again, it swayed me towards a loose fit and a cotton blend.

Today's destination, however, is taking me away

from the differing climates between mountaintops and valley floors. And the further south I travel, the harder it becomes to see the sun. Wall-to-wall blue is being invaded by fluffy and white. Suddenly, short sleeves and a knee-length dress hem feel like ridiculous choices.

As the train starts slowing down for Euston station, the unreadable greying sky makes its intentions clear, with soggy streaks blurring my first look at London in a season.

Before the platform is even in sight, those fellow passengers who cannot wait to begin another eight-hour working day start to queue at the doors. I slowly pull on the white cardigan I brought just in case, wishing I'd opted now for something just in case of a wet emergency.

A familiar face is waiting for me inside the bustling station. When we swap my suitcase and laptop bag for Starbucks' finest and Upper Crust's tastiest, I dig deep for my usual enthusiasm.

'Welcome back, Jo.'

I'm not back, but it's hardly worth correcting someone who only chauffeurs me and my Sharpie pens about during literary matters of business.

'Thanks, Derek.'

***

It's a dash from the car to the office entrance, with my suitcase wheels fighting me every step of the way. At least holding my handbag above my head protects my curls – the ones I got up half an hour early to tong in.

Another coffee is waiting for me at reception, which I will collect after a quick trip to the loo. When my lip gloss, deodorant and perfume have been reapplied, I take a minute in front of the bathroom mirror to compose myself.

Deep breath in and slowly let it out.

And again, in... out... in—

Enough of that shit. I don't believe it works anyway. The same as calming teas and colouring books.

'Amanda and Andrew are waiting for you in the boardroom,' Cal's assistant informs me as she tucks my suitcase and laptop bag behind her desk. 'Would you like anything special ordering in for lunch?'

'Oh, you know me, Fay. Whatever Cal orders will be fine.'

'Cal's dining out today, Jo.'

Is she wondering whether I'll react – or how?

I point along the corridor. 'The boardroom, did you say?'

I've met Amanda a few times, and she scares me in a good way. She's the one who deals with getting my books from the shelves to the screen; she's an adaptation rights consultant/advisor/colonel/ball-buster. I heard she originally came on board because she had a crush on the agency's financial director. Despite walking down the aisle last September, I don't think that's gone away yet.

Everyone thought she was already married, having used 'Mrs' and a double-barrelled surname for years. As well as the platinum band she's always worn on her left ring finger. It's paired with an engagement ring that has a dangerously high-set solitaire diamond. Honestly, when Amanda points to paragraphs in your contract that she fought for, the stone almost takes your bloody eye out.

The woman is polished and posh, and when she's speaking to you, she doesn't blink. She's always on the go; her diary never has a blank space, which also applies to the hours following work o'clock. There's never been time for children, something Amanda has never regretted. That alone would usually be enough for me to like someone. But what sealed it was the first time we met for dinner at a place where they had a dress code, and she loudly called her ex-boss a cunt.

Andrew is one of the marketing people. He does many things, and I was treated to a verbal list at lightning speed the first time we met. No, it wasn't to justify his salary or to get you to question why the man hasn't had a pay rise in ages. It's what he also rattles off when speed dating at Seven Gays in Seven Nights. He's short, sharp and *great* fun to ditch the office Christmas party with, hightailing it away from catered blinis and book talk.

'Shall we get started,' Amanda says. There's no need for a question mark – and no guesses as to who sends her assistant to the morning meetings. She has him text her when the discussion about last night's *Love Island* episode has finished. Only then will she attend.

I look towards the door. 'Shouldn't we wait for Cal?'

'We've already been through this with him,' Amanda insists, turning to the first page of her copy.

She reaches over and turns to the first page of mine.

'More than once,' Andrew reassures me.

I sense his wish to play another role today in my agent's absence. Business-suit support, perhaps, for the woman in the dusky rose day dress.

Amanda's no-nonsense approach is wobbling. 'Are you all right to…?'

I adjust my glasses. 'Rights and restrictions – tell me where I stand with them.'

***

Three hours later, when we reach the bottom of the fifteenth – and final – page, I may need someone to write my name on the back of my hand. The police will need it when they find me trying to eat a shoe as I wander aimlessly along The Embankment.

I vaguely recall raising the odd question during the first three pages, but nothing they couldn't answer. By page eight, however, I was praying for a fire drill or a silo of coffee. Failing either of those, a Holland & Barrett: I thought some emergency omegas and vitamins might help me with my… with my… What was it? Oh, yeah, my concentration.

'And…'

Oh no, Amanda. No more, please.

If she asks me now to look at so much as a receipt to see if she's been overcharged for bananas, I may slide under this table and refuse to come out until the rainforests are saved.

'… we're done.'

My sense of relief wishes it had the energy to slide towards a corner flag on its knees.

'Amanda, Andrew, thank you for all your hard work.'

Amanda's hug is brief but genuine. Andrew's hugs are always the same: legendary in this office, whether for business or pleasure. They're also essential after bad first drafts and break-ups.

'We'll get a copy over to them this afternoon,' Amanda says, enjoying the click of the stapler more than most. She's fastening together the photocopied versions that she has just made, which show the recent notes. 'And we will see you tomorrow for the big sign.'

Andrew reaches for a copy. 'I'll get one of these to Cal. He'll want—'

'I can drop it in if you like,' I suggest, getting to it a millisecond ahead of him – and saving him some nasty paper cuts. 'I need to see him anyway before I go.'

'I think he's in the middle of something.'

He will be in a minute.

I pick up my handbag and swing open the door. 'See you tomorrow.'

***

Have you ever seen anyone pull off a don't-fucking-mess-with-me march in white point-toe flats? Well, that day has come, my friend. I can feel those in the

379

open-plan area watching me over the partitions. The glass-fronted office people are looking up from their red Biro artworks.

'Cal has currently got someone in with him, Jo.'

'I'll be seconds,' I assure Fay, with a smile that would cushion any bad news. I'll make sure she doesn't get the blame.

Cal's office is one of only four here that doesn't have glass walls. He has enough external windows to ward off any changes in his mood during the winter.

I rap on the frosted glass in his door – not too hard, but not like those who tell you they knocked when their knuckles hardly kiss the surface – and walk in.

Andrew wasn't lying. And the 'something' Cal is 'in the middle of' is being conducted from two armchairs angled towards each other. Granted, it's an obtuse angle, and he's sitting back in his seat with his legs loosely crossed.

But if she is one of his other authors, what gives *her* the right to sit forward like that and have one hand on his leg?

Cal jumps to his feet. 'Jo.'

'Sorry to barge in.' I hope clearing my throat will dislodge the unexpected tremble that is threatening to ruin my entrance. 'Here's your copy of the contract.'

I drop it on his desk. *I* say it's a drop. Others may argue that it's verging on a toss – but that's something I don't give right now.

'I was going to call you this afternoon,' Cal says.

I'm not listening. I can't anyway, not while my heart is thump-thump-thumping in my ears. It's loud enough to drown out a rocket launch.

When I find the USB stick in my handbag, I hold it up. 'From Olivia.'

Yes, this is most definitely tossed. It slides past the contract and bumps against someone's monogram canvas Louis Vuitton handbag.

I quickly close the door behind me. I would *love* to slam it hard enough to set off a fire extinguisher, but why give that man the satisfaction?

I rush behind Fay's desk and snatch up my bags. 'See you tomorrow. Thanks for lunch. The cakes were scrummy.'

'You're welcome. Oh, someone phoned for you earlier, and Cal—'

'I'll pick up any messages tomorrow,' I tell her, sprinting down the corridor. 'Sorry. Must dash.'

Two women have just stepped out of the lift; I swerve past them, missing an ankle with my wheelie case by millimetres. The lift doors are closing. I twist sideways and make it through. Once I'm in, I stand back and will the ten-inch gap to close faster than a guillotine.

Or at least faster than the speed at which Cal is moving.

I hear him bang on the closed doors.

The lift gives the merest jolt as it starts to descend seven floors. Six floors. Five. Four.

I take up my starting position.

Three. Two.

On your marks, get set.

One. Groundfl—

I am almost clawing through the narrowest gap to get out, my suitcase clattering behind me. There's a surprised 'Oh!' from one of those waiting to use the lift.

'Sorry. Excuse me. Coming –' by the time I finish my sentence, I should be '– through.'

If memory serves me right, there's a taxi rank just along the street. If so, please let there be some illuminated yellow signs today. Please. *Please!*

There is one black cab remaining, and two other people seem to want it as much as—

'*TAXI!*'

I don't care if I just woke up those people snoring in the back row. Not when the taxi is shooting forward and meeting me at the kerb.

I scramble into the back with my bags. 'Knightsbridge, please. I'm meeting my long-lost brother.'

I'm thrown back in the seat when he puts his foot down, even though I'd slightly braced myself. It's not the first time I've used that line.

***

My hotel is about a mile away by car. By foot, it's only a pleasant amble through the park, which is how I would've preferred to get there. Especially now that the sun is out. Thinking about it, I could've walked. In fact, I'm sure it wouldn't have mattered if I'd strolled outside, bought a muffin from the café next door and savoured it while sitting on his office building's sodding front steps. That's because *I know* the lift wouldn't have reached the fourth floor before Cal was back in his sterile room and... picking up where the leg fondling had left off.

'Good luck, miss,' says the driver as we pull up outside my hotel.

'Hm?'

'Your brother?'

'Oh. Oh, yes. Thank you.'

I shuffle across the seat to the door.

'Is this him?' he asks.

'I doubt—'

The door is yanked open, and a man's frame looms in the doorway.

'Shitting hell!'

Cal grabs my suitcase and laptop bag while I clutch at the region where a beating heart recently evaporated.

'You twat,' I snap. 'You scared me to fucking death.'

I scramble after him up the hotel's white steps. The uniformed doorman touches the brim of his top hat.

'Will you slow down?' I ask in a whispered hiss, almost skipping to catch up with him across the lobby.

There are more white steps, which Cal is taking two at a time. Knowing I won't get an explanation from him in front of the reception staff, I stay on the lower level and stand to the side. To the outside world, it must look like I'm admiring the expanse of marble. Nobody would guess I'm attempting to calm the panicked tempest within.

Sadly, Cal returns before I can find a brown paper

bag to breathe into.

'I'm perfectly capable of giving my name to a hotel receptionist,' I utter.

Cal takes my elbow and leads me towards the lifts, detouring en route to one of the vacant sofas. I drop onto one of the far-too-bouncy cushions.

He crouches in front of me. 'What was all that about?'

Surely my look must be one of disbelief. 'I am here to sign the biggest deal that I will ever – that I will *ever* – be offered.'

'Today, you were only here to read over the contract.'

'And you toss me off for a *skirt*?'

Cal jabs a finger against his shushing lips. 'I've already gone over it with a fine-tooth comb.'

'You *know* how hard it is for me to let go of these books. You, more than anyone.'

'Yes, I know. But as I said—'

'I *needed* you there today.'

'And I had—' Cal checks himself, glancing around again. 'I had planned to be. But something came up.'

'Yeah,' I scoff. 'If I'd left it a few minutes, something would have *come up* all right.'

He shakes his head. It's hard to tell whether he is annoyed with me or giving me five seconds to live. 'You're mistaken.'

'Am I?' To re-enact the scene, I'm forced to invade his personal space. 'I read… *this* wrong?'

'She wasn't…' Cal watches my hand. 'She wasn't

stroking my leg like that.'

'What was she doing, then? Frisking you for POLO Mints?'

'For your information, Jo, that woman in my office is my—'

'No, no,' I beg. 'Let me guess. I'm *really* good at this. Is she your... graynma?'

Maybe my attempt at an Alabama accent is why he doesn't answer.

'Your cousin, perhaps? Are you from a state that allows that sort of behaviour?'

'She is my sister.'

'Whatever,' I snigger.

Cal removes his phone from his pocket. After a few taps and swipes, I am presented with a photo of him with two women.

Two.

The number of sisters he...

'I, erm...' I shrug. 'I didn't get a... good look at her.'

'No, because you were too busy scowling at *me*.'

Why can't the marble floor send some chill to my burning cheeks?

I cross my arms. 'Why didn't you say something at the time?'

'You never gave me a chance,' Cal swiftly answers. 'You threw that stuff on my desk...'

'I didn't... I didn't *throw* it.'

'... and you stormed out.'

'I was angry.'

'Why? Because you saw me with another

385

woman?'

'Yes!'

One of his knees drops to the floor as both eyebrows join the impressive chandelier overhead.

'No,' I correct. 'I was angry because it looked like... like your... *personal* life was getting in the way of... of our professional one.'

The speed at which Cal moves towards me happens too quickly to work out an escape route. That's my excuse, anyway.

'After all these years, Jo,' he whispers, his eyes searching mine, 'and you still think there's someone in my life who comes before you?'

I'm sure staring at him with my mouth open cannot look attractive.

'There should be,' is the response I barely mouth. But Cal is close enough to hear.

'That's a matter of—'

'Hello, Jo.'

The voice that belongs to an unsaved number has only one of us looking up to confirm they're not hearing things.

Sadly, my hearing is fine.

In preppy stone chinos, a preppy pink shirt and a preppy constricting navy blazer, someone who should be lounging on a patio in Cape Cod with other prep-meisters is making an unwanted appearance in a hotel lobby in Knightsbridge instead.

'David.'

It's been so long since I said his name aloud that I'd almost forgotten it.

I'd almost forgotten *him*.

Almost.

How on earth did he know where I…?

The man kneeling in front of me won't even look me in the eye. Fay said there was a call, and Cal… what? What did he do? I left before I could find out.

But now I know.

Cal gets to his feet, taking a small step back when I follow suit. He allows just enough room between us to hold out my key card. 'I'll leave you both to it.'

He is walking away, and my past is stepping forward. I watch them acknowledge each other with the briefest of nods.

'You've changed your hair,' I hear David remark.

'Erm…' My eyes stay on the large patch of sweat on the back of Cal's pale grey shirt until the last second. 'Yeah. Yes. I have.'

'Shall we grab a coffee somewhere?'

Chapter Thirty-Four

There's a coffeehouse close enough to the hotel that I'm hoping to be able to smell the beans from my window.

'One large tea and one cappuccino.'

Oh, no. David has ordered a 'large'. Shit.

'What size would you like the cappuccino, sir?'

'Uhhhhhhhhhhhhhhhh…'

Oh, for—

'Just a tall, please,' I interject. 'And can you make that a latte?'

Leaving him to ooze his charm at the twenty-something who's frothing up the milk, I take a stool at one of the bar tables facing the street. I wouldn't usually advertise myself to this degree, but I'll soon need something to cheer me up.

When our drinks are ready, David brings them over and leaves his smile behind.

Great.

'This new job's stressing me out,' he says.

Why did Cal tell him where I was staying?

'Look at the bags under my eyes.'

Yes, I'd let him pass on this information to David maybe once in the past.

'I hardly sleep.'

All right, more than once. But always after speaking to me first.

'And to top it off...'

Cal always asks for permission. Always. That was the unspoken rule.

'... I was giving it another go with that woman I was seeing?'

Upward-inflexion infection, or is David checking with me that he really *was* seeing her?

'Which one?' I ask.

'The blonde?'

That's like asking someone to pick a card – any card.

He tries again. 'The one who worked in my old building?'

I wish he'd narrow it down to counting only on fingers and toes.

'The one I went to Canada with for six months?'

Ah, he means the one who finally succumbed to his advances the day after our Cambridge round-trip rendezvous. I could've saved on my word count if David had just said that.

'*I* thought we were giving it another shot, but she'd decided to keep her options open.' When he leans forward, I lean back. 'She was seeing other men.'

Did I need him to explain what 'options open' means? I won rosettes for being nothing but an option to him.

David is staring at me. Am I supposed to react or respond?

'You're certain about that?' is what I finally go with.

'I saw the flirty text messages they sent.'

'Were those really proof she was seeing them, though?'

'Of course they were,' he retorts.

That's funny, because they weren't proof when I found some on his phone from his older brother's fiancée.

'It absolutely tore me up, Jo.'

If his words can't convince me, David hopes his Eeyore expression might do the trick.

It won't.

'I was a total mess,' he says. 'I'm sure I was in shock.'

'That's actually just the first stage you go through when—'

'I couldn't understand how this had happened to me.'

That's textbook stage two, but there's no point in saying it out loud.

'All I could feel was *anger*,' David goes on. 'I couldn't eat, I couldn't sleep, I didn't want to get out of bed. I was depressed.'

Two stages back to back; only three more—

'Then, two days after I kicked her out, I went on this *amazing* holiday to Ibiza with the lads.'

Wow. Just... I wish I'd known the secret to David's brief grief success when we broke up.

But if I had, would I have written that first novel?

'I then started seeing this woman…'

I bet that's what she said, too.

'… but she had trust issues.'

No, she could see through the bullshit.

'So now it's just… me, myself and I again.'

That's a lot of David to get stuck in a lift with – or in a coffee shop.

'Is this why you got in touch?' I ask.

He grins. 'You wish.'

No, I don't. If I had a wish, I wouldn't waste it on that.

'The last time we met up, Jo, I got the impression you needed a bit of distance between us.'

Does he want a round of applause for being observant? Or a mention in my Sarcastic Awards acceptance speech?

'Which is what I've done,' he claims.

'Why didn't you just text me?'

'I lost your number.' David doesn't even blink when he says it.

'Didn't you think to look down the back of the sofa?'

When the penny drops, he squeezes my shoulder. I resist the urge to lean sideways against the woman sitting next to me.

'That angry-looking man at your hotel,' he says. 'Is he the rude arsehole I usually speak to when I call your agency?'

'That's right.'

'What does he do there?'

'He's my… He's my agent.'

'*Just* your agent?'

Although that's something Cal has never 'just' been for years now, I save my breath. 'That's all.'

David raises an eyebrow. 'That wasn't the vibe I was getting.'

'I'm not surprised. Before you showed up, we'd had a… a bit of a misunderstanding.'

'It wasn't that kind of vibe,' he mumbles into his cup. 'Therefore, you can thank me by buying me dinner.'

'Thank you for what?'

'Showing up before the two of you made the mistake of taking your tiff *upstairs*.'

Why am I not shocked that he misread the situation as only he could?

'Dinner.' David is still talking. 'Del Tutto's. Have you ever eaten there?'

Is it even worth reminding him? Can I be bothered to dredge up a seven-year-old memory, the one where his work colleague came over and said it was lovely to finally meet Charlotte, the fiancée he had heard so much about? A fiancée I had heard *nothing* about. It must've slipped his mind when David slipped inside me.

'I've eaten there once,' I tell him.

'Who with?'

'A complete bellend.'

'The place is on my doorstep. I can meet you there.' David's phone makes an appearance. 'Tomorrow night. Eight-thirty.'

'I can't.'

'You *can't*?' He seems confused. 'What do you mean?'

I had no idea that word was alien to him.

'I have a train to catch straight after my meeting tomorrow,' I explain.

'But I already have this reservation. I've had it for three weeks.'

I wonder how long David has been fishing for a plus one. When did the original woman he'd booked it to impress fall by the wayside? And how many emergency cumtacts did he get in touch with before me? I'm guessing a few if he had to ring my agency to track me down.

'That's a shame.' My nonchalant tone, were it to join his favourite dating website, would describe itself as 'cool, calm and couldn't care less'.

'A train to where?' David asks his phone screen.

I don't have to think about my word choice. 'Home.'

'You're no longer in London?'

'Not since April.'

'Are you back in Grimsby?'

I am far too over him to correct the town I originate from. He forgets that not everyone grew up in a village where there really was a lord of the manor.

There was also more than one Uncle Dad.

'No. The Lake District.'

David pulls a face. 'Why?'

'I have friends there,' I say with ease.

'I went there once with someone or other.'

I guess that's all I ever was to him.

'A bit too back of beyond for me.'

And that's the best news I've had in ages.

'What is there to do up there except get wet?'

I can think of a hundred things. 'Perhaps it's somewhere that lets you move on without asking why.'

David can't muster up a smidgeon of interest. Not if it doesn't concern him. Either that, or his silence is because of something else. Could it be the realisation that his old reliable won't be waiting for him and his random acts of attention any more?

I look at him and realise something: I don't feel a thing for him. Not a thing. Honestly, there is nothing – nothing – and it's… it's the best feeling in the world.

I get off my stool. 'I have to be somewhere.'

'I don't.'

Just think, my sunshine and David's drizzle would have made a beautiful rainbow.

It wouldn't have made him any less of a limp dick, though.

'Good luck with everything, David.'

'You make it sound like it's the end of the road for us.' His forced laughter follows his words. It's like a lot of things with him.

'It is the end.'

Common sense warned me that my wounds would never heal if I let David dip in and out of my life. A mended heart doesn't sell many books, was always my response – and written on the back of a royalty cheque.

But a heart can often fix itself if you stop fearing what might happen in the next chapter. Allowing others to distract you helps, too. And maybe my stories can be written about what's happening now instead of the experiences of yesterday.

I'll wait to hear the verdict on that.

And the day has arrived when a brief one-armed hug is a final farewell to my fair-weather friend.

Chapter Thirty-Five

I find my hotel suite, change into more appropriate attire, and pinch the complimentary plain mint chocolates off the pillow on my way out. With Harvey Nichols across the street from the hotel and Harrods six minutes away on foot, I slip down Serpentine Walk. Within two minutes, I'm among trees and water again.

Although Hyde Park doesn't have either fells or meres, it has plenty of monuments and fountains. I whizz past them, forgetting to tick them off. There's a bandstand, but no music is playing. Nobody has anything to say right now at Speakers' Corner. The sun and the heavenly scents in the Rose Garden force me to slow down; however, I cannot be tempted today by the pergola's lengthy shade and alluring benches. I have too many thoughts racing through my mind. My muscles and my Nikes must keep moving.

The monarch isn't home, and there are queues outside Westminster Abbey. It's too early for the ice rink at Somerset House, but I'm too late for the fortnight of summer screenings. I didn't see any ghosts in the windows at the Tower of London. The British Museum is open, but I missed the last entry.

At least I can get in to see a Shakespeare production at Regent's Park open-air theatre; one starts in fifteen minutes. But all the seats in my favourite row are taken. I leave my disappointment behind and keep going. If I maintain my speed, although I can't overtake my inner turmoil, there's a chance I'll wear the fucker out.

***

I spend ages in my hotel room's en suite, shampooing my hair twice and conditioning it once in the marble-walled shower. Even then, I still can't answer all the burning questions – the ones that the earlier untimely and unwelcome interruption in the foyer left me with. They are questions that even smashing my previous London best on my step counter couldn't resolve.

As I sit on the balcony with the early evening sun naturally drying my hair, I check the options available on the room service menu. Instead of getting changed, I could have pizza brought up or Thai food. Or do I fancy American?

Or *an* American?

What on earth was David waffling on about when he said he saved me from bringing mine and Cal's argument up to this room? It was an argument, not… not vicious foreplay. Cal doesn't think about me in that way: he has *never* thought about me in that way. After all these years? No.

No!

Remember how he reacted in his Lakeland rental when I inadvertently (shut up, it *was* inadvertently) asked if he *had* to leave? I'm sure the last thing he needs is for me to suddenly see him for who he is.

Or he... could be.

Somebody's phone is ringing. I think it's coming from the balcony below. Or it could be coming from the room next to mine. We have the same ringtone.

Oh. No, we don't.

I look at the name displayed on the screen: Literally Fay. You might see why in a minute.

'Jo, I'm sorry to call,' she quickly says.

'It's fine. Is... everything all right?' What I mean is: Are you at the bottom of a well, and did you accidentally delete every number except mine when you slipped?

'I need to apologise.'

Fay watched my suitcase for a couple of hours. If she took out a pair of my good shoes and wore them to answer the phone, I won't flip out.

'You were literally getting into the lift when that man who called earlier rang again.'

'Was his name David?'

'Yes. He's phoned before, but Cal literally always insists on speaking to him. But I couldn't put any calls through to him again today, and this guy said it was literally a matter of great importance.'

Only David would think the fear of dining alone warranted such drama.

'Then he started getting angry and literally threatening to report me, so I... I told him where you were staying. I'm sorry!'

'Honestly, Fay, it's fine. I saw him a few hours ago. He's an old...' Old, what? Flame? Lesson? Enemy? Sod? 'He's old. I'm sorry he was horrible to you.'

'Thank God! I've literally been worried sick. Cal took off after you, and I wanted to tell him when he got back, but he literally slammed into his office. I've just texted him. God knows what he'll say, but how else was I supposed to tell him? We haven't been allowed to disturb him for two days now because of what's obviously going on with him.'

What is obvious?

'That was his sister with him today, right?' I ask.

'His sister's been with him literally most of today, the big bosses too this afternoon, and his dad literally all of yesterday. I mean, everyone knows, but we all must act like we don't. But if he's leaving, we should be told, yeah? Especially if it's going to affect us. I mean, literally the entire office now knows how *you* feel about it. But I'm only his assistant. Will they keep me on? Or will his replacement keep me on? Will they replace him? You must know, Jo.'

'That's why his family is over here? Because he's leaving?' I grip the phone tighter. 'Why? Why's he leaving?'

There's silence.

'Fay?'

I make sure my old phone hasn't chosen to run out of juice and end things with an *EastEnders*-style cliffhanger. It does that these days without warning.

It goes from three bars of battery to two bars to *Nah, I'm done*.

'We literally thought… That is, everyone kind of… assumed you must… Oh shit!' Fay cries. '*Please* don't tell him I told you.'

'I won't.'

'But when I tell him I've rung you and apologised?'

'Don't tell him. If he asks, say that you'll do it in the morning.'

She breathes a sigh of relief. 'Thanks, Jo. The thing is, we've literally always known he'd be asked to go back and run the family business one day. We think his dad wanted to retire years ago, but Cal literally had his reasons why he couldn't – or, more likely, why he wouldn't. I mean, you know him literally better than anyone.'

'I don't, Fay. He knows *me* better than anyone, yes.'

'But you've been together—'

'Eight years.' I take a bra and my makeup bag from my suitcase. 'We've maintained the highest level of indifference towards each other for eight years. Pretty good going, wouldn't you say?'

'Well, *you* might have managed it.'

Before she goes, Fay apologises again, and I look forward to hearing her apologise again in the morning.

Literally all morning.

Chapter Thirty-Six

I pay the bill and stand outside the restaurant. Turning right would take me to London's lane of luxury retail. If they were open this late in the evening, the shops on Sloane Street would welcome my glittery Jimmy Choos and matching clutch with open arms. However, they might have offered me instant coffee instead of filtered when they saw my long-sleeved polyester bargain. My white, loose-layered dress was described as 'mini' on the website, but it's not too 'mini' on someone who's only five foot four.

I stop pinching my bottom lip and tuck my fancy bag under my arm. Tugging down my cheap hemline, I turn left. Before long, I enter a square with a loop of unassuming brick buildings. They surround a memorial garden with an impeccable lawn and mature trees. It's a green area for those who pay to live in SW1X.

I've never been here before, but I know the address. The number of thank-you gifts I've had delivered to one particular apartment means I know it by heart.

For someone who requires a supermarket time-out to choose between olive oil and sunflower spread, I'm amazed this evening when I don't think twice about pressing a button on a brass intercom. Only when it starts to ring does the desire to run—

'Hello?'

'It's me,' I say.

There's a click to my left.

'Just push on the door.'

***

When I exit the lift, there's only one pair of double front doors on this floor. Cal is waiting in the doorway for me, hands in the pockets of his casual navy joggers. A white T-shirt shows off the tan that he built up while working at my house. The simple colour makes the beautiful blue of his eyes stand out even—

'Nice loafers,' I tell him, interrupting my useless thoughts.

Cal looks down at his suede slip-ons, rocking back on his heels. 'They're slippers.'

'Posh slippers. Do they have to be posh to live in a penthouse?'

He stands aside. The gesture is a welcome without the need for hands.

Hell's Teeth, this place is swish. Shiny off-white floors slide seamlessly into a doorless, glass-walled office opposite, branching out either side to create the lengthiest hallway I've seen in an apartment.

In the lounge, the flooring switches to plush carpeting. The room is dominated by two teal sofas adorned with the perfect number of contrasting pillows, all of which sport this season's trendy chops. The stone-effect coffee table separating them displays a funky chessboard and a marble vase of fresh flowers. There's also a pewter bowl on it containing the greenest apples. They can't be organic, surely.

There's a TV screen above the polished concrete fireplace, with a footstool the size of a child's bed in front of it. Tasteful artwork adorns some of the walls. A dining table with eight chairs appears to be staged for a magazine shoot.

'You did all this?'

'I had a decorator,' Cal informs me.

'And a big bill.'

A kitchen devoid of handles is off the lounge. Recessed lighting subtly highlights hidden appliances and spotless surfaces. During daylight hours, the large skylight must do that job for free.

Cal trails behind me to the other end of the apartment, where the three bathrooms and two bedrooms are located. I was spot on about his walk-in closet.

'That's a massive bed,' I point out in the main bedroom. 'You could fit four in there.'

Do you know when you sometimes say something in your head that sounds perfectly innocent, but then when you say it out loud...?

'Are you asking me, Jo, if I've—?'

'No.'

I stop in the doorway, half-turning my head.

'I have not,' he clarifies.

When I begin the long walk back to the lounge, my stiletto heels click-clacking on the shiny floor, I remember hygiene rules. 'Would you like me to…?'

'No, no. Keep your shoes on.'

'My feet don't smell.' I quickly turn round. 'A handful of times, Cal – and I'm pretty sure I've narrowed it down to those sheepskin boots.'

I know that's why he wants me to keep them on. I mean, what other reason is there? Cheeky bugger. The next time we travel, I will run a marathon in those boots before our flight.

Will there be a next time, though? Will there be another long-haul flight where I can eat Cal's dessert for him?

We step out onto the terrace, which runs the entire length of his apartment.

'Are you on your way out to dinner?' he asks, perching on the arm of a garden sofa chair – one of eight. But an outside area of this size would look odd with just a pair of deck chairs.

'No, I'm on my way back.'

Cal folds his arms. 'Did David take you anywhere nice?'

'I took myself, actually.'

That isn't the response he was expecting.

'I shook him off after half an hour. After he bought me a coffee.'

Cal's eyebrows jump up. 'Will that be in the next book?'

'No, but it'll be going on a water bottle.'

'I apologize for telling him where you were

staying without your permission,' Cal says. 'I shouldn't have done that.'

Is there anything sexier than taking the bullet for someone? Okay, apart from that time when a hot Aussie actor offered me the comfier of the two seats in a green room.

'I won't be seeing him again,' I announce.

'You finally said your goodbyes?'

'I did.'

'Good.'

I admire the beautiful ceiling in the lounge through the terrace doors. 'Do you lease this or...?'

'I own it.'

Cal owns it. He owns, what, nearly two thousand square feet in Knightsbridge? An apartment in—No, a *penthouse* in Knightsbridge? As I'm getting my head around this, he goes inside and takes a throw off the back of a chair in the lounge.

'My fifteen per cent didn't buy you this,' I comment.

When Cal drapes the soft material over my shoulders, it takes all my willpower not to lean back against him when the woody aroma of his aftershave captivates my senses.

'No.' He perches on the arm of the chair again and grips the front edges of the throw. 'No. It didn't.'

Cal's relaxed smile has released from bondage those angry frown lines. They are features I've had to put up with all these years, and not seeing them may take some getting used to.

But soon, I'll have to get used to not seeing that

smile either.

I study the treetop silhouettes in the memorial garden and try to name the different species. I look up at the sky and wonder where the Summer Triangle and Scorpius may be hiding behind the light pollution. The flowers on his coffee table are some variety of white lilac—

'Jo—?'

'I don't get it,' I blurt out. 'I don't... You can afford *this* without me, yet... yet you spend an evening every year haggling with car insurance providers to get me cheap bloody... breakdown cover and legal assistance. You... You spend *weeks* planning unforgettable birthday parties for my family because nobody else can be arsed to even... to even... hang a balloon. You even stop whatever you're doing in another time zone when I want something to distract me. Why, Cal? I mean... *why*?'

He gives the throw a gentle tug. 'Why do you think?'

That's what I'm trying not to do. I'm also trying not to think about how good it would feel to touch Cal's lips with one finger. With two fingers. To brush them with my lips. To taste them with my tongue. And I'm trying not to think about how this could be my last chance to find out.

What if it's my only chance?

I'm reminded of Cal's hold on the throw when I attempt to move one foot back to give me time to assess what the hell—

'My hair,' I remark. 'You've not commented

once.'

'It looks beautiful.'

'No, not now. Although… thank you. No, months ago. You didn't even notice.'

'Of course I did.'

'Then why didn't you say anything?' I snap. 'You flew to LA sitting next to a brunette.'

'I know—'

'Not a word. Nothing. Yet you sit here trying to convince me you drop everything to cater to my whims for reasons other than your percentage—'

'What did you want me to say, Jo?' Cal grips the throw tighter. 'The truth? Okay, here goes. I thought you looked like an absolute fucking knockout. But I couldn't tell you that. I didn't think I could *ever* tell you that. I also didn't think I could ever tell you how *adorable* you look when you pinch your bottom lip when you're thinking. And when you've fallen asleep on my shoulder, I certainly couldn't tell you how many times I've smelled your hair! You've changed your shampoo, right? When you were blonde, your hair smelled of coconut. On that flight from Manchester, it smelled of jasmine.'

I'm not sure I want to know, but I must ask. 'How many times have I fallen asleep on…?'

'Jeez, too many to count. You've also nuzzled my neck on several occasions.'

I'm mortified. 'I thought I was dreaming.'

Cal chuckles. 'Me too.'

I feel my self-correcting mineral powder clocking up time and a half to keep my cheeks looking serene.

'So, yes,' he tells me. 'For the record, I like your hair. I like it very much. It makes—'

'Maria's lovely, don't you think?'

Cal almost hides his reaction to the sudden change in topic. 'Yes, I... She is.'

'I thought you two could've... had something.'

He nods slowly. 'Would that have made you happy?'

'No. Yes. I want to make you happy. No, what I mean is, I want to see you happy,' I quickly clarify. '*See* you... happy. That's all.'

'Yeah?'

I'm now holding the throw on my own. One of Cal's hands is pressing against the small of my back, pulling me against his chest. It's a territory I was allowed to explore back in the Lakes, when I was still trying to convince the world that I didn't require anything else. Or anyone.

This is different, though. Suddenly, the things I convinced myself couldn't be real – couldn't be reciprocal – are only a dress, a throw, and a T-shirt apart.

I place my arms around Cal's neck.

Make that now just a dress and a T-shirt apart.

'There is only one thing, Jo, that would make me happy.'

'What's that?' I whisper.

His fingertips brush my cheek. 'You.'

I don't know who gets there first, but I might have to go back and replace the full stop at the end of Cal's answer with an interrupting em dash. I'm not even sure he manages to say the entire word.

Our lips enjoy a moment together before our mouths open in unison. There's no urgent tongue wrestling, no teeth clashing, no gobbling each other up. It is slow and delicious, and it deserves its own soundtrack.

Cal's hands travel from the small of my back to my hips, but those things don't need any encouragement to push forward. His fingers brush against the sides of my breasts on their journey north, triggering waves of energy to rush between my legs.

My breath catches when he quickly gets to his feet and lifts me under my arms. I'm glad I have no choice but to hook my ankles around his hips. With my back pressed against a brick wall, we miss a gear. No, I think we miss three. Our kisses become hungry and urgent.

Cal carries me through the lounge and down the long corridor. He places one knee on the bed and slowly lowers himself on top of me. Our lips remain locked together as I tug at his T-shirt and jogging bottoms. The desire for more than just our mouths to be—

'Jo?'

My eyes fly open when Cal moves his lips out of reach.

'What's wrong?' I ask.

'If we make love your way first, then we're doing it my way second. Okay?'

I've always approached sex as a sprint. The best words to describe how I tackle it are 'eager' and 'passionate'. And the men I've been with have certainly enjoyed being the centre of all the horizontal attention; therefore, I've had no complaints. For me, sex is all about showing him a good time.

And my good time? Oh, don't worry. I always sort myself out afterwards. But I thank them for the offer.

If they offer.

Yes, all right, don't have a go at me. I've heard it all before. I let Izzie lecture me once about personal control and a fear of giving it up. When she got to the four types of intimacy, I silenced her by asking what the view was like from up her own arse.

And this evening, my way doesn't take long, as usual.

Cal's way, however, is a hell of a lot different from mine.

Chapter Thirty-Seven

With every ring that goes unanswered, my level of worry doesn't creep above 'mild'. Yes, her phone will be next to the bed. Yes, the volume will be maxed out. It will be vibrating its little tungsten heart out too. But with her snoring—

'If somebody hasn't discovered a hole big enough to bury all the fucking hashtags,' a voice croaks, 'I'm putting the phone down.'

'Izzie, I've done something stupid.'

I can picture my aunt shooting up in bed and turning on the light. She'll be putting her glasses on; she can't listen without them.

'Do you need a good solicitor?'

'No.' My heart is pounding, and it's not only because I've just completed a half-mile trot in high heels. 'I've just experienced the best sex of my life.'

'With Cal?'

'Y-Yes. But how…?'

'Finally!'

Have I really been blind to this?

'Are you at his apartment, Bee?'

'I was. I'm almost back at my hotel now.'

'In a taxi, I hope?'

'No. His place is only three streets away,' I explain.

'Didn't Cal offer to walk you home?'

'He was asleep when I left.'

'Just… hold the gravy,' Izzie says. 'You did a fuck and run? Correction: a *fantastic* fuck and run?'

'That's the problem.'

'The fantastic fucking or the running?'

'The first bit.'

'Wrong answer. But that aside for a moment, tell me everything.'

'Not happening, Auntie.'

'If I could get a man to invade my prehistoric pussy, I'd tell you every last detail.'

'No, you wouldn't. All you'd tell me is *how* you got the poor sod to believe the world's about to end.'

'Fine,' she huffs. 'What was the problem with the fantastic fucking, then?'

'Cal likes it… different.'

'*Rrrrrreally?*'

'Out of the gutter,' I order. 'No, he's all about slowing things down and making lots of eye contact. All that bloody tantric shit.'

'You're saying the man likes to make love?'

'Hey, I make love.'

Is no response from her better than—?

'I make love, Izzie!'

'What happened?'

I sit on the edge of a granite planter outside my

hotel. 'I nearly left.'

'You didn't, though.'

'He was willing to compromise.'

'It sounds like you were, too,' she observes.

But only after Cal stopped me from grabbing all my things and making for the door. He sat me down on one of the sofas and seated himself on the coffee table.

'What happened just now?' he asked.

I clutched my shoes closer to my chest and tucked my dress tighter under my arms. Don't ask me why I hadn't put it back on.

'Jo?'

'It's too much,' I blurted out.

Cal looked down at his boxer briefs and raised his eyebrows. '*I'm* too much?'

'No, not… that. No, that's fine. That's good. That's… *very* good,' I insisted. 'No problem there.'

'Where is the problem, then?'

'It's… It's too… It's too intimate.'

He nodded, biting his bottom lip.

'And you kept looking at me like I…'

'Like you… were someone I've wanted to make love to for a while?'

I wasn't expecting Cal to say that. Hoping, yes.

'Even more than that,' I mumbled to my footwear.

'Like you should get as much out of it as I am?'

'My way is simpler. And it does the job.'

He tilted his head to one side. 'That's how you describe having sex?'

'It's what I'm comfortable with.'

'Right.' Cal took my shoes off me. 'Then what do you say about meeting me somewhere in the middle…?'

But I was already shaking my head.

'You've got to give me something, Jo.'

'I did. In the bedroom.'

'That's not what I meant.'

He sat patiently, his elbows on his knees.

'You need to tone it right down,' I traded.

'Okay.'

As Cal turned off most of the lamps, leaving a couple on in the corners to chase away the shadows, he pointed at the other end of the sofa. 'Do you want to get comfortable?'

After we kissed with the same urgency as before, I relished the feel of his mouth as it travelled down my neck, explored my breasts, and visited my navel. I sat up and brought his mouth back to mine. When his lips undertook a second expedition south, they got an inch further than the last time before I intervened again.

With mild irritation in his eyes, Cal asked, 'What are you doing?'

'I'm saving you the hassle. Where you keep heading? It's wasted on me.'

'You're not serious?'

'Totally. I'm sorry, but it doesn't do a thing for me.'

He rubbed his chin. 'May I at least try?'

'You'll get bored,' I said with certainty.

But Cal didn't.

It's hard to say who was enjoying it the most. If I were putting money on it, I would place a safe bet on the person who had an orgasm that was so intense they thought they might pass out. However, it was a bittersweet moment, knowing I would experience nothing like it again.

Until I was sitting astride him.

Then with his mouth again, after we'd stopped to eat some fruit.

And then *with* some of the...

'I'm not usually this greedy,' I said, panting into his neck following another return to earth. 'In fact, I've never...'

Cal pulled his head back. 'Never, what?'

'I've never... you know... during...'

'Should I be flattered?' he asked, stroking my collarbone.

'No, you should be knighted. Where did you learn to—? No, don't tell me.'

It could be any of seven.

Again, Cal started kissing my neck, but this time very gently, very sensually.

Too sensually.

I groaned, covering my eyes. 'I'm sorry.'

'It's okay.'

'It's not you.'

'It's you, Jo. I know.'

The relief I felt when I saw his smile was palpable. Cal knew. Of course he knew. Yet it didn't appear to bother him. In fact, quite the opposite.

When I emerged from his guest bathroom, I

couldn't keep at bay the silliest grin when I found him leaning against the door jamb, waiting to lead me in the opposite direction to the lounge. And doing it all again – in his bed this time – didn't scare me. Well, not that much. Not enough to make me want to leave again.

No, that came later.

'Izzie, it was…' I'm still struggling to put it into words. 'It was truly unbelievable.'

'Oh, Bee. I'm beyond happy for you.'

'I won't regret it. Ever.'

'Why do you say that?' she quickly asks.

'I'll explain later. Now I must go. I've got to be up in a few hours.'

'I'll ring you tomorrow.'

I flash the doorman a warm smile as I hurry past. 'You mean today? Call me at precisely three o'clock.'

'Why?'

'So I'll know not to answer.'

'That does it,' Izzie announces. 'Next time, I'm killing you in your fucking sleep.'

Chapter Thirty-Eight

Before I leave to go anywhere, there are certain things I never, ever forget to do. Making sure my teeth are clean is number one. Then it's a quick brush of my hair, putting on matching shoes, and a cursory glance in a full-length mirror.

This morning, I only managed to do two of the four back at the hotel. That's because I did something else I never, ever do: I fell asleep again after my phone's daily alarm woke me up.

When my phone started ringing, I knew I was somewhere I shouldn't be.

'I'm up.'

And I was. Yes, it had only been for three seconds, but still.

'Is that the good news?' Even in professional mode, images of Cal's lips forming the words made me feel fuzzy everywhere – and not just below deck.

'I'll be there in thirty minutes,' I said, turning on the shower.

'Ten would be better.'

'Fine. Send the jet.'

Thanks to my brilliant budget all-in-one mineral powder, my complexion went from shiny and shadowy to radiant and flawless in seconds. After a couple of blush strokes, a dab of cream eyeshadow, and three sweeps of mascara per eye, I snapped shut my compact mirror. Done.

At least I'm on my way to the office now. As I scowl at a red traffic light, I catch my reflection in the driver's mirror: I'm still wearing my stripy hair claw. I snatch it out and comb my hair with my fingers. My curls from yesterday are just hanging in there, although they resemble lazy waves today. But after what they went through last night, I'm grateful for anything.

As I gloss my lips, I watch the time on the dashboard go from thirty minutes late to thirty-five.

***

I race up the building's front steps and push through the revolving doors. My cardigan is coming off on the way up. I exit the lift to find my headmaster waiting for me, lounging against the wall.

With his arms and ankles crossed, his waistcoat buttoned, and the perfect knot in his tie, Cal looks every inch like the new Boss fragrance man.

And last night, he was definitely *my* 'boss' man.

'First time ever,' I think it's worth saying.

As Fay takes my cardigan and bags, she mouths more apologies when he's not looking. *Literally* mouths them, I should say. She then hands me a white takeaway cup, which sports my favourite green logo.

Usually, I like to take the lid straight off my coffee and admire the perky bubbles. I can't do that today, though, not while Cal is propelling me towards the boardroom. He's also trying to tuck my T-shirt in at the back. You see, that's what happens when you don't look in the full-length mirror before you leave.

Oh well, I suppose it could've been worse.

When his fingers brush the skin above my waistband, I have to tighten the grip on my cup. When they linger, I want to brake without warning and cause a rear-end collision.

Cal will have heard my sharp intake of breath. Hopefully, he'll think it's because I almost dropped my coffee and not because I almost—

'A thousand apologies,' I gush upon entering the boardroom.

'Hey, no problem,' says one of the American guests. 'We got stuck in traffic, too. Ours was because of some accident.'

I almost had one of those in the car that brought me, with every bump and pothole we hit reigniting my undercarriage.

Suddenly, memories of last night are burning brightly in my mind again, making me feel warmer than the devil's armpits. When we finally sit down, I remove my neck scarf. While I'm placing it behind me on the back of the chair, Cal slides one of the paper-clipped contracts between us on the desk.

Synchronised page turning happens around the table as Amanda reads aloud. I sip my coffee and read the people instead, going anti-clockwise. When I get to my agent, he's staring at me in... Wait, is it in disbelief? But why? What did I do? Between taking off a silk print and putting away half my drink, did I unknowingly insult his mother's choice of pie filling?

Once Cal has checked that everyone is concentrating, he tops his glass of water up. In fact, he fills it. Without warning, he picks it up and throws the contents across my chest.

I jump to my feet seconds before everyone else does. It's as though they, too, have just experienced a tepid drenching. With my T-shirt quickly becoming a second skin, Cal snatches up my scarf and thrusts it against my throat and the V-neckline on my top. He holds it in place until I take over.

'Jo, I don't know what just happened,' he says. 'I'm sorry.'

I can feel the water seeping through the front of my trousers and trickling down my legs. I start to lower my scarf, but Cal grabs it and moves it back up.

He shuffles our chairs back. 'Please excuse us for a moment.'

In the hallway, I am marched – yes, marched – towards the ladies' toilets. He ushers me through the door and follows me in.

'Are you *on* something?' I demand to know.

Cal grasps my shoulders from behind and turns me to face the mirror. Without my scarf, the display of bra lace through my now-see-through top is quite something.

However, the dark red trophy bruises decorating my neck and chest are quite something else.

'Seriously, fuck off,' I say resignedly.

But now Cal doesn't seem surprised to see them.

I point at him. 'You gave me these out of spite.'

'I gave you them because you *asked* me to.'

'I did no such thing.'

Why is he nodding when I know full well I didn't...?

Oh, shit.

Last night, it wasn't because Cal was cuddling me that I couldn't fall asleep. Fine, it wasn't *just* because he was... Anyway, knowing this newfound way of spending time with him had an expiration date, I woke him up again in... more ways than one. Maybe it was the lateness of the hour, but he was much more receptive to my way of doing things.

'You realize your nipples are showing?' Cal brings me back to the present by saying.

'You realise whatever you say is going to piss me off?' I serve back.

He does, but the way he wraps an arm around his stomach and laughs says he doesn't care. It's a proper laugh, too, banging his other hand against the door.

'How the *hell* did you not see them?' he asks, wiping away tears.

I pull my T-shirt off. 'I was in a rush this morning, remember?'

Then I am laughing too, which only triggers more hilarity from him. I hold on to the worktop with one hand and Cal's forearm with the other, although he isn't much support right now. And every time we glimpse my new skin artwork, we dissolve into hysterics again.

We lean against the wall on either side of the hand dryer, our merriment slowly fading. As we're catching our breaths, I accidentally meet Cal's gaze. I only hope he's the one with some sense. Especially today of all—

Cal is on my side of the dryer before I can get to his, sandwiching my body between subway tiles and a pale grey, glen plaid wool mix. My fingers are grabbing and ruffling the top of his tapered haircut. We're kissing like two people who survived grocery shopping on a Saturday.

'Mal?' I mumble against his lips.

'Mmm.'

'*Mal*?'

'Hm? Ow!'

My grip on his hair keeps his mouth at bay. 'They're waiting for us.'

Cal takes a moment before exiting the bathroom to regain control of everything below his waist. He returns quickly with my suitcase.

'Take your pants off,' he instructs, locking the door again.

'And who said romance is dead?' I mumble.

'Oh, you want romance?'

After batting both my objections and hands away, Cal lowers my zip and pops the button. He holds my gaze as my trousers pool on the floor around my embellished satin court shoes.

When he lifts me onto the counter between the basins, that's when I know I should protest. But my treacherous grin betrays me, leaving my lips free to claim they were only an accessory to the crime as they join insatiable forces with his.

With one of Cal's hands cradling the back of my head, I encourage the other to check how far the water has seeped through my bra. But when his fingers venture down to the lacy panel on the front of my bikini briefs—

'You can't,' I whisper, stopping his hand.

Cal glances down below the hem of his waistcoat. 'Oh, I can.'

'Then let me put it another way: *I* can't.'

He unwillingly retrieves his hand. 'Did you get your period?'

'No.' After what we did last night (what *didn't* we do last night?), I can't believe that I'd now struggle to tell him anything. 'It's a tad… tender. Down, erm… Down there.'

'How tender are we talking?'

'Change that adjective to a verb. My velvet lounge has been tenderised. Which is great if you're a steak. It's not great if you're sitting on it.'

The backs of Cal's fingers stroke my jawline. 'Surely that just makes it easier to—'

'Don't,' I beg. 'Please don't… say anything sexual or anything I can turn into something sexual. Or just anything remotely… The amount it's throbbing, I might climax before we get to page eight.'

Cal throws his head back. I'm sure they must be able to hear his laughter in reception. I hope they can. Everyone would benefit from hearing it.

'Is it even anything to do with me?' he checks. 'Or is it because you haven't done it in two years?'

I clench my feeble fists. 'That sodding woman. She'll tell anyone who claims to have a disastrous love life that it can't be half as bad as mine.'

'Have you *any* idea how protective your aunt is of you?'

I let my legs swing back and forth, my hands gripping the countertop edge.

'We dined together one evening,' Cal says to one side of my face. 'And before I knew it, I was opening up to her. I don't do that even with my close friends.'

'What, erm... What did you...?'

'Open up about? You, of course.' Cal's smile is visible out of the corner of my eye. 'How I feel about you and... how long I've had feelings for you, which she was aware of; she had guessed as much at your reading in Cleethorpes last October. She must've been some shrink in her day.'

The cold of the countertop and my damp chest make me shiver. As does the realisation that I don't want this man to take those feelings away with him.

Cal finds my limp fingers. 'Izzie said there was no way you'd know. She said... She said that even if you did, you learned a long time ago to—'

'Did you really have to drench me?' I grumble, claiming back my hand.

I slide off the counter, forcing Cal to take a step back. I scoop up my trousers and hold the plate-sized damp patch under the hand dryer.

'Yeah, I don't know what came over me,' he

admits.

'Years of suppressed irritation?'

'More like years of sexual frustration.'

While my trousers and lacy chest are blasted dry, Cal can't stop his spontaneous explosions of laughter. They produce a giggle from him that nobody would believe he kept hidden in his Thom Browne socks. It's highly annoying. It's also highly infectious.

'Yeah, you won't be laughing at Christmas,' I utter, pulling my trousers back on. 'Not when your bonus is put towards protecting blue-footed boobies from extinction.'

Christmas. That's over four months away. Will he have gone by then?

When Cal opens my suitcase, I know what he's—

'I had a choice this morning,' I blurt out. 'I could pack like a pro and piss off those people in there, or I could get here before they changed their minds and only piss off someone in here. What was it to be?'

While I reapply my powdery mineral foundation to my brutally kissed mouth region, Cal riffles through what looks like a well-tossed clothing salad and pulls out a green T-shirt.

'V-neck,' I point out.

He untangles a white polo shirt.

'I went walking in that one yesterday.'

Cal holds it up, examining the front. I immediately cringe when he finds the underarm seams and shoves them against his nose.

'It's fine,' he says, shrugging. 'What?'

'Did you really just smell my T-shirt pits?'

'Do you want to go back in there in just your bra?'

'They say Jesus also liked to answer questions with questions,' I comment.

'Would you thank me for letting you back into a roomful of people reeking of stale sweat?'

I first sniff the top myself before pulling it on, doing up all but one button and flipping the collar up. Because it's fitted, the wrinkles nearly stretch out.

'Will I do?' I ask.

Cal picks up my suitcase and unlocks the door. With the naughtiest bedroom smile hovering on his lips, he murmurs, 'Oh, absolutely.'

***

The meeting takes just over two hours. That is ample time for me to change my mind, grab my best-loved pieces of work to date, and run. But there's a chance I wouldn't stop if I did, not until the line separating fact and fiction broke down. I could then hide forever in the mystical lands of Aeornot, a world over thirty years in the making.

I don't change my mind, though. I don't go back on my word. It's better to do this while I'm alive, to see if the production company loves the books as much as they claim – not just their earning potential.

When the moment arrives for me to sign over a chunk of my literary life, Cal untangles his fingers from mine and turns round in his seat to get his fancy pen from his jacket pocket—

Whoa, hold on a sec. When did Cal take my hand? Was it when I pressed my leg down to stop my stiletto heel from banging a hole through the floor? At one point, people were looking for the source of the noise. I obviously wasn't pressing hard enough on my own.

That must have been it. I mean, there isn't any other reason why…

Wait. No, I recall Cal's hand already being there.

When was it, then?

As I hand him back his pen, I feel my cheeks bloom when everyone in the room claps. Are they congratulating me or expressing their relief? Or is it simply an American thing, which the others around the table join in with to avoid coming across as crusty? Whatever it is, I don't care. It's done.

***

The boardroom doors are propped open as people don their jackets and pick up briefcases. Cal's hand rubs my back and rests briefly on my hip before he walks the visitors to the lift, their exuberant moods smouldering in their wake.

I slump down in my seat, stretching my legs out. I hear the boardroom doors closing again. Cal brings one of his tan, Italian-leather Oxford shoes over my crossed ankles and rests against the edge of the table.

'Thank you, Cal.'

'Don't thank me. This is all you.'

'No. You've always been my driving force, my deadliner, my everything. I mean, my… everything else.'

I want to resist the pull on my hand, but with limited time, why deny myself? With my arms around

427

Cal's neck, I can now enjoy the feel of his hands when they sneak under the hem of my T-shirt.

I momentarily rescue my lips from his. 'I don't know how you've put up with me all these years.'

'It's been my absolute pleasure, Jo.'

'I've relied on you much more than I should have.'

'No, you haven't. I've worked hard to make myself indispensable.'

That's true. And Cal is essential to me now beyond parties and projects and punctuation.

I savour his mouth with urgency while I still can. I feel him trying to prolong the kiss, as unwilling as I am to give it up. But his lips will soon be in another time zone, enjoying another life, another beginning.

Using every ounce of my willpower, I remove Cal's arms from around my waist. Despite his reluctance to let me go, I force myself to step back. I offer a thin smile in response to the lines that have redecorated his forehead.

'My train leaves at half past one,' I explain.

Cal catches my hand and holds it for ransom against his chest. 'Talk to me.'

'I need to get something to eat.'

'Why are you blowing hot and cold?'

I refuse to look at him.

'Is there something you're not telling me, Jo?'

Oh, I'm looking at him now. 'No. Is there something *you're* not telling me?'

Cal's eyes hold mine as he slowly shakes his head. 'No.'

There's a tiny knock on the door.

'Sorry to trouble you.'

I quickly pull my hand away. If Fay is surprised, it doesn't show.

'Henry Tasker is holding, Cal.'

I don't know what Henry does at this agency, but I've heard he has an office on the top floor. A big one.

'He has called literally four times.'

'Then he'll call a fifth,' Cal says. 'Tell him to call back after two.'

'No, Fay.' I straighten the hem of my T-shirt. 'He'll take the call.'

'We're not done here,' he tells me.

'We're done. So, please.' My words combine a conclusion, a request and a challenge, in case the staring contest isn't enough.

'Put him through to my office,' Cal instructs.

In the corridor, Fay scoots past me to her desk and grabs the receiver. 'Sorry about that, Mr Tasker.'

I can almost hear the voice on the other end of the line as I collect my things.

'No, I *do* understand,' Fay tells him.

As the lift doors close, I see her pull a face at the phone. With one finger, she shows how many more calls from him she is *literally* prepared to take.

Chapter Thirty-Nine

As I finish the last dregs of my Starbucks, I know I won't be enjoying another decent coffee until I get to Windermere. Much as my first-class train ticket affords me a free coffee or tea from the trolley as it trundles up and down, up and down, if I can't stand a stirring stick up in the foam until the last mouthful, I'll not bother.

The time of day means the train carriage is quiet, with my little four-seater table having only my reserved ticket on display. Two women are my closest travelling companions, sitting diagonally across from me. As yet, their chatter hasn't paused for ad breaks.

I wonder if they've drawn breath once since they arrived in London for their intensive retail therapy session, scouring the shops for souvenirs for everyone but themselves: red fridge magnets that won't go on the integrated appliances, red tea towels that don't match the colour scheme, and red toys that won't ever be rare or a must-have.

I listen to them battling for friendly one-upmanship regarding their gifted grandchildren.

They're trying not to start each sentence with 'Mine can beat that', and a moment ago, one of them almost – she *almost* – let the other finish speaking before she jumped in.

I take out my train ticket and my current reading material from my bag, as well as the brownie I bought. It needed time to get to room temperature because, as everyone knows, nothing is worse than a chilled brownie.

Well, maybe there's one thing that's worse, but… there's nothing I can do about that.

My rich, fudgy bar of calories still isn't squidgy, so I wrap it in its napkin again and put it back in my bag. I move my backup reading material and my phone further away from it. I don't want a squished brownie. No, they're almost as bad as a chilled—

One second. Did I see the red light on my phone flash?

Cal: Fay wants to know how you get me to do what you say

I haven't even had time to read the text three times, let alone consider what it means or contemplate a response, when another message pops up.

Cal: She thinks either I'm scared of you…

It's vibrating again.

Cal: … or I'm in love with you

A second of euphoria is whipped away quicker than the houses through the window. Why would Cal say that now? Why? What's the point? Why now? It's like the chapters I sometimes take a lifetime to hone that he strikes a red pen through, telling me they're irrelevant to the plot. Well, that's what his text is: irrelevant.

Irrelevant and cruel.

Cal: She also informs me that you know about the meetings with my dad, my sister, and the big bosses

I push my phone away to write the angry text in my head and instantly delete it. I wipe my eyes on my sleeve and think of a sarcastic one to send in its place. More wiping. More deleting. When my shaking hands pick up my phone again, my thumbs struggle with the tiny keyboard.

Me: In the boardroom, I asked you if there was something you're not telling me!

I then send it without even thinking. Any other time, I would pat myself on the back.

Cal: I said to you then that there wasn't

Oh, *then* there wasn't. But between then and now—

Cal: And there still isn't. My dad and sister are discussing business between his company and our agency

I quickly open the next one.

Cal: That doesn't involve me. Except as a handy middleman with an office for them to borrow

Which means…

Cal: Fay isn't getting rid of me

What about…?

Cal: And neither are you

My leaking eyes need more than a sleeve. Thinking fast, I take my brownie out of my bag and steal its napkin.

Cal: Therefore, wipe those tears off that beautiful face, please

As I mop my cheeks, I manage a watery smile. Only one man could correctly guess that I'd be blubbing now.

Cal: And put Charlotte Brontë away

I pop my makeshift bookmark between the pages of *Jane*—

Hang on. How did he…?

I snatch my phone back up.

When travelling on public transport, it's usually polite to ask if the seat next to you is available. The rule, it seems, doesn't apply to everyone. Certainly not to the person who has sat beside me and gently nudged my shoulder. Do they realise such a gesture is wildly intimate if it's the company you desperately crave?

I hope they do.

I keep looking straight ahead. 'I'm not heavily medicated, Cal.'

'Good. Then you know I'm staring at you.'

I know, but it's still nice to hear it confirmed. It's even nicer when I look to my right and see it for myself. The size of my wobbly grin must be proof of that.

I'm trying to imagine how things might have played out if Cal had looked at me this way the first time we met. What would've happened if he had introduced me to those beautiful crinkles around his eyes and that lovely lopsided smile from the start? There wouldn't have been eight years, that's for sure, and knowing this, I offer a huge thank you for our crucial misunderstanding. Our story needed it. Just until it was ready to be told.

'When I thought you were leaving the company.' I swallow back the tears. 'Leaving…'

'You?' Cal smiles gently, shaking his head. 'Had my dad been here trying to persuade me again to leave, it would never have happened. Not now. Not after spending time with you this summer.'

His thumbs must suddenly take turns brushing the uncoordinated leaks from my eyes.

'But, when I… when I asked if you… if you really had to go back to London…'

'Forgive me, Jo. I held back because I wasn't sure you were ready. Yet, the way I did it… Please know that I hated myself afterward.' Cal kisses my damp cheeks. 'As for your feelings toward me at that point, after… after all these years, I just prayed I hadn't misread the earlier signs.'

'Then that wasn't when you initially thought I might, erm… have… feelings for you?'

His eyebrows raise. 'Are you kidding me? No, it was after our hike with Izzie. Or should I say, during? Your hilarious mashed potatoes skit?'

I recall my dabbling with acting on that hillside. I feel as if my cheeks have also been creamed and crushed. Possibly thinking my recollection may be a tad hazy, Cal decides to re-enact it.

'I obviously didn't realise it then,' I say, gently grabbing his hands. 'Or maybe I did, deep down. But it's true: I was jealous.'

'Me too.' Although Cal is smiling, I know when he is serious. 'When you both left after the barbecue, Maria said Nyx planned to tell you about his daughter, and if that went okay, then…' Cal's raised eyebrows finish his sentence. 'So, I hung around after everyone had gone and kept my fingers crossed.'

'Was that why you cleaned her kitchen?'

He chuckles. 'Partly. When Nyx got back, I knew things hadn't gone well, and although I felt sorry for him, I had *never* wanted to kiss another man as much.' When Cal pulls his head back, he has an adorable double chin. 'Speaking of me kissing men…'

'I never thought you were… No, I only said to Izzie… Honestly. That bloody woman!'

Then I'm the one who's kissing men – well, one man – and he is kissing me.

I reclaim my lips, albeit reluctantly. We are on a train, after all. 'Does your boss know you skipped out early?'

Cal holds a lock of my hair to his nose. 'I have permission.'

'Some would call it favouritism.'

'And you would know all about that!'

'Hey, I've worked my fingertips off for preferential treatment,' I state. 'Which is one reason I'm glad I won't have to look for a new… a new…'

Clearly, Cal doesn't have a clue, either. 'Will we

435

ever figure out my actual job title?'

'These things take time.'

'Well, I think we can add something else to my list of duties and responsibilities after last night.' Cal's lips brush a corner of my mouth. 'And... tonight, perhaps?'

'Not tonight.'

His lips brush the other corner. 'Tomorrow night, then?'

'There's a good chance I may *never* fully recover down there.'

When Cal chuckles and his breath dances across my cheek, I want to nestle into his lips with cocoa and thermal socks.

There is one thing I'd like to know. 'Did you hate me this morning?'

'For sneaking out of my bed at three a.m.?'

I look down at Cal's thigh, at my hand resting in his. Support props are holding up my smile. 'How do you know what time it was?'

'What bothered you the most, Jo? Was it that I didn't try to stop you? Or was it that I let you walk back alone at that time?'

I consider my answer. 'The jury's still deliberating.'

Cal's fingers play with mine. 'I would never stop you from doing anything. I know how I feel about you, but if you need time to work out how to let yourself feel that way and not be scared, you can leave whenever you want. But know that when you do, I'll be walking a short distance behind you until you're home safe. Just like I did last night.'

With my free hand, I search Cal's inside jacket pocket for the tissue I know will be there. The subsequent kiss tastes like salty tears, but he gets the picture.

'You, erm... You mentioned tomorrow night.' I try to keep the excitement out of my voice. 'Does that mean you're staying with me for... more than one night?'

'If you'll have me.'

The firmness of my kiss is my answer.

'I'll warn you now, Cal, my rental is small.'

'It's only temporary.'

I keep my expression neutral as I try to remember where I put the folder containing the paperwork from each estate agent. I'll go with the second one if I must. She loved my coffee machine.

'Just until you furnish your cottage.'

I sit up straight. 'You would move for me?'

'Of course,' Cal says without hesitation. 'You love your little house, and you love the Lakes. The people who live there love you too. Seeing you on that market with all those friends you've made?' He holds my hand to his chest. 'And a London apartment is no place to keep a dog.'

I lean towards him, and he lays the gentlest kiss on the tip of my nose.

'But you love the capital,' I remark.

'I do. But I love you a hell of a lot more.'

It's one thing for Cal to mention love in a text, but to say it's a fact while holding my hand...

'And you're Jo when you're in the—'

'I love you too,' I blurt out.

His gaze meets mine. 'Do you mean that?'

'Well, if I can say it when you're not going down on me, then I must do.'

People are smiling when they look over. That's the effect his laughter has.

'Cal, what if, and it's only a what-if right now because hey, who knows?' I quickly add. 'My pink toothbrush and your blue toothbrush love each other as much as we do, but... they don't take kindly straight away to sharing a bathroom seven days a week?'

'And they ask that we keep two addresses going for a while?'

'No, they demand it in blood.'

With a smile, Cal shrugs. He doesn't need time to think. 'Oh well.'

My eyes linger on the small strip of paper poking out between the pages of my book. It is nothing more than the contents of a fortune cookie, which didn't get thrown away when I emptied my shirt pocket. Just a positive quote that came to my rescue when I was short of a bookmark.

No more what-ifs.

Only oh-wells.

'On the plus side,' I advise, 'this... this woman you, erm... you love... can write angry texts in her head and not send them.'

Cal's thumb and forefinger cradle my chin. 'Now that's someone I want to spend the rest of my life with.'

I hold on to the armrest.

'*And* she can make vegetable soup from scratch,' he remembers.

My chest swells with pride. 'Yes. She can.'

'She can also tell you one thing...' Cal removes a USB stick from his waistcoat pocket. '... and then hurl a new story at you the next.'

I touch his lips with my fingers. Why has it taken so long to find them utterly captivating? They're wonderful. And when I press mine against them, it feels real. It... It feels like there can be more to life than just witches and word counts.

Cal places an envelope on the table. 'I have something for you, too.'

It takes me a moment. 'And if I decide to see the house again?'

'I'll come with you.'

I slip it inside my book and thank him in my new way.

Just as my phone starts ringing.

'That'll be my wacky aunt.' I press the green receiver key and the speaker button without looking at the screen. 'Salutations, you slapped twat!'

'Milly, erm, Jo, I've been speaking to Izzie.'

Oops.

'That's nice... Ma.'

'About next month and the surprise party.'

Whoever is having a party, there'll be no surprise. Ma doesn't know the meaning of the word. I have yet to finish opening a birthday present before she tells me what it is.

Cal quickly types something on his phone and tilts it my way. *The twins' fortieth,* he's written. Come on, who do you think buys the cards and posts them?

'She said you won't be coming alone and what have you.'

My aunt's only probable source is shaking his head.

'But I said to her, "Izzie, if there's one thing I can be sure of, it's that our Milly, erm, Jo will always be on her own and what have you.".'

When did they stop burning mothers for bitchcraft?

'My sister, though, is certain you're bringing that fella who works for you.'

I'm going to dropkick Izzie.

'Ma, Cal doesn't work for... I hope she didn't call at silly o'clock this morning to tell you.'

'No, she told me this a fortnight ago.'

Cal's look of surprise matches mine.

'And I said, "Izzie, why on earth would my daughter want to bring him and what have you?".'

When Cal holds out an upturned hand, I shake my head and push it away.

'But then I thought it might be nice for you to bring a friend, Milly, erm, Jo. I know you don't have many.'

I hand him my phone.

'Ms Washington? Hi, this is Cal. How are you?'

I sweep a hand back and forth across my throat, but Cal ignores my warning and gets comfortable. Patiently, he listens to Ma's many alleged ailments and suspicious symptoms. She also treats him to a 1,500-word tale that covers three weeks and skirts the borders of Cornwall. It ends with, '… After all that, it was the wrong milk.'

'About the party, ma'am,' Cal says. 'I hope my coming as Jo's plus one won't put you out.'

'The more, the merrier, and what have you,' Ma declares. 'Tell me, are you courting anyone? If not, I have three eager daughters living under my roof, and I need to find them decent men.'

Eager daughters, yes. Do the men need to be decent? I believe Ma's reached the point where she only cares that they're not deceased.

'Yes, ma'am,' Cal says, smiling. 'I'm… courting someone.'

'Are you sure?'

'Absolutely.'

'Is it serious, though?' Ma wants to know.

'Very.' Cal touches my cheek. 'She's the one.'

I move his hand to my lips. A hand I hope to hold in mine forever.

'Oh, that's a bugger,' Ma utters.

Cal seems surprised. He'll learn.

'Well,' she says, with a side order of sulk, 'I suppose I'll see you both next month then and what have you.'

'I'm looking forward to it, Ms Washington,' he tells her.

'Bye, Ma—'

But my phone is already displaying a photo of my new home.

A photo of… *our* new home.

From one of Cal's bags, I slide out his laptop. He then gently pulls me into this spot between his arm and chest. It's a lovely nook that has my name written all over it. Waiting for me are lips that make me wonder when I should start writing the sequel.

Grudgingly, I pull away from my new favourite pastime. 'We have almost three hours to kill.'

'Spoilsport,' Cal murmurs.

I plug the USB stick into his laptop and open the Word document.

His lips brush my ear as he whispers, 'Let me listen to your amazing voice.'

'*Chapter One*,' I read aloud. '*Have you ever included any of your own romantic encounters in your twelve best-selling novels…?*'

The End

Acknowledgements

Let's start by thanking the most important people: you, the readers. Thank you for investing your money and time in my imagination. I hope you enjoyed reading *You Were Summer* as much as I enjoyed writing and editing it. And I did. I enjoyed every minute I spent in Jo's world. Every minute. There were lots of them, too.

A heartfelt thank you to the lovely ladies who helped me enormously by reading my story during its infancy: Sam Goodhand, Alex Aldous, and Kathy Fillingham. To Paul Tuff, too, for resuscitating my computer and teaching me the importance of backing up my work.

Thanks also to my publisher, The Conrad Press. To Michelle Emerson as well, for her typesetting and cover design.

Jackie Cabas, I'll keep it clean for once. Thank you, Auntie, for 'giving' me Izzie.

Finally, the biggest thank you goes to Ma and Pops for always believing in me. Lynne and Steve Goodhand, I love you beyond words.